# LIGHT IN THE SHADOWS

BOOK 1 OF THE SHADOWS AND LIGHT
SERIES

## GEORGIA C. LEIGH

CASK PUBLISHING

## Dedication

*For my mother, who wrote a book and made me believe I could, too.*

*and*

*For Joy, without her encouragement this story would not exist.*

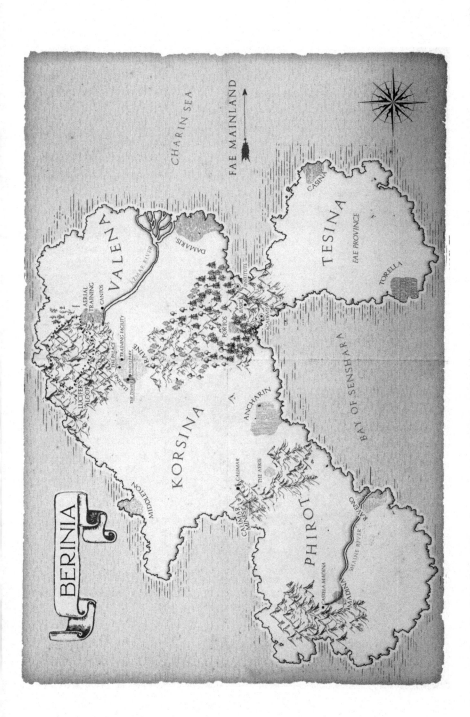

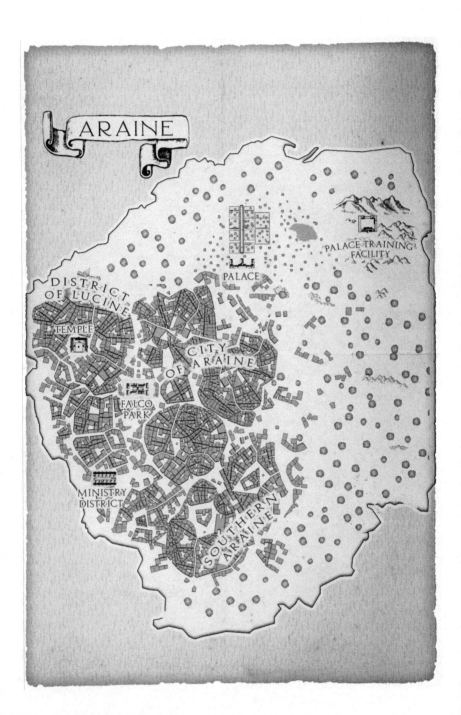

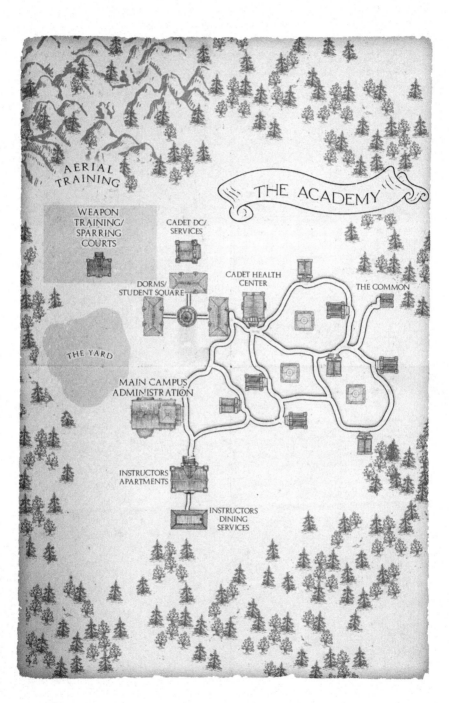

# PART 1

# THE LIGHT

# CHAPTER I
## New York

Ryker leaned against the building under the eaves to escape the swirling drizzle drenching New York. What a miserable night to hunt a demon.

*Any time. Left, right, straight...which way?* he said to Trinity in his mind.

*Hang on. He's on the move. The map is changing,* Trinity replied.

*Tick tock. I've been here for an hour already.*

*I know, I'm working on it.*

Ryker knew he didn't have to remind her. Trinity was a talented Guide and aware of his limits, but he hadn't fully recovered from his last crossing, and the time spent here strained his depleted magic. Recovery would be lengthy once he returned through the Pale to his home in Praesia. But they had tracked this demon for months, chasing it through three worlds. Despite the demon's elusiveness, Trinity found its thread last night in Terra. Her sudden vision of the demon's illegal presence in the human world didn't give them time to fully map a hunt, but they risked the crossing rather than lose the demon again. The moment Ryker stepped into New York, their tenuous plan went to hell. Ryker now waited for Trinity to improvise.

*Trinity, I'm not kidding. We need to move now.* Ryker's magic stuttered, pulling along his spine. He ignored the tension, but if Trinity didn't find the demon soon he couldn't risk a confrontation.

*Shut up, Ryker, don't tell me how to do my job. Your whining is annoying.*

He grumbled but held his tongue.

The meatpacking district was not a place anyone should loiter on a moonless night. Ryker could feel the menace creeping through the deserted streets. While his tall, muscular frame and powerful presence were a deterrent, it did not guarantee unwanted attention. He pulled the hood of his jacket lower over his face, his silver-gray eyes alert and scanning the darkened alley across the street where he heard scuffling and incoherent arguing.

*Okay, left on Eighth Avenue two blocks down, right on Fourteenth. There's an alley on your right halfway down the block.* Ryker strode away, following Trinity's directions. *Bastard just turned in there. It's a dead end. I'll let you know if I see anything, but it looks good.*

*Send me his current form.*

Trinity flashed an image of a man of medium height and slight build, with a short beard, black hoodie, jeans, and tennis shoes.

Ryker rolled his eyes. *That could be half the humans in New York.*

*That's really memorable.*

*Quit complaining. He's alone, even you can't miss him.*

Ryker huffed and turned into the alley where a man crouched in the shadows twenty feet away. Ryker slowed his pace, and his wings unfurled with a soft snicking sound, the onyx steel blades glimmering in the gloomy light above a grimy door.

The man whipped his head toward Ryker, revealing a woman lying on the ground at his feet, her neck covered in blood.

*He's not alone.*

*Yes, I see her. Checking on her now. Kill him,* she hissed.

*Calm. I've got him.* Without breaking his prowling stride, Ryker spread his wings, the multiple broadsword blades flaring from the apex.

"You're a hard one to track," Ryker said, his voice cold and indifferent.

The man's golden eyes blazed, and in a jarring, inhuman rasp, he said, "This is none of your business."

"You know it is. Get away from her." Wisps of smoke swirled down Ryker's arms, growing into a cloud that billowed to the ground and coursed toward the man. Black Bane tendrils whipped within the cloud of Shadow, writhing and thrashing to be free. With a flick of his wrist, Ryker released his magic and a tendril struck the man, wrapping around his wrists and slithering up his body.

The man struggled against the magic tethering him to the ground. Black tendrils seeped from the swirling smoke and gripped the man's neck. The man screamed, then shifted into a daeva.

*Shit*, whispered Ryker.

*Finish it, now. We can't lose this one again.*

*I won't lose it.*

The demon bared its jagged fangs and fought to angle its gaunt, hominid body between Ryker and the unconscious woman. It kept one elongated, clawed hand on her neck and flicked the other toward Ryker. The air around the daeva rippled. Ryker pulled back his Shadow magic from the daeva, creating a shield. The daeva's magic moved around the barrier, the Cancelling magic brushing against Ryker and dimming his magic, but the shield held, deflecting the brunt of it. The daeva's shape was barely visible as it slipped the Shadow's weakened restraints.

The demon's membrane wings emerged, the thin black skin almost transparent. Ryker held his breath against the foul stench of rotting flesh that buffeted him from the demon's flapping wings. The daeva lifted off the ground, dragging the woman with it, her limp body trailing through the pooling rain in the alley.

*Ryker*, Trinity hissed.

*It's a Canceller and a flyer. But I've got it.* Ryker strained his magic, and Shadow enveloped the daeva again. The daeva became opaque as its upward momentum was halted. The woman slipped from the demon's grip, crumpling to the ground in a filthy puddle. Ryker's Shadow bound and collapsed the demon's membrane wings, and it screeched as it fell, landing next to the woman with a splash. Ryker flared his wings as the daeva rose to its hands and knees, crouched and ready to spring. With a rush of swinging blades, the demon crumpled to the ground. Drops of black blood sprinkled into the pool of water as ripples washed around the demon's severed head, the eyes bulging in surprise.

Ryker kicked the daeva's body away from the woman. *Done. Ash it or bring it?*

*Ash it.*

Dark, shadowed smoke laced with Bane engulfed the daeva. The demon's body became gray, then crumbled into a pile of smoldering ash. Ryker knelt beside the prone woman and felt her pulse. Still alive, but not for long if the wound on her neck remained untreated. She had minutes, maybe.

Ryker looked at the woman closely and spotted a hint of gold glinting under her half-closed lids. *This is a djinn, Trinity. Not a human.*

*I know. And now you have another problem. That female? You need to bring her with you. She's been missing for months,* Trinity said.

*You've got to be kidding me. She's alive. You know I don't like crossing live ones. Is Lukas around?*

*No, do it now. Every minute counts for both of you. Farna will be here and ready.*

Ryker swore, the healer's presence a grim reminder of the painful crossing to come. *That doesn't make me feel better.* Even without a passenger, Ryker had been in Terra too long and his magic was compromised from the beginning. The struggle with the daeva had not helped conserve his magic, either. *Starting now.*

*Safe passage. We'll catch you.* Ryker held the female's body to his chest as gray shadow swirled around his feet, snaked up his arms, and enveloped them both.

Silas hovered near Trinity beside a marble dais in the Temple's warded crypt, where Ryker's body drifted between two worlds. Drifting required less magic to walk other worlds, but bringing a body back would push the limits of what little remained of Ryker's magic. Smoke swirled from Ryker's hands and feet, slowly creeping up his transparent body. Too slowly.

"Please, be okay," Trinity said in a shaking voice to Silas, who paced beside the dais. "How is he?"

Silas rubbed the bonding runes tattooed to his forearm. "Heart rate is elevated. Pulse erratic."

"Where in the flaming cracks of Abaddon is Farna?" Trinity grumbled.

"I'm here," Farna said, closing the door to the crossing room behind him. Ryker's arms and legs became solid, the smoky tendrils creeping to his neck and face.

Ryker curled his transparent arms to his chest, and with a pressure wave that made their ears pop, he became solid. His arms fell open, and Silas saw a slight figure with dark brown skin and long, black hair. He quickly lifted the bloody female off Ryker and placed her on a second dais. Farna tended to the djinn, his hands glowing with a pale white light as he gripped the gaping wound in her neck.

Trinity wiped at the blood covering Ryker and took a step back. "Farna," Trinity said. "You need to help Ryker. Now."

Silas noticed a stream of blood trickling from Ryker's mouth and nose. "Oh, shit."

"One minute. We're going to lose her," Farna said.

"We're going to lose *him* if you don't hurry!" Trinity said.

Farna's hands flared bright white. The bleeding wound on the djinn's neck knit together, then sealed. Farna rushed to the dais and placed his glowing hands on Ryker's forehead and chest. Minutes passed, and beads of sweat appeared on Farna's brow.

"I knew he shouldn't have tried this crossing," Silas said.

"We knew the risks. But it was necessary." Trinity's soothing words did little to hide the anxiety in her voice.

Silas rubbed at his bonding runes. "He'll be fine."

Ryker's chest rose and fell, then didn't rise again. Silas slipped a hand in Trinity's and squeezed. Farna's healing Light enveloped Ryker's head and chest, penetrating through him and reflecting off the granite dais beneath his body. Ryker's lips parted in a rattling gasp. Trinity and Silas both exhaled as Ryker's eyes rolled under his lids, then opened.

"You bastard," Trinity breathed as Ryker turned his head toward her. "You scared us to death."

Farna patted Ryker's arm, then returned to the djinn.

Ryker leaned over the edge of the marble dais and coughed, spitting blood on the gray granite floor. Trinity handed him a damp towel. He wiped his nose and mouth, then rested his head on the cushion.

He gritted his teeth and shifted uncomfortably. "Well, if I had died, it would have been your fault for losing the daeva."

Trinity gave him a dirty look. "How do you feel?" she asked, brushing back his short black hair.

"How do you think? Like crap. I could sleep for a week." His eyes closed, and his features relaxed.

Silas held Ryker's arm before he could slip into unconsciousness. "Where do you want to recover?"

"Home," Ryker mumbled. "Take me home, Silas."

"Can you get a Skimmer to the Aerie?" Silas asked Trinity. "I can get you later this afternoon."

"Yes, I'll tap you when I arrive." She stroked Ryker's face. "Take care of him."

Silas nodded and took Ryker's arm, and they vanished.

Silas visualized a small clearing in the woods beyond the outpost town in the mountains bordering Phirot and Korsina. In two heartbeats, Silas's Skimming magic transported them to the new location. In the distance, the Aerie's small cluster of inns, pubs, and markets huddled together on a plateau. Silas lowered Ryker's slack body to the ground.

"Almost there. Just need a minute to rest." The runes on Silas's arm itched and tingled, the sensation alerting him to the clearing's concealing wards.

Silas reached into the base of a large tree. The bark rippled and vanished, revealing a hollowed space in the trunk and a hidden cache of water and food. Silas returned to Ryker and sat beside him. Silas's Skimming magic was powerful, but he wasn't a true Skimmer. To transport Ryker to the Villa from the clearing, Silas would need to rest and eat to replenish his energy and magic. He could sense through his bonding rune that Ryker's vital signs were normal with no signs of pain, so he relaxed against the tree and bit into an apple.

Although it was a lifelong commitment, Silas never regretted his decision to be a part of Ryker's Triad. Ryker and Trinity were the family he never had. Ryker and Silas had trained in the same squad together at the Academy, and at the end of their third year, Ryker had asked Silas to be his Warrior. Silas was responsible for Ryker's safety and the Triad's security. Together, they found Trinity through the fae Institute, the seraphim Academy's sister teaching facility. Trinity was a gifted Seer, a magic more common to fae and more powerful than seraphim readers that allowed her to envision how a person behaved or an event unfolded in the future. She monitored the Pale to feel wrongness and guided Ryker to intercept unauthorized incursions between worlds. The bonding runes they each carried tied them together, but they were more than three people bound by magic. Silas looked down at Ryker's relaxed face. He didn't have any siblings, but Ryker and Trinity were connected to his heart in a way magic could never replicate.

Silas repacked the provisions into the hollowed tree and sealed the wards, making the tree appear solid again. He knelt beside Ryker's unconscious body and gently folded his arms across his chest, then gathered him under his shoulders. They vanished and appeared under the portico of an imposing estate on the southeastern edge of Raveno. The Regency provided a secure retreat to each of Berinia's three Shadowwalker Triads to recover from crossings. The Villa Pandion's powerful warding repelled casual visitors, appearing to any passersby as a modest, unremarkable home that was entirely forgettable.

The entry rune on Silas's arm prickled as he moved Ryker through the Villa's wards. Silas skimmed to the second floor of the east wing and settled Ryker in his bed, checking his vitals again before closing the bedroom door. He walked down the hall to the suite next to Ryker's and knocked.

Shallah opened the door while pulling her long, graying hair into a knot. "You're home," she said, kissing Silas's cheek. "How is he?"

"He's fine but tired. He'll likely sleep through the night. I'll retrieve Trinity later this afternoon from the Aerie," he said, yawning.

"Go get some sleep. Do you want dinner in your suite or together tonight?"

"Together would be great. We missed you."

"I'll arrange it. Go, get your rest." She shooed him away.

Silas walked to his suite in the west wing, fell into bed, and was asleep in minutes.

Ryker felt a hand caress his cheek, stroking his hair back from his forehead. He slowly opened his eyes.

"Hello, baby boy," Shallah said.

Ryker smiled at his grandmother. "I'm not a baby, Mimi."

"Yes, you are. You're my baby," she cooed.

"How long have I been out?"

"Almost a day. Are you able to come to dinner? Or do you want to have something brought up?"

"I'm too tired to eat."

Shallah clucked at him. "No, you're not. I'll have something brought up. You need a shower, too."

He feigned a hurt look. "Are you telling me I smell?"

"Of course not, but you're covered in blood," she said, wrinkling her nose.

He raised an arm crusted with blood from the djinn he crossed yesterday.

"Yuck," he said.

"Come on, it will do you good. Do you need help?"

"No, I can do it." He tried to sit up but fell back onto the bed.

"I'll have Silas help you."

Ryker relaxed, his thoughts drifting back to the edge of sleep. He jerked awake at the sound of a knock.

Silas poked his head around the door. "Look who lives." He offered a steadying arm as Ryker shuffled to the bath, helping him as he showered and dressed. Ryker sat at his dining nook when a platter of food appeared on the table. Shallah hovered in the doorway as Silas left Ryker to his meal.

"Nice timing, Mimi." He ran his hand through his wet hair. "Come, please sit."

"You already look much better."

"I feel better, just starving." Ryker's stomach rumbled.

Shallah sat with him, sipping a cup of tea and watching him devour his food. "Any word from River?"

Ryker paused his eating and swallowed. "Yes, I saw him yesterday before the crossing. He sends his best to you." River hadn't mentioned Shallah in their brief encounter, but she didn't need to know that.

"Does he have plans to come south? We could meet him in Ancharin."

"He didn't mention it." Ryker frowned. He'd accepted River's absences and his indifference to his family, but Shallah's expectations were still high. Disappointment clouded her eyes and dimmed her perpetually sunny spirit. "You know, you can go to Araine. You have a suite at the Garret. Autumn equinox is in two months. Come with us. It would be fun to see you there."

"You know I hate to travel, but I'll think about it. It's been six months since I was last in Araine, and I haven't seen River in two years. It's time."

"It's something River should have fixed. You shouldn't have to chase him down."

"Your brother has his own life."

Ryker huffed. "One you would think he would have outgrown by now."

Shallah clucked at him. "Don't start. He made different choices than you did."

"And is apparently still making them. The gossip at the last ball was embarrassing. And he wasn't even there." Ryker finished his meal and yawned. "Is Trinity here?"

"Yes, Silas skimmed her yesterday afternoon while you slept."

Ryker sat back in his chair. "He's been busy."

"He only woke up an hour before you. Come, you still need to rest." She rose, helped Ryker to his feet, and walked him to his bedroom. "You can visit with Silas and Trinity tomorrow when you've recovered. And we can discuss a trip to Araine, if that would make you happy." Ryker yawned again. She gently pushed him back onto the bed and covered him with a thin blanket. "I'll wake you tomorrow morning."

Ryker heard the click of the door as he drifted into blissful sleep.

# CHAPTER 2
## Portos

Haven was waiting alone on the steps of her parents' estate when the Skimmer appeared at her side. She looked around one last time at , nostalgic, but also eager to move on with her life. "I've never skimmed before," she said to the Skimmer who held her hand.

"Deep breath. It will only be a moment," he said.

In two heartbeats, the estate vanished, and Haven was standing in an open field near a cluster of canvas tents. The new rune on her ribs tingled, and her basic magic faded to a whisper. Haven's head spun and nausea roiled her stomach, and she grabbed the Skimmer's arm to steady herself. The surrounding sounds faded as though a blanket had been thrown over her, dulling her sharp seraphim senses. Other new students sat on benches or lay on cots, adjusting to the strange feel of Portos's protective wardings.

The Skimmer led Haven to a bench. "Rest here. A healer will see you shortly." Then he vanished.

A healer wearing a red Academy uniform approached her. "How do you feel?"

"Awful. I may throw up." Vertigo blurred the edges of her vision and tilted the ground beneath her feet in sickening waves.

"It's an unfortunate process of entering the region around the Academy. The rune that allows you to pass through Portos's wardings also stifles your magic, at least for your first year." He handed her a cup of amber liquid. "Here, drink this. It will help clear your head and calm your stomach." Haven sniffed the cup, scenting peppermint and ginger. "Your reaction appears mild."

"This is mild?" Haven breathed slowly to control her nausea. "I don't even know if I have yet. Why do I feel like this?"

"You may not know what your gift is, but it's there, so the wardings will still affect you. You should feel better soon. Once you are more comfortable, the registration area is to your right." He pointed to an expansive pale limestone building on the southern edge of the arrival clearing. "Good luck, and welcome to Portos."

Haven sat on the bench, watching cadets appear and make their way to first-aid tents, all in varying levels of discomfort. She covered her mouth as one cadet vomited and collapsed. The healer was right, her reaction could have been much worse. She sipped her drink slowly, and within the hour, she felt almost like herself.

She made her way across a broad plaza filled with students milling around in confusion or queuing in clusters at the entrance of the Administration building. The sound of nervous laughter and animated conversation buzzed around her as Academy escorts scattered throughout the square guided students through the registration process. Haven followed the crowd, and a helpful escort showed her to the proper line.

"After registration, how will we get to the Academy?" Haven asked.

The escort blinked. "Portos isn't the Academy. You'll need months of preparation before starting the training program in the fall."

"Oh," Haven said, her cheeks heating.

"It's a common mistake, don't worry. There's more information about the training plan in your orientation package." He nodded and walked away to help another cadet.

Haven tilted her face to the sun, grateful for the mild June day. The cool mountain breeze caressed her skin and lifted her hair off her neck, a relief from the blazing summer heat of her home in Korsina.

Haven waited in line as it inched toward the building, the throng of people bustling around her. She had never seen this many people together in her life. Students greeted one another with excited, warm embraces, and Haven's stomach knotted, both with anticipation and dread. *How do these people make friends like this?* Their conversations seemed so easy. Natural. Even enjoyable.

The sun had dipped behind the tips of the pine trees when Haven finally emerged from the Administration building to a grassy quad surrounded by dormitories. She followed the crowd down the broad central path, the draping branches of oak trees shading her from the sun's last visible rays. Reviewing the slip of paper clipped to her orientation packet, she found her building on the west side of the quad. She walked up the stairs to the second floor and hesitated nervously in the large common room where cadets had gathered. She glanced behind her at the door, to the safety of familiar solitude she could find outside. Squaring her shoulders, she wove through the crowd and opened the door to her assigned room. The chatter in the room silenced as nine sets of eyes fell on her.

A raven-haired seraphim with pale green eyes stepped forward. "Hi, I'm Kit. Welcome to the pod, you're number ten."

A female with black hair patted the bunk above hers. "Last free bunk. I'm Harper." Her vibrant smile reached her forest green eyes.

"I'm Haven." Haven introduced herself, trying to absorb the rapid-fire names.

"I'm Larkin," a male said from the lower bunk across from hers. Larkin's sweeping pointed ears and upturned eyes were distinct from the softer pointed tips and rounder eyes of the seraphim.

Haven raised an eyebrow. "Are you on your way to the fae Institute?"

"No, I'm attending the Academy," Larkin said.

"Oh? Why is that?"

"I'm a Shapeshifter, with a gift for flight. It made sense to train at the Academy, at least for my first year."

"My Skimmer told me the wards dampened our magic. How will you shapeshift without magic?"

He held out his arm, showing her the Academy rune. "Different type of rune limits my magic. The dampening was awful." Larkin shuddered, his dark hair falling over his hypnotic eyes, an unusual pale green that faded to golden amber in the center, ringed in black.

Haven tore her eyes from him and cleared her throat. "How...how long have you been here?"

"About three weeks. Finally feeling like myself."

"That means you must know your way around," said Harper. She pulled Haven to the door. "Come on, I'm starved. Larkin, lead the way."

Larkin's gaze lingered on Haven's, and a slow smile spread across his sensual lips. Heat crept up Haven's neck, and she hurried to follow Harper into the common room.

Larkin led them out of the building, their pod jostling one another, pointing at buildings and asking Larkin questions as they crossed the quad to the dining hall. Larkin held the door for them, and as Haven slipped by, he flashed her a quick smile. Haven sat at the table next to Kit and surveyed the room, noticing other cadets helping themselves to food heaped on the center of their tables.

Larkin saw her confusion at their own empty table. "We all need to be seated." He moved to allow Harper to sit between him and Kit. As soon as she sat, food, plates, and utensils appeared. "See? We need to do everything together. Work together. Nothing happens around here or at the Academy that doesn't benefit the pod." Haven took a plate that Kit handed to her and scooped salad from a bowl passed to her from the cadet to her right.

Larkin blew on a steaming spear of zucchini and said to Kit, "So you and Harper obviously know one another. Are you related?"

Harper huffed. "No, we're neighbors in Damaris."

Kit said, "Our families are close. We've known each other since we were born. I know all her secrets." He winked at her. "Including the first few months of her shift." Kit gave a dramatic shudder.

"Like your shift was so perfect. I remember when your fuzzy brown feathers dropped out and all you had was a bare wing bone. Yuck. You looked like a plucked chicken." Harper pushed Kit, bumping him into Haven. "And I know a few of your secrets, too. Let me know if you are ever in the sharing mood." Kit glared at her and tore off a mouthful of bread.

A tall male with dark brown hair laughed, his green eyes crinkling. "I can confirm. Kit did look like a plucked chicken."

"You're from Damaris, too?" Haven asked, remembering his name was Tristan.

"Yes, I lived close to Kit growing up. The three of us had classes together."

Haven busied herself with her meal, struggling to suppress the surge of envy. These people were more than friends. She tried to imagine what that would be like, to know someone that well, to be close since childhood. She had companions as a child, more than she could remember. But none stayed long enough for Haven to really know them. Haven's fondest memories were the summers spent with Ayden, the only regular companion she had. But Ayden was younger and wouldn't attend the Academy until next year. She'd hoped she would see a familiar face in the crowd when she arrived at Portos, but now that felt silly. Even if she recognized the face of a child she knew for a moment years ago, it wouldn't be the face of a friend.

Haven placed her fork on her empty plate and sat back in her chair. Her eyebrows rose as her plate vanished. She glanced at Larkin.

"Hobs. Pretty cool, aren't they?"

"I've never seen that before."

"I hadn't either before coming here. Hobs are rare."

He stood, and the rest of the pod followed him outside the dining hall. When they returned to their room, Haven found a stack of unfamiliar training fatigues stacked neatly on her bed. As her podmates bustled around her, putting away their clothes in dressers at the foot of each bunk, Haven held up a pair of sturdy but supple black breeches. She also found two pairs of soft cotton pants and t-shirts.

Haven's eyes widened when Kit took off his shirt and pants. Larkin too stripped naked and pulled on a pair of the same cotton pants Haven held in her hand.

Kit snapped his fingers in front of her face. "Quite an eyeful, isn't it, ladies?" he said.

Heat flared over her cheeks, and she quickly averted her eyes. A petite blond female walked by Larkin naked, pulling on a t-shirt. Larkin lifted her by the waist to her bunk over his. Her legs dangled over the edge in Larkin's face as she wiggled into her drawstring pants.

Haven's desperate gaze found Harper, who shrugged and stripped, leaving Haven alone with her embarrassment. With sidelong glances at the others, Haven got dressed as quickly and discreetly as she could, bumping around Harper as she changed. She hopped onto her bunk above Harper and curled away from the chatter of the pod.

Through the small window near her bunk, Haven stared at the dappled shadows of the trees shifting in the light of a single lamppost, a faint beacon in the darkness. She rolled over when the door to their room opened, and the chatter of her bunkmates quieted as a seraphim dressed in fatigues entered.

"I'm Shane, your squad advisor for the next three years. My job is to make sure this squad, all five pods on this floor, function together and abide by the Academy's rules. The rules of your pod, how you live together, are yours to make, but if you stop working together, you'll hear from me. Any questions?"

The blond female bunked above Larkin said, "What are we doing here? When do we go to the Academy?"

Shane said, "Avina, right?" She nodded. "You'll be here for a few days to adjust to the wardings. After that, we'll move to a secondary outpost, Basic, for three months of physical training before entering the Academy."

"Why magic?" asked Kit.

"Our magic has limits. It's just as important to develop your physical capabilities. You'll learn about your magic gift in your second year. Anything else?" They remained silent. "We start early here. Get some rest while you can."

The pod settled into their bunks, and the lights dimmed. Haven stared at the dark ceiling above her bunk, the day's events spinning rapidly through her mind, making sleep impossible. She had imagined this day for months. Maybe even years. Her mind raced around the new people she met, the unfamiliar surroundings and the change in the structured routine of her parents' estate. Thmorning, she said goodbye to her governess and now she was sharing quarters with nine strangers in a new city. Haven turned on her side toward the window and watched the shadows from the lampposts play across the brick building behind her dorm. She eventually closed her eyes and chased away her scattered thoughts, seeking peace in the solitude of sleep.

Haven's pod filed into a cavernous auditorium with a semicircle of raised seating surrounding a stage. Haven took a seat next to Harper, and a tall, broad-shouldered female with short, spiky blond hair sat next to her.

Haven whispered to Harper, "What's her name again?"

"Quinn," Harper whispered back.

Shane stood at a podium with several other instructors.

"Take your seats and quiet down," he boomed. The conversation dulled, then ceased. "By now, you've met your pod and your advisor. This unit, all one thousand of you, will be together for the next three years while you discover the gifts that make you uniquely seraphim." Shane moved from the podium and paced the stage. "Three thousand years ago, the Drankoni, who some of us recognize as gods, created the Pale, the membrane that surrounds worlds and keeps them safe. They gifted seraphim with magic and flight and ordained our race as protectors of the Pale. It is your duty as seraphim to contribute to that objective. At the Academy, we will hone your innate combat skills and explore your gifts.

"For your first year, we will focus on conditioning, basic fighting skills, weapons training, and flight." Shane unfurled his wings, their span at least twelve feet across. The deep brown feathers shimmered under the auditorium lights. "You are here now because you have completed your shift. Your wings are now capable of flight, but as some of you may have discovered, flight is not instinctual. You will need extensive instruction to use your wings safely and effectively.

"Your second year, we will help you uncover your magic. And with magic, you will learn if your wings have a metal phase." With a soft snicking sound, Shane's wings shifted from feathers to iridescent bronze blades. Haven's eyes widened. At least a dozen razor-edged broadswords splayed from the arched metal arm of his wing, the blades curving and bending around him.

"Did you know our wings could be metal?" Haven whispered to Quinn.

Quinn raised an eyebrow. "Of course. You didn't know that?" Haven shook her head.

The female on the other side of Quinn added, "I didn't either."

Quinn looked at her. "How is that possible, Dune?"

Dune shrugged. "My parents are healers, not fighters. I'm not sure they even have a metal form."

"Not everyone has a metal form?" Haven asked.

"Most do," Quinn said. "But it isn't uncommon to not have one. How do you both not know something so basic?"

Haven looked away as Dune said, "Not everyone's childhood was based on fighting. Did you know it usually takes at least three sessions with a healer to fully treat a severe wound?"

"Yes, actually I do," she said.

"Do you know why?" Dune asked. Quinn was silent. "Because magic has limits. If you try to heal everything at once, the magic will undo itself, and the healing will...unravel. The injury will return." Dune smirked at her. "How did you not know this?" Haven suppressed a laugh and Quinn glared at Dune.

Shane continued, "Your third year, we will teach you how to use your gifts together in practical application by teaching you combat strategy." His wings vanished as he furled them into a sheath in his back. "Your pod will remain together for the duration of your time at the Academy. You will share a floor with five other pods and train together as a squad. Over the next two days, we will organize team-building exercises before we leave for Basic, where you will stay for three months. In the fall, you will transfer to the Academy."

Haven and her pod followed Shane toward the Yard, where other pods were being organized into squads. Dune fell into step beside Haven and Quinn.

"Seems like we all have a lot to learn," Dune said.

"Yeah, and it isn't all about fighting. That's what I thought we were going to learn," Quinn said.

Haven smiled at Dune. "Nice to know I'm not the only one in the dark here."

Dune grinned back. "Hardly." She glanced at Larkin and Kit, who were helping organize the rest of the pod. "Although some of us like to think we have it all figured out."

Right now, Haven would settle for anything beyond constant bewilderment. She dug deep for patience to get through the next few months.

# CHAPTER 3

## Araine

Lukas set down the djinn report and reviewed a draft summary of his own crossing into Terra that Calaine, his Guide, had prepared for him. A few months ago, Calaine discovered a new human who could control fire. She monitored the evora, or human magical, then suggested Lukas observe him in his home in Ferrone, a small town outside Florence, Italy. Lukas crossed last week and studied the evora at work in a café. He seemed well-adjusted, easily concealing his magic gift. Lukas added his name to the list of humans Calaine monitored each month. If he or any of the humans showed signs of persecution or distress, Lukas would cross the Pale to Terra and offer to relocate the evora to the human sanctuary in Middleton, in northern Korsina.

Lukas called a windsprite and requested a meeting with Ryker and his Triad. He picked up the recently delivered report detailing Ryker's last crossing to New York and the djinn he had inadvertently rescued.

The windsprite returned a few minutes later, a twinkling whirl illuminated by a pinpoint center of light. For centuries, the faeries maintained a symbiotic relationship with seraphim, energized by the magic used to summon them. Lukas felt a gentle pressure in his mind, and the tiny faerie transmitted a message in Ryker's voice that his Triad would arrive within the hour.

Lukas flipped through the pages of a second binder of requests submitted to the Rift Council for cultural exchange and found a request from a bar in Phirot for a new game called "horseshoes." He pulled the sheet and made a note to forward the description of the game, based on the human variety he'd witnessed during his crossing to Terra.

Xander, his Warrior, leaned into his office. "Ryker and his Triad are here, in the large study."

"Thanks, I'll be there in a moment. Can you let Calaine know?"

"Yes," Xander said, and shut the door behind him.

Lukas closed the binder and folded a summons from the seraphim Rift Council. The fae senate had requested an investigation of a new type of demon sighted in Casina. He would pass the summons to Ryker during their meeting today.

"Thanks for coming on such short notice," Lukas said to Ryker as he entered the study. "Are you fully recovered from your crossing last month?"

"For the most part." Ryker checked with Silas. "Although probably not enough for a crossing." Silas nodded. "And you? Your crossing last week was successful?"

"Yes, I'm fine. I understand yours was much more difficult, but had an excellent result," Lukas said. He handed the investigation request to Trinity.

"How so? I was surprised to find the djinn in New York with a daeva. I wasn't prepared to perform a rescue."

"Neither were we," Calaine said. "We knew the djinn, Silve, was missing. The Rift Council asked me to search for her, but I never saw her until she arrived here in Berinia with you."

"Who is she?" Ryker asked.

"She is a descendant of Suleiman," Lukas said.

"What?" Ryker said, glancing at Trinity and Silas. "I had no idea she was even missing." The blood of Suleiman's descendants bound the Pale around Elsah-ra, the world of the djinn.

"Yes," Lukas said, "A few months ago, the daevas breached the Pale between their world and Tangyra and kidnapped her when she was visiting the faeries on a diplomatic tour."

"How did they enter Tangyra?" Silas asked.

"They have a new Riftmaker," Lukas said. "Their first in three hundred years."

"How did they know Silve was with the faeries?" Trinity asked.

"That is an excellent question," Lukas said. "One we don't have an answer to yet. But since then, the daevas raided Elsah-ra several times and have either killed or abducted the more powerful of the djinn, specifically their Travelers and Serendib. The latter led the djinn to ask us to help find Silve."

"Were the abducted Serendib found?"

"Most of them, but a few are still missing. With Silve returned, the marids mended the rifts and can See into the daeva world again. If they can find a Serendib, they can send a team to break the binding runes."

"Why weren't we told of this?" Ryker asked.

"The djinn asked us to keep it quiet. Their world was vulnerable without Silve in it. So far, they've found most of the missing Serendib. They asked you to track that daeva because they suspected it had Silve. They were hoping you would find her when you found the demon."

"But you knew," Trinity said.

Lukas held her gaze. "It's my job to know."

"But why do you think the daeva wanted to kill Silve?" Trinity asked. "Seems she would be more valuable to the daevas alive."

"Farna said the wound on her neck was bloody, but not deep. The daeva wasn't trying to kill her. I think it was trying to bind her through blood craft."

"That sounds like a bedtime story," Ryker argued.

"It may be. It would be a wild story if it were true," Lukas said.

"Anyway, let me know if they need us to track the Serendib," Ryker said. "It's disturbing to think of a daeva wielding a Serendib's power."

"What can you tell us about the daeva you killed in New York? We don't think it was the daeva that abducted Silve," Calaine said.

Ryker told her everything he knew and described their previous attempts to track the demon. "We think the daeva was working with a Cloak. At least that's what the djinn are speculating."

"Since daevas can't Cloak," Trinity pointed out, "that would be disturbing indeed. But it explains why we had trouble finding it."

Lukas nodded. "The faeries checked their registries for Cloaks and nothing came up. We questioned our seraphim registered Cloaks and they all check out. We also cleared the fae. I'm guessing we have an unregistered Cloak."

"I'm sure there's more than one," Ryker said. "You know there's a seraphim faction resisting any kind of registry."

"And this is exactly why we need it," Lukas said. "There's still work to do, but the djinn are grateful we found Silve. Although I think they wish you'd left the daeva alive."

Ryker shrugged. "We spent so much energy and time looking for that piece of shit, it didn't occur to us someone would want him alive."

"I get it. But if he were still alive, the djinn would know more about Silve's abduction. It makes the search more complicated."

"Have you spoken with Silve?" Trinity asked.

"No, not directly. The djinn are understandably reluctant to let anyone near her."

"It would be helpful to hear what happened in her own words."

"I know. I'm working on it. But so far they've been firm," Lukas said. "The good news is the djinn feel indebted to us, which is always a good thing to have with your allies. I'll let you know if they change their mind."

Ryker's Triad filed into the lobby, but Ryker hung back. "Calaine, a moment?" Calaine paused, then returned to the study. "How are you?" Ryker asked.

"I'm fine," Calaine said.

Ryker moved close to her, taking her hand. "Tell me you've reconsidered."

She slid her hand from his and sat on the sofa. "No, I haven't. Can you tell me you love me? And don't exaggerate. You know I can tell."

Ryker felt the gentle pressure of her Empath gift on his mind. He allowed her probe and opened to her. "You know I wouldn't do that."

"I know." Calaine's hands twisted in her lap.

He felt her magic dissipate. "I care for you. Isn't that enough for now? And I missed you."

"Charming as ever, but no, it isn't enough. Not for either of us. Let this go, and find someone who can hold your heart."

He pulled her to her feet and held her close. "Are you sure you didn't miss me?" His thumb stroked her lips.

"Yes, I did, and I will continue to miss you. But it's for the best. I know how you feel, and as exciting as it is to my body, it leaves my heart empty." She reached up to pull him close and kissed him lightly. "Goodbye, Ryker. And good luck. I hope you find someone you can love."

"Well?" Silas asked as they walked toward the Garret. Ryker glanced at him and said nothing. "So, she dumped you."

"I wouldn't call it a dumping," Ryker said.

"I would," Silas said, grinning. "I'm rather enjoying the shoe being on the other foot for once."

"Very funny." Ryker gave him a dirty look.

"What you need is a night out. A few beers, some dancing, and you could find someone to distract your broken heart."

"The ball is tomorrow. A night out is exactly what I don't need," Ryker grumbled. "And I wouldn't say my heart is broken."

"Which is exactly why she dumped you."

"I thought we agreed she didn't dump me."

"No, that's what you said. You could use a good dumping once in a while. Let me take you out and mend your bruised ego."

"You're a dick, Silas."

Silas barked a laugh and skimmed Ryker away.

Lilith sat at her desk, rolling the agni in her fingers. So much trouble over a stupid rock. The dull, blue-gray stone was warm but dead enough that it wouldn't burn. She brought the stone near her lamp, and the fera light brightened. A newly mined agni was too powerful to touch, even one as small as Lilith held now. A stone the size of her fist could power an entire city the size of Araine for a hundred years. This stone may be too weak to power a grid, but even a used agni took decades to cool. Lilith gripped the stone in her hand, feeling the heat radiating through her fingers. Once dead, a cut agni was a sought-after gem usually reserved for royalty or off-planet trade. She opened her hand and rolled the stone around her palm, the copper veining cooled to a dull brown that would turn black when the stone was truly dead. She could keep this one for herself, or, in a few years, send it to a cutter. Agni were tricky, and even master craftsmen often shattered them. But a cut stone this size would be valuable, particularly outside Praesia where agni were rarely found.

Lilith walked to her window, glancing at the street. Liam was late. She tapped him and heard his voice in her head.

I know I'm late.

That's okay. But if you come here first, we'll be late for the Advisory Board meeting. I'll just meet you there.

But we do need to talk first. I'll meet you outside the chambers. I'm close. Five minutes. Liam severed the link.

Lilith placed the agni stone in an iron mesh cube and turned the dial. The meshing tightened, creating a solid iron box that contained the stone's residual energy. She checked her watch one last time, then tapped a rune on her side and vanished.

Lilith walked down a quiet, narrow hall in the senate chambers to the lobby outside a large conference room. Liam stood and motioned for her to follow him. He took her elbow and pulled her into an alcove when they were out of hearing distance.

"I can't stay for the meeting," Liam said.

Lilith blinked. "You're not showing up to the Trade Panel either? Why not?"

"I'm needed in Damaris."

Lilith huffed. "The king will see it as an insult. He knows you're here in Araine."

Liam waved a hand at her. "He'll get over it."

"Father, really. Why do you antagonize him like this? I know you miss Airon, but Aric is not a terrible king."

"He's a boy. He will never be like his father."

"He isn't a boy. He's four hundred years old," Lilith said, gently scolding him. "I know he didn't expect to be king. The regency usually skips generations. He's still learning, but he's a good person."

"So good he's dismantling everything his father worked to build?" Liam said, anger rising in his voice. "He's incompetent."

"No, he isn't. He has a different philosophy about leadership we need to work with."

"I don't want to talk about Aric right now. We have two objectives in front of the Board, and later, the Panel. I need you to be my eyes and ears, to make sure we keep our edge."

Lilith folded her arms and glared at him. "I could just say no."

"Don't be a child. And you know you're better at this kind of thing than I am, anyway."

Lilith sighed in resignation. "What do you want?"

"Make sure that asshole Jairo doesn't grab more agni distribution rights. Damaris needs to retain off-world distribution."

"It's where the bulk of distribution is. That's obvious. What else?"

"I've heard a rumor he's pushing to have the Aerial transferred to Phirot."

"Really? I haven't heard that."

"It's a rumor, but I also heard it from an admiral. I wanted to prepare you for that. The Aerial must stay in Cantos."

"Agreed." Lilith thought for a moment. "The lull we've had with the daeva attacks for the last twenty years could be advantageous, for many reasons."

"What do you mean?" Liam asked.

"You could help Aric as a military advisor. Honestly, it's a mystery why the attacks ceased after three hundred years. Aric knows you were the cornerstone of building the Aerial into what it is today, and for keeping the attacks contained to Korsina. You would be in a position of strength when the attacks resume."

"*If* they resume, you mean. But I'm no military commander. I found good people to build the Aerial. Besides, I have no interest in babysitting a spoiled playboy."

"Really, Aric is far from that. You need to socialize with him. You have his respect. You just need to gain his trust. Be more political."

Liam squeezed her elbow. "That's why I have you."

"The ball this week will be a perfect opportunity to be seen, to make contacts," Lilith said. She held his arm. "Please stay..."

He gave her a thin smile. "I can't. Be my eyes and ears, and work your magic there. You are the best at influencing the royals. Give your brother my best, and tell him I'm sorry I missed him." He pulled her close and kissed her cheek. "Don't be a stranger. Come home to Damaris soon." Liam vanished.

Lilith looked at the empty space where her father had been and sighed heavily. This meeting would be much more difficult now. As one of Airon's most trusted advisors, Liam didn't recognize the influence he had over Aric simply by being a connection to a father Aric missed terribly after his sudden death forty years ago. But Liam was testing that influence with his erratic disrespect for Aric's new rule.

Lilith walked slowly down the hall to the chamber room where Jairo, the cesare of Phirot, waited outside the closed doors.

"Where's Liam? I thought I heard his voice," Jairo said.

"He had to return to Damaris." Lilith walked past him as the chamber doors swung open.

"He's blowing off the Board meeting?"

Lilith slowly faced him. "I'm here. I'm fully briefed on the agenda for today's meeting. And your agenda as well."

Jairo's eyes grew cold. "I have no idea what you mean."

"Yes, you do. The Aerial stays where it is."

"The demons targeted the Calimar mines in Phirot. They plundered our agni reserves and slaughtered my people. Phirot and Korsina need more direct protection."

"And they have it." Lilith stepped closer to him. "Where were you for three hundred years when my father built the Aerial and protected *your* people? He taught us how to fight the daevas, how to protect ourselves against the shima's deadly venom. You were still pissing in your diaper then." Jairo's face reddened. Lilith saw Aric round the corner and start toward them. "You want to fuck with me? Go ahead. I'll eat you for lunch." She stepped around him and took Aric's arm.

"A pleasure to see you, your Highness." She led the king around Jairo, amused by his slack jaw and wide eyes. "I think we'll have a very productive meeting today."

# CHAPTER 4

## Basic

It was still dark when an alarm blared in the pod's quarters. Light flooded the room, and a seraphim yelled, "On your feet! Muster in the Yard in five minutes. Anyone late will go home!"

Haven leaped out of bed and hastily dressed, then ran with the rest of her pod to the quad. Escorts were yelling at the confused cadets, directing them into formation until the unit of all one thousand cadets was assembled in neat rows.

The seraphim who spoke to them briefly last night at dinner addressed the assembly. "My name is Kilian. I am responsible for your physical training for the next three years. You will hate me. If you do not hate me, I have not done my job. And I am very good at my job. We will hike to Basic, where you will live for the next three months and attain the minimum level of fitness required at the Academy. That I can promise you. Now, *FALL OUT!*"

Shane paced in front of the five pods from Haven's floor. "You heard your sergeant. MARCH!" The rows of cadets took tentative steps forward. "Did you not hear me? March! Keep your lines!" The berating continued as they marched briskly from the Administration center and deep into the forest.

Shane kept a blistering pace and herded the squad into different formations to adapt to the changing terrain. Haven helped her podmates where she could. A helping hand when Avina stumbled, a branch held back for Dax as he rounded a corner, a little push from behind for Harper to encourage her to keep pace. Haven's team helped her as well. Larkin offered a hand to pull her up a boulder, Dune showed her where to step when crossing a stream, and Kit pulled her back to avoid a camouflaged hole in the path.

Sweat poured into Haven's eyes as the summer sun relentlessly beat down on them. Her chest heaved, and she forced her aching legs and feet to keep up. She knew from the orientation lectures that they would drill on physical training over the summer.

Two hours into this hike, and Haven knew she was in trouble. Blisters stung with each step, and her parched mouth begged for the water she finished ages ago.

"First mistake. Learn to stretch your rations," Shane said, shaking his head when Haven tipped her canteen and a lone drop of water touched her tongue.

The sun was well past the apex of its climb when they arrived at a plateaued clearing in the forest. Basic's cluster of buildings was visible in the distance, a small, walled outpost in a sunken flat valley dotted with pine and oak trees. They worked their way down the rolling hills and assembled in an open, grassy field in front of the gated entrance.

Kilian addressed the exhausted unit. "We're late for our first day of training. We'll start with a two-mile run, after which your instructors will lead you through today's fitness drills."

Haven looked at Harper in shock. "Are you shitting me? After marching all day, now we have fitness training?" Harper's face was as miserable as her own.

"You heard the Sergeant. RUN!" Shane turned on his heel and took off at a brisk jog, and the squad stumbled behind him. Haven could feel the blisters on her feet bursting, the wetness seeping into her socks. When they returned, Haven was near collapse, but she took an ounce of pride in at least staying on her feet, which was better than most of the cadets. Shane then led them through another hour of grueling exercises.

At last, Shane guided them to the dormitories, similar to their quarters in Portos. On the second floor, five doors surrounded a common living space. Haven and her pod found their assigned bunk room and sorted out the new clothing left for them. Harper, Tristan, and Haven headed to the communal bath on the far side of the common room for a shower. Feeling at least clean, Haven trudged with her pod to the dining hall. They wolfed their meal and returned to their quarters, too dead on their feet for conversation. Haven was asleep minutes after her head hit the pillow.

Haven was sure she had just closed her eyes when a blaring horn jolted her awake.

A voice loud enough to rattle her teeth shouted, "Muster in five minutes!"

She groaned and pulled her pillow over her head.

Harper yanked her covers back. "On your feet, cadet. You know how much Shane loves the lazy ones." Haven threw her pillow at Harper. Harper whacked Haven over the head with it.

"Fine, I'm up," Haven griped. She swung her legs over the edge of the bunk and carefully slid to the floor, gingerly testing her blistered feet. Her aching thighs barely held her weight as she stripped and dressed in fatigues and boots.

Standing in formation in the fields, Haven thought she would legitimately kill for a cup of tea.

Shane and Kilian faced their squad, and Kilian's voice boomed, "We've stressed the importance of teamwork. To reinforce this, you will be tethered to a new partner every week for the first month of Basic."

Haven stared at Harper in silent protest. Tethered to someone for a *week*? Gods above, what the hell? Haven's mind raced to the most embarrassing loss of privacy possible.

"The purpose of tethering is to break down barriers between you and your pod," Kilian said, "to teach you self-control, and to value the group above your own personal needs. On the battlefield, the only thing that matters is the safety of your squad."

Shane walked down the center of their pod, lined up in two rows of five. He placed a leather cuff on Haven's wrist. With a muted click, the cuff sealed into a seamless band. Attached to the cuff was a three-foot braided rope, with a single metal carabiner at the end. He attached the link to the one on Kit's rope.

Kilian said, "Learn to love your partner. You will learn to live together, work together, and protect each other. If one falls, the other will fail. Squad leaders, fall out."

Despite their rocky start, she and Kit made a good team. Kit helped her in hand-to-hand combat training, and Haven paced him on their runs and worked on his archery technique.

"How can you know so much about fighting but be so awful with a bow?" Haven asked as he missed the target completely. Again.

Kit swore in frustration. "My father didn't think archery was a necessary skill."

"Stop rotating your elbow when you draw the bow," Haven said, demonstrating a straight arm. "It's one reason your arrows are veering right." Kit released, and the arrow clipped the side of the target before bouncing off to the right. "Better." Haven drew her bow with practiced confidence and let the arrow fly, hitting the center of the target.

Kit whistled low. "Nice. How did you learn archery?"

"One of my tutors taught me. I liked it, so it became a hobby."

Kit worked with her to develop a center of balance where her speed, her best natural attribute so far, could be an effective weapon. But Kit's defenses were impossible to break. Only once did Haven outmaneuver him, and he easily overpowered her and pushed her to the ground. Haven landed on her back, the air rushing out of her lungs. She lay gasping as Kit offered her a hand, helping her to her feet.

"You need to get stronger. Keep working at it," he encouraged her.

They returned to the barracks to clean up before dinner. Haven averted her eyes as Kit stripped and wrapped a towel around his waist. He reconnected the tether after their undressing, and they left for the showers. Kit groaned under his breath as the hot water poured over him.

She glanced at him and said, "My feelings exactly." He bowed his head, braced his free arm against the wall, and groaned louder. "What, no lewd comments, Kit?"

"I'm too tired. Too sore."

Haven's small laugh became a long moan of her own. They finished the shower, dressed, and trudged to the dining common. Hot beef stew, crusty bread, vegetables, and fruit appeared on the table once they were seated, and they dug in as if they had not eaten in a week.

Haven sat next to Maddox, his longer sandy blond hair pulled into a ponytail. "Do you know if you have magic?" she asked.

Maddox's amber eyes flicked up to her. "Nothing yet. How about you?"

Haven shook her head. Maddox looked around the table. "Anyone else?"

"Glamour," Kit said.

"What do you expect to do with that after the Academy?" Haven asked.

"Probably nothing, other than look fabulous." Harper huffed and rolled her eyes. "I'll likely work for my father's merchant shipping business, eventually."

Haven furrowed her brow. "So, why are you here?"

Kit looked at her in surprise. "Why wouldn't I be? As a seraphim, we should all know how to protect our country. And I will probably enter the Aerial after the Academy for the traditional two years of military service. Besides, the Academy is the best place to learn how to fly. I don't know about you, but I've never flown. And who knows? I may have another magic." Haven nodded. "Why are you here?"

"Same," Haven said. "But mostly because I don't know what magic I have yet. And I know it will be very difficult to use my wings. I'm hoping training and building strength will help with that. And to learn what is out there. I'm not even sure where I fit in."

"I think we all feel that way to some degree," Dax said.

"Well, the way my body aches every day, it better mean I'm at least getting in shape," Tristan said.

"Will you join the Aerial after the Academy?" Maddox asked Haven.

"I'm not sure. If I have a talent for it, maybe. But I have a long way to go."

"Same here," Dune chimed in. "Sparring is not something I enjoy so far."

"I don't dislike it," Haven said. "I'm just not very good at it. Yet." Kit nudged her and grinned.

"Your family are healers," Haven said to Dune. "Is that what you want to do?"

"I would love to, if that's what my magic is. But if not, then..." Dune shrugged.

After dinner, Kit and Haven collapsed on his bottom bunk.

"I hope you don't snore," Kit said. Harper tossed Haven a pillow. Kit caught it and handed it to Haven.

"I'm so tired, I hope I remember to breathe."

"Gods, I didn't know this many types of weapons existed," Haven grumbled as she picked up two short swords, awkwardly hefting their weight.

"People are always thinking of new ways to kill each other," said Kit.

Haven raised an eyebrow. "That's a little dark."

"Not everyone is nice," he said, clapping her on the shoulder.

They spent each morning learning sparring techniques in choreographed sequences from their instructors, then the afternoons practicing the moves in pairs with instructor critique. For the entire week, no matter what Haven had in her hand, Kit bested her. Not only were his fighting skills more advanced, he was at least six inches taller and outweighed her by seventy pounds. After hours of repeatedly getting her feet swept out from under her, knocked to the ground by his elbow, or slammed by his body,

Haven lay on the ground and screamed in frustration.

Kit helped her to her feet. "Your stance is all wrong for fighting someone bigger than you." He put his hands on her waist, shifting her body into a new stance. He instructed Haven for the next hour until she could finally knock him backward. "Good, keep practicing. When you get stronger, that move will send me to the ground."

"Thanks for helping me," Haven said.

"Of course," he said.

The next morning in formation, they switched partners and Haven was tethered to Quinn. The instructors used Quinn and Avina, who had skillfully sparred with daggers last week, as examples for new training sequences. During practice, Quinn further showed Haven how to wield a variety of daggers, from short knives effective in close combat to longer, wickedly curved blades that were almost as deadly as a sword. It didn't matter what kind of dagger Quinn had in her hand; she had a natural talent for fighting with the smaller blades. Haven quickly understood that a light dagger handled with skill and speed could easily be her weapon of choice.

At the end of the week, Haven was partnered with Dax. They worked on strength training and using a broadsword, which Haven detested. The sparring sequences the instructors taught did little to help her wield the heavy, ungainly weapon.

On their last night together, Haven and Dax rolled into his bunk after dinner, and she draped her arm over her eyes. She was dying for sleep and bruised from hours of afternoon training with a staff, which Dax used with deadly efficiency to pummel her from head to toe. Dax had come away unscathed, and her brain mulled over several creative ways to get back at him without actually killing either of them in the process. She glanced at Dax, who grinned at her. She wouldn't mind it if he bled a little.

"You look like you're plotting my death," Dax said.

"I am. I'm trying to decide between a clean beheading or a nice, slow bloodletting."

Dax chuckled. "Roll onto your stomach." She did, and he worked the muscles along her spine with his thumbs. Haven groaned loudly, flinching under the pressure of his hands on her sore back.

"Can't you two take that somewhere private?" Tristan commented. Avina giggled with Quinn.

"Don't you dare stop," Haven said.

"Not a chance, princess," Dax said, his thumbs and fingers moving to her neck, down her spine, and up her ribs.

"Don't call me that."

He bowed his head. "Yes, my queen."

"Don't call me that either."

"Certainly, my holy empress." Harper and Larkin joined in the laughter.

"Jerk," Haven said, trying to suppress a laugh.

Dax lay next to her on his side and draped his tethered arm across her hip, and Haven snuggled into his warmth.

The fourth week, Shane paired Haven with Larkin, which gained her a deep look of sympathy from Harper. She had been unusually quiet for the prior week, when she had been tethered to Larkin. Harper's face seemed to be perpetually red, particularly each time she and Larkin emerged from the shower.

Since Larkin was fae, Haven assumed he would be strong and fast, but after the first day, she knew he was in a class of his own. Larkin moved with deadly efficiency.

"Your best skill right now is your speed," Larkin said. "I've seen your training and have some ideas about how you can use this to your advantage." He showed her the basic defensive stances of either moving away from your opponent, going around, or moving forward into their body.

"Defensively, I'd focus on moving away or around. You can use your speed to wear down larger opponents," Larkin said. He moved her body into different positions.

"Your feet should be apart to help carry your weight, and just a little more on your back foot. And you need to keep your knees bent and hips loose," he said. Haven tested the new stance, and Larkin shook his head. He stood behind her and placed his hands on her hips, rotating them to the left and right.

"Looser, keep them flexible. Don't lock them up, or you'll be slow to react." He kept his hands low on her hips. "Pretend you're striking out at someone in front of you." Haven punched at the space in front of her while Larkin moved her hips. She lost her balance and stumbled forward. "You need to practice keeping your hips loose and your balance in your legs."

Larkin helped her with her stances until she was breathless and drenched in sweat.

"How did you learn to spar?" Haven asked, using the bottom of her shirt to wipe her eyes. They walked across the Yard to the dorms together.

"I took a prep course for a year before arriving here. Didn't you?"

"No," Haven said. "I didn't know you could do that." She looked around at the pairs of cadets walking with them. "It's pretty easy to guess who did."

When they arrived at their room, Larkin said, "I need a shower. Are you okay with that?"

Haven swallowed nervously but tried to keep her voice casual. "Sure."

Larkin untethered them and stripped off his shirt, exposing his lean stomach and the corded muscles of his shoulders and arms. He unbuttoned his breeches, and Haven quickly looked away, grimacing with Harper.

Kit walked by Haven and leered at her. "About to get hot and wet, Haven?" She made a face and flipped him off. Kit laughed and followed Haven and Larkin to the showers. "It's going to be a long three years if you keep holding on to your modesty like this," he said from behind her.

Haven ignored his ribbing and chose a corner shower. Next to her, Larkin turned on the water, dropped his towel and stepped into the spray. Looking up and asking the gods for help, she did the same. The hot water hit her face, and she closed her eyes and showered by touch as quickly as she could. She shut off the water and tucked her towel around her, then opened her eyes. Larkin was staring at her, towel slung low on his hips.

"That was impressive. You showered the entire time with your eyes closed." Haven flushed and said nothing as they returned to their room. They untethered, and she dressed quickly with her back to him.

"Well, how was the show?" Kit asked. "Was it feature length? Or a short story?" Dax snickered behind her. Haven brushed him off, but she could feel the heat in her face.

Larkin covered his eyes with his hands. "Well, if Haven ever goes blind, I know she'll get around just fine." Haven glared at him and he winked back.

"You mean you didn't peek? Not even a little?" Kit asked.

"Fuck off, Kit," Haven said, pulling her shirt over her head. Harper kicked Kit in the shin as he walked by. He yelped in pain and hopped to his bunk, and the entire room roared with laughter.

Haven lay next to Larkin that night, thinking of what she had learned with his help. She practiced the new stances in her mind, planning new drills for the next day. Her thoughts drifted at the feel of his hands on her hips and thighs. Haven squirmed, trying to move her thoughts back to the mechanics of the lesson, but her brain and body wouldn't budge. She moved as far away from Larkin as she could in the narrow bunk.

He whispered to her, "It's ok, Haven. It's a natural reaction." She stiffened, remembering his keen fae senses could discern what was on her mind.

"I'm sure you have females draped at your feet all day with your devastating good looks," she snipped.

"Not as many as you'd think. In the fae provinces, I'm rather common."

Gods, she hoped she never went to Tesina. Haven looked at him, the dim moonlight illuminating his hypnotic, amber green eyes.

"I'll try not to ravish you this week," she said.

"Don't try too hard."

"Saying things like that doesn't help."

He snorted and nudged her with his elbow. She smiled and nudged him back.

Haven endured the tether with Larkin, and Kit's horrid humor, for the next six days. Despite the torture of showering, Haven's hand-to-hand sparring techniques improved rapidly with Larkin's help. The most Haven offered Larkin was a good pacer on their morning runs. The squad trained together as a unit, but the week Larkin and Haven were tethered, their pod encouraged them to challenge each other. Their speed became a contest, and Larkin pushed Haven to her limit. At the end of the week, they ended a five-mile run with Larkin falling to the ground gulping for air. Haven heaved next to him, bent over at the waist but still on her feet.

"Ha!" she taunted. "I thought fae were fast!"

He grinned, looking up at her from the ground. "You've improved. Getting fitter every day."

"Get up, fleet-foot," she teased. Larkin chuckled and took her helping hand. He rose and kissed her cheek. Haven pushed him away. "Ew, you're all sweaty."

"Mmmmm, so are you." He brushed a damp strand of hair from her cheek.

Haven's stomach tightened at the brush of his fingertips along her jaw, his hypnotic eyes that seemed to see inside her, and that small curve of his lips that knew too much. She cleared her throat and moved away from him, tugging on their tether. "Come on, let's go eat."

In their room, they stripped and re-tethered, then walked to the shower. Haven turned in the warm spray and washed her hair. Larkin did the same, the bubbles cascading down his chest and over the rippled muscles of his stomach. Haven's gaze wandered over him, then found him looking at her. She tried to casually avert her eyes.

"Look all you want," he said. She glanced at him. "But don't expect me not to react." Haven's eyes dropped and widened slightly, then quickly looked away. She heard him laugh softly.

"Gods, Larkin, really?" she said under her breath.

He shut off the water. "You started it. It's just biology." She scowled at him and grabbed her own towel.

That night Haven couldn't sleep, her mind stubbornly fixated on Larkin's body in the shower. She lay with her back to him and listened to the quiet slumbering sounds of the pod. Even with the limited options on her parents' estate, Haven had two brief romances during the year of her shift, when hormones raged and a seraphim's body matured. Her last relationship with the son of her governess had lasted six months, but she broke it off before leaving for the Academy, seeing no point in maintaining a long-distance relationship that was meaningless to both of them. Haven couldn't relax. The hope of a new relationship—*this one different?*—kept her tense and far from sleep.

Larkin nestled behind her, his fingertips a featherlight touch along her ribs, then rested his hand on her hip. She covered his hand with her own, and his fingers traced the bare skin between her shirt and pants, his touch sending jolts of anticipation—and pleasure—through her body as his warm breath tickled her neck. Soft lips grazed her skin, and his hand drifted to her stomach as he pulled her closer. Their legs tangled together, and he hissed when she pressed into his hard body. He stroked her skin in slow circles that inched up her abdomen until his fingers traced the curve of her breast. She gasped as he cupped her, his thumb grazing her nipple. Haven rolled over to face him, and he leaned over her.

"You're beautiful," Larkin whispered into her ear. He looked at her, then kissed her. She ran her hands along his back, down his perfect backside, and pulled him harder to her. He kissed her cheek, her neck, then tucked her head to his chest.

"Sleep, Haven," he said.

"That's unlikely," she whispered into his neck. She could feel the rumble of a silent laugh in his chest. He stroked her back as her lips tingled. She drank in his scent of rich, earthy woods and enjoyed the luxurious feeling of being held.

In the Yard the next morning, Kilian paced in front of the unit as Shane moved through the squad, removing the tether cuffs. Haven rubbed at her chafed wrist. Kilian said, "Value your team above yourself. For the remainder of Basic, you will be untethered. However, your squad advisor can tether for any reason, so remember the lessons you've learned this month."

Haven struggled to sleep the first night alone in her own bunk without the feel of another body beside her. When she woke the next morning, she saw she wasn't the only one. Tristan and Dune shared a bunk, as did Avina and Larkin. She caught Larkin's eye as he looked at her over Avina's shoulder. She stared at Avina, then back at Larkin's unapologetic eyes. Haven looked away to hide the sting as she pulled on her fatigues.

The next eight weeks passed in an endless cycle of instruction, practice, fitness drills, and aching muscles and constant fatigue. The summer days grew shorter as hints of orange touched the leaves of the trees, and the pod anxiously anticipated the next phase of their training.

"You will move to the Academy in a week," Shane informed them on their last day of Basic. He was interrupted by grumbling throughout the squad.

"Another fucking week of Basic?" Maddox said to Dax.

"I'm over it," Dax whispered back.

Shane held up his hand. "Quiet." The squad's protests faded to sullen silence. "No more training. For this squad and three others, you'll spend the week in Araine to attend the Autumn Ball." Haven's eyes brightened and she glanced at Harper, who clapped her hands in glee. "You have an hour to shower and change. Skimmers will be in the courtyard to take you to the Academy apartments in Falco Park. Enjoy your break. You've earned it. Dismissed."

Harper grabbed Haven's hands. "Oh, this is going to be so much fun."

"I've never been to a ball," Haven said. "What do I do? What do I wear? Oh my gods, help!"

Harper laughed. "You're in safe hands," she said, tucking Haven's hand into her elbow. "Shopping, a dresser, and let's get that hair of yours done properly!"

They both squealed and ran to the dorms.

# CHAPTER 5
## Autumn Equinox

Lukas entered the ballroom flanked by his Triad and strolled through the throng of guests, greeting fae and faerie diplomats, djinn emissaries, and seraphim courtiers. He made his way to the king's dais and took his place next to the other Shadowalkers, where he had a panoramic view of the spectacle.

Lukas scanned the crowd, pausing for a moment on the group of new Academy cadets wandering through the crush of people. He smiled and wondered if he ever looked that young and bewildered at his first ball.

He greeted Finnian, who took up a position alongside him. Approaching his sixth century, the senior Shadowalker's brown hair was touched with gray at the temples, and fine lines appeared around his golden eyes as he smiled at his mate, Corde, who stood by his side.

Ryker lounged casually off the king's dais, apart from the royals' receiving line. He nodded to Lukas, his unusual silver eyes shifting to a dark gray as he looked past Lukas to the crowded room.

Lukas turned his attention back to the crowd and saw his sister make her entrance. Even alone, Lilith's presence commanded attention. Her long, straight black hair rippled in a sheet down her back, setting off her pale skin and dark green eyes. She wove her way through the throng of diplomats and courtiers eager to be seen with her. She stepped onto the dais, and Lukas kissed her cheek.

"You look lovely."

Lilith draped her arm through his. "Always a pleasure. Will you stay near me tonight?"

"If it pleases you."

"It does." Lilith greeted a group of faeries who hovered off the dais. "Make sure you speak with them tonight. We need to develop a better relationship with the new ambassador and his team."

"Of course."

Lukas had entered Lilith's service two years ago and had to admit he liked the work. It was a perfect complement to his role as a diplomatic Shadowalker, although he was still adjusting to working with Lilith. His sister was one hundred years older, and they barely knew each other. She was a professional, a brilliant strategist, but also a private person, which made her an enigma.

King Aric and Queen Tegan entered the ballroom and ascended the dais, acknowledging Lilith and Lukas, then Ryker and Finnian before taking their seats.

The king greeted Jairo, then Kira, the cesare of Korsina. "Where is Liam?" the king asked Lilith.

"My apologies, your Highness," Lilith said. "Unfortunately, a last-minute obligation took him back to Damaris."

The king's gaze grew dark. "That's bullshit and you know it. He was here yesterday. I thought I made it clear he was to come tonight."

Lilith lowered her head, and Lukas shifted uncomfortably. "I'm sorry, your Highness," she said.

"Tell him next time he publicly disobeys me like this, the repercussions won't be only my anger."

"Yes, your Highness," she said. Both Lilith and Lukas bowed deeply, and King Aric turned his attention away from them.

"Gods, Lilith, why didn't you convince him to stay?" Lukas said under his breath.

"I tried. He was adamant," she whispered.

"This petty spat with the king will not end well."

She nodded and sighed. "He's still angry about Airon's death, then the transfer of domestic distribution rights to Phirot. And his anger is getting worse."

"Well, he better get his shit together."

"I agree." She tugged on his arm, leading him off the dais.

Haven entered the ballroom and stopped in her tracks, gaping at the crowded room. The soft light emanating from three magnificent chandeliers warmed the ornate white walls and danced across the splashes of burgundy, green, gold, and brown silks and velvets amongst a sea of black, with dots of crimson in the dress uniform coats of the Aerial commanders. Across the room, the last pink and violet glows of sunset softly lit six massive windows framed in dark wood. A stunning view of the patio and Palace gardens beyond was still visible in the fading light. Servers in white jackets and dove gray slacks passed among the guests with small silver trays, offering delicacies that tantalized Haven's rumbling stomach. The balcony orchestra's lilting music filtered through the rumbling din of voices and clattering shoes on the rich, dark hardwood floor. She could feel the heat on her bare skin from the bodies crowding the room, chasing away the chill of the autumn evening.

Haven and her pod had arrived in Araine four days ago, and she quickly fell in love with Falco Park, a quaint residential district between the shops of Araine and the Temple district of Lucine. They spent the week roaming Araine, delighting in losing their way in the labyrinth of cobblestone streets. Even a few days was enough to understand how small Portos was by comparison.

Harper had dragged her through Araine's many shops and restaurants where they sampled foods she had never heard of. Yesterday at a boutique, Harper chose the burgundy silk gown Haven now wore. She was uncertain of the style Harper selected and crossed her arms over her chest. The plunging neckline and tight brocade bodice that hugged her hips left her feeling a little exposed.

Harper pulled her arms down. "Relax, you look lovely."

Looking around the ballroom, Haven realized there was a lot of skin on display, so she tried to relax and let Harper lead her around.

The king and queen entered the ballroom with their grand-children, Prince Ayden and Princess Tallys, following closely behind. Haven caught Ayden's eye and gave him a small wave from her hip. The prince's eyes lit up, and he noticeably waved at her from across the room.

"You know the prince?"

"Yes," Haven said, chewing her lip. "He visited our home in Korsina during the summers when I was growing up." Harper's eyes narrowed when Haven nudged her. "Come on, let's keep moving."

Harper worked her way down the royal receiving line and in-troduced Haven to a couple near the King's seat. "Lilith, this is Haven and Dax. We are in the same pod at the Academy. Lilith is a member of the Rift Council."

"It's an honor to meet you," Haven said.

Lilith's calculating gaze fell on her for a moment before turning to the male standing next to her. "Lukas, this is Dax and Haven, from Korsina." Lukas barely noticed Dax but studied Haven intently. She shifted awkwardly under his scrutiny. "Lukas is my brother."

Yes, she could see the resemblance, except their eyes. Lukas's bright blue eyes sparkled with friendly mischief. Lilith was attrac-tive in a cold, distant way. Her dark green eyes hovered on Haven but didn't smile, even when her mouth did.

Haven politely excused herself and allowed Harper to pull her to the next group of people.

"Hello, Harper. Having fun with your herd tonight?"

Haven stopped short, and Dax bumped into her from behind. She barely heard his apology. The male speaking to Harper eclipsed the room of beautiful people. Almost a foot taller than Harper, he stood with his hands clasped behind his back, exuding an air of relaxed confidence bordering on arrogance. His short, black hair set off his unusual silver-gray eyes framed by thick, dark lashes. His straight nose and full lips softened the masculine angles of his face. He wore black slacks and a traditional charcoal gray stand collar jacket with black embroidery on the right chest and cuff, expertly tailored to emphasize his broad shoulders and trim waist.

Harper tugged on her hand and pulled Haven from her daze. "Haven, this is Ryker. And this is his Guide, Trinity, and his Warrior, Silas," Harper said.

So, Ryker was a Shadowalker.

Trinity greeted Haven, revealing white teeth and slightly elongated canines of the fae. Haven had never seen someone so beautiful with her ebony skin, gold eyes, and short, tightly curled black hair. She tore her eyes from Trinity, only to see Silas's imposing presence standing an inch or two taller than Ryker and towering a foot over Trinity.

"Haven?" Harper said to her.

Haven blinked. "Sorry, I missed what you said."

Ryker chuckled softly, and Harper scowled at him. She took Haven's arm. "You didn't miss anything. Come on, let's find better company." Ryker laughed.

Harper's rudeness to a Shadowalker shocked her. "Harper, you shouldn't talk that way to him," Haven whispered as they walked by Ryker.

Ryker huffed at Harper. "Yes, she's right. You shouldn't talk to me like that."

Harper gave him a nasty look and pulled Haven to the next group. They continued down the receiving line until they were in front of the king and queen. Haven curtsied low. Ayden grinned at her, and she winked back.

King Aric said, "Hello, Haven. What a surprise to see you here. A very pleasant surprise."

"Thank you for allowing me to attend the Equinox this year," she said, rising to her feet.

Queen Tegan said, "Of course, child. It's long overdue, and a gross oversight on your mother's part."

Haven flushed. "Thank you. The Palace is stunning."

The Queen thanked them, and Harper and Haven moved on.

The music quieted, and a tinkling bell announced the dinner hour. They made their way with the crowd to the dining hall and found their assigned table with the other Academy cadets. Haven took her seat across from Kit and gaped.

"What is with Kit tonight?" she whispered to Harper.

Harper stared at him, too. "Kit's magic is Glamour. He can use it away from the Academy wards. Kit always 'polishes' himself for balls." He was flawless tonight. "I wish he wouldn't do it," Harper said irritably.

"Why?" Haven asked. "I think he's fabulous."

"Yes, and so does every other female here."

"Are you jealous?" Dune needled from Harper's other side.

"Of course not," Harper said too quickly.

"Yes, you are." Haven admired Kit's perfect face, his shining hair, those beautiful green eyes. "What's with you two?"

"Nothing, let's drop it," Harper said, squirming in her seat.

Kit blew Harper a kiss.

Haven left Kit and Harper to their visual battle and turned her attention to Larkin, seated next to Avina. He was just as stunning as Kit tonight. Larkin caught her staring, and she blushed at his curved, sensual smile. She focused on her meal and tried to ignore the room full of dazzlingly handsome males.

Harper rose and tugged at Haven's elbow when the soft dinner music subtly crescendoed and a server removed their plates.

"Come on, time to dance."

"Dance?" Haven said, a flood of anxiety churning her full stomach. "I...I don't know how."

"You've never danced?" Harper said. Haven shook her head but allowed Harper to lead her to the main ballroom.

The king led the queen past her to the dance floor, and Haven was entranced as he swept the Queen around the ballroom, their steps in perfect harmony with the flowing melody.

When the music paused, the queen waved to a cluster in the crowd. "Please, join us."

The Shadowalkers and their Triads led their partners to the dance floor. The couples moved together in the traditional Autumn Waltz, the intricate, uptempo steps dazzling to follow.

The dance ended and the king and queen retired for the evening, taking Ayden and Tallys with them. Ayden gave Haven an overdone pout as he walked by her, sticking out his tongue.

Haven stuck out her tongue, too.

Harper's eyebrows rose. "How well do you know the prince?"

"Very well. He lived near me, and we didn't have siblings of our own, so our parents brought us together often. We terrorized the staff at my parents' house, I'm afraid. He's as close as I have to a brother." Haven cut off Harper's next question. "So, what happens now? Is it over? Do we go back to the apartments?"

"Oh no." Harper flashed her a sunny smile. "Now is when the fun starts." They found their pod as the lights dimmed and the music increased in volume and tempo. Modern dance music piped in from an unseen DJ, replacing the orchestra. "Come on, Kit, let's go." Harper took Kit's hand and waved to Haven to follow.

Harper and Kit weaved their way through the writhing crowd to an empty spot where they danced entirely too close. Feeling awkward, Haven turned to leave the floor and ran into Larkin.

His hands found her waist. "Dance with me, Haven?"

She swallowed. "Sure. But I don't know how to dance like this."

"It's easy. Just move to the music." His hands guided her body, and Haven followed his motion, letting the music inspire her. Their bodies synchronized, and their steps adjusted to the new rhythms, always remaining close. Haven lost track of time and her surroundings as she focused on Larkin, the feel of his hands on her back, on her waist, and how they drifted lower, pulling her close, their hips swaying together in an ancient rhythm.

The music faded and the couples slowed, then dispersed. Harper walked by Haven, her arm linked in Kit's, her cheeks rosy and her eyes bright as she looked at only him. Haven hung back, uncertain, then moved to follow them when Larkin took her hand.

"Some fresh air?" he asked. They walked across the dance floor to a patio surrounded by a waist-high balustrade. Haven leaned on the rail, the light from the ballroom falling on the gardens, hinting at the elaborate maze of topiaries.

Larkin's fingers trailed down her cheek to the line of her jaw. "You look beautiful tonight." He tipped her chin, and his lips slowly brushed hers.

"That's not much of a kiss," she said.

He grinned and pulled her closer. "Wasn't sure if you wanted one," he whispered, his lips tracing the shell of her ear.

"You love to flirt, don't you?"

"With you? I do." His lips trailed across her cheek, then found her mouth. His kiss was deeper, soft and warm as his tongue traced her lips, then touched her tongue.

Haven backed away from him, a little breathless and unsure what to make of him. The kiss they shared in his bed was thrilling, but seeing him willingly sharing a bed with Avina the next day made her hesitate.

"What are we going to do with you?" she murmured, almost to herself. "So, who is it going to be? Me? Avina? Quinn? I'm pretty sure you know you can choose. Unfortunately, you can't have us all."

Larkin's beautiful eyes held her gaze, but he remained silent. Haven brushed by him toward the ballroom. "Think about it. Find me when you decide."

Ryker's temples throbbed. He wished he had not let Silas drag him out last night. To make it worse, Silas seemed fine, and Calaine was taking their breakup seriously and was avoiding him. Ryker lurked in the back of the ballroom until Trinity scolded him, dragging him into the crowd to mingle.

"Will a dance shake you out of this funk?" Trinity asked, leading him to the dance floor. They merged into the swirling flow of couples.

"I doubt it." Normally dancing lifted his spirits, but tonight the black cloud over his mood was relentless. "When can I leave?"

"Hours. Don't even ask. You just got here."

Ryker swore under his breath. "I hate this part of my job sometimes."

Trinity smiled and nodded to a fae senator who passed by. "Be nice."

"I'm always nice."

"No, you aren't."

"Are you going to bail me out and be my partner for the Autumn Waltz?" The music paused and Ryker led Trinity off the dance floor.

"Fine. But only if you can't find someone else. Pick an ambassador. Or a senator. And not Harper. Don't be lazy."

He threw up his hands. "That sounds horrid. I'm getting a drink."

"Hopefully something non-alcoholic." Ryker glared at her, and she laughed.

He walked to the bar and ordered water with lime.

"It's good to see you tonight. It's been too long," Lilith said, sliding up beside him.

Ryker's head pounded. "Really, we saw each other last month," he said with forced politeness.

"Too long," she purred.

Ryker dismissed her tone. "You don't need my company. Seems like you could find a lot of enjoyable conversations at an event like this. It's filled with your kind of people."

"You know I prefer you."

Ryker kept his face still, remembering Trinity's advice. He swallowed the nasty retort on the tip of his tongue. "I wouldn't want to monopolize your time. But please, save me a dance tonight."

Her dark green eyes brightened. "Of course. Hopefully not just one."

Ryker politely extracted his arm and left the bar, regretting his attempt at being civil.

"That must have made you happy," Silas said, smirking as Ryker approached him through the crowd.

"Just what I wanted, Calaine avoiding me and Lilith flirting. Gods," Ryker grumbled.

Silas laughed under his breath.

The crowd stilled, and the conversation dropped to a low hum as the king led the queen to the floor for the traditional waltz. When the queen asked the Shadowalkers to join them, Ryker felt a hand on his arm.

"That dance you promised?" Lilith said in a forced, sultry tone.

*Gods, could she have picked a more public dance?* Ryker sighed and led her to the floor, fluidly moving Lilith in the dance but keeping his gaze over her head and on the others in the room. He saw Silas dancing with Calaine and caught a wink. Tomorrow on the sparring field, he was going to kick his ass.

"We missed seeing you in Araine last month at the Rift Council meeting. Your recovery went well?"

"Yes, I'm fine."

"Will you be staying?"

"For now. The crossing calendar looks light for the next month." Lilith's hand on his arm tensed, but he brushed her off.

"Why don't we discuss it over dinner tomorrow night?"

Ryker's fluid movements faltered, and his attention returned to her. "That sounds more like a social invitation."

"It is," Lilith said, stroking his arm. "It would be fun to get to know each other a little more personally."

"That doesn't sound like a good idea. We work together."

"Don't be so grumpy. It's just dinner," she chided.

"Nothing is ever 'just' with you." The music ended and Ryker stepped away from her. "Thank you for the dance," he said brusquely. He glimpsed a flash of indignant anger on her face as he left her on the dance floor. He lingered with Trinity and a group of faerie ambassadors and fae senators who were deeply embroiled in a discussion of trade routes. Ryker caught Trinity's gaze and rolled his eyes. She slid a hand to his elbow and pinched him. He nudged her, then excused himself and headed to the bar for something stronger.

He found Harper there with her Academy friends and kissed her cheek. "Hey, punk."

"I haven't seen you in three months and that's the best you can do?"

"Yep," he said, ordering a scotch and soda. "Where's your other half?"

"Around. Where's yours?"

"And which one is that? Silas?" Ryker pointed to a cluster of people. Silas's traditional black dress coat, short, wavy blond hair, and broad shoulders stood out in the group of Aerial commanders.

"No, the female variety," Harper said.

"Trinity?" Harper's hands went to her hips. Ryker waved her off. "I'm done with that kind of distraction for a while. More trouble than it's worth," he said, downing half his drink.

"Distraction? That's kind of rude."

"Should I be more specific? How about pain in the ass?" Ryker said.

"You're in a foul mood tonight." Harper pulled Haven forward. "You need to mingle and lighten up. Here, dance with Haven."

"No, that's okay," Haven stammered, trying to keep her feet under her as Harper dragged her forward. "He doesn't have to."

Ryker forgot his irritation at the sight of the female stumbling in front of him. Harper's friend was a beauty. Her height was unusual. Even wobbling in her heels, her eyes came nearly to his chin. Her thick chestnut hair was swept up on the sides and curled down her back in waves, shimmering gold and red in the ballroom's low lights. And her eyes, a deep ocean blue framed by long, dark lashes. Her high cheekbones broke the soft curve of her oval face and set off her full lips. Ryker found it difficult not to notice her lush figure in the dress that barely covered her.

His eyes narrowed as he observed her more closely. He realized he knew this female. Another spoiled, entitled debutante.

"Are you afraid, princess?" Ryker's silver eyes glittered.

Haven bristled. "Of course not. But I don't need to dance with males who don't want me around."

"Yes, I'm sure you have quite a string of followers," Ryker said, his voice flat.

"Probably as long as yours," she snapped.

They glared at each other, neither moving.

"Gods, you two." Harper dragged both Haven and Ryker to the dance floor. The music changed, and the beat and tempo slowed as the orchestra resumed. Harper left them facing each other.

Haven turned to walk away.

Ryker stepped in front of her and slid a hand to her waist. Before she could react, he held her close and swept her through the crowded floor.

Haven felt stiff and unsure in his arms. Ryker pressed her against him. "Relax. Let me guide you," he said. He felt her falter, then her body loosened and she moved with him.

"That's it. Just like that," he whispered. He felt her melt into him, and he swept her around the ballroom, blending gracefully with the soft rhythms of the violin. He slowly smiled. She looked away, a red flush creeping up her pretty face. Ryker laughed to himself. *So easy to fluster the naïve ones.* Her movements improved with every step they took together. He felt her hips follow his, felt the curve of her body under his hand, the brush of her breast against his jacket. Her fresh jasmine scent deepened, shifting into a sweet, rich honey. Ryker's hand on her waist dropped an inch, feeling a hint of the swell of her backside.

When the music faded, Ryker hesitated. He started to move his hand from her waist, but instead pulled her an inch closer, his thumb stroking the silky fabric of her dress. She didn't move away either. Ryker forgot his headache, and for a moment lost himself in her blue eyes. A tentative smile played across her lips.

"You're a lovely dancer," Haven said.

"Thank you."

"And thanks for your patience. I'm just learning." Haven looked around at the other couples who had started to move again to an energetic piano and flute concerto.

"Would you—"

"Excuse me," a firm voice said from behind Ryker. He released Haven and turned to see a fae male behind him. "May I?"

"Of course," Ryker said. He nodded to both of them and left without another word.

Haven watched Ryker walk away, curious to know what he didn't ask. But Larkin consumed her attention as he took her by the waist and swept her into the swirling couples.

"Enjoying the dancing?"

"Yes," she said breathlessly. "But I'm still learning. Sorry in advance to your toes."

Larkin laughed. "You're doing fine. Just stay relaxed."

Larkin was a proficient dancer, but there was something missing. His steps matched the music, but it felt more mechanical, like he was practicing one of their sparring routines. With Ryker, Haven had felt the flow of the music in his movements, the perfect rhythm of his step, and the way he guided her without seeming to force her. She tripped as Larkin turned her abruptly.

"Sorry, maybe it's the tempo of this music. It's a lot faster," Haven said.

"Not a problem. I'm happy to help you learn, even if it takes all night."

"Oh really," she said, a hint of sarcasm in her voice.

He dipped his head to her ear. "I hear you, and I choose *you*." Larkin grazed her cheek with his fingers, tipping her chin, and kissed her lightly, his lips soft and warm on hers. Thoughts of dancing with Ryker vanished as she looked into his amber green eyes. She saw a sparking playfulness, and something deeper. A wanting, one that matched her own. And one she hadn't seen in someone else's eyes in a long time. And to be wanted was thrilling.

Larkin kept her on the dance floor, through slower tempos and energetic staccato melodies until Haven begged for a break. He led her to the dessert table and found Harper, Kit, and Dax speaking to Trinity and Silas. Larkin handed Haven a glass of ice water, which she gulped.

Ryker approached Trinity from behind. "When can we leave?"

Trinity looked around, then at her watch. "Soon."

"How about now. It's close enough."

"I've barely seen you tonight. You're not having fun?" Harper asked, a little disappointed.

"It's a ball. I tolerate them." He studied the crowd around Harper, his gaze passing over Haven. "I'm tired and have no reason to stay."

"Don't be a jerk," Harper snapped.

Ryker pecked Harper's cheek and tickled her ribs. "My deepest apologies."

She flinched and pushed him away with an irked sigh. He grabbed her and pulled her close, kissing her other cheek.

"Come to dinner tomorrow night," he said before walking away. Haven moved closer to Harper.

"Are you okay?" Haven said, staring at Ryker's back.

"Of course." Harper said. "He's my brother. Such an annoying shit."

Haven's mouth dropped, then slowly closed. "Well, you're full of surprises."

Larkin's hand slipped into hers. "Only a few more minutes until the night ends. Last dance?"

"Sure," she said, and followed him back to the floor.

Haven and Larkin later joined their pod in a queue waiting for Skimmers. Haven noticed Kit holding Harper's hand and caught her eye with a raised brow. Harper glanced at Haven's own hand in Larkin's, and they smiled at one another.

A Skimmer took them to their apartment building lobby, and they walked up the stairs to the long corridor of small guest rooms. Haven unlocked the door to the apartment she shared with Harper and looked up when Harper brushed by and followed Kit into his room. Harper winked at Haven over her shoulder and closed the door behind her.

Haven washed her face, brushed her hair, and changed into leggings and a t-shirt. She flopped onto the sofa, still too energized from the evening to sleep. Her ears rang from the clamor of voices and music. Socializing was exciting, but also overwhelming. She closed her eyes and replayed the evening in her mind, from the very beginning when she and Harper dressed for the ball. The giggling and excitement of anticipating the evening had made the process entirely longer than it should have been and made them run a little late. But that had been fun too, and a new experience for her. She almost enjoyed those moments with Harper more than any of the evening.

She thought of learning to dance, the splendor of the Palace, and meeting a faerie for the first time, with their faintly green, opalescent skin and strangely vertical pupils. And the music. Familiar classics that her tutors had drilled into her head, but also the quick, peppy beat of modern music that she instantly loved. The new foods she tried at dinner, and the amazing desserts, some from foreign places she'd never heard of. She recalled a bite of a fluffy cream-filled pastry that tasted of cinnamon, but also had a flare of heat. She would have to ask Harper what that was and try it again before she left Araine.

And the dresses, the splashes of autumn colors contrasting against the formal, dark clothes of the handsome males. She felt an echo of a warm hand on her waist and powerful arms guiding her, with trim hips pressed close. And hypnotic silver eyes. Haven's lips parted as her breathing shallowed. She saw his full lips curl into a half smile.

Haven's eyes popped open as a knock on her door abruptly broke her thoughts. She heaved a sigh as the memories of the evening vanished. She opened her door and found Larkin standing in the hallway, leaning against the doorframe.

"Hi. Kit kicked me out. Can I bunk with you?"

"Wouldn't you rather stay with Dax or Maddox?"

"And sleep on the floor? I know Harper's bed is empty." He gave her a lazy smile.

Haven moved away from the door and allowed him to enter. She pointed to the door on the other side of the small living room. "Harper's bedroom is there."

Larkin moved closer to Haven and stroked her cheek, then traced her lips. "I'm happy to stay there. But I'd rather share yours." He leaned close, and his lips found hers.

An ache she hadn't felt in a long time tingled through her body. His lips were soft, careful, and tentative. He released her and stepped away, but she held his hand. She wanted that closeness. To feel desired. To be cared for. Cared about. And if she walked away now, she might be passing on a chance for a real connection. And that was worth taking a risk. She took his hand and led him to her room.

# Chapter 6

## The Outpost

Haven woke in the dark early morning, her hand drifting to the empty space next to her. She sat up, listening for movement in the silent apartment.

Larkin really left without saying goodbye.

She made herself tea and ordered breakfast, but neither helped settle the knot in her stomach. Looking for a way to ease her anxiety, Haven changed into running clothes and stepped into the dusky morning. She ran through the broad, tree-lined streets of Falco Park that narrowed before winding their way into Araine's shopping district. Shadows of merchants bustled silently in the depths of their shops, the brighter lights of open cafés catering to a scant few early risers. Loneliness and the embarrassment of waking up alone wrestled with the pleasant memories of the night with Larkin in a tangled mess in her heart. But the brisk autumn morning and solitude of the neighborhood helped settle her tangled emotions and cleared her mind. By the time she returned to her apartment and showered, her tension had eased.

Fuck him. She had enjoyed being with him last night, and if it was just sex, that was fine.

Haven was considering ordering lunch when Harper returned.

"Have fun last night?" Haven asked with a grin.

Harper flopped on the couch and stretched. "It was spectacular. I'm in desperate need of a shower and food. Want to go to lunch?"

"Sure," Haven said.

"Where are we going?" Haven asked as they wandered by eclectic shops to an obscure alley.

"Damaris is home, but Ryker has a residence nearby. I know this area well. Check this out." Harper dragged her into a trendy clothing store, where they shuffled through racks of dresses ranging from practical to distinctive and off-beat. Haven tried on a few, but the quirky styles were beyond her comfort zone. Harper tried to talk her into a flouncy orange sundress.

"Where the hell would I ever wear this?" Haven asked, turning to view herself in the mirror.

"Anywhere. How about on a date?"

Haven snorted and slipped into the dressing room. "No. I look like an ice cream cone." She could hear Harper's gale of laughter through the curtain, which set Haven to laughing with her.

They found their way to an open café serving unique delicacies imported from Tangyra.

"The faeries have the best sweets. Here, try this." Harper passed her a fork with a glistening black and green lump. Haven eyed it suspiciously. "Trust me," Harper said.

Haven took the fork and ate the sweet. "Oh wow," she gasped, tasting a balanced blend of chocolate, pistachio, and a fresh fruity flavor she couldn't place. "That's amazing. What is it?"

"Kora berries. Sylphs grow them in Tangyra. Delicious, right?"

"Mmm...yes," Haven stole another bite of Harper's dessert. "So, tell me, what did you do last night?" she asked, licking the chocolate off her fork.

Harper grinned at her. "I don't kiss and tell."

"Ha! I knew there was something between you two."

"This isn't the first time Kit and I have been together. We've always had a close relationship. But this time it's different. I think we're ready for one another."

"What do you mean?"

"We're both in a place where being together feels right, you know?"

Haven picked at the remnants of her salad. "No, not really. I suppose I could imagine it, but I've never felt like that. I've dated a few males, boys really, but nothing serious. It took the edge off the shift, if you know what I mean."

"Gods, yes. Hormones raging. It was the worst," Harper said, and shuddered. "Kit and I, we, uh, helped each other then, too." Harper's face reddened. "But this time feels different. I can feel him here," she said, her hand over her heart.

Haven stared at Harper's hand for a moment. "I'm happy for you both," she said, with a hint of wistfulness. And maybe a touch of envy.

"Dinner plans for tonight?" Haven asked.

"I'm meeting Ryker at a local pub," Harper said. "It's fun, and the food is good."

"I thought you were going to his house."

"He's running late, so change of plans. Come with us. It'll be fun."

Haven and her pod walked the short distance to the Outpost later that evening, but there was still no sign of Larkin. She swallowed the disappointment souring her stomach and pushed him from her mind, determined to have fun her last night in the city with her friends.

Dax spotted a pool table as they finished eating. "Are you up for a game?"

"I've never played before, but sure."

"Come on, I'll show you." Dax led her to the tables and showed her how to rack the colorful balls, explained the basics of the game, and helped her hold the cue stick.

"Choke up on it and lean over the table. Hitting the ball low gives it backspin," he instructed. He hit the white ball with his cue stick and it bounced into another ball with a yellow stripe, stopping short and sending the yellow ball down the table.

"Well, that's clever. Let me try."

Dax helped her through the first few games, which she enjoyed, although she wasn't very good. She got the hang of it by the end of the evening and gave Dax a good run before he sank the black ball on the last shot. Harper, Kit, and Maddox joined them, and they took turns playing. Haven was surprised to find she wasn't the worst. Kit seemed to sink the white cue ball every time it was his turn, and they roasted him mercilessly. Even Kit started laughing when he scratched on the eight ball and lost the game for his team when they were clearly ahead of Dax and Haven.

"Gods, you suck," Maddox said, tossing his stick on the table. "I had them beat by myself. All you had to do was tap the eight ball."

"It isn't my best game," Kit said.

"Buy me a beer and I'll forgive you," Maddox said, clapping Kit on the back and dragging him to the bar.

Around midnight, Haven stifled a yawn. "I'm beat," she said to Dax. "Ready to go?"

Dax stowed the cue stick and followed Haven to their table to retrieve her jacket. Haven saw Harper speaking with Ryker and Trinity, and behind him, in a darkened booth in an alcove, sat Larkin with a seraphim female. They held hands across the table and appeared to be deep in conversation. Haven's throat tightened, and the light joy of the evening with her friends fled. Larkin looked at her and tipped his chin, then turned his attention back to his companion. Haven's mouth dropped.

The only thought left in her head was the need to leave.

She turned toward the door and bumped into Harper. "Oh, sorry," Haven mumbled.

Harper caught her arm. "Are you okay? You look like you saw a ghost."

"Yes, I'm fine." Haven glanced at Larkin, feeling desperate for solitude and some fresh air. "Do me a favor. Don't kick Larkin out of Kit's apartment tonight," she said.

Harper followed Haven's gaze. "Did Larkin stay with you last night?"

Haven nodded. "I need to go. Stay here with Dax. I'll see you later."

"Are you sure? You're upset."

"I'm fine. I'm tired and I need some air." Harper's eyes narrowed. "I promise. I'm fine. Have fun. I'll see you tomorrow."

"Do you need someone to walk you back?" Ryker asked. "It's on my way."

"If you want," Haven said, ready to traipse through the flaming gates of Abaddon if it meant she could leave. Ryker's hand on her back guided her through the crowded bar into the crisp night air. They walked in silence for a few blocks.

"I heard your conversation with Harper. Are you okay?" Ryker asked.

"Yes."

"You don't sound okay. It's none of my business, but you don't seem like the type to tolerate disrespect from any male."

"I can stand up for myself. I just wasn't aware before ten minutes ago I needed to," she said, maybe a little harsher than she intended.

"I didn't mean to imply you should have stayed. What I'm trying to say is I can understand why you would be upset, that your feelings are justified."

"I don't need you to tell me how I should feel," she snapped.

"Of course not," he said stiffly.

The cobblestones under her feet slowly released the sun's heat from the day, a pleasant, warm contrast to the cool autumn night. Their steps echoed down the tranquil streets, but Haven found no comfort for her scattered mind and knotted stomach. They reached her apartment, and Ryker opened the door for her.

"Good night," he said.

She paused in the doorway. "I'm sorry if I was rude. This isn't one of my finest moments." She turned toward the stairs, desperate for solitude.

"I understand. I hope your night gets better," she faintly heard him say as the door clicked closed behind her.

# CHAPTER 7

## Araine

Ryker sat at his desk, reviewing the summary of his next crossing. He heard voices from the floor below and closed the report and stood as Silas and Trinity walked up the stairs to his loft.

"You went to the new djinn restaurant? I've been dying to try it. How was it?" Trinity said.

"Excellent. Food is hot as hell, though," Silas said, plopping onto the couch.

Trinity wrinkled her nose. "You know I don't like really spicy stuff."

"My favorite," Ryker said, sitting next to Silas.

Ryker offered Trinity a glass of wine set out on the low table in front of them, but she shook her head. "Water, please. Still not recovered from the ball."

"Same," Silas said, pouring her a glass from a pitcher. "What's for dinner? I'm starved."

"Roasted chicken. Thought we could all do with something a little lighter. The hobs should deliver it within the hour," Ryker said.

"Where's Shallah?" Trinity asked.

"With River at the Temple. I expect them any minute."

"The Temple? Is everything okay?"

"Yes, she's fine. She's been tired lately, so we thought she should see a healer."

"River is still in town? I didn't see him at the ball," Silas said.

"You know he doesn't like them," Ryker said. "By the way, I spoke with Lance at the ball."

Silas's eyebrows rose. "The chancellor of the Academy? What did he want?"

"He and Finnian asked me to teach."

"You had to know that was coming," Trinity said.

Ryker nodded. "Yes, I'm surprised they waited this long, to be honest. The Academy needs strategists to help with third years. I'll train with Finn for the next two years, then we'll trade off every other year."

"No first-year teaching?" Silas asked.

"Hell no," Ryker said with a shudder.

"What's wrong with teaching first years?" River asked from the stairs.

"Nothing. But I'd prefer to teach cadets after they have some basic skills."

"I like teaching first years," River said, leading Shallah to the sofa. "Fewer arrogant asses." He gave Ryker an arched look.

Ryker ignored him. "How are you?" he asked Shallah. "What did the healer say?"

"I'm fine," she said, waving a hand at him.

River frowned. "She's anemic." Shallah glared at him. "The healer treated her and gave her a prescription of herbs." He folded his arms and fixed his gaze on her. "Which you will take every evening, right?"

"Fine, fine. Don't henpeck me," she said.

"Take care of yourself and we won't have to," River said.

"So, are you starting at the Academy this year? Or next?" Trinity asked.

"Ideally, this year, but what do you think? It really depends on our schedule."

"It's been quiet," Trinity said. "The daeva we finally caught in New York is the only thing I've seen for months."

"I heard the shima queen is waning," River said.

Ryker stared at him in disbelief. "Where did you hear that?"

"You're not the only one privy to demon information," River said with a sneer.

"I didn't say I was."

"You don't believe me?"

Ryker shrugged. "Depends on who told you."

"I heard it in a meeting with the senior leadership of the Aerial and the king."

"When did you start attending meetings with the king?" Silas asked.

"Since I was promoted to unit commander last month," River said.

Shallah gasped and clasped her hands together. "Oh, that's wonderful! Congratulations."

"Thank you," River said.

Ryker said, "Yes, congratulations. Much deserved." River briefly bowed his head.

Trinity asked, "So what of the shima queen? Does the Rift Council know?"

"Not yet," River said. "They're being briefed this week. But I expect the shima will stay bound to Shimar until they spawn a new queen."

"That could take decades," Trinity said.

"It could," River said. "But I've heard there's already a new one. We'll know for sure in a few months. If she truly is a queen, it will take that long for her magic to strengthen enough to push demons through the Pale."

Dinner appeared on the counter in the loft's kitchen. Ryker glanced at the balcony where the sun blazed on the sofas and over-stuffed chairs. Despite the shade of an enormous umbrella, heat danced over the metal railing and concrete decking.

"Looks too hot to eat outside," Ryker said. Trinity and Shallah rose and helped Ryker unpack the steaming food and bring the dishes to the dining table.

"Must be nice having hobs," River said.

Ryker didn't react to River's needling, but Shallah chided him. "Don't start, River."

"What? Hobs are rare. But nothing but the best for our Shadowalker," River said.

"You don't mind riding Ryker's coattails, using the Garret as your flophouse when you come to Araine," Silas said.

"I think I'm owed some comforts," River said. "After all, I'm the one who got you here in one piece, don't you think?"

Silas rolled his eyes, but Ryker remained silent and focused on his dinner. "How many times are you going to pull the 'I'm my brother's protector' card?" Silas asked. "That song gets so old. I think Ryker's success is his own now."

"It's okay, Silas," Ryker said, looking at River. "I've been fortunate. I don't mind sharing what I have." Silence fell over them as the clink of silverware on plates echoed throughout the room.

River wiped his mouth with his napkin and placed it on the table. "Hate to eat and run, but I'm out."

Ryker saw Shallah's face fall. "We haven't seen you in months," he said.

River rose and kissed Shallah's cheek. "I'll come by tomorrow around lunch to see you before I return to Cantos."

She gave River a wan smile. "I'd enjoy that."

Ryker followed River down the stairs and caught his arm before he walked into his guest suite. "Where are you going?" Ryker asked.

"I told you. Out."

Ryker couldn't hide his rising contempt. "You haven't seen Shallah in two years, and you spend less than an hour with her. You leave her to get drunk at a club somewhere?"

River pulled his arm from Ryker's grasp and stepped closer to him with a grin. "Yes. And I'll probably get laid too."

"Don't you ever get tired of the same thing? Booze, sex, and then regret?"

"You're the one that felt regret. I still know how to have fun." He glanced up the stairs. "You'd sit around all night talking. Politics, gossip, boring shit that doesn't matter."

"Like partying matters?"

"No, it doesn't. But it doesn't pretend to be important either. It's just fun, pure and simple. You used to agree with me."

"There's more important things than booze and fucking," Ryker said, his voice cold.

"Okay, Dad, if you say so," River said as he walked into his suite and slammed the door.

Ryker looked up from his book as Trinity walked up the stairs to the loft. The morning sun streamed through the open doors, and a crisp breeze cooled the room. Ryker could feel the heat in the rays pouring in, already warming the dark hardwood floor beneath his bare feet.

"Hey," Trinity said.

"Morning," Ryker said. "Tea?" Trinity nodded and took a seat on the overstuffed chair across from him. Ryker walked to the kitchen and brought her a cup. "There's muffins and fruit if you want something."

"Thanks, I'm good." Trinity blew on the steaming liquid she poured from the pot on the low table between them. "The Council Linked with me this morning. River was right, they know about the shima queen. They want to meet this afternoon to update us. I'm assuming they want me, Calaine, and Tanner to scan for a new queen."

"Can you See it?"

"No, not yet. I'll have to work on it over the next few weeks. Tanner is much better at Seeing into Shimar." She set her cup on the table. "River didn't come home last night. Just thought you should know."

Ryker sighed and ran his hands through his still damp hair. "I think he might be getting worse."

"He's an adult. He's not your responsibility."

"I know. But I wish he would get help."

"You need to recognize you have a problem before you will accept help. River doesn't think there's anything wrong with his lifestyle. His promotion reinforces that he's doing everything right."

"Well, I don't think he knows what he got himself into. This promotion will bring him into politics, which he hates. It will also shine a light on his personal life." Ryker gave her a weary look. "If you want to call it that."

Trinity snorted. "He's been in Araine for a week, and there was already gossip at the ball. And he wasn't even there."

Ryker cringed a little. "I know. I heard. But not the details."

"It was...colorful."

Ryker held up his hands in surrender. "I'm not sure I need to hear more."

"Well, so you know, he's been making the rounds among the courtiers. Apparently, he had a fling with one who was also seeing Prince Archer."

"Oh, shit."

"Yea, it wasn't pretty. Brought the entire thing out to Princess Tylar. You know Tylar and Archer are really just friends, but it was embarrassing."

"Gods, what was he thinking," Ryker mumbled, almost to himself. "Why does he do this?"

"Who knows. He likes to stir the pot. But I think you're right. His new colleagues won't let River drag them through the mud. He'll have to learn discretion."

"He's not good at that," Ryker said, shaking his head.

Trinity drained her cup. "I'll let Silas know about the meeting this afternoon." She paused, and said softly, "Calaine will be there too."

He kept his gaze neutral. "I'm fine."

"I can see that. I think that's what bothers me most."

Ryker frowned. "What do you mean?"

"You know, you and River are the same but opposite sides of the coin."

"Did you just call me a drunk playboy?"

Trinity laughed. "Hardly. But River doesn't let anyone in, and neither do you."

"I don't need anyone. I have you and Silas. My work. Shallah and Harper. That's enough."

"That's flattering, but ridiculous. Calaine really cared for you."

Ryker looked away to the slate rooftops of Araine. "Relationships never work out for someone like me."

Trinity gave him a small smile. "Not everyone is a social climber."

"Yea, but how do you know? I've tried, and it didn't work out so well for me."

"So you're never going to trust anyone again?" Ryker ignored her. "You deserve someone." She kissed his cheek and ruffled his hair. He growled at her. "I'll come get you later for the Council meeting."

Ryker squirmed in his seat on the hard wooden bench as Lilith directed the discussion with the Rift Council to Finnian's latest crossing into Tangyra. A fellow Council member detailed a new rift into Hura and the faeries' plan to map it and secure beacon runes. Ryker sighed and shifted again.

"Stop fidgeting," Trinity hissed.

"Fucking boring," Ryker hissed back. "I thought we were here to talk about the shima queen."

"We will. Eventually," Trinity whispered.

Ryker swore under his breath. "My ass is asleep."

Silas chuckled, and Ryker grinned at him.

"Stop it, you two," Trinity said.

Lilith said, "Thank you for the update. The last topic for today is the shima queen. I think we've all heard the news that she's waning and they've spawned a new queen. Tanner will lead the effort to monitor the queens. I expect a weekly progress update."

Tanner, Finnian's Guide, nodded to her. "In the meantime, the shima are vulnerable. Without a powerful queen, the Pale around their world thins, and other races, like the daevas, easily influence their demons. We have agreed to open negotiations with the daevas."

Ryker stiffened. "We've had an embargo with them for three hundred years. Why change that?"

"Because we need more than warriors to keep them at bay and away from Shimar. We need a new treaty to keep them from using the shima to invade other worlds."

Ryker huffed. "They'll never abide by a treaty."

"They will if they get access to agni again." Voices rose in protest throughout the Council chamber. Lilith raised her hand, and the din of outrage ceased. "We're just starting discussions. Nothing has been decided yet."

"What does the king say to this?" Finnian asked.

"As I said, we are discussing it," Lilith said. Rumbling voices echoed again.

"I think this is ill-advised," Finnian said. "We don't know why the daevas stopped invading twenty years ago. And twenty years isn't enough time to forget the devastation in Korsina over the last three hundred years."

Lilith sighed. "I know all this. We're establishing an advisory group to deal with the daevas. We will allow them to come to Praesia—" The Council room erupted, drowning out Lilith's explanation.

Finnian leapt to his feet. "You're allowing daevas to come *here?* I'm filing a formal protest with the king."

Ryker rose with Finnian. "It will be a joint filing." Ryker glanced at Lukas, who remained in his seat and kept his gaze on Lilith.

Lilith rapped a gavel on her desk, and the din faded to silence. "I understand your feelings. Truly I do. But this is necessary. If you had let me finish, I was planning on inviting you, Finnian, to the advisory group."

"I don't like it," Ryker said.

"Neither do I," Finnian said. "Do you remember how this country suffered at the hands of the daevas? The food shortages because the daevas burned the fields of Korsina, razed villages, and slaughtered livestock? And the plundering of Calimar?" The silence in the chamber was complete. "I do. I remember three hundred years of death. Losing civilians by the tens of thousands. Hundreds of our Aerial soldiers killed by shima poison. A thousand years would not be long enough for me to agree to allow daevas here in Praesia. Find another solution, Lilith." Finnian stormed out of the Council chamber, followed by his Triad.

Ryker held Lilith's gaze for a moment. "I don't know what you're thinking, proposing something like this. Did you ever think to ask us first? We are the front line, keeping the demons at bay." His eyes traveled over the faces of each of the seven Council members. "Finn and I see demons crossing to other worlds, killing faeries, humans, and djinn to take what they want. None of you see what we see. I would rethink this plan." Ryker left his seat and paused by Lukas. Lukas remained seated but looked up.

Ryker said in a low voice, "One day, you'll have to pick a side." Lukas looked away. Ryker shook his head, then left the chamber with Trinity and Silas. In the hall, he caught sight of Finnian crossing the main lobby toward the exit. He jogged to catch up to him. "Finn," he called. Finnian halted with Griffin, his Warrior, and waited for Ryker.

"I'm sorry," Finnian said. "I shouldn't have left the Council like that. But I can't believe what I just heard..."

"I know. It's understandable. You've seen more than anyone in that room. I barely remember the demon attacks. They stopped my last year at the Academy, and Damaris was far away from Calimar and Korsina. The demon attacks seemed remote to us, something that happened to other people."

"Sometimes I feel these Council members live in another world." Finnian's mouth set in a thin line. "I'll let you know what the king says."

"You have my support," Ryker said.

# Chapter 8
## Flight

Haven appeared with a Skimmer in a large square surrounded on three sides by imposing, five-story red brick and white limestone buildings. This was her first look at the Academy, despite having been in the training program for months. Shane met their squad and led them along a path bisecting the square, past a large fountain that dominated the center. Seraphim lounged in grassy areas off the paths, enjoying the warm autumn day.

Haven and her pod jostled each other as they passed through the courtyard.

"Gods, this place is huge," Haven said.

"It's a little scary," Harper said.

"You've never been here?"

"No, not to the actual Academy campus. I had a weekend orientation with my parents last spring, but we could only enter Portos. You didn't attend orientation?"

"No," Haven said, frustrated once again by how unprepared she was.

Harper linked her arm in hers. "That's okay. I know a lot who didn't. Stick with me. We can get lost together."

Haven laughed with nervous relief. The pod walked up the expansive steps of the eastern dormitory. On the second floor, they followed Shane into a large common room surrounded by five bunkrooms.

"Your pod assignments are on the doors. You know the drill. Baths are at the end of the hall and shared by the entire squad. The dining common is in the building behind this one, off the square. Same rules apply here as in Basic. Settle in today, your flight training starts tomorrow morning."

Haven and her pod found their assigned quarters and spent the afternoon sorting through the gear and clothing left on the bunks. Haven avoided Larkin's attempts to catch her attention, refusing to let what happened between them take away from the excitement of finally arriving at the Academy.

On the way to dinner, he finally caught her. "Are you upset with me?"

"Why? Should I be?" she snapped.

"I don't understand," he said, giving her a puzzled look.

The rest of the pod walked by them. "What is it you don't understand?" she spat. "That you slept with me, then vanished, and you haven't spoken to me since? Then I saw you last night with another female?"

"I can see why you're upset. My family was here in Araine for the day. I needed to leave early to see them and didn't want to wake you. The female I was with last night was my cousin. We grew up together, and I haven't seen her in more than a year. Yes, I should have told you. And I'm sorry for that."

"Your cousin is seraphim? Not fae?" Haven asked. Larkin said nothing. "This isn't a great start."

He touched her arm. "You're right. I'm truly sorry."

They walked together to the dining commons, but Haven's stomach tensed. *Maybe his apology came too easily,* she thought. He smiled at her, but the warmth she had seen at the ball was absent in his beautiful eyes.

The next morning, the squad assembled in the Yard, where Shane stood speaking with a tall, powerfully built seraphim who seemed familiar.

"Your flight training begins today," Shane said once they settled. "This is River, your instructor, who will work with you once a week for your first year."

River? The new instructor was identical to Ryker. Haven caught Harper's eye, and Harper nodded.

"I am a commander in the Aerial division and will teach flight techniques each Monday," River said, his voice echoing among the silent cadets. "During the week, you will work on general fitness, combat skills, and drills from each lesson." He paced in front of the squad. "How many of you have flown yet?"

Three cadets raised their hands. He pointed to one of them. "Unfurl your wings." The cadet's gray feather wings emerged from his back, where his wings' magic created a space in his shirt to emerge, then sealed the fabric around the joint.

River inspected the broad span and thick feathers. "Good. And how did your first flight go?"

"Not well. I flew into the air and then didn't know how to come down. So, I ended up falling twenty feet." The cadet winced, and muffled snickers filtered through the crowd.

"While seraphim are gifted with wings, using them isn't an instinct, unfortunately. An irony of our species." Laughter rippled through the squad again. "Injuries are common when learning flight. Fair warning." River walked back to the front of the squad. "The most common type of flight wings are feathers. But seraphim can also have membrane wings." River unfurled his wings, flaring the fourteen-foot span of black leathery skin to display the fine, subtly spotted charcoal fur covering the apex. "Membrane wings are less common, and stronger, built for speed and distance. The fur on the apex protects the wing from the cold of higher altitudes. Are there any membrane wings in this squad?"

Six cadets raised their hand, including Haven. She noticed she was the only female.

River pointed to her. "Cadet, let's see yours." Haven unfurled her wings and spread the twelve-foot span. The leathery brown skin was covered at the apex in a fine tan fur, with gray and black serpentined throughout.

Dax swore under his breath. "Holy shit, those are huge."

Haven glanced at him and saw Kit's eyes bulging. "Gods, Haven..." he said.

River walked around Haven. "You're undersized for your wingspan. Training will be difficult in the beginning, but I'll provide exercises to build the muscles in your back and shoulders." He pointed to her place in line.

Haven withdrew her wings and stepped back to her pod.

Harper whispered from behind her, "Girl, those wings are badass." Haven looked at the ground, trying to suppress a grin.

River continued, "Membrane wings are difficult to control and master, but once you do, they will be one of your strongest assets, and highly valued by the Aerial. We will look to add you to our ranks."

River continued his lecture for the next hour, then they broke into pods.

Haven found Harper once the squad dispersed. "Who is River? And why does he look exactly like Ryker?"

"River and Ryker are twins," Harper said.

"Twins?" Haven stared at River as he instructed another pod. The resemblance was uncanny, except for River's pale, icy blue eyes.

Harper said, "They are the only successful birth of twins I've ever heard of. Unfortunately, their mother didn't survive." Haven wasn't surprised. Seraphim pregnancies were difficult enough with a single birth.

"Is he a Shadowalker like Ryker?"

"No, there are only three Shadowalkers in Berinia. You met them at the ball. Ryker, Lukas, and Finnian."

"Why didn't you mention Ryker had a twin?"

Harper shrugged. "River and I have never been close. I barely know him."

"And Ryker?"

"Ryker and I have been close my whole life," Harper said. "Even though he's twenty years older, he always made time for me when

I was a child. I love my brother very much."

"It's remarkable how much they look alike."

River moved through the pod, laughing with a cadet. "I suppose if you are meeting them for the first time, I can see how you would think they are similar," Harper said. "But they are very different to me."

After lunch, the pod spent an hour of individual instruction with River. He explained the basics of flight: acceleration, braking, drifting, and banking. The cadets practiced the movements on the ground, and Haven knew she was in trouble. After ten minutes, her back ached, and she could barely hold up her wings.

River circled her. "I told you this would be difficult. Wings this size are more commonly found on males with larger frames. You should complete the exercises I give you at least twice a day to build the muscles in your upper body." He moved near her and dipped his head close to her ear. "But nice set of wings." His blue eyes held hers as he moved around her. Haven flushed. "Keep working at it, cadet," he said louder, and moved away to work with Dax. Haven's wings drooped as she saw Dax fan his wings, tilt them to one side, and raise them over his head, simulating a landing.

"Hey, your wings are in the dirt," Maddox said.

"Gods, I can barely lift them."

Maddox tucked his amber wings behind him. "You'll get there. I'll help if I can."

"Thanks," she said. "But I'm not sure there's anything you can do. Unless you want to loan me your back muscles."

Maddox flexed his biceps and growled at her, making her laugh.

Through October, Haven's squad practiced flight techniques on the ground. While she grasped the basics of flight and felt stronger, she was still well behind others in her pod. On one of the last warm mornings of autumn, Haven and her squad assembled in the Yard. She felt a nervous buzz among the cadets.

"We are airborne today," Dax said, his eyes bright.

Haven's face fell. She noticed a female in a healer's white coat standing with River and Shane.

River walked to the front of the squad. "As you may have guessed, today you're airborne. While the first flight isn't technically challenging, you'll find it a strange sensation." Haven swallowed the lump in her throat. She knew the rest of her pod were eager to get in the air, but she still struggled with basic control and wasn't keen on the idea of falling from the sky.

After lunch, their pod met with River and Shane in the training field for their individual instruction.

River reminded the pod of the drill and moved to Haven. "You, come with me," he said. Shane organized the pod as wings unfurled around Haven.

"My first time in the air, I flew so high I couldn't get down. My instructor had to retrieve me." Haven laughed nervously at River's admission. "The first few times are hard, but you'll get the hang of it. Ready?"

"Sure. Might as well," Haven said, glancing with uncertainty at the sky. She unfurled her wings, spreading them wide.

"Remember, your first downstroke should be a fraction of what you think it should be. Give it a try."

Letting gravity move her, Haven let her wings fall gently to the ground. She shot ten feet in the air, panicked, and fell to the ground.

River caught her arm and helped her land on her feet.

"Holy crap," she gasped.

"I told you, these wings are powerful," River said. "But that wasn't too bad."

"I didn't even bring them down. I just let them fall."

"That's perfect. Try it again."

Haven let her wings fall, and she shot into the air, but this time she spread her wings as River and Shane had instructed and let them slow her return to the ground.

"Excellent. Looks like you'll be a natural. But don't get cocky," he joked.

She lowered her wings again with a small push and launched fifty feet into the air. She yelped, panicked a little, and fell, but spread her wings again and lessened her fall to the ground.

River helped ease her down. "There is an art to finding the right power off the ground. That was a little too much. Try again."

She did, and rose a little slower, then coasted to the ground.

"Perfect," River said.

He worked with her for the next hour until she could rise fifty feet into the air and descend and land on her feet. Sweat ran down her forehead and neck into her shirt, and her body ached mercilessly. But overall, their pod had done well. A few falls and some mild bruising, but nothing a healer couldn't easily mend. She walked back to the dorms with her pod, relieved at coming out of the day with only a scratch on her elbow and a sore knee. Her expectations had been so much worse, and a little pride crept into her bouncing stride.

In early November, Haven's pod gathered at the northeast corner of the Academy grounds in a clearing inside the forest.

"We've focused on launching, simple aerial maneuvering, and landing over the past few weeks," Shane recapped. "Today, we'll work on the first of five beginner obstacle courses, which will help you practice banking, deceleration, and turning around objects."

The pod lined up single file while Shane described the course. One by one, Shane sent them into one of five breaks in the trees scattered around the clearing.

For Haven's turn, Shane said, "When you enter the course, your first maneuver will be a bank to the right. The course will be obvious after that. Medium speed to start. For you, controlling your speed will be essential. Don't go in hot." Haven nodded and unfurled her wings. Gently, she launched into the forest.

A wall of trees appeared in front of her, and she banked right as Shane had instructed. She immediately encountered another wall of trees and turned around it, but her right wing thumped across the trunks. Haven hissed as the bark scraped the apex of her wing, leaving tufts of fur behind. The course then demanded another bank, but this time her left wing caught a tree, and she spun out of control and tumbled into the loamy dirt. Haven lay on her back, out of breath. She slapped her hand on the ground, sending a cloud of dust into her face. She coughed and waved it away, then picked herself up and launched again. She slowed her pace a little and maneuvered successfully through the zigzagging labyrinth.

As she rounded a curve, she saw a short wall in front of the next turn. She elevated over the wall and banked at the same time. She overshot the turn, hit her head on a branch, and once again tumbled to the ground and lay there until the world stopped spinning. Picking herself up, she brushed the dirt and needles off her breeches and stood for a moment. The next curve had a similar low wall. She launched a little higher, cleared the wall, and rounded the curve successfully. The next bend had planks hung high overhead, which forced Haven to fly lower, then bank again. Her wingtip dragged through the dirt and caught a tree root. Haven spun into the trees, completely off the main course. Her back slammed into a trunk, and she lay moaning on the ground. She slowly climbed to her feet and walked back to the course. The next curve had planks hung on the left side and looked like a switchback. She launched, cleared the curve, but missed the next one and flew face first into the planking.

Haven made it through the next few curves and came out the other side of the course and found her pod assembled. She landed next to Dax and gingerly touched a scrape on her cheek.

"That was great," Dax said, a huge smile lighting his face.

"It sucked," Haven mumbled.

"What do you mean?"

"How many times did you fall?"

"Uh, none? I scraped a wing on a plank the first time I had to turn harder to the right, but I didn't fall."

Harper said, "That sharp bank got me, too. I caught a wing on a tree and fell. But otherwise, it was fun."

"So you only fell once?" Haven asked. Harper nodded.

"You fell more than that?" Dax asked.

"Yes," Haven said. "A lot." Dax gave her a look of sympathy.

Shane sent the pod back through the course from the opposite direction. Haven's results were about the same. Shane then switched courses, and Haven struggled through the next one with the same outcome. For the next hour, Haven practiced each of the five courses.

Her back and shoulders were screaming in pain, and halfway through the last course, she gave up, furled her wings, and walked the rest of the way. She found Shane and the pod seated on logs and the ground, waiting for her. She sat next to Tristan, fighting back tears of frustration.

Shane dismissed her pod, and Haven rose stiffly.

"Wait for a minute," Shane called to her, waving off Dax and Harper, who hung back waiting for Haven. When they flew away, Shane said to Haven, "I know this is difficult."

"You think?" Haven said dryly.

Shane smiled, his tone supportive. "River warned you it would be a struggle to master flight. Keep practicing. It will come." Haven sighed deeply and unfurled her wings. Shane examined the cuts and scrapes on the leathery membrane. "See a healer before dinner tonight. It will help with the soreness that will come later."

"Great. I can't wait. Just when I think I'm getting the hang of something, I find out I don't know shit."

Shane laughed. "Welcome to the Academy."

By the end of November, the pod had mastered the beginners' obstacle course and moved on to the intermediate level. Haven, however, did not. Banking was still impossible for her to control with any kind of precision.

"It will take time," Shane encouraged. "River will be here tomorrow and will work separately with the membrane group. Accuracy and control will come."

"It's really frustrating," Haven grumbled.

"I know, but your progress is normal."

The next day, River gathered the membrane-winged cadets in the Yard. Haven saw the rest of her pod follow Shane to the obstacle course, and with a pang of disappointment, wished she was like them.

"I know you all feel you are not progressing with your pods, but you shouldn't compare yourselves to them. Today, I have an exercise that will show you how different your wings are." River unfurled his wings and motioned for the six cadets to do the same. "I want you to fly with me in a V formation," he said, flashing them a wicked smile, "and try to keep up." With a powerful downstroke, River launched into the air. The cadets all did the same, and Haven left the earth behind. She flew into formation, third in line to River's right.

River shouted to them, "Now keep up with me." And River was *gone*.

Haven's heart pounded as she stroked her wings, racing through the air at a speed she didn't know was possible. The cadets eventually caught up with River, and he continued to push them at a breakneck pace. Haven blinked rapidly as a thin film slid across her eyes. Her vision cleared, and her eyes stopped watering.

River led them in a large circle, then slowed, bringing them back to the ground. As they slowed, the film across Haven's eyes retracted, and the wind blistered her vision again. River landed in the Yard, the cadets landing beside him. Haven tucked her wings behind her, heaving and grinning from ear to ear.

"Your wings are better than feathers. They are harder to control, but once you learn, you'll outfly any feather-winged seraphim and it won't even be close. So don't compare your progress to other cadets. Who noticed a change in their eyes during flight?"

They all raised their hands.

River said, "With your membrane wings also comes added eye protection. It's like the fur on the apex of your wings. You will eventually learn to unsheathe it at will. Now, let's work on that obstacle course."

The cadets groaned and complained.

"More speed flying!" one cadet yelled.

River laughed and clapped the cadet on the back. "Not until you learn how to bank without running into a tree."

After the group lesson, Haven walked with River back to the dorms.

"I like speed flying more," Haven said.

"I did too when I was learning how to fly," River said. "It's hard with our wings to master agility."

"How long did it take you?"

"Almost a year. Have patience. You'll get there."

Haven stole a sidelong glance at River's striking features. "How long have you been teaching flight?"

"Ten years. I joined the Aerial after graduating from the Academy, and I took to the military right away. The Academy asked me to give a seminar on flight, and I enjoyed teaching. Now, part of my responsibilities with the Aerial includes teaching once a week and leading the flight session during the summer."

Haven moped at the mention of the summer session. "No time off, then."

"You'll need the extra training to keep pace with your pod. You'll get a few weeks off in August."

"Thanks for your help today."

"Sure, anytime." He appraised her arms and torso. "You're doing really well. I can see the change in your musculature from when we first started. You're fitter, stronger."

Haven flexed her biceps. "I'll be a bruiser before you know it."

He gripped her arm and whistled. "Remind me not to arm wrestle you at the end of the year."

Haven rejoined her pod but watched River from a distance as he spoke to Shane. He glanced her way, his gaze settling on hers. Haven averted her eyes, flustered by getting caught staring.

Larkin moved to her side, and Haven dragged her attention from River. "Ready for dinner?" he said, taking her hand.

"Sure." His hand in hers felt strange. Unfamiliar. She saw him staring over her shoulder. His eyes were cold, and his lips compressed into a thin line. He tightened his grip, almost pinching her fingers. Haven followed his gaze and caught River's taunting smile. Larkin tugged on her hand, pulling her away.

Haven looked at Larkin, then at his hand in hers. Since the ball, they had remained close, but Larkin preferred to keep their relationship discrete when around their pod. They found privacy when they could. A few stolen kisses in the common study, or fumbling, hurried touches in the dark behind the dorms, and occasionally they escaped into the woods for sex. But the longer she played this hiding game with Larkin, the more frustrated she became.

As soon as Haven and Larkin approached the dining hall, he dropped her hand. They sat together at dinner, but he kept his back to her, engrossed in a discussion of the intermediate flight course with Tristan. Dax squeezed her shoulder, and she gave him a thin smile. Haven picked at her dinner, half listening to Larkin's conversation that didn't include her. She scowled at him, but he didn't seem to notice. Or maybe he just didn't care.

# CHAPTER 9
## The Common

The winter passed quickly in a haze of training. Haven doubled her lessons, training with her pod while juggling separate sessions with the other membrane-winged cadets, and occasionally one-on-one with Shane and River. In late April, during an individual session with Shane, he ended their lesson early.

"You need to rest your body. You've been dropping weight. If you keep pushing yourself like this, you'll start dropping muscle, which is counter to what you are trying to accomplish," Shane warned.

Haven looked up to see her pod practicing advanced combat maneuvers in the sky above the Yard. "I'm falling farther behind, even behind the other cadets with membrane wings. I need to master these techniques."

"They are males, with bigger frames and heavier musculature. You are the only female with membrane wings, so I understand why you feel isolated. You'll make it up and catch your pod this summer." Shane turned her toward the dorms, giving her a little push. "It's Friday. Take the night off. Have a drink with your pod. Sleep in tomorrow. If I find you at the obstacle course over the weekend, I'll bind your wings in iron for a week."

Haven glowered at him but left for the dorms. She showered, and brooded over Shane's comments as she dressed. She liked the changes in her body that came from the intense training this year. Her tall frame was athletic in a feminine, curvy way. The long muscles in her thighs were stronger, her arms toned. Her endurance had improved, along with her core strength, which showed in her flat, defined abdomen. She was learning to trust her body, her coordination more balanced and instinctive. But she still worried the changes weren't enough to keep up with her squad.

After dinner, her pod headed for The Common, a pub on the Academy campus. She casually surveyed the bar and saw Larkin sitting at a table with Avina. He glanced at her, nodded, then returned his attention to Avina.

Haven huffed and sat next to Dax at a table near the entrance, her back to Larkin. Dax shrugged. "Forget him. I'll buy you a beer."

"A beer will help forget him?"

"Eh, probably not. But I bet you won't care as much."

"Maybe. Maybe it might make me want to punch him in the face."

"I'll get you two." She laughed at his waggling eyebrows.

Haven noticed River and Shane enter the bar. River saw her from the doorway, and Haven waved him to their table.

"What brings you to the Academy on a Friday?" Haven asked as he neared them.

"The flight advisors had a review session with the regents today that ran late, so I stayed over," River said.

"Well, welcome. Please, sit." She motioned to the free chairs at their table.

"You look thin. You've dropped weight," River said.

"So I've heard," she said to River, and glared at Shane.

"You shouldn't. You need to be gaining," River said, thanking the server who delivered their drinks.

Shane sat back in a chair and crossed his arms. "I love being right," he gloated.

Haven made a face at Shane. "Can we not talk about my weight? Or any part of my body."

"Sorry, I didn't mean to offend," River said. "It's hard to not be an instructor all the time. But since it's a Friday and I'm off duty, I can say you look stunning."

Haven looked at him in surprise. "I didn't think you noticed."

"I may be an instructor, but I'm not dead. I can't think of any male who wouldn't agree."

"Dax wouldn't."

"You're wrong about that," Dax chimed. "You're hot." He sipped his beer and continued his conversation with Shane.

Haven gaped at him. What the hell just happened?

River laughed at her reaction. "Dax is a mature male and understands he is your podmate. But it doesn't mean he doesn't think you're attractive."

"Okay, this is a weird conversation."

"So, you don't think people can speak objectively of beauty?" River said.

"Sure." She studied his almost perfect face. "I think you're beautiful."

He leaned closer. "I know."

Haven choked on her beer. "Fair enough," she said, wiping her chin.

"Anyone up for a game of pool?" Dax asked. They moved to the tables and rotated games for the next hour. While still learning, Haven had a natural talent for the game and took her fair share of wins.

Shane swore after Tristan sank the eight ball again. "This is ridiculous. I'm starting to think you have a trick ball on the table."

Tristan said, "Nah, you're just old and blind." Dax and Haven snickered at Shane.

"Keep it up and you'll be running extra laps around the Academy after our session tomorrow."

"Ah, here come the revenge threats," Tristan said. "Not very professional, *professor*."

"Oh, I think it's very professional," Shane said, circling Tristan and poking him in the ribs with the cue stick. "You're getting thick around the middle."

Tristan rubbed his flat, muscled stomach. "I think I'm good. But watch your own. Eating too much humble pie these days." River, Haven, and Dax roared with laughter.

Haven fought a stitch in her side as she racked the balls. From behind her, Larkin said, "Interested in playing teams?" Haven glanced at him but said nothing.

River said, "Sure. I'll take Haven. You can have Tristan."

"I'd prefer Haven," Larkin said.

"I bet you do. But you're a newcomer, so I get to pick my team. Or you can wait your turn and play one-on-one." River pointed to Haven. "You get the break." He reached for a cue stick, his free hand trailing across her waist.

Larkin's face hardened. River smirked and casually guided her to the end of the pool table. The warmth and weight of his touch sent a tingling sensation curling in her stomach. She dragged her mind away from River and focused on the game.

River insisted on using her cue stick, a lighter version that she found easier to wield. Every time they exchanged cues, he would brush her hand or hip. Haven figured it out after the first few times, then it became a game. He would find a new way to stroke a finger, brush her shoulder or hip, and Haven would evade him. She weaved around him once, and his chest bumped hers. Haven bounced off him and laughed at his bluntness after being so subtle. She looked at Larkin, who was also acutely aware of their side game. Red blotches tinted his cheeks. And she found she really didn't care. The game was close, but she and River claimed the win.

Larkin put his cue away and in a clipped voice said to Haven, "Nice game. It's late. Walk you back to the dorm?"

"I'm not ready to leave," Haven said, handing her cue stick to Dax.

"I would have thought you'd be exhausted from the *game*," he said, forcing a smile through his obvious anger.

Haven held his gaze and used one of his indifferent expressions she knew too well. She noticed a muscle tic in his cheek, and she turned back to the game to hide her smile.

"When you're ready, I'm happy to see you back," River offered. "Although, I'm not sure why you need an escort. You look perfectly capable of handling yourself."

"I am," she replied. She turned to Larkin. "If you're tired, I'm sure Avina can see you home."

Dax choked back a laugh. Larkin's expression darkened, then he walked away.

River leaned close to her, his hand on her waist. "Well done." She shot him a sideways glance as he smiled and focused on his next play.

They stumbled out into the black night, the lights of The Common flickering off before their feet hit the stone path.

"I think we pissed off Darius," Dax said, falling into Tristan.

"He'll get over it," Tristan said. "At least he cleaned the entire bar before we left."

"We did worse when we were cadets. Darius has seen it all," Shane said. He clapped Haven on the shoulder as he turned toward the instructors' apartments. "This is exactly what you needed."

"You may be right. I feel relaxed for the first time in months," Haven said.

"Do you need an escort back to the dorm?" Dax said, mocking Larkin in a falsetto voice. Tristan snorted with laughter.

Haven pushed Dax's chest. "You can barely stand up. A lot of good you would be as an escort."

"I'll see you home," River said, letting Shane walk ahead as he waited at the branch in the path that would lead him away from the student dorms. He seemed relaxed and composed compared to her bumbling podmates. He offered Haven his hand. "A walk?" She hesitated, then took his hand and let him lead her in the opposite direction from her dorm. When they were alone, River's flirty, friendly tone vanished. "You need to dump Larkin."

Haven's eyes snapped to him. "I really don't think that is any of your business, *professor*."

River stopped her. "You're right. It isn't. But I don't think you can see what he's doing. He only pays attention to you when he thinks someone else will steal you from him. Trust me, I know the type."

Haven continued walking, the silence heavy between them until they reached the steps of her dorm. "Good night. I enjoyed the evening," River said, his voice distant and polite.

She watched him walk away, his tall, muscular frame fading into the darkness. The sullen mood he left behind was a stark contrast to the playful, light banter they had shared earlier tonight that, if she was being completely honest, she had relished. Then it occurred to her that she may have misread him. That she had missed a chance, maybe, to connect with someone who intrigued her. And excited her. And who maybe felt that way about her, too.

Haven met River the following Monday for another late afternoon lesson. He took her to the advanced obstacle course for the first time and coached her through the difficult banking, deceleration, and agility the course demanded. Their conversations were professional; River kept the personal side she had glimpsed at The Common to himself. But Haven took pride in her performance on the course. She only fell once and walked away from the challenging flight lesson with a light heart and a quick step. River walked with her to the medical center to treat her black eye and bruised ribs.

"I'm looking forward to the day when I don't have to see a healer after every lesson," Haven said.

River chuckled. "Be patient." He paused in front of the medical center and gently held her chin. He turned her face, examining the purpling bruise below her eye. Haven's heart skipped a beat at his warm touch. "It's not that bad," he whispered. He released her face, his fingers tracing her jaw. Goosebumps prickled the skin on her arms.

He said goodbye, but Haven lingered on the steps. "River?" He looked back at her. "Thank you." She walked toward him.

"My pleasure," he replied, his full lips curving into a brief smile before he dipped his head. Haven opened her mouth, but words failed her. "What's on your mind?" River asked.

"I'm not sure. But I'm not interested in hanging out at the dorm tonight."

"Would you like to have dinner with me?"

Haven cocked her head. "Isn't there some kind of Academy rule about instructors and students?"

"I suppose, but I really don't give a shit. It's just dinner."

"Okay," Haven said slowly. "But how will that work? My pod can't eat without me."

"I can clear it with Shane, who can sort it out with the hobs. They're cranky, but not unreasonable. Meet me at the instructors' apartments in an hour?"

Haven agreed and hurried to her dorms, taking the stairs two at a time, her stomach fluttering with anticipation for a change.

Harper walked into the bathroom and dropped her shower bag near a stall where Haven was touching up her makeup.

"You look fancy. What are you up to tonight?" Harper asked.

Haven gave her lips a quick swipe with a blush lipstick. "I'm having dinner with River. Are you okay with that?"

Harper was silent. Her concern caught Haven's attention. "Are you sure you want to see him?" Harper asked.

"Why wouldn't I?"

"You don't know him very well, do you?"

"I guess not. Is there something I should know?"

"River is different. I don't want you hurt."

"He's been nothing but pleasant and polite to me."

Harper watched her for a minute. "Be careful."

"You worry too much. I'm fine," she said, turning back to her mascara.

Haven arrived in the lobby of the instructors' apartments and found River waiting for her. He led her to his top floor apartment, which was small, but modern and elegant. Haven trailed her hand over the polished concrete counters as she passed by the kitchen. Her shoes echoed on the hardwood floors as she sat on the sofa River offered her.

"This place is nice," she said, noticing the table set on the balcony.

"The Academy takes care of its instructors. One reason we don't mind volunteering to teach. Glass of wine?" he offered.

"Sure," she said, taking the glass from him. She looked around the apartment, then her gaze settled on River's dark hair and blue eyes, his broad shoulders stretching the tailored white dress shirt tucked into black jeans. "This must work really well for you with other cadets," Haven teased.

River stiffened, and his smile faded a little. "You're the first cadet I've ever invited here. You make it sound like I prey on students."

"Sorry, that's not what I meant," she said, looking down and fidgeting with her hands.

"Just because I don't care too much for the Academy rules doesn't mean I go out of my way to break them." He leaned back on the sofa and crossed his legs. "I do try to be respectful. But, I don't know, you're different. I'm intrigued. But if you feel this is some kind of trap, you're free to leave any time."

"I...I'm sorry. I didn't mean to insult you. But I obviously did. Sometimes I don't know when to keep my mouth shut," she said.

River refreshed her glass of wine. "Forgiven. The hobs set the table outside, but it's chilly. Are you okay with that?"

"Yes, that sounds fine." He rose to turn on a heat lamp, and food appeared on the counter in the kitchen. They brought dinner outside and ate under the stars. River was funny and charming, and seemed to have forgotten her poor attempt at humor earlier in the evening.

After dinner, Haven helped him clear the table and rinse the dishes.

"Leave them in the sink. The hobs will finish cleaning later." He refilled her glass and slid the balcony door closed. Haven shivered a little.

"Still not quite summer," she said. He sat across from her and sipped his wine.

"So, did you like your first year at the Academy?" he asked.

"Very much. I've learned a lot, and I love the friends I've made in my pod and the squad."

"They are the most important relationships you'll have in your life."

"Are you still close with your pod from the Academy?"

"Some," he said. "A few stayed in the Aerial, and we remain close. But after twenty years, most of us have moved on to other lives."

"I think it's an effort worth making to stay close to friends." Haven finished her wine and noticed the lights winking into darkness in the neighboring buildings.

"It's probably time for me to leave."

They rose, and he took her hand. "Thank you for coming tonight." He kissed her fingers, his lips moving across her hand, warm and soft.

Her stomach tensed and tingled when she felt the tip of his tongue. His ice-blue eyes roved her face, studying her reaction. Haven flushed and dropped his hand.

He stepped closer. "Do you want me...to walk you home?"

Haven smiled at his pause. "I think I would enjoy you...walking me home."

He stepped even closer, their bodies almost touching. "Is there anything special I can do for you? Anything you desire?" he said, his eyes glittering.

"No, I don't think so. Just a walk home before I tuck into bed."

He pulled her close, their bodies fitting together perfectly. "Did you say tuck? With a T?"

Haven laughed. "I did." Her hands rested on his hips, gliding over his trim waist.

"I wasn't sure, so thought I'd ask."

"Flirting?"

He grinned. "Maybe a little. I can't seem to help myself around you."

She slid her hands down his arms and clasped his hands but backed away. They walked together across the campus to the entrance of her dorm. Haven stepped up on the first stair, now eye level with him.

"Thank you for the evening. I had a great time."

He leaned a little closer. "Would it be improper for me to kiss you good night?"

"Definitely," she said. "You are my instructor, after all. I wouldn't want to be accused of manipulating you."

"I'm fine treating you differently." His blue eyes and full lips smiled in a way that made Haven's heart flutter and her pulse quicken. River looked at the dormitory building. "Is this where you want to stay tonight?"

"It's where I need to be."

"But what do you want?"

Haven stepped up another step, moving away from him. "Good night, River." She backed up the steps, but River remained where he was, watching her, until she turned to enter the dorm.

Larkin was waiting for Haven in the common room, lounging on a sofa. "Did you enjoy your night out?" he asked, the tension in his voice a sharp contrast to his relaxed posture.

"I did. Very much." She neared the door to their room, but Larkin stood and held her arm.

"Are you seeing River now?" he asked.

Haven wrenched out of his grip. "I wasn't aware you cared who I'm seeing."

"Why would you think that?"

Haven was stunned into silence. "Really, Larkin? You actually have to ask that? I'm tired of being ignored. And maybe I'm tired of being lonely. And I think it's true. You only pay attention to me when you think someone else is interested." Haven walked around him.

"Maybe I haven't been fair. I can see that. But I do care for you. And seeing you with River hurts."

"Then maybe you should think of my feelings for once. And do you know what I feel right now? I feel like we're a bad habit. One that needs breaking." Haven sighed. "I know I've said this before, and I guess this time I mean it. You need to decide what you want."

"I want you," he said, reaching for her hand. She backed away from him.

"I'm sure you do. But I'm not convinced you want only me."

In late May, as the first year of the Academy came to a close, Haven's flight skills had steadily improved, and she felt ready for the advanced flight session over the summer.

After a grueling session with the other membrane-winged cadets, River walked beside her across the courtyard toward her dorm.

"Dinner with me tonight?" He had asked her every week since their dinner together.

"You know the answer to that," she said.

"Had to check, wondering if I'd worn you down yet."

"My life is complicated, and you're still my instructor. Not exactly proper, don't you think?"

"You know what I think of the Academy rules. And when are you going to dump Larkin? He's unworthy of you," River said. They had repeated this conversation for more than a month, too.

She huffed. "And you think you should take his place?"

"It's a thought." He stopped and held her arm. "Seriously, Haven, no more playing. I enjoyed our dinner together and would like to see where this goes between us."

Haven and Larkin were still trying to make their relationship work. She had agreed to keep a distance from River, and while Larkin seemed more at ease now, Haven's heart was empty. She had been with Larkin a few days after her date with River, but their sex had been unemotional, and she avoided any physical contact with him since. Sex certainly wouldn't fix what was broken between them, and that needed to be mended first.

"I'm still your student. And I'm not comfortable with that kind of relationship," she said.

"Should I quit being an instructor? I'm happy to give it up."

"I'm trying to be serious, and you're being ridiculous."

River took her hand and pulled her into a secluded alcove behind the dorm.

"I think it's unfair you punish me for my chosen profession," he said half-heartedly. She knew he was trying to be funny, but she also knew whatever this was between them didn't fit in her life right now.

"I'm already struggling with one relationship I have to hide. Why would I run to another? It's exhausting," she said, shaking her head.

"Well, we don't have to call this a relationship. I'm happy being...a distraction."

"So, what, you're looking for sex?"

"Sure, if that's what you want. I also enjoy spending time with you. I like you. But I won't lie and tell you I'm not attracted to you. I am. Very much. I think we could have a lot of fun together." His hand ran down her arm and settled on her hip. He pulled her toward him, their hips fitting together in a way that let Haven know what was on his mind.

"As tempting as it is," she said, backing away from him, "I'm not interested in another purely physical relationship. But I'll keep you in mind if I feel I need one."

River gripped her and pulled her hips back to him. He pushed her against the side of the building, pinning her against the wall. His icy blue eyes flared, and for a moment, Haven glimpsed a predator she hadn't seen before.

The hair on the back of her neck prickled. "River, let me go," she whispered. He pressed harder, then released her. She slid from between him and the wall, trying to calm her racing heart and jangled nerves.

"I think you're lying to yourself. I can feel you want me."

"We can't always have what we want." With a chilled tone, she added, "I'll see you in two weeks for the start of the summer session."

A mask of indifference dropped over River's face, then he walked away.

Haven lingered in the building's shadow, her racing heart pounding in rhythm with the thoughts in her head, tumbling from disappointment to disbelief. And a hint of something new. Fear, maybe. She walked to the dorms, her steps as heavy as her heart and mind.

"Are you okay?" Dax asked as she entered their room. "You look like you've seen a demon."

"I...I'm fine."

Dax's eyes narrowed.

"Ready for dinner?" Harper glanced at Dax, then took Haven's hand, leading her to the dining common.

Harper and Dax both tried to draw Haven into conversation, but she kept to herself during dinner, eating slowly, but mostly picking at her food. She sat in the common room afterward, listening to the conversations around her but not talking, feeling disconnected from her pod.

Harper sat next to her on the sofa. "What's bothering you? And don't say nothing."

"I'm not sure." Haven thought for a moment, then asked, "Why are you not close to River?"

Harper started. "He wasn't around much when I was growing up. And his time in the Aerial made him...I don't know. Hard? There's something about him that makes me uncomfortable. He's always been polite to me, but I can't deny what my instincts tell me."

"And what is that?"

"That I shouldn't turn my back on him. Why do you ask?"

"I'm starting to think I have zero judgment when it comes to males."

Harper put an arm around her and gave her a squeeze. "Relationships are tough, but don't give up. There's someone out there for you."

Haven sighed, then walked toward the door. "I'm going for a walk. Hopefully, I can find my brain with some fresh air."

The forest surrounding the Academy couldn't decide if it was the mountains or the plains. The crisp, pungent smell of pines mingled with the tangy, earthy smell of oaks, with a few maples sprinkled in, just enough to put on a colorful show when the seasons turned in autumn. Haven loved the thick canopy of trees, so different from the open plains of Korsina. Fractured sunlight filtered through the branches, shining thin spotlights on the dust dancing in the air from the soft, loamy dirt under her feet. The surrounding silence quieted her mind and let her focus on her own thoughts.

She knew her relationship with Larkin had run its course, but her heart wasn't ready to give up. She imagined Larkin holding her hand, kissing her with affection, spending time with her, talking and laughing. The way she thought it should be with a lover. The way Kit behaved with Harper. Despite its flaws, her relationship with Larkin had been the longest of her life. Part of her felt like it could have been more if she had done something different, given him something more of her. But a part of her also knew she couldn't force someone to have feelings they didn't have. She had never ended a relationship like this. With her emotions tangled up with Larkin, she wasn't sure how to end it without crushing her own heart. And flirting with River, while a thrill, didn't seem to help. She also couldn't shake the feeling she was playing with fire. A tear of frustration fell on her cheek, and she angrily swiped it away.

Haven rounded a large redwood tree and stopped in her tracks. In a small clearing, Larkin held Avina on his lap. They were both naked, with Larkin buried inside her. Haven tried to leave but her feet wouldn't move. She watched them as Avina moved on him, her head thrown back. Larkin's hands cupped her backside as he moved with her. Their pace quickened and Avina cried out.

Larkin noticed Haven over Avina's shoulder. He held Haven's eyes as he thrust into Avina and shuddered.

Haven's heart died. She left the woods, tears streaming down her face.

Dax found her an hour later in the shadows behind the dorm.

"What are you doing here? Where have you been?" Haven turned toward him, and the dim light from the windows fell across her face. "Ah. So you know about Larkin and Avina."

"You all knew?" Haven sniffled.

"Yes." He wiped at the tear dripping from her jaw. "And you should have, too. It was pretty obvious. But I don't think you wanted to see it."

"I feel like an idiot." She hugged her arms around her body as another tear slipped down her face.

"We all do stupid things when our hearts lead our minds. You're not an idiot, Haven. You have feelings. Emotions. Which is normal. Larkin doesn't, not like the rest of us."

"I watched him fuck Avina. He saw me watching, and I think he liked it," she said, hiccupping. "Gods, how could I be so wrong about someone?" He reached for her hand. She squeezed it, and he pulled her in and hugged her tight.

"I'm sorry. As your friend, my heart breaks for you." He pulled her back and wiped her face again. "But as your podmate, I'm telling you now, you need to fix this. Our pod needs you, and we can all feel the tension between you, Larkin, and Avina. We have two more years together. Next year, hopefully Larkin will leave for the Institute, but Avina will be here. You made the choice to have a physical relationship with someone in our pod. You owe it to us to not let that choice damage us."

Haven was speechless. "You're right. I'm sorry. What I'm hearing from you is it's time I grew up."

"If it's any consolation, Larkin is a piece of shit and doesn't deserve you."

Haven hugged him. "Thanks. And thank you for being my friend. Even if it means kicking my ass and telling me to stop being a child."

"That's what friends are for. Come on. No more tears over Larkin." Dax pulled her to her feet. "There are way better options out there."

The next morning, Haven found Larkin in the common room. "Can I speak with you?" she said. He followed her to a study. She closed the door behind her and rested against it. Larkin perched on the edge of a table. "We both know I caught you with Avina yesterday." Larkin folded his arms across his chest and nodded. "And I know it didn't bother you in the slightest." His bored expression turned Haven's nerves to anger. "I've been clear from the beginning I expected our relationship to be exclusive. You obviously didn't respect that, so it's over between us. I needed to say it to you, so there's no misunderstanding. You've hurt me, and I don't think highly of you right now."

A hint of a smile played on his lips. "That's disappointing. And I'll miss you."

Haven abruptly laughed. "Fuck off, Larkin. You actually have to care about someone to miss them, and we all know you don't care for anyone but yourself. Our pod comes first from now on, and these types of flings make everyone uncomfortable. So keep your dick in your pants."

She left the study and found Avina, Dax, and Maddox in their quarters changing into flight gear.

"Avina, can I speak with you?" Haven asked.

Dax quickly took Maddox's arm and dragged him away.

Haven closed the door behind them. "I saw you last night with Larkin. In the woods." Avina flushed. "Larkin and I are done. But you knew I was seeing Larkin, yet you thought it was okay to fuck him."

"I wasn't sure what was between you," Avina stammered.

"And you didn't think to ask? Come on, that's bullshit and you know it."

"Honestly, I thought you felt the same. He's fun and expects nothing from me. And it's common knowledge he sleeps with anyone."

"Yes, well, I guess that makes me the village idiot because I certainly didn't feel that way," Haven snapped. Avina's cheeks blushed an even deeper shade of red. "Whatever, it's over. I won't let my feelings toward you or Larkin interfere with this pod any longer. I've spoken to Larkin about keeping it in his pants, and I'm saying the same to you. It's time we all thought of our pod and not what's between our legs. Myself included. Understood?"

Avina's eyes dropped, and she nodded.

"And by the way, Larkin saw me watching you have sex last night, and that's what made him come."

Haven left the room, slamming the door behind her.

# CHAPTER 10

## Magic

Haven's second year started with a grueling three-week stay at Basic. For once, Haven felt ahead of her pod since she had spent her summer working hard to master the advanced aerial flight training instead of lounging at the beach. She squeezed in a quick two-week break in Araine, meeting up with Dax, Tristan, and Quinn for the last week in a whirlwind of exploring the city she had grown to love. Dax had even taken her to her first live theater performance, and they spent the evening howling at the comedy.

In mid-September, on their first day back at the Academy, the squad gathered in a large seminar auditorium.

"Well, this is different," Dax said. Shane and two instructors she didn't recognize were speaking together on a raised dais in front of the amphitheater as the cadets filled the room.

"I thought this year we were learning magic," Tristan said, sliding into the seat next to Dax.

Shane rapped on the podium. "Take your seats and quiet down." The cadets rustled into silence. "I'm pleased to introduce two new instructors." An older seraphim of medium height, with dark green eyes and black hair graying at the temples, stepped forward. "This is Adrien, a gifted guardian and scholar with extensive knowledge of seraphim history." He gestured to a fae male with sandy blond hair and cornflower blue eyes. "This is Kaden, who leads the Academy's magic training. This year, you will explore your magic gifts with Kaden and his team and learn our history with Adrien."

Tristan groaned. "Gods, a history lesson? I'm already dying of boredom."

Dax snickered under his breath.

Haven scolded them both. Seraphim history had been her favorite subject with her tutors, and she perked up at the idea of learning from a scholar. An hour later, however, Haven was squirming in her seat, trying to stay focused on Adrien's monotone, droning voice.

Dax's head drooped, then jerked as he fought sleep. Tristan had given up the fight half an hour ago and snored softly.

Finally, Adrien's lecture ended, and Kaden took the podium.

Haven swatted Tristan and his head snapped up. "What?" he shouted. Dax snorted.

Kaden said, "Who here already knows what kind of magic they have?" Half the students raised their hands. Kaden pointed at one cadet.

"I can control water," the cadet said.

Kaden pointed at another. "Wind, I think."

Kaden nodded. "Elemental magic is the most common type of magical gifts. Whether you can feel your gift now has no bearing on whether you have an actual gift. Some of you will have more than one. Does anyone here know if they have multiple magics?"

Two cadets raised their hands. Kaden pointed at one of them. "What do you have?"

"Wind and Skimming," the cadet said. "Although I've only skimmed a few feet twice."

"Skimming is a common, non-elemental gift. It needs to be developed slowly to prevent injury, and it varies in strength. Some of you may have magic strong enough to skim others.

"Our magical gifts fall into three categories. Elemental magic, as I mentioned earlier. That's Water, Wind or air, Fire, and Light. Of the four, Light is the strongest. It also produces heat and is the strongest foundation for healing. Phrenic magics, or those involving the mind or emotions, are the next category. Phrenics are our empaths and sympaths, the fae Seers and Linkers. It also includes Skimmers, but we still debate whether Skimming is a Phrenic gift or if it belongs in the third category, Strophae." Kaden asked the cadets, "Anyone here have Glamour magic?"

Kit raised his hand.

Kaden said, "Strophae magics consist of Echo, Glamour, Persuasion, Amplifier, Cloaks, and a few others. We think of them as trickster magics, or deceivers. In Berinia, we require all Strophae gifts to be registered to ensure these gifts are used properly. For example, if you develop Persuasion magic, it is illegal to use this to force someone to do something against their will. Repeated abuse of a Strophae gift may be punished by permanent warding that will dampen your magical abilities. Strophae gifts used properly can be very beneficial to our society. Our guardians who apply wardings and runes usually have either Echo or Amplifier magics, or sometimes both.

"There are certain magics that can be combined into a learned magic, mostly based on Amplify and Echo. Seraphim readers, guardians, and healers are examples of these, and where a seraphim lands really depends on the strength and characteristics of their magics. For example, most of our healers have a combination of elemental magic and a Strophic gift. Elementals have a passive healing capability inside the magic. Wind is particularly useful for respiratory and cardiac health. Water is best with circulatory and digestive. Fire is effective on the mind and nervous system. Light is universal. Amplify can enhance the healing properties of elemental magics, particularly Light. Later this year, you will have a guest lecturer, Farna, who will describe our healers in more depth. Farna's primary magic is Light, and he's one of the strongest elementals I've seen. His secondary magic, Amplify, is almost as strong, which is why he is our Master Healer."

Adrien moved forward to stand beside Kaden and said, "The three categories of magic come from the offspring of our original seraphim founders, Gabriel and his partner, Fenix. The Drankoni, our gods, helped Gabriel and Fenix divide their magics amongst their children. Caspian, their oldest son, was an Elemental. Their daughter, Kensal, was a Phrenic, the line of mental and healing gifts. The youngest son, Loeki, was gifted the Strophae magical line. Gabriel and Fenix themselves had unique magical gifts that don't fall into these categories.

"When the Drankoni created the Pale and chose the seraphim as its protectors, they gifted Gabriel Shadowalking magic. He was our original world walker and had the gift of Bane that is unique to seraphim. We consider Shadowalking one of the most essential magics in the role of seraphim as guardians of worlds. Berinia has three Shadowalkers, and only two have Bane magic.

"The Drankoni transformed Fenix, replacing her magic with raw power through Pairing."

A cadet raised her hand. Adrien pointed to her. "Why Fenix?"

"She was a warrior, the leader of the elite Valkyria, the King's Guard," Adrien said. "She was loyal and a fierce fighter. The Drankoni further divided the magical gifts to the next generation, limiting the power of future seraphim."

Kaden continued, "Those of you who develop multiple gifts will receive one-on-one instruction. Magic is tricky and takes patience. To understand how to use your magic, it is helpful to understand our origins. Adrien will return once a month for additional seminars on magical history. We look forward to his talks."

"Great. More mid-morning naps," Tristan grumbled. Dax yawned in agreement. The auditorium filled with the sound of scraping chairs and low voices as they filed out of the seminar hall into the plaza. Haven stretched and yawned herself, trying to clear the dulling fog of Adrien's lecture from her head. She squinted in the midday sun. "Come on," Haven said. "We all need a strong cup of tea after that."

"Forget tea. More of those lessons and I'll start bringing a flask," Tristan said.

Larkin walked away from their pod alone. She had not seen him over the summer and didn't miss him. But she regretted the tension she caused, which had only worsened when they returned for the new academic year. Larkin had withdrawn from their pod and spent most of his time sullen and quiet. He was quick to anger when Dax or Tristan reminded him of their rules about no casual relationships within the pod. Avina kept her distance from Larkin, which seemed to anger him even further.

The next day, the squad gathered in the Yard and Shane introduced them to their instructor, Tannys. Haven stood next to Larkin, who kept his eyes forward and away from her, except for the occasional brief stare filled with cold malice. She glanced at Dax, who shrugged. She wasn't sure how to repair their relationship with Larkin, and hoped time would soothe the tension between them. Or at least show her a way to mend this fence.

Haven sighed and turned her attention to the lesson.

The petite fae female stepped forward and said, "We will start with some basics. Accessing your magic should be an instinct. It's sort of like riding a bicycle. Some people can instinctively do it, and some need training wheels."

Laughter rippled through the squad.

"Who has used their magic already?" Half the squad raised their hands, including Larkin, Kit, Tristan, and Avina. Tannys gestured at Larkin. "What type of magic do you have?"

"I can shapeshift. But only flight animals."

"Have you ever completely shifted to an animal?"

"No. So far, I can only shift to wings. And it's pretty easy for me to produce seraphim flight wings."

"That's because you share the same anatomy with seraphim. You're only really shifting part way and producing wings. You will need detailed anatomy instruction to fully shift into a bird."

"What about other animals?" Larkin asked. "I've never been able to produce fur. Not even the membrane wings like Haven and River have."

"Most fae shifters are limited to one species. The only true shapeshifters I've ever heard of are certain types of demons."

Tannys said to Larkin, "I can understand why you trained here at the Academy last year, but you should think carefully about continuing your education at the Institute. They have several master shifters on staff, and peers to learn with." She queried the rest of the squad. "Anyone else?"

The squad had a scattering of elementals, a few Skimmers, and an Echo.

"An Echo is a rare Strophic gift. I'll set up one-on-one instruction with you for the first few months to show you how to use your gift within our laws."

That afternoon, Tannys worked with Haven's pod. Dax found he had Fire magic, and Tristan discovered he could control Wind. Unlocking magic perplexed Haven.

"It's a pull inside your stomach," Dax explained after their lesson. "Focus on it and the magic appears." Haven focused on her stomach but felt no pull, just a rumbling telling her it was dinnertime.

By the end of October, most of the pod had uncovered their gifts. Harper and Quinn discovered they had Water magic, and Maddox found he could Skim, but Dune and Haven still had no evidence of magic. Tannys worked with Dune and Haven separately.

"Your gifts may be less common," she said. "For example, it took Lukas several months before his Shadowalking magic appeared."

A look of horror crossed Dune's face. "Gods, I hope that's not my magic."

"I doubt it's Shadowalking," Tannys said, resting a comforting hand on Dune's shoulder. "That truly is a rare gift. Although you should have seen Lukas's face when his arm disappeared in a cloud of smoke. I must admit, we were all shocked since Ryker was in the same class as Lukas. Two cadets with that rare gift caused quite the stir around the Academy."

Tannys next instructed Haven and Dune on meditation techniques. Haven cleared her mind and relaxed, controlling her breathing in a deep, slow rhythm. She felt inside for any kind of pull. She focused on her mind rather than on her stomach like her podmates had, and felt a thread, a presence that was *different*. Strong and wild.

Her hands burst into Light.

Tannys's face brightened. "You found it!"

Haven felt a strength flow through her. The Light brightened, and Haven felt heat. And it was *hot*.

"Okay, you need to let it go," Tannys said.

Haven hissed in pain as her hands burned. "How?" Haven asked, shaking her hands.

"Let the thread go, Haven, now."

Haven's hands erupted in flames. "Oh, *fuck*." She shook her hands, trying to extinguish the flames.

"*Let it go!*" Tannys shouted, breaking Haven's concentration.

The Light vanished, and Haven swore under her breath.

Tannys gingerly turned her hands over, examining the blistering red welts. "Well, it's a start. Now let's find a healer and get you patched up."

Through November, Tannys worked with the pod, helping them control their gifts. Dune eventually uncovered her Amplify magic and was thrilled when days later her second magic, Wind, appeared, giving her the tools she needed to be a healer.

"I was hoping for Light," Dune said, holding out her palm where a leaf swirled in an invisible tornado. "But Wind is good, too. My mother has Wind, and it's an excellent healing source, particularly with respiratory ailments."

Dune had an abundance of opportunities to learn how to combine her magics to heal the basic injuries that seemed to plague the squad. Haven learned to control the heat of her Light, but it still occasionally got away from her. Dune graduated to more complicated injuries and took to following Haven around, hoping she'd have a magic mishap. Dune suggested Haven's gift might lead to a career path in healing. Haven wasn't sure healing interested her but tried to keep an open mind. As the months passed and a second Strophic gift didn't appear, the possibility of training to be a healer faded.

By January, Haven's pod had mastered basic control of their magic. After being segregated from flight training last year, magic training gave Haven the chance to progress alongside her pod. While Haven's Light magic was a powerful gift, she learned to master it at the same tempo as others in her pod, and faster than others who were challenged with more difficult gifts. Knox, a male from another pod in her dorm, discovered a strong Echo gift and still struggled to use it properly. For once, Haven wasn't the one singled out for individual instruction. She didn't envy Knox, although she sympathized with him.

The past few months of unity without romantic entanglement had brought Haven closer to her pod. She found a new level of friendship, particularly with Dax and Maddox, and Harper, when she could catch her alone in between lessons and dates with Kit. She felt a deeper connection and relished the comfort of finally growing in community, struggles and all.

On an unusually bright, crisp winter day, both Ryker and River joined them as guest speakers. The brothers stood before them with unfurled wings, Ryker's raven-black feathers crossing with River's black membrane.

Tannys said, "You have all progressed well with your gifts. The next step is to discover whether your wings can shift." In a blink, River and Ryker's apex wing bone became a series of metal rods. Ryker's black feathers vanished, and more than a dozen broadsword blades, gleaming black as night, fanned from the metal arch of his wing. River's membrane shifted to matte charcoal blades that absorbed all light. Haven gaped, transfixed by the bending metal.

Tannys pointed to River's blades. "Carbon steel. Very tough, very sharp." She turned to Ryker. "Onyx steel, a metal unique to seraphim. The only thing harder is diamonds. Extremely sharp."

Tannys walked among the cadets. "Shifting your wings usually comes with discovering your magic gifts. You focus those same sensations on the sheaths in your back, on your wings. And if you have a metal phase, your wings should shift."

She approached Dax. "Unfurl your wings. You're our test case today." Dax's black feathered wings unfurled with a sigh. "Now focus here." She touched the place where his wings connected to his back.

Dax's eyes unfocused, lost in concentration, then his wings shifted from feathers to broadswords. He glanced behind him, turning the shimmering black steel blades. A hint of deep red glistened across the edges.

Tannys's eyes narrowed as she examined Dax's blades. "Not onyx. Carbon steel, with a hint of garnet copper, I think. Another unique seraphim metal, very rare. Beautiful," Tannys said. "And strong. Focus on the same place again and they will shift back to feathers. You can also retract them and they won't cut you. Try it."

Dax withdrew his steel wings, and they vanished, his back unmarred. "Amazing," he said, beaming.

"We will work with you to monitor your first shift. Membrane wings may feel a little different, so River, help Haven." River gestured for Haven to follow him. He walked by Larkin and gave him a smug look. Larkin's face became rigid, his eyes cold.

"Nice to see you again," River said to Haven. "Let's see what these wings can do." She unfurled her wings.

He walked behind her, placing his hand at the joint. "Your magic is Light, right?"

"Yes," Haven said.

"So, the feeling you have is more like a thread in your mind? Imagine that same thread right here." His fingers traced the base of her wing, and her body tingled at his touch. Pleasantly.

Haven did as River asked and felt a pressure on her wings.

"Excellent. Very pretty."

Haven looked behind her at the apex of her wing, which was now a solid jointed silver bar supporting over two dozen thin rapier blades. She splayed her sharp blades and marveled at the silver white that glistened in the sunlight.

"These may look delicate, but they are quite strong. They aren't silver, but more like rhodium. Hard and strong, and extremely sharp. Now, try retracting them and see how that feels."

She did as he asked. "Huh. It didn't feel any different."

"It shouldn't. Don't be afraid of the metal cutting you. It won't. Your wings work with you, to protect you."

Haven unfurled her wings again. They appeared in the metal form. She shifted between metal and membrane a few times. "That is too cool." River circled her. She felt a pressure in her mind, and a sharp pain lanced behind her eyes. Her stomach turned, and she staggered back.

River reached for her arm, holding her steady. "Are you okay?" he asked. The feel of his touch sent Haven's head reeling again.

"Ugh, I don't feel well," she said. He led her to a bench away from the other cadets.

"Here, sit for a moment. It may be from your first shift."

"Thank you," she said, breathing deeply to control the nausea. River sat beside her. His black hair curled over his forehead and collar, making his blue eyes even bluer. She had forgotten how beautiful he was.

"Did you miss me this year?" he said, his voice soft as silk.

"I did, yes," she said, surprised to realize she really had missed him.

"So, have dinner with me tonight."

Distracted by his broad shoulders and the healthy glow on his sculpted cheeks, Haven blurted, "Yes, I'd like that."

His face froze, then he laughed. "I didn't think you'd say yes."

"Neither did I, to be honest," she said.

"How do you feel? Better?"

"Yes, I'm fine," Haven said, and walked with River back to her squad. His hand drifted to her waist, and Larkin visibly tensed, his eyes narrowed. His possessiveness bewildered her. Apparently, for some people, bad habits were hard to kill. Tannys called the squad into formation, and Haven took a place in line in front of him.

"What a waste of a day," Larkin growled behind her.

"Why?" Haven asked. "Because for once this day wasn't about you? Suck it up."

"Speaking of sucking, planning on doing a little of that tonight?"

She turned slowly and glared at him.

"Shut your mouth, Larkin. Uncalled for," Dax said.

Larkin shot him a dirty look but held his tongue.

Tannys said, "If you're wondering why we brought a Shadowalker and a commander of the Aerial here today, Ryker and River are both gifted seraphim and will show you ways to use your gifts together."

Ryker stepped forward and shifted his black raven wings to onyx. Gray smoke swirled around his blades, and black tendrils slithered on the ground, drifting into the squad.

Haven's skin felt clammy, and an aching tension pulled at her neck and back. The black tendrils writhed between the cadets, and Haven's heart slammed in her chest. She shifted away from the magic, bumping into Dax, who also broke ranks to move away from the black tendrils flicking toward them. Haven reached behind her for his hand, and he gripped her tight. She could see the same reaction from her pod as the tendrils crept down the row between them. Everyone cringed and moved away, and Haven's heart raced so fast she felt it skipping beats, her breathing rapid and shallow.

"What you're feeling is Bane," Tannys said. "One of our next lessons will be how to recognize the influence of different magics."

Ryker stepped back, and his magic vanished. Everyone around Haven visibly relaxed. Haven's own shoulders slumped, and her pulse slowed. She finally let go of Dax's hand. He rubbed his cramped fingers.

"Sorry," she mumbled sheepishly.

"River?" Tannys said.

River stepped forward and unfurled his membrane wings. A breeze lifted Haven's hair. The breeze became a strong wind, lifting River off the ground. His wings billowed and sliced the wind.

Haven could see if he angled his wings, the wind would propel him.

"Next year we will train you to use all three of your gifts—wings, blades, and magic—together. And you will learn to use your gifts strategically, in battle and to defend yourself."

The squad broke up, and Ryker and River walked together through the crowd of cadets. Ryker passed Haven and stopped to speak with Harper.

Larkin sized up the brothers. "I don't get what's special about them. They seem pretty average to me," he sneered. Haven shook her head and ignored him.

Dax said, "Right, a Shadowalker is so common." Tristan snickered.

"Haven, if you can't make it with River, you can always try his brother." Ryker's penetrating gaze landed on Larkin.

"You're an asshole," Haven said, walking by him. "Stay away from me and mind your own business."

"Or you could have them together. I bet you couldn't tell which one you were blowing or fucking."

Dax walked over and slammed his fist into Larkin's face.

Haven grabbed Dax's arm and stopped him from landing a second blow. "He's not worth it."

"You've got a big mouth, cadet," Ryker said from behind Haven.

Larkin wiped the blood off his split lip. "You want to see a big mouth, check out hers. Feels great around your cock. Trust me."

"What is your fucking problem today," Dax snarled.

Larkin scuttled backward as gray smoke slithered around his legs.

Harper whispered, "Larkin, be quiet."

Ryker's eyes were a dark, storming gray. The raven feathers of his wings shifted into broad blades, and wisps of Shadow weaved around the black metal as they arched around his body. The billowing smoke wrapped around Larkin's legs, and his face paled.

Ryker nudged Haven to the side as the smoke drifted up Larkin's body and twisted around his throat. One of his blades brushed Larkin's cheek, the lightest feather of a touch. Blood welled at the line and dripped down his cheek.

Haven flinched, and the rest of the pod froze.

Harper hissed, "Ryker, that's enough. Let him go."

Ryker's eyes flashed, and the dark gray went platinum. Black tendrils snaked around Ryker's wings and arms. Waves of nothingness rolled from him, a penetrating sense of dread and anxiety that spiked Haven's pulse.

Tristan and Dax backed away, fear flooding their faces. A black thread reached for Larkin, circling his wrist. Larkin's eyes widened, and a small whimper escaped his lips. The thread snaked up his arm, and Larkin's whimpers became a scream until the thread wrapped around Larkin's neck and choked off all sound as his mouth froze in a wide O.

"Stop it!" Haven shouted and stepped between Ryker and Larkin. She pulsed a wave of Light and heat at Ryker, who flicked a shield of gray smoke that consumed her magic.

"Let him go. Now."

Ryker's cold eyes landed on her. His fist tightened, and Larkin screamed. Then Ryker released him. His magic vanished, and he tucked his raven-feathered wings discreetly behind him.

Larkin lay on his back, his eyes wide, his chest heaving.

"Keep your mouth shut, boy. And learn some manners before you open it again," Ryker seethed. He looked at them with contempt. "Some pod you have, Harper. Only two of you stepped up to help. Worthless." He walked away.

Haven's face flushed. Ryker wasn't wrong. She whirled to her team. "What the hell is wrong with you all," she snapped. "We just spent a year and a half backing each other up, and you leave him? He's still one of us!"

Avina rushed to Larkin's side and helped him to his feet while wiping the blood from his face.

Harper said to Larkin, "You disrespected him. He will never allow that kind of insult. You have no idea the power he can wield."

"Well, I think we have a good idea now." Dax said to Larkin, "Haven's right, but it's a two-way street. And I think you showed us all how you feel about the pod. I'm speaking with Shane today. You're out." Dax took Haven by the arm and led her away.

Larkin left for Portos that afternoon and transferred to the Institute the next day.

Haven squinted at the setting sun as she hurried through the drizzle toward the instructors' apartments. Now that she was on her way to meet River for dinner, the initial excitement she felt during afternoon training was fading. She was sure dating him again wasn't the best idea, but the two thoughts seemed at war in her head. His attention was flattering and she found him attractive, but she also had not forgotten the moment behind the student dorm building when she caught a glimpse of darkness. The more time passed, the more she dreaded the evening, but also felt curious whether he was worth a second chance.

Haven entered the lobby and noticed River speaking with another instructor. She walked to him, her heated, glowing hands quickly drying her misted hair.

River rose to greet her. "Haven, this is Adrien."

"Yes, I've heard your lectures this year. It's a pleasure to meet you."

"Thank you, and likewise," Adrien said. He finished his conversation with River and excused himself.

River said, "So, what would you like to do tonight? I wanted to give you a choice of dinner in my apartment or at Falcon Ridge."

"What's Falcon Ridge?"

"It's a decent restaurant off the instructors' dining hall. It has a main hall but also semi-private dining booths."

"I didn't know that existed." Haven liked the idea of keeping their dinner public. "That sounds like fun." With his hand on her waist, River guided her to a building behind the instructors' apartments, his Wind magic moving the heavy rain away from them. They walked up three flights of stairs to a reception area and were led to a bay with floor-to-ceiling glass windows on two sides. Haven sat at the table, captivated by the open, rolling fields leading to the woods behind the Academy. The sun's last rays danced along the bottom of the clouds in bright pinks and oranges, reflecting off the falling rain like glittering stars on earth.

"Wine with dinner?" River asked. Haven nodded, and he discussed options with the waiter. "So how are you liking Academy this year?"

"It's okay. It was cool finding out my magic and new wings, but I have to admit the history lessons are...a little dry." Haven sipped the wine the server poured for her.

River chuckled. "I've known Adrien my entire life. He knew my mother and was close to my father. He has a passion for history, but his delivery could use a little creativity."

They talked through dinner, gossiping about the new class of cadets.

"I have a friend who's a new cadet," Haven said. "Maybe you know him? His name is Ayden."

"You mean the prince?" River asked. "Yes, I know him, but he isn't in the squad I teach. He's doing well, I understand." The server appeared at their table to remove their dinner dishes.

"Dessert?" he asked. "We have a specialty on the menu tonight, a chocolate berry torte from Tangyra."

Haven's eyes brightened. "Oh! That's a good one."

"Split it?" River offered. The server left, and River asked, "So you were mentioning spring break?"

"Yes, my pod is planning to go to Maddox's home in Phirot. I'd love a vacation in a new place. It would be fun to see more of Berinia."

"Come to Damaris. It's Berinia's second largest city and my home. I'll admit I'm biased, but there is nothing like it."

"I would like that. But right now, a beach and sunshine sounds great."

The server brought the dessert and two forks. It was as good as Haven remembered. River settled the bill, and they left the building. The rain had stopped, but the air felt heavy around them. The clean smell of wet stones and earth chilled her lungs but cleared her head.

River asked, "Nightcap at my place?"

"That sounds like a terrible idea, professor," Haven said, smiling.

His face fell in mock disappointment. "And here I thought we had moved beyond the teacher-student relationship. I'm not teaching you this year, after all."

"Maybe next time. Walk me back?"

"So you're saying there will be a next time?"

"If you're lucky." His pale blue eyes sparkled with playful mischief, and his face was friendly and open. This version of River was the one she remembered. She took his arm and leaned into his warmth.

Through the dissipating clouds, the full moons transformed the stone path into a glittering trail that snaked between the shadowed buildings. They leisurely strolled past the instructors' apartments. River led her around the students' square to the far side of her dorms at the modest back entry. The dim light above the simple single door illuminated a narrow brick stairway.

River took her hand. "I really missed you. Thank you for agreeing to see me tonight. I feel like I got a second chance."

"I had fun. It was a lovely evening. Thank you." Haven watched him closely. She saw nothing but kindness in his beautiful face.

He stepped a little closer and kissed her cheek. "I'd love one kiss good night."

"You just got one," she said.

"That's not what I had in mind." His mouth was captivating, and she was tempted to feel those full lips on hers. "One kiss. I want you to think of me when you're lying in bed tonight," he whispered, pressing into her. His words, the sound of his voice, set loose a flutter of butterflies in her stomach. She didn't move as his lips brushed hers. He studied her face, then his mouth found hers. *He feels as good as he looks*, Haven thought as he softly explored her lips. The butterflies in her stomach became a thrilling ache. His hand tugged at her hip, and she stepped closer to him, running her hands up his arms. He deepened the kiss and pulled her closer to him until there was no space between them. She could feel a strength in his grip that was rigid and hard, unmovable. She lessened the kiss and tried to move away from him, but his hands on her hips kept their bodies together.

"Come back with me. I promise you won't regret it. You have no idea the things I could do to you, what I can make you feel." His lips found hers again, and Haven pushed away from him harder, the thrill vanishing as fear slipped into her mind. For the first time, it occurred to her that she could lose control of the level of intimacy with a male, something she had never experienced or expected. River held her tight, her efforts to get some space between them ineffective. His hand drifted down her backside and cupped her low, his fingers inching between her legs. She squirmed to free herself, and River groaned at her movements. Haven thrashed against him, nearing panic.

River's grip lessened suddenly as a flash of light sparked in the dark. Haven's thoughts blurred, and her surroundings dimmed. She sensed River as he pulled back in surprise and caught a look at his face before a second flash of light distorted her senses again.

"Let her go," Harper said. River broke away from Haven with a start, and Haven stumbled backward into Kit, who gently moved her behind him.

"Hello, Harper," River said. "What a pleasure to see you." His forced smile did not reach his cold eyes, nor warm his voice. He said to Haven, "Thank you for dinner tonight. Maybe next week when I return to the Academy, we can do it again." He backed away and disappeared into the dark.

Haven held Kit's arm, shivering. He kept her close as they walked into the dorm.

Before she opened their door, Harper asked, "Are you okay?"

"Yes, I think so. Thank you."

"I won't say I didn't warn you. But you need to be careful with River."

"I feel so stupid. But I'm done making that mistake. It won't happen again."

Harper squeezed her hand. "I'm sorry, Haven. Do you want to go for a walk? To talk?"

Haven gave her a trembling smile. "No, I'm fine."

"Are you sure? I'm here for you, if you need someone."

"I know. But I just want to forget about it." Haven exhaled a shuddering breath. Kit held her waist, his solid presence a comfort as he led her into their bunk room.

Haven dressed for bed and lay in her bed, listening to the soft sounds of her pod sleeping. Every time she closed her eyes and drifted off, she felt hard hands pinning her, holding her as she struggled to run, and she jerked awake, her heart racing and her skin clammy. She slid off her bunk and into Dax's. He pulled her close and she finally slept.

# CHAPTER 11

## Spring Break

Haven stood at the foot of her bed with her hands on her hips and took inventory of her sparse selection of civilian clothing. "I have nothing beachy to wear," she said, watching Harper struggle with the zipper of her overstuffed bag.

"One more reason to shop," Harper said. "We're staying in Raveno for a few days. We can pick something up." Haven followed Harper to the square in front of the dorm where Dax and the rest of her pod waited with four Skimmers. She pulled her collar up against the drizzling rain, ready for a reprieve from winter.

"Have you ever been to Phirot?" Haven asked as they skimmed to a bustling urban residential area.

"Yes, many times," Dax said. "My family vacationed in Raveno and the southern beaches in the summer. You'll like the city." The rest of the pod appeared, and Maddox led them inside a large, three-story brownstone. Maddox's parents, Mason and Keryl, greeted them in the expansive foyer and led them to a living room that opened through glass doors to a large garden patio. Climbing vines blooming in a riot of colors curtained the eaves of the house.

Lunch waited for them on a long wooden table draped with a white tablecloth. A bouquet of early spring wildflowers gave a festive air to the semi-formal setting. A hint of roasted chicken fought its way through the flowers' perfume, reminding Haven she was starving.

After they ate, Keryl showed the pod to the top floor of the brownstone, an open loft area set up with cots and bunks. "There's two bathrooms, one on either side of the floor," she said, motioning to the room. "We have windsprites and hobs, so make yourself comfortable."

Haven opened the sliding glass doors, stepped onto the expansive balcony, and immediately felt the difference in the balmy, warm climate of the south from the chilly mountains of the Academy. She admired the views of the garden below, the narrow, winding streets, and an eclectic mix of brick buildings with terra-cotta and gray slate rooftops. She could hear the voice of the city, a buzz of people passing through the streets mixed with the distant roar of the Shaine River.

"Ready to explore?" Harper said, leaning on the railing next to her.

Haven nodded enthusiastically. "Where do we start?"

"The Ridge Walk," Harper said.

"I'm in," Dax said, joining them on the balcony.

The Shaine River passed through an asymmetrical ravine, cleaving the city of Raveno in half, with the southern side of the city resting on a fifty-foot cliff known as the Wedge. Maddox's parents lived in the residential district that sprawled behind the Wedge, with brownstone row houses clustered together near the urban center and estates in the rolling hills to the south and east.

Haven and her pod flew over Raveno's theater, artist, and commercial districts that lined the cliff's edge, which offered spectacular views of the ports in the distance. They landed in a plaza on the Ridge Walk, a series of grassy parks, undulating hills, and clusters of trees that ran along the edge of the Wedge. Haven walked to the edge of the ravine and leaned on the railing. Thirty feet below, Raveno's market and warehouse districts and shipping ports sprawled on the other side of the river to the north.

Haven and her pod walked across the Walk and back into the theater district, through the winding streets to the retail shops where Haven and Harper lost the rest of their day. That night, the pod explored the city, eating dinner at a local pub. Crowds of people strolled along the cobblestone streets, drawn from their houses to enjoy a break from winter, courtesy of a fleeting visit from spring.

Later that night, Haven and her pod wandered back to the Walk, where more crowds gathered, listening to live music and snacking from vendor carts. The tangled smell of roasting meats, popcorn, and coffee wafted around Haven in the fresh, crisp air.

Dax handed Haven a paper cup, steam curling over the rim. Haven sipped the rich chocolate, a hint of mint liqueur cool on her tongue. "Mmmm, delicious," she said.

Haven stood near the edge of the ravine, watching the tumbling water race and the flickering lights of the still-bustling city across the river.

"What a beautiful city," she said over the roar of the river below.

"Isn't it? I like it better than Ancharin," Dax said.

"I could never imagine a place this lovely."

"You haven't seen many cities, but this one is extraordinary. One of my favorites in Berinia."

"I wish I had seen more of Korsina. I love Araine, and I think I like Raveno even more." She nudged him in the side. "It's also fun to see it with you guys. I think that's what makes these cities even more exciting."

Dax smiled at her. "We are waiting for you, you know."

"What do you mean?"

"You have real friends here, in this pod. Myself included. But you also need to let us in. I feel like we know only bits and pieces of you."

Haven stared at him, then sipped her drink. "I don't know how to do that."

"I know." He slid an arm around her and gave her a squeeze. She rested her head on his broad shoulder. "We're here—I'm here—when you decide you want to know. You tell real friends everything. Not just the good stuff. All the bad stuff, too. Like what happened with River." Haven stiffened, and he squeezed her again. "You're a strong person. One of the things I admire most about you. But you don't have to be strong alone. It's okay to need someone."

"That hasn't ever worked well for me."

"Well, you need to choose better friends."

"Like you?" she said, poking him in the side.

"It's a decent start. I'm not all that bad," he said, grinning at her.

"You're the best," she said softly, leaning into him again.

On her way to the garden for dinner on their last night in Raveno, Haven passed a small study and noticed Maddox's parents through the doorway. She slowed, knowing she shouldn't intrude. Keryl nestled into Mason's arms, her head resting on his chest, their arms wrapped tightly around one another. He kissed her forehead, then her lips in a slow, deep kiss. Dax paused next to Haven, then gently took her arm and led her away.

After dinner, the pod visited a local bar for a nightcap and roamed the bustling theater district.

"Does this place ever sleep?" Haven asked, as they weaved their way through the throng of people on the street.

"Come here in the morning," Maddox said. "It's like a ghost town. Artists are night owls."

"I can see why. I love it. Thank you for sharing your home with us." Maddox squeezed her in a hug.

Haven gripped the sand with her toes as a warm wave lapped at her ankles. She shifted as the wave withdrew, taking the sand under her feet with it. She pulled her light slipover around her as the clean, salty breeze tickled her bare stomach. The sun touched the horizon, and the deep blue water reflected the last glittering rays in a fond farewell, the sky joining in with a fanfare of pinks and oranges.

Dax stood beside Haven, and she looped her arm through his. "Dinner is in half an hour," he said.

"Thanks." She nodded at the sun's showy finale. "This place is beautiful."

"I loved coming here with my family as a kid. The last day was always the hardest."

"Ancharin doesn't have beaches like this?"

"No. The water there is much colder, and the shores are pebbles, not sand like this." Haven dragged her toe through the granules, the next wave erasing her mark. "You're from Ancharin. How do you not know what the city is like?"

She eyed him warily. "I told you, I never left my parents' estate. And it wasn't near the water."

Dax waited, but Haven didn't explain further. "And?" he asked. Haven kicked at a wave. "I'm not trying to pry." Haven scowled at him. "Okay, maybe I am, but remember what I said earlier? About letting people in?" He gestured to the peaceful, lapping ocean and scenic sky. "What a perfect opportunity to open up to a *friend.*" He nudged her ribs. "So why didn't you leave your parents' estate?"

"I don't know." She gazed at the sunset and let him take her hand. "I don't know why my parents left me there, why they chose not to be a part of my life."

"I know there's more to this. There's something you hold back."

The sun's reflection rippled across the water, alive, sparkling gold and white. Haven sighed. "My father is Prince Astor."

Dax's eyebrows rose. "Prince? You're a princess."

"Maybe one that was stuffed in a tower and forgotten." Haven gave a short laugh. "I'm a walking cliché."

Dax wrapped an arm around her. "There is very little about you that's common." He kissed the top of her head. "You know you can trust us. All of us."

"I know. But I don't want to be judged by my family. I have a hard enough time reading people's intentions as is."

"You read me fine," he said.

"You're easy. You're honest. Not everyone is that way."

"Like River?" Dax said.

Haven gave him a steady look. "He's beautiful and sexy, but I learned my lesson. I've no interest in tangling with someone like him again."

Dax sighed. "Don't blame yourself too much. Guys like Larkin and River, they can tell when someone isn't experienced. You drew them to you because you were vulnerable."

"You mean gullible."

"I like the way I said it better. It's not your fault you weren't more aware that there are males like that out there. Ones that would take advantage of you."

Haven looked up at him. "I feel lucky to have a friend like you."

"And I am that. Your friend. At least it will be easy to avoid River next year. And I'm always happy to be your gallant knight," he said, flexing his biceps. Haven giggled. "Come on, let's eat." He took her hand and led her back to the beach house.

The pod was tidying up the dishes after dinner when two large picnic baskets appeared on the cleared table. Maddox opened one and gasped. "I love the hobs here," he said. Tristan helped him carry the baskets to the beach, where a large stack of firewood was ready to be lit. "Dax, do the honors," Maddox said. Dax focused, and red and gold flames licked the wood.

Maddox opened one basket and removed a bottle of amber liquor. He poured each of them a glass, then opened the second basket. Haven sipped her drink, the light almond-flavored liquor pleasantly burning her throat. Maddox removed sticks, and on a platter placed bars of chocolate, golden cracker-type biscuits, and white squishy blobs.

Haven asked, "What the heck is all that?"

"You haven't ever had a fire pie?" Maddox asked. Quinn and Tristan took a stick and skewered one of the white blobs and stuck it in the flames. Quinn squealed when her blob caught fire. She quickly blew it out and placed a square of chocolate on one golden biscuit and squished the white blob between another, withdrawing the skewer. She bit into it and groaned.

Dax handed Haven a skewer with a blob on it. "It's best if the mallow is toasted and not burned." He twisted his skewer in the fire.

"I disagree," Tristan said. "I like mine kinda burnt. Then they're extra melty."

Maddox and Tristan began a lengthy debate on proper mallow toasting methods. Haven twisted her skewer in the fire until the mallow was golden brown, then took the biscuit and chocolate Maddox handed her and squished the melting mallow between the biscuits. She bit into it and almost died.

"Gods." Her eyes rolled in ecstasy.

"The best, right?" Dax asked through a mouthful of mallow and chocolate. Haven nodded enthusiastically, licking the sticky white goo from her fingers.

Maddox sipped his drink and asked Haven, "What was your favorite vacation when you were a kid?"

"I didn't go on vacation," Haven said, tensing.

"Ever?" Maddox asked. "Did you ever go anywhere?"

"You know I didn't. Why are you asking?"

"Sorry, but you're an enigma, sometimes. We know you're keeping something private." Haven glanced at Dax, who gave her an encouraging look. She picked at the seam of her sweater and swallowed hard.

Haven said, "Lord Astor is my father."

"Lord Astor. You mean Prince Astor. The king's younger son," said Maddox.

"I didn't know Prince Astor had children," Harper said.

Haven shrugged. "Very few people do. The day I arrived in Portos, the day we met, was my first time away from home." She looked up at Maddox. "I never had friends before I met you. My parents hired companions, but they were rotated often."

Dax pulled her between his legs, and she snuggled into his warmth. "You have us," he said, squeezing her tight. She felt safe with Dax, the warmth of a friend who had no expectations other than enjoying her company.

"Maddox, your parents are in love," she said.

"Very much so. They are mated. They have been since they were young."

"I've seen my parents in the same room maybe twice in my life. I've never seen adults have...affection for one another like yours do," Haven said. "They're lucky."

"They are indeed," Dax said. "Being mated is uncommon."

"Why didn't you tell us?" Quinn asked.

Haven looked down at Dax's arm wrapped around her stomach and played with the cuff of his shirt. "I guess I didn't want to be treated differently. I want to be, I don't know, normal. One of you."

"You are one of us," Tristan said. "You should know by now it doesn't matter where you come from or who your family is. We care about *you*." Haven's throat tightened, and she hugged Dax closer, feeling the security and warmth from a sense of belonging, of being accepted by people she cared for. And who cared for her in return.

# CHAPTER 12

## Araine

Lilith looked past Lukas and saw Liam arrive in the ballroom, late even by his standards.

"I really didn't think he would show," Lukas grumbled when he spied his father. Liam escorted a tall brunette, her arm draped through his. "And really? Have you met this tramp?"

Lilith elbowed him. "Be nice, Lukas. And no, I haven't met her."

Liam greeted Lilith warmly, kissing her cheek. "It's good to see you," he said to her.

"Yes, it's been too long. You need to come to Araine more often."

"You know I'm not a fan of this city," he said, glancing across the room to the royals on the dais. His gaze fell on Lukas briefly. "Too many self-important people here." Lilith saw the red flush creeping up Lukas's neck.

"It's good for you to be seen at these events. And the king expects your attendance," Lilith said, a hint of scolding in her voice.

"That's why I have you." Liam gestured to the female next to him. "This is Kya. My children, Lilith and Lukas."

"Does mother know you're here?" Lukas said, ignoring the introduction.

"Don't be rude, Lukas," Liam snapped.

"Me? You don't think it's rude to my mother to bring..." Lukas's eyes roved over Kya's low-cut dress and full figure, "...her, to such a public event?"

Liam's lips pressed into a thin line. "One day we will choose an enosi for you, and then maybe you'll understand the difference between obligation and love."

Lukas snorted. "Love? Give me a break." He waved a hand at Kya. "Does she know about the blonde you brought to dinner with the Council last autumn? I can't even remember her name. You rotate *loves* like I have new shoes." Lilith's hand tightened on his arm, but he pulled away from her. "And I don't need you to arrange a partner for me. You want an alliance? Find an enosi for Lilith. I've seen enough. Excuse me."

Lilith watched Lukas walk away to join Ryker and Silas, then gave her father an exasperated sigh. "Really, you shouldn't pick fights with Lukas," she said. Liam turned his attention to Kya, dismissing her. "But you're right, you should partner Lukas soon. It would be a good time to find a new alliance."

"It would be a stronger connection if he were a real Shadowalker," Liam said.

"Father, please. You need his cooperation. Antagonizing him makes any alliance harder." Lilith followed his piercing gaze and saw Lukas and Ryker joined by the latest group of cadets from the Academy. "I suppose it's too much to ask if you've spoken to Ronan again." She watched Ryker follow Silas as they each led a cadet to the dance floor.

"Not recently. I know you want Ryker as your enosi. I do too. But his father has no influence over him. His brother is a possibility, but unlikely as well, and not nearly as advantageous as an alliance with Ryker." He smiled softly at his daughter. "You'll have to convince him yourself."

"I'll see what I can do," she said. The soft classical music silenced, and a tone echoed through the ballroom. "Come, walk me to dinner."

Liam led Lilith to her seat at the Council table, one of three set near the King. He stroked her hair, then led Kya to find his seat with the other cesares at the king's table. He faltered for a moment at the seat placement and flashed an angry look at the king before sitting next to Jairo. After greeting him formally, he draped his napkin on his lap and busied himself with the appetizer.

"Liam, we haven't seen you in Araine in months," King Aric said.

"My apologies. The needs of Valena keep me in Damaris," Liam said.

Jairo said, "Really? And what needs are those? I would think the demands on your time have declined over the last two decades."

Liam could feel heat rising on his neck. "Actually, trade in Damaris's ports and distribution centers is higher than ever since we also compensate for your inefficiencies when Aric transferred local distribution to Raveno."

The King's face grew cold. "I expect your continued courtesy and obedience," he said to Liam. "You may have been a favorite of my father, but he's dead."

"My apologies, your Highness," Liam said curtly, bowing his head. "I meant no disrespect."

Jairo said, "Yes, Phirot is still learning distribution practices, and Raveno has made great strides in our ports and Skimming centers." His mouth curved into a smug sneer. "It's kind of Damaris to fill in for us while we build our infrastructure." Liam brushed him off and focused on his salad. "Although the peace we've had for the past twenty years has been a tremendous help," Jairo said to the king, "It may be a good time to transfer the Aerial base back to Madina."

Liam dropped his fork to his plate with a clatter. "Absolutely not. Cantos has been the Aerial's base for three hundred years, with well-established training facilities. Transferring them now would be disruptive."

King Aric considered Jairo's suggestion. "I agree with Liam. We don't want to disrupt the Aerial right now. This lapse in the daevas' incursions into Berinia worries me. I feel this may build into a major movement."

"Maybe now is the time to transfer them," the cesare of Korsina said.

"Why do you care, Kira? Korsina doesn't control agni mining or distribution, and never has," Liam said.

"I care because the rift is in our lands, and Korsina has always borne the brunt of daeva attacks. Our people die. Is agni the only thing that matters to you?" Liam rolled his eyes and said nothing. "I like the idea of the Aerial being closer to the mines. It made sense to have the Aerial in Valena when distribution ran through Damaris, but now that Phirot controls some of it, maybe in this unusual lull we can strengthen a local presence."

"Phirot has on-world distribution. The majority of distribution, all off-world trade, still runs through Damaris. The military belongs in Valena," Liam insisted.

"For now," Jairo taunted. Liam's face contorted with barely contained rage.

"Enough bickering. You're worse than my grandchildren," the king said. "It's something to discuss at our scheduled meeting next month. It's an interesting suggestion, but for now, we should keep the Aerial in Valena. Liam has done a remarkable job maintaining the Aerial's elite capabilities. And the distance to Phirot isn't unwieldy."

Liam breathed a sigh of relief.

"Enough business and politics. This is a social event," the king said.

Kira eyed Kya, then asked Liam, "And how is Skye? We haven't seen my niece in years in Araine."

"She is well. You know she doesn't like these types of events," Liam said.

"I remember her enjoying balls when she was younger, before we committed her to you," Kira snapped.

"Yes, well, things change, don't they?" Liam said, his eyes wandering over Kya, who squirmed under his scrutiny.

King Aric leaned back in his chair. "Liam, we discussed this at the Council dinner last autumn. Bring Skye the next time you are here. I know your relationship is by contract, but bringing your mistresses to royal events is tasteless." Liam's eyes blazed at the public slight. "In the future, exercise more discretion. And don't disregard my wishes again."

Lilith slapped the letter down on her desk and paced her office. She stopped to look out to the street of Falco Park at the drenched people scurrying by. Black clouds dimmed the afternoon, and the wind whipped the spring rain against the windows with a steady, splattered pinging.

After months of endless discussions about the daevas, the king had finally decided. He summoned the Council for a meeting that afternoon, invoking his arbiter rights. Lilith knew the news wouldn't be what she wanted. Gods damned Finnian. And the king.

She glanced behind her at the summons on her desk. King Airon never would have treated her like this. A brief note, as if she were a common Council member. Airon had appointed her head of the Rift Council almost a century ago and had valued her input and counsel for even longer. She was young, only fifty years old, when Airon appointed her as Council chair. She had been a Council member for ten years and leapfrogged over other members, some of whom openly resented her and protested to the king. Airon had quickly replaced them, and no one dared to defy him since. Lilith earned the king's trust and effectively led the

Council through the demon incursions, the transition in the Regency after Airon's death, and now that the attacks had ceased, through the tentative peace.

When Airon died forty years ago, she mourned his loss as deeply as Liam. Lilith struggled with Aric's ruling style, even more than her father, but kept her misgivings private. She needed Aric's support, but these small disrespects grated her. Lilith fumed, already thinking of ways around limitations the king was sure to place on daevas entering Praesia.

She yanked her cloak from the stand and slung it around her shoulders. With a tap to her Echo rune, she vanished, then reappeared in an alley a block from the ministry building. She hurried through the pouring rain and into the lobby, shaking the water from her hood. Her feet moved gingerly across the marble floor, treacherously wet from others tracking in the rain. Lukas sat outside the Council chamber with Calaine and Xander.

"What is this about?" Lukas asked.

"I don't know, but I'm guessing it's a resolution on the daevas."

Lukas's eyebrows rose. "The king didn't tell you?"

Lilith gave him a surly look, then shook her head.

Ryker, Silas, and Trinity appeared in the hall, looking annoyingly dry.

"I don't suppose you know what the king will tell us?" Lilith asked Ryker.

Ryker ignored her and entered the chamber. Lilith and Lukas followed close behind. Ryker took his usual seat on the curved benches facing the Council risers. Lilith stood in front of him and folded her arms.

"What?" Ryker said.

"You didn't answer me."

"You're right. I didn't."

Lilith's face heated, then she spun on her heel and marched to her seat.

King Aric entered the chamber, followed closely by Finnian and his Triad. Finnian sat next to Lukas, and the king took the arbiter's seat, a single plush chair between the wooden benches and the Council's arched risers.

"I've listened carefully to both sides of the daeva issue. And while I agree we need more than Shadowwalkers to control the daevas, I am also sympathetic to their reluctance to allow daevas into Praesia. We will open discussions with the daevas." Lilith heaved a silent sigh of relief. "However, there will be strict conditions."

"First, under no circumstances will we allow any seraphim to cross the Pale to Alja-hin. We cannot trust the daevas in their own world, and I will not risk the life of any seraphim, nor have a seraphim exposed to the risk of kidnap and ransom."

"Second, the Daeva Council will approve daeva crossings, and Finnian will chair that panel. Lilith, you may select two Council members. I will appoint a fourth. All crossing approvals must be unanimous." Lilith gritted her teeth but said nothing.

"Third, we will construct a chamber with an iron floor here at the ministry."

"What?" Lilith blurted out.

"Don't interrupt," Aric snapped. Lilith flushed. "No magic is allowed with the daevas. They may pass into Praesia only through a new rift directly into this room. The djinn's marids will work with a fae Caster to set and ward the new rift. We will assign an Aerial squad to be present during all crossings."

"And finally, any negotiations with the daevas will not include agni."

Lilith gaped. "With all due respect, your Majesty, what leverage will we have? We can't ask for anything without something to offer."

Finnian said, "We have an agreement with the faeries to trade in nectar."

"What...how did you do that?" Lilith spluttered.

"We are making allowances in a large order for agni the faeries plan to place in the coming months to resupply the coast of their largest continent," said the king.

Finnian said, "Agni amplifies the daevas' magic. It's too dangerous to have it in their hands."

"Agreed," the king said. "Nectar is a universal food source, which will benefit their people without risking a power imbalance. We know the new shima queen's magic is strong enough to push demons through the Pale."

"How do you know that?" Lilith said.

"The faeries have a source and informed me. The queens will transition in the next few weeks. With a young queen in place, we expect shima to cross the Pale again."

Finnian said, "While the queen's magic is strong, she is still young and easily influenced. We can't have the daevas interfering and potentially gaining control of the queen. That would be devastating to many worlds."

"I agree," King Aric said. "The daevas need to be kept in their world." He turned to Lilith. "You will be consulted in discussions with the daevas, but Finnian and the Daeva Council set all terms of negotiations."

Lilith sat back in her chair, fuming but trying to regain her composure. "As you wish, your Majesty."

The rest of the Council meeting was a blur. She listened to the details of the king's decree with half a mind. For the first time in the forty years since Aric assumed the throne, she felt the shift in power. Her father complained about it constantly, but it had never affected her until today. She knew the king didn't value her counsel as Airon had. The king had effectively diminished the influence of the Rift Council. And her own.

Her gaze fell on Ryker.

The king stood, and Lilith rapped her gavel and called an end to the meeting. She left her seat and strode to Ryker as he rose from the bench.

"A word? In my office?" she asked in a clipped voice. Ryker nodded and Silas followed him. "Alone."

Silas stiffened. "It's fine," Ryker said to him. "I'll meet you at the Garret."

Lilith marched down the hall to her office and stepped aside to allow Ryker to enter, then closed the door behind him.

"You knew of the king's decree," she said.

"Yes. I worked with Finnian and the king to devise the plan."

"And why aren't you on the Daeva Council?"

"The king offered, but I declined. Finnian is better suited to negotiations."

"What of Lukas? Will the king select him as the fourth panel member?"

"No."

"Why?"

"Honestly? Because he's too closely aligned with you."

Lilith tensed and looked out the window. "Who will it be?"

"Likely an Aerial leader. A commander, or someone of higher rank."

Lilith turned to him. "Your brother?"

Ryker laughed. "No. He's only been a commander for a year and a half, and River likes politics even less than I do." Lilith looked back at the window. "Why are you so opposed to this?"

"It undermines the role of the Rift Council."

"Ah. And yours, by proxy."

Lilith sat on a leather sofa. "Tea?"

"No, thank you."

She motioned to the space next to her. "Please, have a seat." Ryker watched her warily, then sat next to her. "You are no longer seeing Calaine."

Ryker bristled. "I can't see how that is any of your business."

"It makes things cleaner," she said.

"What things?"

"An alliance. Between us." She saw his face pale and a muscle in his jaw tick. "It could be in name only," she hurried on. "Enosi contracts are flexible. We could come up with our own terms. But our union would be a powerful one."

"No, thanks."

"Why?"

Ryker sighed. "I have plenty of people in my life who are interested in me only for my status. I certainly don't need another."

"I'm interested in more than your status," she said, touching his knee. He moved away from her and stood. She rose with him, her hand sliding to his hip. "We could have a lot of fun, I think."

Ryker removed her hand, squeezing it tightly. Lilith flinched. "Don't touch me," he said, a whisper of venom in his voice. His silver eyes darkened to a shimmering charcoal gray. Lilith backed away as a tendril of Bane slid down Ryker's arm. "Don't ever touch me again." Lilith swallowed the fear choking her throat, her pulse pounding in her temples. Ryker abruptly left her office.

Lilith clutched her chest and sank to the sofa, breathing deeply to slow her racing heart. The fear abated, and her cheeks burned. She pounded her fist into her thigh. She was an idiot. She knew better than to push Ryker like that. Accessing his magic had been her goal for a decade, and his growing influence only added to the importance of an alliance. But now her impatience had set a new hurdle between them. She would have to fix that later.

More importantly, she had to address the outcome of the king's decree. The Daeva Council was a serious obstacle, and there was very little time to work around it. Lilith leaned forward and rubbed her temples. Fucking Finnian. He'd pay for this complication. But right now, she had to decide her path. She had tried to work within the system, and Finnian ruined it. There was only one other way now, but she had to decide if her goal was worth the risk.

Lilith leaned back on the sofa, gathering her magic. She tapped the Linker rune on her hip and forced the magic through Praesia's rigid Pale into Alja-hin. *Come now*, she gasped, then the Link vanished. A bead of sweat dripped down her shoulder blades, and pain stabbed behind her eyes. Her magic faded to a whisper.

A shadowy figure appeared in her office. "I can't maintain this for long," Vannin said.

"You need to form a rift," Lilith ordered. She briefly explained the advisory panel and the room where they would hold negotiations. "Under these conditions, in a room like that, we can't meet."

The daeva swore. "I thought you had more influence than this," Vannin said. "Maybe we are speaking to the wrong person."

Lilith barked a laugh. "Go ahead and try. Most people in Praesia would kill you on sight. If you want agni, I'm the only one who can help. Form a rift in Damaris, near my father's estate. Do it on the same day they form the rift here at the ministry and it should go unnoticed. We can move agni through the rift in Damaris."

The dark figure faded. "The second queen is mature."

Lilith smiled. "No one knows the shima spawned a second queen?"

"No. They believe she was destroyed as a nymph. The daeva that transported her to me is...no longer. There are only three of us that know—you, me, and her keeper. Two queens shouldn't exist, but she is bound to us now, and we can keep her hidden."

"Then our bargain is sealed. Agni for universal currency and control of demons."

"You never said why you want to control shima," Vannin said, his voice fading.

Lilith smiled as Vannin vanished. "A little chaos is always good for business," she said to the empty room.

# CHAPTER 13

## The Phoenix

The first day back from spring break started with a lecture from Adrien. Even the topic of demons wasn't enough to keep the pod from nodding off. Haven and the squad walked into the bright sunlight from the amphitheater and crossed the square to the Yard. Tristan yawned and rubbed his eyes.

"That's what happens when you fall asleep in lectures," Dax said.

"What the hell," Tristan said, jumping and high-stepping his knees to get his blood moving again. "I thought lectures were over for the year."

"Nope. One more after this. The history of our Regency." Dax said.

"Riveting," Tristan said, rolling his eyes.

"Quiet down," Shane said as the squad assembled in the Yard.

Ryker, Silas, and River stood behind Shane, hands clasped behind their backs. The brothers wore black combat leathers covered in a fine, supple armored scaling, with reinforced vests over fitted long-sleeved shirts. Silas wore a similar charcoal gray uniform, with heavier plating on his vest and thighs under the leathers. They were armed with an array of daggers, knives, and swords.

"Next year you will learn military strategy, problem solving, and how to use your gifts together with your wings," Shane said. "I know many of you will seek careers outside the military, but there are many benefits to learning strategy that can carry over to non-military settings, such as analytics and problem-solving. Whatever your path may be after the Academy, we encourage you to join the Aerial for the traditional two-year rotation, and hope some of you will find a career there."

"Ryker and River both volunteer their time at the Academy. You all remember River from your first year, and some of you will get to know Ryker next year. He is an advisor for our war gaming. I've asked both to stop by and show you how your gifts can be used together."

Silas stepped forward and said, "You've experienced the influence of different magics. River's magic is Wind, and you know he can use it to control respiration. You've also felt the effects of Bane. I think we can all agree it is one of the deadliest magics we seraphim have. Ryker and River will now walk through several sparring routines you will need to master as the foundation for your training next year."

Ryker and River's wings switched to blades, and Silas spent the next hour describing the stances and movements of several sparring routines. "These routines are like the ones you've used in the past but differ in complexity." He selected teams of cadets to move through the stances with Ryker and River. The first set focused on hand-to-hand combat, and the second incorporated wings.

On the last rotation, Silas selected three cadets and paired Haven with River. "The third stage of the sparring routine incorporates magic." Silas and his partner began the sparring routine, but Silas vanished, then appeared behind the unsuspecting cadet, tripping him and pressing his bladed wing to his throat.

Ryker bound his cadet in Shadow, and the cadet struggled against the immobilizing magic.

Haven faced River, his mouth curving cruelly. Haven's lungs constricted as the surrounding air became impossibly thick. She grabbed her throat and fell to her knees. Blood rushed to her face, and spots clouded her vision as she gulped for air.

"That's enough, River," Silas said, then continued his lecture. The squad turned its attention away from River and Haven.

"Come on, cadet, show me a real fight," River taunted in a low voice meant only for her.

Haven held her throat as her lungs were denied even a wisp of air. She looked up at River as her lungs burned and her throat closed. River's lips curved into a cruel smile, and Haven saw the predator she'd encountered behind the dorms. Anger rushed through her, and her world went dark.

Haven's blue eyes paled to a glowing white. River frowned and took a step away.

"Haven? What's wrong with your eyes?" She snarled, and red feathered wings burst from her back. "What the hell," River yelled.

Ryker and Silas paused their routines, and the entire squad froze.

Then Haven erupted in flames. She roared at River and lunged for him.

"Holy shit," River said, stumbling back.

A cloud of smoke enveloped Haven, tethering her to the ground inches from River's face. Bane laced from Ryker's hands as he struggled to restrain her. Haven hissed at River, a guttural rumbling deep in her throat. Long, curved fangs punched from her upper and lower jaw, slicing her mouth. Blood pooled on her lips and spilled down her chin.

"Get away!" Ryker shouted to River. River yelped and scrambled to his feet. Ryker's Shadow wrapped around her neck, Bane threads flickering within the smoke. Haven struggled against his magic, growling and lurching toward River.

"Haven!" Dax called out, rushing to her side.

Silas grabbed him around the waist and flung him to the ground. "Stay away from her," he said. "For your own safety." Dax struggled underneath Silas, swearing at him and kicking to break free from his grasp.

Ryker clenched his fist, and the Bane threads tightened around Haven's throat. She wrenched away from him, slipping his restraints as she lunged for River again.

"Fucking hell's fire," River shouted as her fingers raked his arm, her nails leaving bloody grooves in his skin. Ryker's magic surged around her again as River jumped back from her. Haven fell to her knees, struggling against Ryker's magic. She choked and gasped for air until her wings shifted back to membrane and she collapsed unconscious to the ground.

Shane swirled her in a cloud of fog, extinguishing the flames still burning across her wings.

River froze, his eyes wide, staring at his brother. Silas let Dax up and moved among the cadets, attempting to settle their nervous chatter. The smell of burned flesh and hair permeated the squad. "Harper," Silas called, motioning to the cadet he was assisting, her face pale and clammy. Harper led the cadet away from the crowd for fresh air and a seat.

Ryker rushed to Haven and felt her neck for a pulse. He jerked away, shaking his hand from the heat of her skin. He gingerly pulled her hair back, exposing her blistering red scalp. Her blackened shoulders smoldered, and charred skin peeled from the edges of her wing joints.

Dax knelt beside her and covered his nose with his hand. "Holy gods, the smell."

"Your first taste of burnt flesh," River said, gagging as he brought the collar of his shirt to shield his nose from the acrid smoke curling from Haven's wings. "Is she dead?"

"No, but her pulse is weak. Someone get Farna. *Now*," Ryker shouted. Maddox skimmed away to fetch the healer. Ryker rolled Haven to her stomach to avoid pressure on the burns. His voice was tense as he said to Shane, "Keep the fog on her wings. She can't flare again."

Farna and a Skimmer appeared beside Haven. Farna knelt and probed her burned shoulders with softly glowing hands, and the angry red burns eased in color.

Ryker felt her forehead. "Her body is cooling."

"She needs to be moved to the medical wing," the healer said.

Dax moved to help, but Ryker stepped in front of him, his raven wings emerging. He gently rolled her onto her back and slid his arm under her burned shoulders. Half unconscious, Haven whimpered at the contact. Ryker lifted her in his arms, and with a whoosh of warm air, launched into the air.

River watched his brother fly away, then turned back to the squad. "Well, where were we?"

Ryker turned from the window in his instructor's apartment toward the knock at his door. "I have a feeling I know why you're here," he said, feeling dread as Shane entered the apartment.

"Yes, I'm sure you do. She needs you to train her. It has to be you. Only Shadowalking can restrain that kind of magic. And she will need your Bane to induce a shift."

"She's not up for this," Ryker argued. "A fae should train her first. Give her a chance to learn about her Light before she delves into this form."

"Did anyone give you a chance?" Shane asked. Ryker said nothing. "She doesn't have any time. You know, *you know*, what's in store for her if she can't control this."

Ryker paced the room. "I understand what you're saying. And I eventually understood why you and Finn trained me the way you did. But it will be much more difficult for her. I knew my magic for over fifteen years before I had to work with Bane. She should have some time and training to ease into this."

"I disagree," Shane said. "She'll be released from medical in a few days, and we'll need to start right away. No holding back. She needs to be provoked for another shift. This time was an accident. Next time will be the hardest. Her mind and body know what it is now and will fight it, so you'll need to go at her hard."

"She's just a kid, Shane," Ryker snapped.

"Yes, a kid with a dangerous gift she can't control. Of all people, you know what happens to kids who have powerful gifts." Ryker's face shut down, and he gave Shane a hard look. "You managed to live through your Bane training."

"I wasn't as naïve as she is. And for the record, my Bane training was horrible."

"I remember it. Do you think Finnian felt good about your sessions with him? But it's necessary. You know this."

Ryker sighed and ran his hand through his hair, pacing in distracted circles. "Fine. I need to work out the details with Silas, but tell me when you want to start."

Haven woke two days later, her back and wing joints achy but not pained. She heard a knock on her door, and Farna entered.

"Ah, welcome back. How are you feeling?"

"Okay, I guess." She felt her shoulders, the soft skin eerily smooth and new. Farna asked her to unfurl her wings and gently probed her back. "What happened? *Where is my hair?*" she yelped, gingerly touching the large bald patch on the back of her head.

"Ah, that. Well, I can restore it, but I thought you should be awake first to tell me how you wanted it to look," he said cheerily.

"What happened to me?" Haven said, an edge of panic in her voice.

"You don't remember?"

"No. The only thing I remember is sparring with River and not being able to breathe."

"Ah. Perhaps it's best if you speak to Ryker and Shane. Now, your hair. Short? Medium? Long?"

"Longer, I guess." She worked with Farna for the next hour repairing her scalp and growing her hair.

Shane knocked on her door and poked his head in. "You look much better. Ready to eat?"

Haven eyed the plate heaped with sandwiches and fruit. Her mouth watered and her stomach growled, almost painfully. "Yes, I'm starving." Shane handed her the plate, and she dug in like she had not eaten in a week. "What happened?"

Shane sat next to her bed. "You shifted into a Phoenix. You caught fire."

Haven's hand stilled halfway to her open mouth. "What's a Phoenix?"

"It's a very rare magic, even less common than Shadowalking."

"Great," she said, focusing her attention back on her food.

"Your flight and magic training will change for the rest of this year, and next."

"Why?"

"For your own safety and the safety of others. It's best if we keep you isolated until you learn how to control the shift."

"Does Tannys have experience with shifting magic? I know she advised Larkin to go to the Institute."

"Tannys won't be training you. You will train away from your pod, with me and Ryker."

She wrinkled her nose. "Why? Why drag Ryker into this?"

"Because his gifts can control you when you shift."

"But he's a jerk," she said.

Shane shook his head. "No, he isn't. But he doesn't tolerate bullshit. There's a difference. He takes his work seriously. Something you should, too. You almost burned your wings off. You were lucky to have Farna as your healer. A less experienced healer would have left you grounded for months. Maybe permanently."

Haven groaned. "I don't understand this. How is this even possible?"

His hand fell to her shoulder. "I don't know. But it's not important right now. Rest, and focus on healing. We can talk later."

Lilith sat at the desk in her ministry office, distracted by the report she'd just received from the Academy. Each fall, the Academy sent their annual report to the Rift Council detailing second-year cadets who uncovered rare magics, typically a few Echoes, Cloaks, and Amplifiers, as well as any truly gifted healers. Receiving a magic report in the spring meant an unusual emergence. Lilith reread the report in disbelief. A Phoenix. The Council was in an uproar. There hadn't been a Phoenix in Berinia for three millennia.

Lilith's office door opened, and a hooded figure slipped in and closed the door silently, then flipped their hood back.

"Princess Hope," Lilith said, standing abruptly and moving from behind her desk. "What brings you here? Please, have a seat." Lilith gestured to the chair across from her.

"I can't stay." Hope stood rigid by the door, her hands clasped in front of her. "I came to ask a favor."

"Of course. But you didn't need to come here. I would have come to the Palace."

"It's better if this conversation happens away from the Palace. Somewhere more private. I need you to go to Damaris and meet with an acquaintance of mine," Hope said.

"This isn't a great time for me. We're very busy right now. I received a report from the Academy—"

"Yes, about my daughter, Haven," Hope interrupted. "I'm aware of this report. I think my friend Roque could be useful to you."

"Useful? In what way?"

Hope paced the room. "We've had conversations in the past about working together to change Berinia. To create a more traditional, centralized approach to the Regency."

"Yes, I still want a return to the old ways. But what does that have to do with your daughter?"

Hope pulled her hood over her head. "Speak with Roque. He can fill you in. I would appreciate your time." Hope turned and abruptly left.

Lilith stared into the space where Hope had stood, perplexed.

She cleared her calendar, and the next morning, a Skimmer took her to the eastern shipping district of Damaris. The warm spring day was thick and humid, the sun glinting off the waves of the broad Azmar delta. Towering crates appeared on loading docks near the banks of the river, spurring a rush of activity as seraphim pried open the crates and inspected the contents. Lilith had spent hours in the shipping district with her father as a child, playing amongst the crates and hitching rides on the wagons that wove through the streets of Damaris, delivering goods to shops or Transport locations for off-world distribution. Vivid memories danced through her mind of the bustle and excitement when an agni shipment arrived, the massive onyx steel crates glowing slightly, barely containing the raw energy of the freshly mined stones.

She walked away from the docks and into a short alley, checked the address on the slip of paper in her hand, and climbed the steps of a modest apartment building. Lilith rang the door and tapped her foot impatiently. This request from Hope was unusual, but intriguing. Lilith found few people in the upper social circle of Berinia who appreciated the regency era of King Airon as she did. Hope's shared political views had drawn them together, and over the last ten years, Lilith and Hope had grown close. Lilith wasn't sure she would call it a friendship, but she certainly thought of Hope as a confidante and ally. Even more so recently, with Aric's decentralized policies trickling down to her domain. Hope's influence had helped push back on Aric, re-establishing some boundaries he had recently crossed.

The door buzzed, and Lilith entered the aged but clean lobby and walked up two flights of stairs, checking the apartment number again. She knocked and took a step back when a hulking male filled the opened doorway.

"Lilith?" he said in a deep baritone voice.

"Yes. You are Roque?" The male nodded and opened the door wide for her. Lilith entered the small but well-furnished apartment.

"Thank you for making time to see me. Hope thought it best if we met away from Araine for now." He gestured to a sofa. Tea service was set on a low table, the silver pot polished to a gleaming shine and the elegant cups a fine, almost translucent porcelain. Roque poured them each a cup.

Lilith asked, "How do you know Princess Hope?"

Roque handed her the cup. "I've known Hope since she was a teenager, well before she was bound in a mating contract to the prince. We are close and share many of the same interests. I think of Hope as a sister."

"How can I help you?" Lilith asked, sipping her steaming tea.

"I know Hope has spoken to you in the past about your mutual interest in seeing the Regency restored to its more centralized, traditional roots," Roque said.

"Yes, but I understand we are in the minority."

"Agreed, you are. But the emergence of the Phoenix offers a very intriguing opportunity, one where our interests may align."

"Oh? And what exactly are your interests?"

"Mine are simple. I want the Phoenix...controlled. By someone who can also be under our influence. Hope thinks you may have access to someone who would be ideal."

"Really? And who is that?"

"A commander in the Aerial. River. You know him?"

"Yes, I've known him since he was a child. Our families have long been connected in Damaris. How would River control the Phoenix? And why is this important to you?" Lilith asked.

"That is my business for now. But River...how should I say...-doesn't always walk the straight and narrow."

Lilith smirked. "Yes, you are correct."

"But he also has influence within the military."

"Correct again. But what does this have to do with the Phoenix?"

"If River were bound to the Phoenix, he could direct her magic," Roque said.

Lilith sat up, realizing what he was suggesting. "The Phoenix is a powerful source of magic. If she were bound to a commander of the Aerial, and the commander was under our influence, we would effectively control the military of Berinia," Lilith said.

"It's an important first step," he agreed as she rose and paced the study.

"What do you need me to do?" Lilith asked.

"Arrange a meeting with River. Let's see where we get with him."

Lilith appeared in the living room of her townhouse in Falco Park. She quickly changed her clothes and glanced at her watch. The Council meeting would start soon, and she was running late. She rushed down the stairs to the first floor study to retrieve the Phoenix report and halted.

"Where have you been?" Liam asked, rising from the sofa and downing the rest of his drink.

"How long have you been here?" she asked.

"An hour," he said. Lilith walked around him and retrieved the report.

"I don't have time to talk," she said.

"Make time. The news of the Phoenix. This is the best thing I've heard in a decade."

Lilith frowned. "How so?"

"Come on, Lilith. You're supposed to be the strategic one. Can't you see this?" He shook his head at her puzzled expression. "You were the one who said Lukas needed an enosi."

"You want Lukas bound to the Phoenix?"

"Bound? I'm not sure what you mean. But committed, yes. Think of the status we could gain from an alliance with a princess with that kind of power."

"I can't believe how much time I've spent talking about the Phoenix today," Lilith grumbled under her breath. "Seems like everyone has bright ideas for her. Would Lukas do it?"

Liam shrugged. "I'm sure we can convince him. But we need leverage now. Jairo's influence is growing with the king. If you were committed to Ryker, this wouldn't be so urgent." Lilith bristled at his barb. Liam walked to the door. "You're chummy with Hope. Talk to her and have her petition the king for a commitment contract. And do it quickly. Astor is bound to have a long list of suitors once this news gets out. I want Lukas at the top of the list."

Roque opened his liquor cabinet and pushed aside the bottles of whiskey and liqueurs, reaching for a small flask nestled in a corner. He poured a splash in an empty glass and shot the clear liquid, grimacing as the raw alcohol hit the back of his throat. He'd found this blend, an illegal, distilled thujone-heavy absinthe that was as close as he had ever found to the blend from home, in the market near the Damaris docks. The mild hallucinogen took effect immediately, euphoria easing the pounding headache from the stress of the last few months.

He finally relaxed, although he wasn't pleased at leaving his fate in Lilith's hands. But he had little choice. He needed someone with Lilith's motivations, cunning, and connections. She was an ideal ally on paper, but he also knew Lilith's own agenda would take priority over any alliance.

For two hundred years, Roque had carefully controlled the rise of a Phoenix in Berinia. But twenty years ago, Astor fathered a child. He had wrestled with the unpleasant idea of killing the infant, crossing a moral line he could never reverse. After a bitter argument with Astor, he'd watched the small infant girl skimmed from the medical wing in Lucine to Astor's heavily warded estate in Korsina. He often thought of the moment as the biggest failure of his life. For twenty years, he'd dreaded this day, hoping the Ignisian bloodline would remain dormant.

Roque dropped his head back to the wall and focused his magic on the silence he hated. He pushed harder, but the barrier held and the whispers were absent, as they had been since Haven's arrival. He ground his teeth in frustration and pushed harder. Beads of sweat broke on his temple, and blood trickled from his nose. He released his magic as pain lanced through his head and blinded him. He rose and washed his face in the bathroom and looked at his reflection in the mirror. Other than a profound weariness and a single red vein in his eye that bled into the brown iris, he couldn't see any real damage that would require a healer. He knew better than to try to reach through the Pale.

Roque dried his face and sat at his desk, rereading the report from the Academy. The Phoenix was a disaster that needed to be neutralized. Ideally, she needed to die. But the Academy's wards protected her, and she was visible to their Seers. He couldn't risk exposure. The best plan he could come up with was binding her to River. Then he needed to break her.

# PART 2 :

# THE DARK

# CHAPTER 14

## The Academy

Haven recovered in medical for a day, then was released. Shane stopped by as she was leaving the building.

"How are you?" he asked.

"Fine. A little tired, but the soreness is gone."

"Ryker will be here Monday. We'll start your training then. Get some rest." Haven watched him walk into the building, feeling his words were a little ominous. She returned to the dorms to catch up with her pod, but as she passed through the common room, she noticed a few stares and whispers from some of the squad. She tried to ignore them but hurried to her room, where Harper, Tristan, and Dax sat on their bunks.

"Where's everyone?" Haven asked.

"Guest lecture from Lukas on faeries," Dax said.

"It was optional. But we knew you were being released today," Harper said. "We're waiting for you."

"Thanks, but you didn't have to do that," Haven said.

"We know. Is it okay to want to?" Tristan said.

"Yes," Haven drawled as she hopped up on her bunk. "Tell me what happened." Dax described her shift, her injuries, and what happened in the Yard. "No one was hurt?" Haven whispered.

"Just you." Harper gave her a wry grin. "And maybe River's ego. I think you scared the shit out of him."

"You scared the shit out of me for sure," Tristan said.

"Are you okay?" Harper asked.

"Yes, I feel fine."

"What happens now?" Dax asked.

"I have to train with Shane and Ryker."

Harper blinked. "That sounds like Ryker's training. I don't envy you if it is."

"That's what I hear. Honestly, how bad could it be? It can't be any worse than my wings or being burned by Light," Haven said. Harper, Dax, and Tristan looked at each other with uncertainty. "Seriously. I'll be fine."

Shane led Haven through the forest to a clearing just inside the tree line.

"We'll train here. It will give us privacy, and the clearing is large enough we won't catch anything on fire."

A few moments later, Ryker walked into the clearing, took off his light jacket, and stuffed it inside his bag without a word to either of them. He dropped the bag on the ground, pushed up the sleeves of his snug black shirt, and rolled his shoulders.

"Okay, let's get started," Shane said to Haven. "We'll need to provoke your Phoenix magic to make it surface. As with all powerful magics, it will resist at first and be slow to develop. Fair warning, the training will be grueling."

"So how—?" She choked on her words as Bane threads writhed up her legs. Her heart raced, and sweat beaded down her spine. A Bane thread wrapped around her wrist; the frigid magic numbed her fingers and toes, and icy fear lanced through her heart.

"Fight back," Ryker hissed, flaring his raven wings. Haven stumbled away from him and pulsed a panicked Light wave. He waved it off with a wall of smoke. "Please. That's pathetic. You're not even trying." He clenched his fist, and the Bane around her wrist tightened painfully. "Try to break my magic," he said.

Haven pushed away her confusion and the fear his magic forced into her mind. She wrapped the Bane in Light and heat. Ryker gripped his hand tighter, and the Bane cut into her wrist and her Light vanished.

"Focus. Try harder. You're boring me."

Haven glared at him, then flared her Light and heat at the Bane around her wrist again. Ryker let go and the Bane vanished. Haven hissed as her Light scorched her bare wrist. As soon as she withdrew her Light, Ryker's Bane was around her again, squeezing harder. Blood dripped from the cuts and burns on her arm.

Ryker laughed. "Why would you burn your own arm? Be more strategic with your magic."

Haven's face flushed. She formed her Light into a thin rope that mirrored the Bane thread, but a wall of smoke flew at her and knocked her to her back ten feet behind where she'd stood. Air flew from her lungs and she writhed on the ground, fighting to gain her breath.

Ryker loomed over her. "I've seen children with better control of their magic," he sneered.

Her vision narrowed in fury, and a wall of heated Light erupted from her. He shielded it with Shadow and with a flick of his wrist flung her magic back at her, singeing her eyebrows and burning her face. Haven yelped as her cheeks blistered.

"That didn't work the first two times you tried it. Why do you think it would work a third?" Ryker stepped over her and walked back to Shane.

Haven lay on her back, furious with herself for letting anger get the best of her. She sparred with Ryker for the next hour. He had hundreds of ways to destroy her defenses, and effortlessly evaded her feeble attempts at offense. Cuts and burns covered her arms and neck, and she rubbed at a burn on her stomach through a hole in her shirt.

Ryker's wings snicked to his metal form. "Now, your lesson with wings."

Haven did her best to defend herself against his ruthless attacks, but she spent more time on the ground than on her feet.

After another hour of sparring, she screamed and swung wildly at Ryker. He easily sidestepped her and kicked her legs from under her. Haven dug her fingers into the dirt as she lay writhing, refusing to give in to the tears that burned the back of her eyes and threatened to spill down her face.

"That's enough for today," Shane said.

Ryker furled his wings and picked up his bag. Haven watched from the ground as he strolled away. She shook and breathed through the pain from the damage to her body.

Shane extended his hand. "There's a method here. I know it seems harsh, but Ryker knows what he's doing."

"Leave me alone," she whispered, turning her head away from him and his help. Shane hesitated, then retreated and left her.

Haven exhaled sharply and let her control crumble. The tears slid from her eyes and down her temples into her hair. The year's progress was worthless. The control Ryker had over his magic was unnerving. She was no match for him, not even in the same league. She slowly rolled to her feet and made her way to the healers.

The next week, she trained with Shane, Kaden, and Tannys individually to develop her magic more strategically and learn more advanced metal phase techniques. But her next session with Ryker was much the same. At the end of the second hour, she lay on her back again, covered in new burns and cuts, her chest heaving.

"Did you even practice at all?" Ryker said, shaking his head. Haven stayed silent, refusing to take the bait of his scathing insults.

Maddox later caught Haven on her way to the healer. "What the hell happened to you?" he asked, turning her arm over. She winced as he gingerly touched a long, bleeding cut.

"It's nothing," she snapped, and walked away from him.

Maddox moved in front of her, blocking her way. "The hell it isn't."

Haven's anger vanished, and tears welled in her eyes. She bowed her head and exhaled a bitter laugh. She withdrew her arm from Maddox's grip and silently walked around him.

Through the end of May, Haven worked with the instructors during the week, and on Mondays, Ryker showed her how much she didn't know.

One Monday, after Ryker left her in the dirt again, Shane caught up to her and held her arm.

"Don't be discouraged. You're improving. You need to keep working at it."

She yanked her arm from his grip. "Did I land one blow?" He remained silent. "Does Ryker have a single cut? Did he fall once? Does he have one burn?"

"No."

Haven laughed bitterly. "I'm not improving. I don't understand why I have to do this. I'm no warrior. I don't even want to be one."

"Your magic is powerful. You will be targeted. You need to know how to use it and at least defend yourself."

Haven's lip quivered. She shook her head and walked away.

Haven's pod dispersed to their homes for the summer, but she stayed behind. The Academy was empty except for the first-year cadets with membrane wings in training with River. She spent her mornings with the magic trainers and her afternoons watching the flight lessons with River and the other instructors. Eventually, River included her in the exercises. They became the lone moments of joy she had that summer, flying at speed in the aerial maneuvers River had taught her last year. A few times the cadets even asked her to join them at The Common, and while she enjoyed their company, it wasn't the same as being with her pod.

After one of the many frustrating and pointless training sessions with Ryker, she left the medical facility and trudged up the stairs to her squad's empty floor. She stared at the nine neatly made bunks of their room, and rather than the familiar, curious longing to know what real friends felt like, she now ached for the laughter, the sound of their voices, the warm embraces of the companionship she now cherished.

She never felt so alone in her life.

One afternoon in late August, Shane stopped by her dorm. "Ryker is recovering from a crossing and out for the rest of the summer. Kaden and I are sending you to Araine for two weeks. You can return here with your pod for the start of your third year."

Haven knew she should welcome the reprieve but found it difficult to be happy about anything. "Thank you," she said.

A shadow passed across his face. "Get some rest. Enjoy some time with your friends."

She left him in the common room without reply.

Haven was assigned her own apartment in Araine and found solitary peace for the first time in months. She slept most of her first two days, but eventually connected with Dax and Tristan. The rest of her pod had scattered to their homes in Berinia.

At the end of her first week, Haven received an invitation to lunch at the Palace. She peered at the neatly printed message and realized she had no idea if this was her mother or father's hand-writing. She wouldn't know. She crumpled the note and threw it in the trash, then walked to the cooler and poured herself an orange juice. Her shoulders slumped, and she plodded to the trash, picked up the note, smoothed it, and shoved it into her bag.

When Haven arrived at the Palace, an attendant escorted her to a small private dining room on the second floor. She halted in the doorway at the sight of her mother seated next to the king and queen, and two people she had never met before. And Lukas.

Astor kissed her cheek. "Welcome. It's good to see you." Hope sat next to the queen, her empty brown eyes set on Haven.

"Thank you. Father, Mother, I hope you are both well," Haven said.

Hope spoke privately to the queen without acknowledging Haven's greeting.

Astor said, "I think you may have met Lukas."

"Yes, we met at the Autumn Ball two years ago. It's nice to see you again," Haven said.

Lukas gave her a tight smile. "Hello, Haven." She watched his face, puzzled by his stiff demeanor.

Astor continued, "This is Lukas's father, Liam, and his mother, Skye." Haven politely greeted each of them. Her father offered her a chair next to Lukas.

"I'll get straight to the point," Hope said, finally acknowledging her presence. "We have agreed to an enosi contract with Lukas's parents, which we'll sign next summer." Haven gaped at her father. Lukas kept his gaze fixed on his empty plate.

"I know this is a surprise," said Astor, "but given your recently discovered gift, your mother and I felt it was important for your own safety to have you committed now. Lukas is from one of the most prominent families in Berinia, and as a Shadowalker, he can provide a uniquely secure and safe environment for you."

Haven said to the king, "If security is an issue, why an enosi contract? Why can't I have my own security?"

"And you would ask that of the Regency? To support you. You must be so special," Hope scoffed. "What would you give them in return?"

"I don't know," Haven said sullenly.

"So you would propose being a burden to the king." Haven's face heated.

"You aren't a burden," the king said kindly, his eyes flashing with irritation at Hope. "But your mother is right. The protection we offer a Shadowalker is costly. And asking another person to devote their entire life to you is something we don't take lightly. Shadowalking Triads are a unique arrangement for a specific purpose." He sighed. "I realize enosi contracts are difficult, but both your families want this arrangement. It seems like something we should consider."

The queen said, "Your father and I and the king agreed you should finish your training at the Academy. You both need time to get acquainted before agreeing to this."

"Agreeing?" Haven said in a quiet voice.

"Yes," Astor said. "You will need to agree to it."

"It will be an advantageous alignment for both our families," her mother added. "You want what's best for us all, I'm assuming."

Haven shifted uncomfortably but said nothing. Her mind reeled at the thought of giving up her newfound friends and the taste of freedom she experienced at the Academy. Her adventures in Araine. In Raveno. And she thought of her childhood, trapped on an estate. Alone. She sipped her water, trying to loosen her tightening throat and fight the tears that burned the back of her eyes.

"I won't force two people into a contract," King Aric assured her. "But there must be a good reason I shouldn't certify it. And I won't accept petulant rebellion as the sole reason."

Lunch was served, but Haven's stomach soured. She picked at her salad and tuned out the polite conversation buzzing around her, which was easy because no one spoke to her. She knew Lukas was watching, but she avoided his gaze. She would find no answers there, and certainly no relief from the creeping dread she felt. No one at the table was interested in what she felt anyway.

After lunch, Lukas rose and offered his hand. "Will you walk with me?" She took it and allowed Lukas to lead her into the gardens.

"I was told yesterday. I'm truly sorry they sprang this on you." Haven kept her eyes on the path in front of her. "I've had a whole day to think about this," he spat. Haven glanced at him, surprised by the frustration on his face and in his tone. "And I have my own deal for you." Haven stopped walking and faced him. "I'm not opposed to this contract. Your father is right, I can offer you protection and a safe environment. I'm willing to do this for you. But I've seen the contract, and there is a requirement that we produce a child."

Haven could feel her cheeks burn. The feeling of dread flared to horror.

"That won't happen unless you agree to it," he said, his eyes set hard. "I won't let a piece of paper dictate how your body is used, and I'm not in the habit of forcing my attention on unwilling females. Are we clear on that?"

She relaxed a little. "Yes. Thank you. What is your deal?"

"First, we decide if we can stand each other. If we decide it's possible, then we decide how we live together. We don't have to live in the same house, either. I have two houses, one here in Araine and another you can have access to if you choose. It's heavily warded, and the grounds are extensive. You could live there your entire life and we would likely never see each other."

The tangle of dread and horror solidified into a reality she knew only too well. "Sounds like a cage."

Lukas said, "Well, that's a harsh description. But yes, there would be no visitors except my Triad. You can also live at the Hollow here in Araine, but the living space is tighter. We could adjust that if you wanted." Lukas took her hand. "I can make this work for you in whatever way makes you the happiest."

"What about us?" Haven asked.

"Us?"

Haven glanced at him nervously. "At some point we will both have...needs." Her face heated again.

"Most contracts like this don't involve love. But some couples find affection and friendship. And yes, occasionally sex. But there is no requirement you stay celibate or faithful to me. Or I to you. The only thing I ask for is discretion, and I will do the same. But first, let's see if we can even stand to be around each other. This will be our decision."

"Why are you doing this? What's in it for you?"

"Does there have to be something in it for me? My family asked me. And I'm able to offer you protection, which you will need. Those of us with powerful magic need a space to feel safe."

Haven looked down at her hands, not sure what to think of his generosity. "Thank you. I know this is a sacrifice for you."

Lukas tipped her chin to him. "From what I've seen, you're a good person. It's not such a big sacrifice." Lukas tucked her arm in his and they walked to the Palace together.

Haven told Dax about the commitment over dinner that night.

"That's really archaic. I didn't think contracts like that still existed," he said in disbelief.

"Yes, well, looks like I'm digging up every extinct seraphim tradition. I have to come to Araine once a month to meet with Lukas as part of our agreement to get to know one another. I don't know. My whole life I've been living in a cage of one kind or another. I just do what others tell me is best for me. I didn't choose to go to the Academy, but honestly, it's the first time something has meant anything to me." She glanced at him. "And I found people who really care for me. And whom I care about." Her eyes welled, and she wiped at them in frustration. "I want my own life."

"You can start making your own choices now. You said Lukas won't force you. Take the next year to decide what you really want. For you, and only you. You have that right."

She held her head in her hands and rubbed her face. "I'm not sure I even know how to do that. How do you tell the king that he can take his contract and shove it?"

"Uh, wow. I have no idea," Dax said, chuckling. "But my first suggestion would be to find a gentler way of saying it." They both laughed a little.

"Why can't I be committed to you." Haven tossed her napkin in her lap. "I already know I like you."

"Yes, but I can't offer you a secure environment. There's something to be said for the security around a Shadowalker. Besides, I've seen you sweat, bleed, and roll in the mud way too many times. I could never think of you in a romantic way."

"I thought you said I was hot," she said, resting her chin on her clasped hands and fluttering her lashes.

Dax chuckled. "You are. But also like my sister, so that would be kinda gross."

She laughed with him, then her smile faded. "Well, I doubt Lukas has romantic feelings for me anyway."

"You never know. You may be pleasantly surprised."

Haven looked at him doubtfully.

# Chapter 15

## Silve

Ryker and his Triad stepped out of the Garret into the swelter-ing summer day, the still air adding to the suffocating heat rippling off the smooth, cobblestone streets of Falco Park.

"Are you sure you want to walk?" Silas said. "I can skim us. It's only a few blocks to the ministry."

Trinity wiped her sweating brow. "Maybe walking wasn't a great idea."

Silas took her arm. "Ryker?"

Ryker looked at the sky, the vibrant blue of summer retreating into a bleached haze from the relentless, angry sun. "I can fly. No sense in wasting your magic."

Silas shrugged. "It's a short distance. I can manage."

Ryker unfurled his wings. "I'm good. Take Trinity. I'll be right behind you." They vanished, and Ryker launched into the sky. Once away from the streets, the air cooled, but still hung heavy from the summer sun. Ryker flew the short distance to the ministry building on the southern border of Lucine and Araine and landed next to Silas and Trinity, who waited in the shelter of the limestone portico with Lukas and his Triad. They walked in together, leaving the heat behind them in the cavernous, cool marble foyer.

Lukas led them to the west wing Council chambers. "We will need to be efficient with our questions," Lukas said. "Silve has agreed to appear here, but she won't stay long."

"What's her rush?" Silas asked.

"When she leaves Elsah-ra, it weakens the Pale," Ryker said.

"Yes, which is also why we weren't given any notice of this meeting," Lukas said. "Her departure from Elsah-ra isn't widely known, and Seers will only feel it now."

"No time to plan an assault," Xander said.

"Exactly," Lukas said.

The clicking echo of their shoes on the marble floor quieted as Lukas opened the heavy mahogany double doors of the Council chamber. The Triads filed in and took their usual seats on the curved benches facing the seven Council members whose conversation echoed in a muted buzz. Lilith waited from her elevated spot in the center until the Triads took their seats, then called the meeting to order.

"Thank you for assembling so quickly," Lilith said. "We don't have much time, so I'd like to introduce you to Silve." A petite female with long black hair rose from a table set between the risers and the benches where the Triads sat. She acknowledged the Council and the Triads, then took her seat.

She turned her deep brown eyes to Ryker. "You are the Shadowalker who freed me?" He nodded. "Thank you."

Ryker bowed his head to her. "Sometimes my work has moments of good fortune, of being in the right place at the right time. I'm glad I could help."

Lukas asked, "How did you come to be in Terra with a daeva? Are they the ones who abducted you?"

"Yes," Silve said. "I crossed the Pale to meet with the faerie council in Tangyra. It is standard procedure to have my meetings spontaneously. Someone inside my circle, a djinn, betrayed me and told the daevas my plans."

"Do you know who?" Lilith asked.

"No, not yet. We're questioning everyone and have tightened my guard. But the risk remains."

"So why are you here?" Ryker asked. "Seems like an unnecessary risk."

"Because of your Phoenix," Silve said. "Your Pale will change. Moving across the Pale will be almost impossible for anyone other than a Shadowalker as soon as she bonds with someone."

"What do you mean, 'bonds'?" Lukas asked.

"A Phoenix is a Paired magic. Very ancient, similar to my own. By instinct, she will seek someone to bond with. That bonding will strengthen her magic, and depending on the magic of her bonded partner, it will alter your Pale. The stronger the magic, the tighter the Pale will be."

"Our Pale is already one of the strongest there is," Lilith said.

"Second only to Terra," Silve said in agreement.

"Why is the Pale around Praesia and Terra so different?" Ryker asked.

Silve cocked her head. "You don't know?"

"Know what?" Ryker asked.

"The Pale was a gift from the Drankoni," Silve said. "Suleiman received this gift, and as long as there is a descendant, our Pale remains."

"But demons can cross to Elsah-ra," Lukas said.

"Yes. Because I am the sole descendant of Suleiman. The gift was intended to be tied to two beings. A Pair. With only one living descendant, our Pale is intact, but the daevas can still make rifts. And I am also unbound," Silve said. She sighed. "My gift is complicated among our species. I cannot bind with a marid or Serendib. Our laws forbid it. And those are the most magical of our species. Any other djinn magic would have very little effect on our Pale, even a Traveler. An ideal Pair for me would be another descendant of Suleiman, but I am the last of our line."

"I would think your Council would make an exception," Lukas said.

Silve gave him a grim smile. "Our social structure doesn't permit it. While I'm a descendant of Suleiman, I'm also a commoner. Marids view themselves as gods, and Serendib a close cousin. No marid or Serendib would subjugate themselves to someone like me, even if it's in the best interests of our world. Which is why having your services," she said, nodding at Ryker, "is so important."

"While this is interesting, it doesn't really explain how the Pale around Praesia is different. We only have one unbound Phoenix, and she is twenty. Our Pale has been in place for three millennia," Ryker said.

Silve's penetrating gaze landed on Ryker, her deep brown eyes studying him. "You are astute. I suggest you discuss this with your king."

Silas and Ryker shared a confused look. "So why are you here?" Ryker asked. "As far as I know, you have our support."

"Because we need continued access to Praesia. You need to adjust your diplomatic rifts to allow our djinn to pass."

"Of course. The fae have a Caster who can make the necessary adjustments," Lilith said.

Silve shuffled in her seat. "I'm also here to ask about your relationship with the daevas."

Lilith frowned. "And why is that?"

"It's our understanding, from a dependable source, that the daevas have received agni."

"We opened limited discussions with the daeva only a few weeks ago," Lilith said. "Our dealings do not involve agni. We've made our limits clear."

"We know they have it. They replenished a long-dormant agni stone in their capital."

"If not from us, where could they get a stone that large?" Ryker asked.

"I'm not sure. Aefa has a productive mine, but the elves do not trade with anyone. And the daeva have a new Riftmaker, but it would have to be a powerful one to form a rift into Aefa. Hura is a possibility. They have a very small agni mine, but it is barely enough to keep their world's needs satisfied. It would be an improbable coincidence that the stone came from Hura. Huraks don't have the resources to engage in off-world trade. It's one reason they invade other worlds so often. It's more likely Praesia has a leak. Someone here may be smuggling stones."

"That's highly unlikely," Lilith said.

"But not impossible," Silve retorted. "What of the rift in Korsina?"

"It remains," Finnian said. "But it was tightened twenty years ago. It's almost impossible to pass through. Only Ryker and I can move through it, and I can assure you, neither of us would supply daevas with agni."

"I would never suggest that," Silve said quickly. "What of an undocumented rift?"

The room fell silent. "It's possible," Ryker said. "It's possible that it's the elves, too."

"We can check Praesia, but the elves don't allow us to pass through to Aefa," Finnian said.

Silve sighed. "Yes, I know. If it's the elves, there's no way to stop them. We don't have a diplomatic relationship with them."

"No one does, to my knowledge," Lilith said.

"Can you try to reach them?" Silve asked. "We've tried but were rebuffed."

"Yes, we will contact them, but we too have been unsuccessful in the past. I don't want to give you any false hope," Lilith said.

"I understand." Silve rose. "We cannot allow the daevas to rise in power. Elsah-ra has always been a target for the daevas. They have stated their goal of inhabiting our planet."

"Why?" Ryker asked.

Silve looked at him. "Their planet is dying. The sun that shines on Alja-hin wanes. They will eventually share the same fate as the fae."

"Faesa is a dead planet. We offered the fae sanctuary here in Praesia thousands of years ago," Lilith said.

"Yes, but no planet will offer the same to the daevas. They mean to invade and replace. I will not allow that to happen to my people. With a source of power like agni, the daevas could rise again, and that threatens the existence of my people."

"We understand," Lilith said. "We will search for any illegal activity here in Praesia and try reaching out to the elves." She looked at the rest of the Council. "But I think we should also bear in mind there may be another source, another mine on a world we don't know of. There are thousands of worlds, most are unexplored."

"We realize that," Silve said. "We can only control what we can." She rose from her seat. "While I was gone from Elsah-ra, the daevas plundered our planet. They have a symbiotic relationship with Shimar, as you know. The daevas created many rifts and sent teams of shima to destroy our cities. We are still repairing the rifts, but it will take time. And our djinn still die. You have opened diplomatic discussions with the daevas. I hope you understand their motivation and why we beseech you to support our cause."

"You have our support," Finnian said.

Lilith's stony gaze fell on Finnian. "Yes, as chair of the Rift Council, who determines all diplomatic relations and Pale crossings, I can assure you of our support."

Finnian was unflinching. "And here I thought the king set our policies."

Lilith said through clenched teeth, "Of course. But on this topic, we are aligned."

"I certainly hope so," Finnian said, and walked to Silve. "I speak for myself and Ryker," he said, glancing at Ryker. "The Shadowalkers will help you and your country."

A red flush crept over Lilith's furious face.

Silve left the chamber with her escort, and Lilith adjourned the meeting. Ryker walked toward the exit with Finnian, and his eyebrows rose when he saw Lilith hold Finnian's arm. Griffin's hand shot out and gripped her wrist. Lilith winced at the pressure and released him.

"Hands off," Griffin growled.

Lilith ignored Finnian's Warrior, but rubbed the red mark on her wrist. "We need to work together. It isn't helpful when you expose our internal disagreements in front of people like Silve. It makes us all look bad."

"You know what? I really don't give a shit," Finnian said. "You care more about appearances, particularly your own, than the issues we're facing right now."

Lilith's face grew cold. "Careful," she whispered.

He stepped near her. "Or what?"

"I'm not without influence. Do you really want our relationship going this direction?"

"I want a functional conversation. But let me make myself clear. I don't work for you. No Shadowalker does."

Lilith's mouth curved into a bitter smile. "The Rift Council authorizes your crossings. And ensures your *safety*."

"Is that a threat?" Griffin said.

"It's a reminder," Lilith said, her eyes never leaving Finnian.

"That's enough," Ryker snapped at Lilith.

Lilith's icy eyes fell on him, then she smiled sweetly. "We're on the same side. I'm simply trying to present a dignified, united front in our diplomatic conversations." She turned her attention back to Finnian. "Seems like some of you need a refresher course on politics before being allowed at the grownups' table. Excuse me."

Ryker and Finnian watched Lilith's back as she made her way through the crowd. "She's getting bolder," Finnian said under his breath.

"She's desperate," Ryker said. "She doesn't like your appointment to lead the Daeva Council. She's grasping at whatever she thinks will give her the upper hand."

"Careful. She may grasp for you," Finnian said.

"She tried," Ryker admitted. Trinity gave him a sharp look. "I turned her down."

"When did she do that?" Trinity asked.

"After the Spring Ball last year, when the king set the rules for daeva relations."

"You never said anything," Trinity said.

Ryker shrugged. "What was there to say? I didn't take her seriously."

Silas watched Lilith as she spoke with two Rift Council members. "You may not have taken it seriously, but I'm sure she was dead serious."

"It doesn't matter. It's not the first time it's happened. I'm sure it won't be the last."

Trinity touched Ryker's arm, and he gave her a grim smile.

# CHAPTER 16

## Araine

River sat in his suite at the Garret, fuming. The last thing he wanted to do with his brief break after summer flight training was spend a minute in Araine. Lilith had asked for a meeting; more like issued a summons. But that was two days ago. Gods damn Council. They acted like royalty.

A windsprite fluttered in his face, and Ryker's voice asked him to stop by the small study. Great. Another command from a self-important prick.

River sauntered down to the first floor and took a seat across from Ryker's desk.

"What?" River said. "I'm leaving soon."

"I know. I was hoping to catch you. I have the short list of rec-ommendations for the King's appointment to the Daeva Council and wanted your opinion."

River raised an eyebrow. "You want my opinion."

"Of course. The list has three Aerial commanders. I would assume you know them." Ryker handed River the list.

"Yes, I do," River said. "Forget Dekkar. Talented soldier, but an idiot."

"He's the commander of Special Forces and he's an idiot?"

River snorted. "Rumor is he got the position because of his father's connections. Or maybe because his partner is Liam's cousin's daughter. But it certainly wasn't because of his brains."

"How does the division perform, then?"

"His lieutenant, Callah, is brilliant. If it weren't for her, Special Forces would be a joke."

"What of the others on the list?"

River scanned the names. "They are both good. Danmar is a superb strategist, and Shaia has a lot of experience with demons. She was a commander for the last century of the demon invasions. Very low casualty rate in her unit."

"If you had to pick one for the panel, who would you choose?" Ryker asked.

"Probably Shaia. Her practical experience would balance the politics I'm assuming would be rampant with that group."

Ryker snorted. "Only one open position left, and gods, the jockeying. It's exhausting."

"You're not taking it?"

"Hell no. I'm helping the king and Finn fill this last position, and I'm out." Ryker eyed him carefully. "Your name was on the list, but I took it off. Assuming you didn't want it either. I can add it again, if you want it."

"Gods, no," River said. "I have to be in Araine for unit meetings way too often as is."

"I figured, but thought I'd check."

River stood. "Anything else?"

Ryker opened his mouth to say something, then closed it. "No, that's it. Thanks for your input."

"Shallah is still at your safe house?" River asked. Ryker nodded. "Give her my best, and let me know the next time she comes to Araine."

River left the Garret and walked the few blocks to Lilith's townhome, where an attendant waited for him in the lobby and led him to a study. He threw himself onto the sofa and stretched his arms across the back. From the time he met Lilith as a child, everything had been a power play. She never passed up a chance to remind him of her superior position. River had half a mind to ignore her request altogether, but curiosity got the best of him, so he waited. And seethed.

Lilith joined him in the study with a tall seraphim male River didn't recognize. "It's been years, River. It's good to see you again, thank you for coming. And for your patience. I apologize for the delay. I was waiting for Roque to arrive in Araine to speak with you both." She turned to the male behind her. "Roque, this is River, a commander in our Aerial. Roque's specialty is ancient history, in particular dark magic."

"What is this about?" River said. He studied Roque's imposing figure as he sat in a chair across from River and folded a long leg over his knee.

"We'd like to discuss the Phoenix," Lilith said.

"You mean Haven?"

Lilith waved a hand at him and sat in a chair. "Whatever. I'm only interested in her magic."

"We need your help," Roque said. "As you know, Haven only recently discovered her Phoenix form. You've seen its raw power. But she's in training and will soon gain control. We are looking for a way to contain her."

River's eyes narrowed. "What do you mean 'contain'?"

"Are you aware of the power of a Phoenix? Do you know what the magic is capable of?" Lilith asked.

"Not really. Other than I've seen her burn in flames, hiss at me, and try to bite me."

"Her magic is flexible," Roque said. "It can take any form except Shadowalking and Bane. The Phoenix is part of a Pair. Right now, the Phoenix is unbound, unpaired, if you will."

River gave her a blank stare. "Who cares? Why does any of this matter?"

Lilith breathed an irritated sigh. "Think bigger, River. Think strategically." River glared at her. "If she were bound to, say, an elite soldier in our military, think how you could direct her power."

"How the hell would I direct her power?"

"It's part of a Pair magic. Didn't you ever listen to Adrien's lectures?"

"Hell no," River said. "The most gods awful, boring part of the Academy, hands down. I like Adrien, but I couldn't bear his lectures."

"Well, if you had listened, you would know this. The Phoenix will seek a Pair. We want that to be you."

"I have no interest in a mate. Ever."

"It's not a mating," Roque said. "It's a Pairing. Your magic will be linked. You could direct her magic."

Lilith eyed River. "And with your second magic, you could effectively control her."

River bristled. "What are you talking about?"

"I know your secrets. I know why you've excelled in the Aerial, why you've advanced so quickly."

River stood. "I've advanced because I'm good at what I do." He walked to the door. "Find someone else for your schemes. I'm not interested."

Lilith said, "Someday you will be. Let me know when you change your mind. But don't take too long. We don't have a lot of time."

"I won't change my mind." He slammed the door behind him.

River walked to the Temple, needing the time to gather his thoughts. *How the hell did Lilith know?* Only two people in this world knew River's second magic. His grandmother would never tell anyone, not even Ryker. It had to be Adrien. That fucking asshole.

River marched to the Temple and paced the hall until he caught sight of Adrien walking toward him. He followed Adrien into his office and closed the door.

"What are you doing here?" Adrien asked.

"Why did you tell Lilith about my magic?" River blurted out, his anger boiling over.

"I didn't," he said, sitting behind his desk.

"Well, she knows, and you're the only one who would say something."

"I would never, *never* say anything. I'm actually shocked you would think that, after everything I've done to protect those with magical gifts," he said curtly.

"Well, Shallah isn't the one who told her. And you two are the only people who know, so you do the math here."

"Have you considered Lilith found out on her own?"

"How the hell would she do that?" River snapped.

"Because she is an unregistered Echo."

River blinked. "What?"

"You heard me. She can feel your magic. And use it."

"Why are you telling me this? I thought you didn't tell secrets."

Adrien paced away from River. "I'm guessing Lilith tried to blackmail you."

"Basically, yes."

"I don't condone using someone's secrets against them. I'm telling you hers to balance the scales again."

River smirked. "Adrien, you're as devious as they come."

"No, I'm not. I believe in fair play and privacy. I hope this now settles your mind."

"It does." River moved to the door.

"A word of advice. Be careful of Lilith. She's a master deceiver. Being involved with her is playing with fire."

"Well, that didn't go well," Lilith said to Roque. "I still think Pairing her with Lukas is ideal. I know I can control Lukas. River is a wild card."

"Absolutely not," Roque said, cutting her off. "There is no way she can be bound to a Shadowalker. I'll kill her before I let that happen."

"But he doesn't have Bane," she argued, dismissing his harsh words as overdone dramatics. "How bad could that Pairing be?"

"I said no. It's not a risk I'm willing to take. Hope only agreed to support the commitment contract with Lukas, not the Pairing." A darkness fell over Roque's face, and his voice grew cold. "I can access her through Lukas, which will not seem unusual to a Seer."

"Why do you need access to her?" Lilith asked. Roque stared at her but said nothing. "You and Hope know something you're not telling me."

Roque smiled, then shifted to a female fae.

Lilith's eyes widened. "I didn't know you were a Shifter. I thought you were seraphim."

"Do your part, Lilith, and don't ask questions about things that don't concern you." Roque rose and moved to the door. "I'll follow River. I'm guessing he went to speak with Adrien."

The fae female waited in the hall outside Adrien's office until River left, then Roque shifted to Lilith's face and body, and entered Adrien's office.

"What did River want?" she asked him.

Adrien looked up from the reports on his desk and glared at her. "You crossed the line. Don't threaten River again. I told him about your magic," he said.

"You have your own secrets, don't you? I'm assuming you want to keep those," she said, her voice cold.

"You should know me by now. Go ahead, tell all my secrets. I have nothing left in my life I couldn't live without and haven't for forty years. Can you say the same?" Adrien turned his attention back to the paperwork.

"Stay out of my business, Adrien. Particularly concerning River."

Adrien ignored her, and she stormed from his office.

Roque had one or two shifts left before he depleted his magic. He shifted back to the fae female and sent a windsprite to Lilith, *River knows you're an Echo.*

# CHAPTER 17

## The Academy

Haven threw her bag on her bed in the pod's Basic quarters and noticed an extra empty bunk. "Where's Avina?" Haven asked Dax.

"She transferred to the Institute for her third year to train with other readers and Seers," Quinn said.

Haven's mood lifted, but with a twinge of guilt. She had never warmed to Avina after their confrontation over Larkin, but was glad at least she could avoid that tension for her final year at the Academy.

For the next three weeks, Kilian led her squad through intensive physical training to shake off the summer and get them back into shape. The last night at Basic, Shane pulled Haven aside.

"When we return to the Academy tomorrow, you'll resume your private lessons."

Haven tensed. Over the last month, she'd almost put her Phoenix training out of her mind. The normalcy of being with her friends in Araine and at Basic had revived her. At Shane's words, a dark anger and frustration settled over her like a skin she thought she had shed. She turned to leave, but Shane held her arm.

"Haven, I know this is hard."

She frowned. "What exactly do you think you know? When you were at the Academy, barely figuring out what kind of magic you had, did you ever have one-on-one sessions with a warrior Shadowalker who kicked your ass every week for four months?" she spat. Shane said nothing. "Well, did you?"

"No, I didn't."

"Then don't tell me you know what I'm going through. You have no fucking idea," she said, and walked away.

Haven's pod hiked from Basic to the Academy the next morning, arriving in the Yard late afternoon. Shane, Kaden, and Ryker met them as the squad lined up in formation under the September sun.

"Welcome back," Shane greeted them. "This year you will focus on strategy." He introduced Ryker and Silas. "Ryker will advise this squad on field training and war gaming. Once a month, you will compete against another squad in a game of capture the flag. You will also receive instruction from guest speakers, like Silas, who will give seminars on strategy and advanced training in flight, weapons, and sparring." Shane outlined the goals of war gaming and the schedule they would follow over the next year, culminating next summer in a month-long exercise—Combat Simulation, or ComSim.

The squad disbanded to the dorms amidst noisy chatter, excited and a little nervous to finally apply the skills they had learned over the last two years to real-world situations. Haven, however, was held back.

"Ryker is advising four squads, so he'll be here every Monday," Shane informed her. "He's agreed to stay and teach you Tuesday mornings."

Haven stared dead-eyed at Ryker. "Lucky me."

His face in return was stone. "We begin tomorrow."

The pod sat waiting in the dining common with empty dishes until almost the end of lunch break.

"Where the hell is Haven?" Maddox grumbled to Dax.

"I think she has training again," Harper said.

Haven appeared and slid onto the bench next to Dax, and food finally appeared on their table. "Sorry I'm late," she mumbled.

"Where have you been?" he asked, handing her a basket of bread. His eyes widened. "What the hell happened to you?"

"Nothing," Haven said, pulling her sleeve down to hide the burns and cuts on her arms.

Dax pulled it back. "That is not nothing."

She flinched. "Let it go. Eat your lunch."

Haven sat at the table in silence until the pod finished serving themselves, then left the dining common, her plate untouched.

"Did you see her arms?" Harper said. Dax nodded. "What the hell are they doing to her?"

"I don't know. She goes into the woods with Ryker. Why don't you ask him?" Dax said.

"I'll try, but I doubt he'll say anything."

The squad met Shane on the training courts the following week. He reviewed the sparring routines they had learned last spring, then divided the squad in half for their first rotation. Haven and Tristan sparred with two short swords, and Haven beat him. Soundly. She didn't acknowledge the win, but rather moved to the next station and picked up two daggers. Dax watched her wield them against Maddox and best him in minutes. Dax and Tristan stared at her in disbelief.

When it was Dax's turn to spar with her, they picked up their staves, knowing this was Haven's weakest weapon in the sparring circuit. She shifted her weight into her knees, taking an offensive stance. Dax did the same. Months ago, she would have fallen back defensively, but this time she didn't budge. They clashed, and Haven spun so fast Dax never saw her staff until it hit him in the head. He went down hard.

Over the course of the match, Dax landed a few hits, but he spent most of the time on the ground or dancing away with rapped knuckles and bruised ribs and thighs, or ducking his head to avoid getting clocked. He knew he was the loser in the match.

Haven replaced the staff and walked away without a word. Before she rotated to the next sparring station, Shane pulled her away with a firm grip on her arm and escorted her into the woods. A few minutes later, Ryker followed. Dax glanced at Maddox and Tristan, then headed toward the woods too. Kaden blocked his way.

"Let it go," he said.

Dax's face darkened. "What the hell are you all doing to her?"

"She needs the training. They won't hurt her."

"The fuck they won't. Have you seen her after one of your little sessions?"

Kaden stepped near him, his gaze like steel. "Get back in rotation, *cadet*. Now." Dax stood his ground, but Tristan dragged him away.

They paced in the empty Yard. "I've had enough of this," Dax said brusquely.

"Me too. But Kaden and Shane are keeping this under wraps," Tristan said.

"We're also taught to stick up for one another."

Haven later emerged from the forest on Shane's steadying arm, visibly limping. Dax leapt to his feet and supported her other side as they crossed the square. Blood dripped from a cut on her arm, and her cheeks were burned and blistered. The hair on one side of her head was scorched, her scalp red and raw. He brushed the hair back from her forehead, and she winced away from his touch. Dax gave Shane a furious look over Haven's head but remained silent.

They helped her up the steps of the medical center to a treatment room, and a healer shooed them out and closed the door. Dax wheeled to Shane. "What the fuck are you doing to her?"

"You need to back off and let this happen," Shane said. Dax opened his mouth to argue, but Shane held up his hand and stopped him. "Have you seen an improvement in her skills?"

"A profound change. But I've also seen a change in her. She's withdrawn, losing weight, crabby. And the wounds. Good gods, Shane..."

"I know what this looks like, but it's necessary."

"All of it?"

"Yes. Powerful gifts are difficult to learn. But she will gain from it, too."

"But at what cost? Her soul? And what about what she wants?"

"She lost the luxury of choosing her own path when she became a Phoenix," Shane said. "Make sure she gets something to eat tonight."

He left Dax gaping at him.

Dax didn't find Haven when he returned to their room after the day's training ended. He stripped and grabbed a towel and headed to the showers, passing Harper in the hallway. She paused, then shook her head. Dax found Haven and turned on the shower next to her. She braced herself against the tiles as the steaming water beat over her. He couldn't see any visible marks, but exhaustion showed in her sagging shoulders and slow, deliberate movements. She groaned under her breath.

"Are you okay?" he asked.

She nodded. "Just sore."

"What's with you?"

"What do you mean?" she asked, scrubbing shampoo into her hair.

"Do you even know what you did today during sparring?" He took the bar of soap she handed him.

"What did I do this time?"

"Haven, what is *wrong* with you? You're fighting like a beast and you're not happy," he said, rinsing the soap off his body.

"It's the training with Ryker. I hate it."

"We can see what happens to you afterward. Does this have to do with your Phoenix form?"

"Yes."

"What can I do to help?"

She shut off her water and mopped her face. "Just be my friend," she said, slinging the towel around her body.

"Always. But—"

She didn't let him finish as she closed the door behind her.

The cycle continued for the next few weeks, with no reprieve for Haven and no answers for Dax. He waited for her in the Yard every Tuesday and helped her to medical afterwards. She knew he was trying to help, but there was nothing he could do. The growing frustration and anger on Dax's face every week was just another burden to her, something she caused and couldn't ease or resolve. With each training session, she withdrew a little more; the only solace that comforted her was, once again, her familiar solitude.

In early October, their squad met Ryker in the Yard. He stood near a cache of bows, arrows, swords, and daggers.

"These training weapons are the same ones you've used for two years. They still disintegrate on contact and aren't meant to inflict wounds, but strikes from these will sting like hell. If it's a killing strike, you'll glow blue. If you accumulate enough wounds, the magic will also determine if you can survive, and glow blue when you can't. You're eliminated from the exercise if you are killed. Gear up."

The squad distributed the weapons, unfurled their wings, and followed Ryker two miles into the forest outside the Academy.

Haven landed and furled her wings tight behind her. The site was small but elevated, giving them a view of the hazy morning mist filling the valley below. Dax and Maddox landed beside Haven and surveyed the site.

"Well, at least we aren't stuck in a hole," Haven said.

Dax scanned the mountain behind him. "We should scout the other side of this ridge." He and Tristan flew away as Ryker assembled the rest of the squad. When they returned a few minutes later, Dax said to Haven and Maddox, "The other squad is a mile away, pushed up against a hill in a depression. It looks like they are trapped."

"It can't be that easy," Haven said, watching Ryker instruct the squad on the opposite side of the clearing. "I'm going to scout."

"The other squad will see you," Maddox said.

"Not if I fly high enough and approach from the far side. It will only take a few minutes." She launched into the sky and vanished from sight. Later, she returned and landed beside Dax and Maddox. "It's a trap," she said.

Ryker strode across the clearing, his face a dark storm. "Why aren't you with the rest of the squad? You don't think the instruction is worth your time?" he snapped. "Who said you could leave?"

"I did," she said.

"You're not in charge," Ryker said.

"My understanding is this is a cadet-led exercise. So fuck off."

Ryker's scowl softened, and a smile played across his lips. "So you're a leader, now? Right out of the gate? By all means, lead, princess."

She ignored him and turned to Maddox and Tristan. "In the mountain behind their staging site is a cave system. If we approach from the top of this ridge, which they would expect us to do, they'll see us coming and escape through the caves. On the other side of the cave is a bowl. If we follow them through, they'll be waiting for us and pin us like cattle in a pen. It will be a slaughter."

"So, what should we do?" Dax said.

"Slaughter *them* like cattle," Haven said. She gathered Harper and Kit and had them split the squad in two. "Wait at the ridgeline until you see my signal. Once we are in position, move in from the top of the ridge, and be loud. They'll spring their trap, and when they come through the caves, we'll be waiting for them. Your job then will be to seal the caves and prevent them from retreating."

Haven and twenty of her squad flew around the site, staying below the trees and out of view. They circled back and hiked a mile on foot, creeping under the canopy of trees and pausing when aerial scouts were visible above. Once in position, Haven sent a flash of Light toward the ridge a mile away. She heard the war cries of the team led by Kit and Tristan as they flew over the crest of the ridge, skimming the tops of the trees.

As they neared, the opposing team flooded into the bowl, where Dax, Maddox, and Haven's team waited along the elevated edge. Haven, Dax, and half their team leapt into the bowl, with Maddox and the remaining team spaced evenly along the ridge, their arrows picking off the opposing cadets with deadly accuracy. Together, Dax and Haven entered the chaos of the other squad, protecting each other's blind side. She swept her dagger across the throat of a cadet, who screamed and glowed blue. She quickly leapt to the side, avoiding the thrust of a cadet's sword. The cadet erupted into a glowing blue as Dax's sword burst from the cadet's chest before disintegrating.

Haven heard the squad leader call for a retreat just as Kit's team emerged from the caves, attacking the floundering squad from the opposite side. The opposing squad collapsed into chaos, and Haven's squad left no survivors.

Haven and Dax held their opponent's flag while the entire opposing squad lined up in defeat, glowing blue. Haven's team lost only three cadets.

She beamed, her cheeks glowing with the thrill of their win, and for the first time since her vacation in Araine, she felt a sense of accomplishment and pride in their victory, and the joy of sharing it with friends. She remembered what it felt like to be happy.

"It's good to see you smile," Dax said, nudging her.

The next day, Haven and Shane met Ryker in the forest clearing for her lesson.

"Nice work yesterday," Ryker remarked. She didn't respond, only removed her jacket and faced him, rolling her neck and loosening her shoulders. Ryker stared at her, crossing his arms.

Haven waited. "Well? Get on with it."

"Why don't you approach these sessions with the creativity and insight of yesterday's team exercise?"

"And how exactly am I supposed to do that?" she asked. "There's no terrain to scout here. No puzzle to figure out. Just an experienced warrior beating the shit out of a cadet every week. So, have your fun and let's get this over with."

Ryker's eyes darkened to a cold gray. "I don't think it's fun to beat the shit out of you."

She laughed. "Really, I don't give a shit what you think."

His face grew stony, and he began.

The pod waited for Haven in the plaza until she and Shane emerged from the woods, trudging toward the medical building. Tristan nudged Dax and pointed to the other side of the plaza at Silas and Ryker as they walked to the instructors' apartments. Silas draped an arm across Ryker's shoulders, and Ryker leaned into him.

Dax said, almost to himself, "This is a mess."

"Did Ryker say anything to you?" Tristan asked Harper.

"No. In not so many words, he told me to butt out," Harper said.

"This can't go on much longer," Maddox said.

At dinner that night, Haven picked at her food. Tristan caught Dax's eye and gestured toward her.

"You look like shit," Dax commented.

Haven glared at him. "Thanks a lot."

"Seriously, you look like you haven't slept in a month."

"You need to eat your food, not chase it around your plate," Tristan added.

"I don't need a nanny," she snapped. Haven put her fork down. "I'm not hungry."

She rose, but Dax held her arm. "We are going to The Common tonight. You haven't come with us in weeks."

"I'm not in the mood. I'm going for a walk." Haven hitched her pants up her gaunt frame as she walked away.

"I think we're losing her," Tristan murmured.

"Not if I can help it," Harper said. The pod followed Haven to the courtyard. Harper caught Haven's elbow.

"Don't run from us," Harper said to Haven.

"I just want to be alone," Haven said, trying to pull out of Harper's grip. Harper held her tight.

"I know what's happening to you," Harper said.

"Oh? And how is that? Are you there in the clearing when your precious brother beats the shit out of me every week?"

"Obviously not. But I know what happened to him. I was an infant when Ryker trained to control his Bane. I heard the stories growing up, from Shallah, Trinity, and Silas. It was awful. Ryker almost quit the Academy."

"I'm happy for him," Haven sneered.

"He made it because he relied on his pod. And Silas, even before they were bound. We are here for you. Don't shut us out."

"Shut you out? I didn't realize you were in."

"Haven, that's not fair," Dax said.

"All of you. You all have everything." Haven looked at Harper and Kit. "A lover who cares." She looked past her to Dax and Maddox. "Friends. A family that wants the best for you. Actually, for *you*. How do any of you know how to help me?"

"That's easy," Harper said, her eyes blazing. "We are in. All of us. Even if you don't want our help, we're inside your heart and we aren't going anywhere. Let us help you."

Haven stared silently at Harper for a minute, then her shoulders sagged. "You can't."

Harper stroked her arms. "I can't help you with training, but I can help you deal with it afterward." She looked behind her to Quinn, Dune, and Tristan. "We all can. Let us be your friends. Real friends."

Haven squeezed Harper's hands, but slowly removed them from her arms. "I appreciate what you're doing and what you're saying. And you're right, I love you all. But please," she said, her breath catching in her throat, "I need some space. Some time to think." Haven backed away and hurried across the Yard, slipping inside the forest alone.

Dax said, "It was a start. We need to keep after her."

"Gods, I'm starting to hate her family," Harper said.

"What about Ryker? Can you talk to him? Can he ease up?"

Harper sighed, then shook her head. "It won't work. It can't be a simulation. The threats need to feel real, or her magic won't come out." Harper looked at Dax. "Ryker and Shane's method may seem brutal, but it works." She looked back at the woods. "We just need to figure out a way to help her get through it."

The pod's second session of war gaming in November was like the first. Haven, Dax, Maddox, and Tristan led the exercise, with their pod executing their plans. They won the next game within two hours and were back at the Academy by lunch.

Ryker met Shane and Haven in the forest clearing the day after the game.

Ryker paced in front of her, glowering at her in frustration. "It's been over two months since you came back from summer break, since we started training again. You're not using your mind in these lessons. *Think*, Haven."

Haven put her hands on her hips but kept a neutral face and said nothing.

Ryker glared at her. "You're clearly capable of thinking. I know after talking with Dax, you're the one who came up with the diversion strategy, which was a good one. So maybe you come here to pout like a brat? Because you sure as shit aren't applying yourself to these lessons."

"Maybe you are really that shitty of a teacher," she seethed.

Ryker's rough laugh grated on her ears. "That's not true," he said. "You've learned a lot. But you're not willing to admit it." He dipped his head to her ear and whispered, "Confess it. I'll keep your secrets."

Haven could feel the heat in her face, and replied through gritted teeth, "There is nothing of value in sparring with you. I hate it. I hate being near you."

"Now we're getting somewhere." Ryker stepped close, their bodies inches apart. Her anger stormed to the surface. "Lie to me again about how much you hate me."

"That is no lie," she shot back.

Ryker inhaled deeply, as if scenting her anger and fear. "Ah, I love a good lie," he said, his platinum eyes dancing, taunting her.

The edges of Haven's vision narrowed as her rage focused on Ryker's mocking smile. She felt the familiar panic of his Bane threads wrapping around her wrists, and she shoved away the feeling, embracing the flow of her rage, letting it give her the strength she needed to endure another session with him.

He leaned closer to her and laughed. "Fight me, Haven, if you can. Use your brain. Master this and you can be free of me forever. But I don't think you really want to. I think you like being near me."

Haven snapped.

Ryker took a step back as Haven's eyes paled and fangs erupted from her mouth. Blood trickled down her chin from the gaping holes around the elongated, razor-sharp teeth.

Ryker's magic swirled around her, holding her away from him. "That's it," he said.

Her wings sprung from her back, red feathers flaring away from her and bursting into flames. "Shane," Ryker said, his voice urgent.

"Got it." Shane enveloped her wings in a cloud of mist, keeping the flames from her back and neck.

Ryker could smell burning hair. "Haven, can you hear me?"

Haven hissed and lunged for him.

He grunted but held her with his magic. "Feel this magic. It's unique, different from your Light. When you know it, you can use it, control it." Ryker kept a steady stream of words flowing to her, but Haven struggled against his magic. He jerked his head to the side as she bit at him, her teeth inches from his face. Ryker held her tighter and she roared at him, her eyes flaring brighter.

"Holy shit," Shane said.

"Keep water around her," Ryker said, straining to keep her contained. "Haven, pull back your magic. Control it. Make it listen to you."

Haven lunged at Ryker again and slipped through his magic. She grabbed him and bit at his neck, a fang furrowing the skin on his cheek.

"Ryker," Shane hissed.

"I know," Ryker said, fending her off and avoiding her snapping jaws. "She's fucking strong!" Flames danced down Haven's arms, encircling his hands that held her shoulders and burning his skin. Ryker yelped in pain but didn't let her go. She pushed into him, the flames creeping up and blistering his forearms.

"End it!" Shane yelled as he sent a soothing mist over Ryker.

Bane slipped from the Shadow binding her and slithered around her throat. Ryker clenched his hand on her shoulder and the dark magic tightened. Haven choked but broke through Ryker's Shadow and gripped him around the neck. Flames scorched his cheeks.

"Harder," Shane said. "Do it now!"

Ryker clenched his hand tighter, and the Bane constricted. Haven's mouth opened in a silent scream. She released Ryker and fell back, thrashing against the Bane encircling her throat like an iron band. Her eyes darkened back to blue before she fell to the ground unconscious.

Haven sat up slowly, rubbing her eyes to clear a disorienting fog. She sighed at the now-familiar room in the medical building and gingerly lifted the thin gown she wore instead of her training uniform. The skin on her legs tingled with the itchy heat of burns no longer there. She touched her face, feeling smooth skin instead of the blisters she expected. Grimacing at the stiffness in her back and shoulders, she reclined on the pillow, rubbing at her temples to ease the blinding ache behind her eyes. Her presence in medical and the echoes of her injuries told her she'd shifted, but she still had no memory of it. Haven rubbed her eyes in frustration. Without memory of her shift, how was she supposed to learn about it? Her chin quivered at the prospect of this endless training cycle she was trapped in.

Shane knocked on her open door and sat in a chair. "How are you?"

"Tired. And sore. My head is killing me." She propped herself up on the pillows. "What happened?"

"You shifted to your Phoenix form."

"I'm not burned," Haven said, glancing at her arms.

"We controlled your flames this time. The healers mended a few scorches, but nothing serious. Do you remember anything?"

"Not really. It's hazy." She covered her eyes with her hand. "I'm so tired, Shane." Her voice was thick and quavering.

"I know. Your magic, it's powerful. I've never seen anything like it. It will take time for you to gain control, but you need to shift and experience it. It's a brutal process. But you're not alone. We're here to help you."

"Who is 'we'?"

"Me. And Ryker."

Haven laughed bitterly. "Then I'm truly alone." She rolled to her side, shunning Shane's support that felt like a mockery.

Haven woke in the early hours of the morning before the sun's shadows had appeared through the trees. Her gaze lingered on the forest, then she took a deep breath. She was done with the Academy. None of it was worth the pain. She found her clothes from yesterday folded on a chair next to her. She dressed and shuffled down the silent halls. The dark morning air was fresh on her face and cool in her lungs, easing the pain still throbbing behind her eyes. She unfurled her wings, and with a powerful downstroke, shot into the air.

# Chapter 18

## Portos

Ryker woke to a pounding on his door. He opened it, rubbing his eyes, and blinked at Shane.

"She's gone," Shane said.

"Shit. Give me a few minutes."

Ryker ran a hand through his wet hair as he met Shane in the lobby moments later. "Tell me what you know."

"She's in Portos. She flew there early this morning." Ryker's eyes widened. "I know. It's far. But her wings." Shane shrugged. "We got lucky. She barely made it there before she collapsed in front of the Admin building. I don't think she knew how taxing it is to use magic. I have a Skimmer waiting to take us to Portos, if you want to go."

"Of course I do," Ryker said.

A healer met them upon arrival and escorted them through the ward toward Haven's room.

"She's resting," she said. "We tried to get her to eat, but she refused. She's asking for a Skimmer. Honestly, I don't think she should go anywhere for a few days. She's really weak."

"Can we see her?" Shane asked. The healer nodded as they stopped outside Haven's room. Shane entered first, and Ryker lingered behind. Haven glanced at them, then turned her attention to the view of the forest through her window.

"Are you okay?" Shane asked. She said nothing.

Ryker stepped around Shane. "Haven, are you okay?" Ryker could see her jaw set and a tear roll down her face. "I know this has been hard."

She slowly faced them, her eyes flat and dull. "Get out," she spat, then looked back at the window and said nothing more.

Shane returned to the Academy to cover classes while Ryker stayed in Portos to monitor Haven's condition. The healers finally convinced her to eat, which improved her coloring and energy. She slept for most of the next three days but eventually was strong enough to take short walks. Ryker kept his distance, though he stopped by each morning. She refused to look at him or speak to him. By the end of the week, the healer told Ryker she was well enough to leave.

"She hasn't asked for a Skimmer since the first day, but she can finish her recovery somewhere else if she wants. As I'm sure you know, when you deplete your magic like that, it often takes a week or two to fully recover." Ryker nodded, intimately familiar with that sensation.

"I think it's best she stays here, if that's okay with you," Ryker said.

"Of course. It's up to her, but she's not asking to leave, so I won't push it."

That night, Ryker lingered in his usual place in the hall outside Haven's room and caught her slipping out of the medical ward. She walked into the woods and Ryker followed her, fearing she would try to fly away again. She strolled through the silent forest, often stopping to pick up a leaf or twig or a stray flower that found a patch of sunlight to bloom. Ryker trailed behind, but kept his distance.

She paused in the dark shadow of a tree. "I know you're there."

"Where are you going?" he asked.

"Nowhere. I have nowhere to go."

"You were asking for a Skimmer. Where did you want to go?"

"Away."

Ryker was silent, then said, "If I can, I'd like to tell you a story. And after, if you never want to see me again, I'll respect your wishes." She sighed, and he added softly, "It seems like a small price to pay to get rid of me forever."

She crossed her arms and leaned against a tree. "Tell your story."

"I was five years old when my Shadowalking magic appeared. Until that time, Shallah was trying to raise me and River. My mother died giving birth to us. My father was a powerful figure in Damaris who had an affair with a poor dressmaker. He abandoned her, refusing to help her through her pregnancy and birth. If she had a skilled healer with her, she may have survived. Once my father discovered I was a Shadowalker, he took us into his home, but we weren't a family. I lived with Shallah and River in a separate wing of my father's house. Ronan made it clear that when I came of age, he would arrange an enosi contract for me. There were many suitors. I was on display like a prize bull for almost fifteen years until I went through my shift. Then the real trouble started. My father offered me as breeding stock for those of elevated status who wanted a daughter bred to a Shadowalker."

Haven turned to look at him.

"It never happened. I realized the only way I could protect myself from people determined to use me was to control my magic. I made a life for myself by aligning with the king and accepting the Regency's security. But I made sure everyone knew they couldn't manipulate me. There would be a price to pay for threatening me. I won't stand by and let this happen to you. But the only way you can have independence is to control your magic. I've been provoking you for six months, trying to get you to shift into your Phoenix to feel it, learn it, and understand it. Those are the first steps for control. You're already incredibly brave and strong.

"I understand why you want to leave, but there is no place in this world you will truly be safe. Someone will find you. There are people who will bind you and use you for your power." He backed away into the forest. "Think about it. Dax will be here tomorrow. Talk to him. I'm here to help if I can."

Ryker walked slowly through the forest to the inn in Portos. He could only imagine the thoughts running through her mind. He remembered his many conversations with Silas through his Bane training, the only thing that had kept him sane through the brutal lessons with Finnian. It was the main reason he had chosen Silas as his Warrior. In his room, he stuffed his clothes into a backpack and slung it over his shoulder. Hopefully, Dax could help her tomorrow. But she had to stay at the Academy. He would hunt her down in any dark corner of Praesia to make sure she was safe.

Dax knocked on Haven's door the next morning. She sat on her bed, her legs tucked under her.

"Hey there," he said, sitting next to her.

"Hi," she said.

"It's good to see you. Will you tell me what's happening?"

Haven told him everything.

Dax dragged his hand through his hair. "What do you want to do?"

She looked away from him, her chin quivering. "I don't know. I just feel dead inside."

"What Shane and Ryker did to you doesn't sit well with me, but I can understand it. And I can see why Ryker has taken an interest in your situation. I'm guessing his magic is the only kind that can contain you?"

"I guess."

"So, how else can you explore your Phoenix form safely? Without a Shadowalker to bind you?"

"Honestly, I don't think there is another way. And I think I need them both. Shane's Water magic lessened the burns." Her voice shook. "I swear, Dax, I feel cursed."

He held her to him. "Maybe there's a better way to uncover your magic instead of provoking you."

"How?"

"I don't know, but there must be something. For very selfish reasons, I want you to come home." Haven couldn't suppress a small smile. "But also, Ryker's story kinda scares the shit out of me. He has a point. You were already committed to Lukas without your permission. Frankly, without even your knowledge."

"I know. And honestly, after hearing Ryker's story, I'm afraid that may only be the beginning. I want to control my own life, make my own choices. I guess I also have to decide how hard I want to fight for it."

"You're a fighter, for sure. I'd put my money on you any day." Dax reached for her hand. "Come home. Let me help you fight this one, too."

The following Monday, Haven and Dax met Ryker and Shane in the common room of the instructors' apartments.

Haven said, "I'm willing to continue training, but I have rules. If you don't agree, I'll try it my way alone or quit training altogether. At this point, I really don't care either way."

Ryker leaned forward. "Let's hear it. I'm open to suggestions."

"Dax comes with me from now on. I need someone on my side."

"We are all on your side."

"Bullshit. No one is on my side but me. And stop interrupting." Ryker grinned. "Rule number two. I know you're trying to provoke me to shift. But there are other ways to do that without being a dick." Ryker's grin broadened. "If those don't work, you can be a dick again. On a very limited scale. Rule number three. We separate wing training from magic. It's too much, all the time." Haven was silent.

"Is that it?"

Haven turned away from them. "I know what you're trying to do. And maybe it was the right thing. I don't know if this will work either. But I need something new."

Ryker conceded. "We'll try it your way and see what happens."

Shane and Ryker met Dax and Haven in the forest clearing the next day.

"I've been thinking about what you said, of other ways to get you to shift," Ryker said. He paced around her. "Do you remember what your wings felt like when they shifted?"

Haven thought for a moment. "They felt hot."

Ryker huffed a laugh, circling her. "Let's see your blades. Maybe we can start there." Haven unfurled her silver wings. "Imagine your blades are feathers. Focus on shifting even one blade to a feather." Haven tried to shift for several minutes and got nowhere. "Okay, that's not working." Bane swirled around Ryker's hands. Haven stiffened, and Dax stepped in front of her. "I'm doing this your way, but you also need to trust me."

Haven moved Dax behind her as Ryker's Bane wound around her legs. She swallowed hard and focused on pushing away the fear, fighting the feeling of panic.

"Don't fight the fear. Use it. Focus on it," Ryker said.

Haven settled her thoughts, centering on Dax's hand in hers. She closed her eyes and let go. Fear engulfed her, and her heart raced as her skin grew clammy and sweat beaded on her forehead. She fought the overwhelming instinct to flee, and a hint of red feathers appeared at the tips of her blades.

"Hold it, no more," Ryker hissed. "That feeling? Feel that?"

"Yes, I can feel it."

"What does it feel like? A pull in your stomach? A thread in your mind? Describe it to us."

Haven's brow furrowed. "It's like a wave in my chest. In my heart."

Ryker started, then looked at Shane.

"That's like your Bane, isn't it," Shane said.

Ryker nodded, then released her. Haven exhaled, and her shoulders relaxed. Ryker paced in front of them. "That's why we use fear to induce the shift. When you feel fear, doesn't it feel like chest pain?"

"Is that what your Bane feels like?" Haven asked.

"Not now. But when I was discovering it, yes. It was fear and panic. That's what I had to feel to develop Bane. And we know your Phoenix responds to threats."

"Is that like your Bane, too?"

"A little, but not like your magic." He scowled at her and folded his arms. "And since you don't scare easily, it's hard to get it to come out. This would be a lot easier if you were more of a pansy," he said, a teasing smile curving his lips. She relaxed and laughed a little. "Okay, now that you know where it comes from, let's see if you can control a shift." They tried for another hour, but Haven couldn't get any response without Ryker's Bane provoking her.

"That's enough for today. This is progress. You should be happy with this."

"Well, I'm not convinced this will work, but it's a start," she said. As they approached the dorms together, Ryker turned towards the instructors' apartments.

Haven called to him, and he looked back at her.

"Thank you," she said.

"You're welcome."

# CHAPTER 19

## Araine

Lilith impatiently tapped her foot under her desk and looked at her watch for what felt like the hundredth time in the last hour. Dekkar was late. If he didn't show up soon, they would miss their window. She rose and paced her office, peering out to the street to watch for him. She heard a knock on her door.

"Enter."

Lukas stuck his head in. "Father isn't coming to the Advisory Board meeting. He just linked with me."

Lilith swore under her breath. "This is the third month in a row. Why did he tell you?"

Lukas smirked as he pushed the door wider. "Why do you think? Take a look in the mirror. Smoke is coming out your ears."

She gave her brother a dirty look. He laughed as she turned back to the window to look at the street.

"Who are you waiting for?" Lukas asked.

"A colleague." Lukas rolled his hand, asking for more detail. Lilith waved him off. "He's not important. It's a private matter."

"Oh? Anything scandalous I should know?" Lukas wagged his eyebrows.

"Give me a break. And that's none of your business." Lukas chuckled and moved toward the door. "How about you?" she asked.

Lukas paused in the doorway. "What about me?"

"Are you getting to know Haven?"

"A little. She's a nice kid."

"Kid? She's twenty-one, isn't she?"

"Yes, I think so. Something like that. She's just young. I like her. But she's sheltered in a lot of ways. And private. Keeps me from knowing her."

"Well, you better get to know her. You'll be seeing a lot of her in the next centuries."

"Maybe. We haven't decided that yet."

"Really. You'd go against Father's wishes?"

"Yes, if Haven doesn't want the arrangement. Why would I force her to live with me? That sounds horrible."

"Well, convince her."

Lukas shook his head. "It's her decision. How did you put it? It's none of your business."

A hulking figure filled the doorway behind Lukas. He turned, then took a step back. Lilith hurried across the room and gently pushed Lukas into the hallway.

"We'll discuss this later. Thank you, Lukas."

She closed the door in Lukas's curious face, then wheeled to Dekkar. "You're late," she snapped.

"Blame River. He kept us late this morning on an exercise."

Lilith walked back to her desk and swung a picture from the wall. As she punched in the combination code, she said, "I thought you were the commander of Special Forces. What does River have to do with your group?"

"Any commander can request Special Forces to work with their unit." Lilith swung open the safe door and removed a large iron cube. Dekkar took a step back. "Abaddon's flames, that one is big. Are you sure it's safe to handle?"

"Yes. The containment system is perfect." She lifted the cube with two hands and handed it to Dekkar. "We don't have long. The

Daeva Council meets just after the Advisory Board meeting. I need to leave now to be on time."

Dekkar hefted the cube. "Vannin knows the timing?"

"Yes, of course. His timing through the rift has to coincide with the daeva representative passing through to the Iron Room. He knows his job."

"Last time he was a little off."

Lilith gave him an annoyed look. "Two minutes off doesn't matter. But you being late doesn't help."

"I'll be where I'm supposed to be. I always am. Why is this one so big? Won't it be missed?"

"No. A huge shipment came in for the djinn. It was easy to take the stone. And now the daevas owe me." Lilith closed the safe and swung the picture back into place. "Hurry. And send me a message after Vannin leaves."

"Easy. The transfer shouldn't take more than a few seconds."

"Not too soon. I have to be seen in both council meetings for cover."

"We know," Dekkar snapped. Lilith opened her mouth to speak and Dekkar vanished. *Gods, he's an ass*, she thought as she gathered her bag. But useful. Thank gods he didn't have to think too much. Lilith walked out to the street, unfurled her dove gray wings, and flew toward the ministry.

Lilith exited the conference room behind King Aric, listening carefully to the end of his conversation with Jairo. Seemed benign enough. An enosi contract with his son Julian and Princess Tallys when she came of age in fifteen years. Liam had inadvertently resurrected the enosi tradition, and more prominent families were scrambling to embrace the trend. Lilith stayed by the King's side as he walked toward the Iron Room. Finnian waited with the rest of the Council outside.

"The ambassador should be here shortly," Finnian said.

"Excellent," the king said, saying goodbye to Jairo as he continued down the hall with Kira.

Finnian stared at Lilith. "Can I help you?" he asked, his voice curt.

"You? No," Lilith said, her tone equally short.

"You're not part of the Daeva Council. Don't you have somewhere to be?"

The king chuckled. "Come now, Finnian. Lilith. You two have been snipping at each other for two years now. Can't we put our differences aside?"

Lilith smiled sweetly. "Of course. You first, Finnian."

Finnian wrinkled his nose in distaste, and said to the king, "You ask an awful lot."

King Aric laughed and clapped Finnian on the back. "Let's get this over with. What's the topic today?"

Finnian waved the king inside the open door to the Iron Room. "I'll fill you in once we're inside. Where it's more *secure*."

The king entered the room and Finnian followed him, wagging goodbye to Lilith with his fingers.

Gods, she fucking hated him. She stormed down the hall and noticed Princess Hope lingering outside the conference room.

"Are you sitting in on the Aerial meeting today?" Lilith asked.

"I doubt it." Hope sighed heavily. "The beginning of the month is so hectic. We should space out these Council meetings. It gets tedious."

"We tried that, but then all we do is travel back and forth for meetings. Yes, it's tedious, but more efficient this way."

"Are you taking your father's place at the Aerial meeting?"

"Yes." Lilith gestured to a branching hallway. "Walk with me?"

Princess Hope fell into step with Lilith. "Did you meet my friend, Roque?"

Lilith glanced at her. "I did."

"And?"

"He had an interesting request. River is resistant, but we're working on it."

"Let me know if I can help," Hope said.

They stopped outside the conference room. Lilith caught sight of River approaching behind Hope. "Funny you should say that.

Let me introduce you to someone."

Lilith waved River over to her. "River, do you know the princess?"

"Yes, we've met a few times," he said. "Always a pleasure to see you."

"Likewise," Hope said. "Lilith was just mentioning how much she admires your leadership with the Aerial." River couldn't hide his surprise. Lilith expertly hid her own unease with the direction of the conversation. "Your command is relatively new, isn't it?"

"It is. I've been a unit commander for just over two years now. I like to think I've learned a lot during that time."

"Rave reviews from the admirals regarding your military leadership. But that's not the only skill you need as a commander." Hope nodded towards Lilith. "You also need to hone your political instincts. I can't think of a better teacher than Lilith. You would be wise to take opportunities to work with her."

Lilith noticed River's eyes narrow. Hope was laying it on thick. Maybe too thick. "I'm sure River has many good examples to follow," Lilith said.

Hope glanced at her watch. "None that have as much natural talent as you. It was nice to see you again, River. Lilith."

River watched Hope until she rounded a corner out of sight. He walked into the conference room and said to Lilith as he passed her, "Must be nice to have a princess as your biggest fan."

"It's not a bad thing," Lilith said, following him inside and breathing a sigh of relief.

# Chapter 20

## The Phoenix

Haven continued her training with Ryker and Shane throughout the winter, with Dax by her side. While her mental and emotional state improved, she learned no more about her Phoenix form. Three months of training and she was still only able to have the tips of her wings shift if Ryker provoked her. She caught glimpses of her magic in her subconscious, feeling it as she surfaced from sleep or drifted into dreams. But as soon as she opened her eyes, hoping to hold on to the feel of her magic, to understand it, it vanished into a frustrating haze, lurking just behind clarity.

Ryker passed her weapons training to Silas, but after a few sessions, Haven almost wished for Ryker again. Silas towered over her by eight inches. Even her speed was not an advantage when sparring with him. Despite his size, he was shockingly fast. During one of their sessions, he easily blocked her wing strike and tripped her in one fluid movement. She screamed in frustration as she lay in the dirt. He offered her a hand and helped her to her feet.

"I want to kill you. But I can understand why Ryker picked you for his Triad," Haven grumbled.

"You're doing fine. Look." He showed her a long scratch on his forearm. "You got me."

Haven rolled her eyes. "That will take a healer thirty seconds to mend. And I think you let me do that."

He winked. "Now, why would I do that?"

She huffed a laugh. Even though Silas put her in the dirt more often than Ryker had and was brutal with wing training, she genuinely liked him. His warm sense of humor, quick and easy smile, and underlying gentle heart made him impossible to resist.

As much as she enjoyed being around Silas, she had not warmed to Ryker. By late January, their sessions had stalled into the doldrums. Haven refused to let him bait her, and he withdrew into cold detachment.

Their lack of progress frustrated Shane, and their sessions often ended abruptly in heated arguments. One morning, after losing the battle again, Shane threw up his hands in disgust and left the clearing.

Haven packed her things to leave while Dax stood near her, his arms crossed. "This isn't working."

"Obviously," Haven said in a clipped voice.

"Let him push you."

Haven slung her pack over her shoulder. "Is that what you want?" she said to Ryker.

He shrugged. "It's up to you." He walked away through the trees.

Dax kicked the dirt in frustration. "Come on, Haven. We need to try something new."

She stared at him for a moment, then left the clearing. She could hear him swearing softly to himself behind her.

When Ryker arrived in the clearing the following week, Dax and Haven weren't speaking to each other. Dax ignored her sullen glare and walked by Ryker. "Do it," he said, and paced the edge of the tree line behind them.

Ryker looked at Haven, surprised—and a little relieved—at the chance for progress. The past months had been a frustrating waste of time, but he knew after her breakdown that Haven needed to control the process. And if that meant he had to come to the woods once a week and play senseless games with her, fine. But Shane wasn't the only one losing patience.

Haven tipped her chin up, bracing herself, her eyes glistening. Ryker wrapped Bane around her legs.

"Breathe, and use it," he said, and squeezed. Hard.

Haven screamed as her silver wings sprung from her back. She lowered her head and fought through the pain and fear.

"Don't resist it. Use it. Use me." His Bane swirled up her arms. He tightened his fist, and blood dripped down her fingers into the dirt. Her eyes flared white. "Shane," Ryker said softly.

"I'm ready." Fog swirled around Haven's legs.

Bane tendrils wound around her chest. Ryker clenched his hand, his knuckles turning white. "Come on. Stop screwing around. Let it out, *princess*," he seethed.

Haven's white eyes set on him. She growled, and flames bloomed across her wings. Dax raced to her side.

"Stay back!" Ryker yelled.

Haven lunged at Dax. He stopped, stumbled backward, and fell.

Ryker wrapped his magic around her torso, holding her back, inches away from Dax. "Get away from her, now!" Ryker shouted.

Dax scrambled away. Haven hissed at Ryker, baring her long fangs.

"Good gods," Dax said.

Ryker spoke to Haven in a calm voice, encouraging her to reel in her power, control her magic. But Haven roared and lunged for Ryker, breaking through his magic. Her fangs ripped through his coat, tearing his shirt.

"Careful, Ryker," Shane hissed.

"I know," he said under his breath as Haven snarled at him. Ryker slid his magic around her neck and squeezed until she dropped unconscious to the ground. He knelt beside her, checking for burns.

"Is she okay?" Dax asked from behind him.

"Yes, she's fine. Her skin is cool," Ryker said. He gently pushed her hair from her face. "She still needs a healer, though." Ryker picked her up and Dax followed them through the forest.

Haven slept for an entire day. Ryker, Shane, and Dax were there when she finally woke.

"Did I hurt anyone?" she asked.

"No, we're fine." Dax sat on her bed and described what happened.

"I'm hopeless." Haven curled against Dax. "It's nothing, or I'm a wild animal."

"It will take time." Shane reminded her. "You need to keep shifting, keep experiencing the form."

Haven's gaze fell on Ryker, and he saw her frustration, and a little fear. He knew that look too well. She closed her eyes, and he slipped away, escaping his own disappointment. He knew she was where she needed to be. With friends.

The next week, Ryker forced her to shift again with the same result. The hate she felt toward him that had tempered over the last months returned as he taunted and tortured her into shifting. She knew he was trying to help her, but she couldn't help turning her dread and pain on him.

In late February, the night before their next session, she was walking through the plaza when Ryker passed by with Silas, headed toward the instructors' apartments. At the sight of him, apprehension and anxiety flooded her heart.

In a flash of bitterness, she called to him. He stopped and slowly turned to her. "Do you enjoy this?" she spat.

Shock flickered across his face before his eyes shifted to a cold, dark gray. "Enjoy it? No, I don't enjoy this."

"Then why do you keep coming here?"

"Who else can help you? Get some sleep." He walked away with Silas.

Haven watched him go, then trudged back to the dorms. Ryker's words burned her heart, and loneliness overwhelmed her once again. She had her pod, and even though they were her friends, she could feel another sweeping change approaching with the end of the Academy now in sight. Their circumstances connected them, but they had their own lives, their families who loved them. Her sullen resentment tormented her, a persistent, cruel reminder of her isolation.

That night Haven dreamed she burned, her body engulfed in flames. She felt a presence lurking in her mind, hiding in the shadows. She fought it, driving it away, fearing its need to consume her.

*Let me in,* the fire said from the shadow.

*You'll hurt me,* Haven said, circling the shadow, tapping her magic and flooding her mind with Light.

*Maybe,* the fire said. But I can make you stronger.

*How?*

*Let me show you. Trust me.*

Haven hesitated, then fatigue overwhelmed her. She just didn't care anymore. She was tired of being alone, afraid, and powerless. She dimmed her Light, and the magic slipped from the shadows and wrapped around her heart. And she burned. She whimpered, folding in on herself, but heard Ryker's voice telling her to control it, to use her anger and fear, and fight.

She embraced the flames and fought. And the fire loved her.

Haven woke the next morning with a new clarity that eased her heart and mind. In her dreams, she found someone who loved her, who would help her and always protect her. That person had been in front of her the entire time. Her confidence, intelligence, and strength would always be there for her. No one could take that away. Haven's heart no longer hurt because now it was her own.

Haven arrived in the clearing without Dax.

"Where's your nanny?" Ryker snarled.

She didn't respond, and said to Shane, "Leave."

"That's not a good idea," Ryker said.

"Yes, well, looks like I'm full of great ideas these days."

Shane walked toward the edge of the clearing and said to Ryker, "I'll get Farna."

"Just you and me, princess," he said, his eyes a twisting shift of silver and gray.

Haven held her voice steady. "What are you waiting for? Set me on fire." She held his gaze and backed away.

Ryker touched her with Bane, and wicked, curved fangs slid from her jaw, and her red wings flamed. Ryker could smell her hair burning and a darker smell of burning flesh. Haven hissed at him but kept her distance. Ryker drifted Shadow down her wings, stroking her, the magic swirling around her face, her arms, her torso. She stood her ground but didn't attack.

"Haven, can you hear me?" he asked.

"Yes."

Ryker stepped back at the sound of her deep voice. "Can you see your magic, in your mind, in your body?"

"Yes. And I can see yours. I can feel you."

Ryker let out a sharp gasp. He could feel Haven. He could sense her mind and the cage wrapped tightly around her heart. And he felt her hate. Ryker tensed with surprise and a twinge of disappointment. He knew he deserved it, but it was hard to take.

"You are sad," Haven said.

"Yes."

"Here," she said. "See." He felt a shift and saw the other side of her heart. He felt her loneliness, and a warmth that longed for a connection, someone to trust with her heart, someone who would care about her. Haven's wings shifted to membrane, and the flames vanished. And the glimpse inside her closed off behind a cold wall.

"You did it," he said as he reached for her.

She groaned, then collapsed.

The following week, Haven's squad returned to the mountains for war gaming. As they had since the first game, Haven and her pod led the exercise, with Ryker guiding and advising when asked, which wasn't often.

Haven and Maddox lured the opposing squad into a concealed pit at the base of a ridgeline, and Haven's team guarded the only way out. While Haven and her squad sprang the trap, a team of four led by Dax ambushed the six cadets guarding the squad's flag, easily capturing it.

When they returned to the Academy that afternoon, Ryker reviewed the game with them, then dismissed the squad from the Yard. He left with Silas without a word. He hadn't spoken to her all day.

That night Haven lay on her bunk, restless and unable to sleep despite the comforting sounds of her pod sleeping around her. She glanced at Dax on the bunk across from her and saw him tuck an arm behind his head. "Want to grab a drink?" she whispered.

"Sure," he said. They dressed silently, bundled in thick coats against the freezing February night, and crossed the slumbering dark campus to The Common. Haven ordered a shot of whiskey and a beer.

Dax took the seat next to her at the bar. "Planning on walking home? Or should I expect to carry you?"

"Keep up with me, and let's see who carries who home." She dropped the shot in the beer and downed the entire drink, then belched loudly. Dax howled and downed his own beer. Darius placed another shot and a beer in front of them.

"Wait, we didn't order this," she said. The bartender pointed over her shoulder. Haven looked behind and saw Ryker and Silas.

Ryker winked at her and sipped his beer. Haven tipped the whiskey at him and shot it. His mouth curved in a half smile, and even from a distance, Haven could see the flash of his silver eyes.

Her stomach tightened. She saw River's strikingly handsome face, but it was different. There was none of River's cool, malignant hardness. Of the two brothers, she knew Ryker was more of a threat. She had felt a fraction of his power firsthand and knew the depths of fear and pain he could inflict. But there was a moral center to him and a warmth she could see in his features. For the first time since she met him at the Autumn Ball over two years ago, she realized how beautiful he was. Annoyed at herself, she turned around and faced Dax, her cheeks flushed.

"Are you only now realizing how good looking he is?" Dax asked, nudging her.

"Shut up. You think he's good looking, you go chase him," she muttered, sipping her beer.

Dax chuckled. "He could turn me. But I like females too much. And I think he does, too."

"Right. I'm sure he has a string of them in every city."

"If I looked like that, I would."

"This is not helpful." She sighed. "Obviously, he's good looking. I'm not blind, and it's not even debatable. But I learned my lesson with Larkin. No more pretty boys."

"Ryker is not a boy. He's as far away from Larkin's type as you can get."

"Way too much shit between us, after the last six months. I can't even think of him that way."

"Sure. Keep telling yourself that."

"You saw for yourself what happened between us. Impossible. And no more males," she said firmly.

"I know you've had terrible experiences. We've all had our fair share of disappointments. But the pain you felt with Larkin? It's part of learning what a good relationship feels like."

"What are you saying? I need my heart crushed to feel love?" she said.

"Maybe. But I think it makes you ready when real love comes your way."

"I wouldn't know what that is."

"Someday you will. But don't close yourself off to the possibility. You are worthy of being loved."

"I'm skeptical," she said, dismissing him with a wave of her hand. "Anyway, it wouldn't be with someone like Ryker."

Dax shook his head in defeat, and they clinked glasses. They closed the bar and somehow made it back to their dorm.

Haven trudged her way to the clearing the next morning, wishing she had stopped by the healer to take the edge off her raging hangover. Dax seemed worse. Shane was alone in the clearing.

"Where's Ryker?" Haven said.

"He and Silas left this morning for Araine. Your Phoenix training with him is over." Kaden walked through the trees into the clearing. "From now on, it's me and Kaden."

Haven busied herself with her bag to hide her frustration at having to start all over with someone new.

Kaden worked with her on her shift, attempting to teach her to ease into her Phoenix form without an external threat. After an hour of trying, Haven ended the session in frustration.

"Why did Ryker quit when I was starting to get it?" Haven said.

"Did you ever consider how hard this was for him? Do you really think he enjoyed hurting you?" Shane asked. "You know he did all of this, all this training, to help you. He put aside dredging up his own terrible memories or having to deal with appearing like an asshole so you could free your magic. I'm really surprised you can't see that. And frankly, that's disappointing." Haven watched Shane walk away.

Dax stared at her, hands on his hips.

She left the clearing without speaking to him, but walking back to the dorms, she couldn't shake the guilty feeling twisting in her stomach.

# CHAPTER 21

## The Academy

Adrien's voice droned on about the history of the Regency. Haven was astounded that he could turn political intrigue, a civil war, and the creation of magic from the gods into a mind-numbing experience. Quinn had covered a sheet of paper with doodles, and they lost Maddox a half hour ago. He rested his head on his desk, snoring softly.

She couldn't get the conversation she'd had with Shane last week out of her head. Her thoughts wandered back to her training with Ryker and their conversation in the forest. She hadn't faced what he had. Yet. She had tried to visualize his life before the Academy. While she knew the isolation she had grown up in wasn't right, Ryker's childhood had been worse. And left on her own without training, she could also envision a life of no choices. Of being forced into isolation again with Lukas. Or worse. There had to be a way to convince Ryker to continue training her. She was sure Kaden was a competent teacher, but Ryker's experience was unique. He knew what she needed. Maybe even more than she did.

Quinn rose and tapped her on the shoulder, bringing her out of her reverie.

"Come on, time to go." Haven looked up as Adrien walked off the stage. She shook Maddox, who rubbed his face and yawned, then followed her out of the lecture hall. The squads spilled out around them into the plaza, warmed by the brilliant winter sunlight.

Haven lingered with Dax and Harper in the square and noticed Ryker walking from the Yard where his squad was dispersing from a war game debrief. Haven hurried across the plaza and fell in step beside him. He glanced at her but didn't pause his stride.

"Well?" she said.

"Well what?"

"Did you win?"

"The squad won, yes," he said.

"Can I speak with you?" she asked, holding his arm. He stilled, and Silas left them. "Why did you stop training me?"

"Because you don't need me. From here, a fae expert can train you."

"Well, my first session with Kaden was a washout."

"It will take time," he said, glancing across the square to the instructors' apartments. "But it will be more enjoyable for you."

"What if I said I wanted to train with you?"

He looked back at her, and his eyes faded to a dull gray. "I'd say you are lying to yourself. You didn't enjoy working with me. And I wouldn't expect you to have liked the sessions. I know how bad they were. It's better for you to learn to use your magic without involving hate and fear."

"I don't hate you," Haven said.

"Yes, you do. I felt it. You showed it to me when you were a Phoenix."

Haven dropped her gaze. "Maybe that isn't fair of me."

"Fair or not, it's what you feel. I remember my feelings toward Finnian after my Bane training, and I wouldn't describe them as warm. But we are friends now."

Light in the Shadows

Her frustration rose, bringing a little anger to the surface. "You want to know how I feel? Right now, I feel like every time I need someone, they walk away."

Ryker's mouth softened and curved at the corner. "That's not true, and I think you know it. Dax, Harper, and your whole pod have always been there, waiting for you. And I never walked away from you when you needed me. Shane will keep me informed of your progress, but you don't need me anymore."

Haven watched him cross the square and catch up to Silas. Her eyes stung and her cheeks burned at her outburst. She wasn't sure what she hated more, the fact that he was right about her friends, or his implication that she was the one that walked away from them, which was painfully true. She slowly walked back to Dax and Harper. The more she thought of the conversation, the more her resolve grew. Ryker wasn't entirely right. He may have never walked away from her. But she did still need him.

In late March, Haven's pod assembled in the Yard for a war game exercise. From her place in formation, Haven could see Shane and Ryker waiting for the squad, deep in conversation. Ryker listened intently to Shane, his weight shifted to one leg, his shoulders relaxed, and his fingers stuck into his jeans pockets. His eyes crinkled as a smile spread across his face and they both burst into laughter. Shane clapped him on the arm, and they joined the squad. Haven noticed a glow on Ryker's face she hadn't seen in months. And a spark in his eye. He seemed...*happy*.

She listened to him describe the game situation and potential strategies and tried to focus on his words, but her thoughts drifted to their last few private sessions. With Ryker's help she had shifted to her Phoenix form, but Kaden's approach, using meditation and relaxation techniques, was so far ineffective. She knew Ryker had helped her, but seeing him now, relaxed, smiling, and even laughing, the toll her training had taken on him was obvious. And he'd willingly paid that price because she needed him.

The sound of droning voices quieted, and Haven's attention returned to the lecture. Ryker gave her a questioning look.

237

"Are we boring you?" he asked. She realized he was waiting for a response to a question she hadn't heard.

"No, I...sorry," she mumbled. He repeated his question. Haven stalled but knew she couldn't answer because she hadn't listened to him at all.

Dax scowled at her. "I don't know," she admitted.

"I suggest you stop daydreaming and join us, or you can stay here," he said. Haven could feel the heat rising from her neck to her ears.

The squad flew to a staging area at the foot of a ravine. As the squad assembled, Tristan, Dax, and Maddox scouted the area. Haven walked to the edge of the clearing five hundred feet from the mouth of the ravine and peered over the edge. There was a short, twenty-foot drop that led to a steep, heavily wooded mountainside.

The squad gathered around Ryker as he described the surrounding terrain.

Maddox said to Haven, "I walked fifty yards into the ravine and saw nothing unusual. The ravine is pretty wide, maybe six abreast."

"The walls around the mouth of the ravine are steep and bare," Tristan added. "But the woods start thirty feet away from the cliffs, so that's ideal."

Dax waited for Haven, but she said nothing. "Haven, what did you see?" Tristan asked.

"The far edge of this clearing is a twenty-foot drop that tapers into a dense forest. It would be unlikely for the opposing squad to approach us from that side."

"Where do you think the squad is right now?" Dax asked.

"I don't know," Haven said slowly.

Dax waited, but she didn't continue. "And...?"

Haven opened her mouth, but closed it, saying nothing.

Dax frowned at her. "What's with you today? You're distracted."

"Nothing."

"Scout the ravine from the air," Tristan suggested.

"Okay." She unfurled her wings, grateful for a moment alone.

Haven flew up the ravine to where it widened into a large circular bowl. She landed on the ridge, which dropped at a steep angle to the smooth, flat floor forty feet below. Haven squatted on the edge, her arms resting on her knees. From the elevated position, she imagined the river that had once flowed through the bulge in the ravine, leaving permanent evidence of an extinct, eddying current in the swirled carvings in the cliffs and rocks. Haven scooped a handful of red silty dirt and let the fine powder sift through her fingers. The dust caught the breeze, and the smell of earthy clay billowed around her until only a few small pebbles remained in her hand.

Without her podmates near, images of Ryker's smile, the sound of his laugh, the way he strolled with Shane, and his animated gestures when explaining the game dominated her already distracted thoughts. *What was it about Ryker that felt different?* He normally irritated her in the extreme just by breathing. But today when she looked at him, an empty feeling gnawed at her stomach. Maybe because after everything they went through this winter, it was so easy for him to be happy. He had a life to return to.

Her new magic was an obstacle, a moat around the ever-present uncertainty that was her life. No matter how she reached out and tried to build bridges, she always returned to the solitude that plagued her. Ryker's unwillingness to train her put control of her magic in limbo, at best. And potentially out of reach. It seemed like every time she thought she had a way to climb out of her prison, the walls got higher, or someone removed the ladder. She should have been furious that he quit to return to his wonderful, fulfilling life, while she...did what? Floundered?

She hung her head, then slowly rose and flung the pebbles into the bowl. She could hear them plink softly in the extinct riverbed. Behind her, across the rocky, uneven terrain, the tree line began a hundred yards from the edge of the bowl. The opposing squad was nowhere to be found.

She spread her wings and flew back to the staging area, landed softly next to Dax, and gave her report.

Tristan asked, "Did you see the opposing squad?"

"No, they weren't there. But if we camp in the bowl, we can wait for them there. There's only one other way into the bowl, and if we set archers on the rim, we'll know when they arrive and can attack them as they enter through the ravine from either side."

Dax paced around them. "I don't like this. We need to know where the other squad is before we commit to a strategy."

"I agree," said Tristan. "But this might work. If we get there first, it won't matter what the other squad does. They will need to come to us."

They debated the strategy for a few minutes, but Dax held out for a better plan. Haven's attention drifted from the discussion to the other side of the clearing, where Ryker was absorbed in a discussion with several cadets. He pointed to the ridge, then gestured to the edge of the staging area. He turned back to the cadets, and the group laughed at something he said. Her stomach churned and her gaze dropped to the ground. She kicked at a rock absently, then looked back at Ryker and caught his eye. His brow knit, then a slow smile crept across his face. Haven looked away, her stomach twisting in new knots.

Maddox said, "It's a decent idea, and Haven is usually right about these things. Let's try it."

Dax finally relented. "What do you want to do with our flag?" he asked.

Haven hesitated. "Bring it with us."

"Uh, that's not a great idea," Tristan warned.

"If whoever is holding the flag gets killed, we lose," Dax said. "You want to bring the flag into a bowl with only two ways in or out when we don't know where the other team is?"

Haven winced at the obvious mistake.

"There's a landing halfway up the cliff face," Maddox said, pointing at the side of the ravine. "Three cadets will bunker there with the flag, and we'll put three archers in the tree line thirty yards away. They can shoot anyone trying to scale the wall."

As they organized the squad, Ryker listened to their plan, his brows furrowed. "As your advisor, I need to tell you there are holes in your strategy. Have you scouted the area thoroughly?"

"Yes," Haven said.

"So thoroughly you know where the other squad is?" Ryker asked.

"We haven't found them yet," Tristan said. "But if we move now, we can set up in a good defensive position and wait for the squad to find us."

"It's risky," Ryker said. "But this is your exercise and your decision."

Dax arranged their flag's defense, and the rest of the squad marched into the ravine. As soon as the squad filtered into the bowl, their plan fell apart. The opposing squad rushed from the far side of the ravine, and the front line of Haven's squad glowed blue as they fell under a barrage of arrows.

"Back! Against the walls!" Dax yelled.

"In the air, now!" Tristan called out to the squad's best archers.

Four cadets flew into the air in a storm of arrows, and two of their archers immediately glowed blue and fell from the sky. Tristan sent a gale of Wind at their archers, momentarily deflecting the incoming arrows and creating a window that allowed their archers to land on the ridge before the other squad's Wind wielders could counter his magic. Dax and Tristan pulled additional archers forward and begin a counterassault. They lost several more archers, but two fought their way to the rim, and the tide of the battle turned in their favor. The archers kept the opposing squad pinned as Dax led a team through the onslaught to engage the squad on the ground.

Haven followed behind him and noticed a team breaking off and retreating into the ravine behind the battle. She held Maddox's arm and pointed to the escaping team. Maddox took two cadets around the right flank, sending two more archers into the air to give them cover. Maddox fought his way through the brawling cadets and chased the team into the ravine, while the archers in the air prevented the opposing team from following. An archer covering their advance jerked backward and glowed blue. A team from the opposing squad broke through the now unprotected side and pursued Maddox.

Haven fought her way through the line, pulling Dax with her. She followed Maddox and found a staging area hidden from above by the curve of the eroded walls a short distance up the ravine.

Maddox and another cadet from her team glowed blue, but the third teammate held the opposing team's flag.

Haven sagged in relief.

"I've never been killed on an exercise before," Maddox said to Haven, grimacing. "Stings like hell."

When they returned to the Academy, Ryker had the squad stand in the Yard for an hour as he lectured them on what they did wrong.

"You won by sheer luck and the incompetence of the other team," he said, pacing in front of the squad. "Sloppy planning, and even sloppier execution. Did you scout the far side of the bowl?" he demanded of Maddox and Dax. "Did you even know there was a staging area to the north?"

Dax avoided Haven's silent plea for help, frustration plain on his face. Ryker stilled and waited for a response.

"I...I didn't scout the northern ravine," Haven admitted. Dax glared at her.

Ryker's intense gaze fell on her. "Let me see if I got this right. You led your squad into a blind bowl without knowing the location of the opposing squad and without fully scouting the area."

Haven gritted her teeth but held her tongue.

Ryker continued, "You lost half your squad and would have lost the exercise completely if the other squad had set archers on the ridge. The only good part of your shitty plan was the flag defense. That was genius." Ryker turned from her in disgust, and Haven glanced at Maddox, who had finally stopped glowing. He kept his eyes forward, avoiding her.

Ryker dismissed them, but held Haven, Dax, Tristan, and Maddox back. When the rest of the squad had left, he wheeled on them. "What the hell happened today?" The team was silent. He walked to Haven, his piercing gaze filled with contempt. "How did you put it? 'This is a cadet-led exercise, so fuck off'? Spectacular leadership skills you showed out there. If this were real, your squad would be dead. And that would be on you."

Haven held her ground and didn't look away.

"You want to lead? No problem. But you better fucking lead. I don't give a shit what is going on in your personal life. When you're a leader, your only job is the safety of your squad." He glowered at the team. "Are there questions?" They remained silent, eyes anywhere but on Ryker.

"If this happens again, I'll leave you four behind to listen to an invigorating history lecture. Dismissed." Ryker stormed through the Yard toward his apartment.

Haven caught up with him as he was walking up the stairs to the lobby. "Today was my fault. I was distracted and didn't take the exercise seriously. Don't blame the rest of the team."

He turned to her. "Yes, it was your fault. I saw what happened. You put yourself in a position where your team depends on you, and then you abandoned them today."

"I know what I did. I don't need you to tell me," she snapped.

"I think you do." His eyes blazed. "This may be a game to you, but some day the lessons you learn here may save your life. Or someone else's."

"Yes, you excel at teaching people how to depend on someone, then abandon them. I learned that lesson really well from you," she blurted. Humor and condescension flickered on his face, and she immediately wished she could take back her impulsive words.

Ryker's eyes dimmed to a dark gray. "And what exactly are you depending on me for, *princess*?" Haven ground her teeth but didn't flinch. "What did I offer, that you think you need so badly? That you can't get from someone else?" He stepped closer to her.

Haven's body tensed and her pulse raced.

"Well? I'm waiting."

"Nothing," Haven said, and walked away.

Haven took her pod out to The Common for drinks that night as an apology for her dismal performance. After two rounds and letting Dax beat her three times at pool, they all finally relaxed. Walking with Dax and Tristan late that night, she realized how much she had missed her friends over the last few months. She had been so wrapped up in her miserable training that she had neglected her friendships. Dax threw his arm around her and almost knocked her over as Tristan barreled into him. Dax chased Tristan across the square and tackled him on the grass. Maddox and Haven howled with laughter.

"You two are children," Haven said as the two males wrestled on the lawn. When she passed by, Tristan hit her on the hip, picking her up and throwing her over his shoulder. Haven squealed as he carried her up the steps to their dorm.

"Gods, you weigh a ton," he said, opening the door with one hand. Dax snickered behind her.

"Fuck off, Tristan. Put me DOWN!" she screamed. He flung her on a sofa in the common room. She bounced before settling on her back, her arms flung over her head. Dax and Harper helped her up and laughed with her as they stumbled into their room together.

Her magic lesson with Shane and Kaden the next day was the same as the previous weeks. Kaden had her practice meditation and breathing techniques, and while she felt more relaxed after the debacle of the previous day's war game, her Phoenix form remained elusive.

"I'm not progressing," Haven said, following Shane out of the forest.

"It's slower this way, but Kaden is also teaching you ways to manage your magic once you finally gain control over it."

"It's so complicated. Way more than managing Light."

"It is." Shane paused in the dorm plaza. "Listen, you'll be on break in two weeks. Kaden and I are sending you to Araine a little early. You haven't had a real break from the Academy in two years. Take some time for yourself. No magic, no flight, and no strategy."

Haven spent the next two weeks in Araine doing exactly what Shane told her to do. Nothing. She prowled the city streets, sat in the park behind her apartment complex, and enjoyed the early spring weather. And even read a book. In the weeks after her training with Ryker, she had made a real effort with Dax and Harper to overcome her instinct to keep them on the fringes of her life. Now that she had let them in, she felt a dull ache at their absence. While she loved being back in Araine, the solitary week reinforced in her mind that being alone wasn't something she wanted to repeat.

At the end of the first week, Haven received an invitation from the queen to attend the Spring Ball. Technically, third-year cadets couldn't attend balls, but her Phoenix status was the source of a lot of rule breaking these days. She sent a response to the queen saying she would be there, asking if she could also invite Kit, Harper, and Dax. Haven's heart felt lighter. She was excited about the ball, and to see her friends.

Haven packed her book into her bag and sat on the couch, pulling on her sneakers. Tomorrow, Dax, Harper, and Kit would arrive in Araine. She had been eyeing a new pub a few blocks away from her apartment, and it sounded perfect for her last solo night. She entered the bar, her eyes adjusting to the dim room. Elaborate iron wall sconces scattered throughout the room emitted faint pools of light. Despite the early hour, the main room was half filled with diners seated at dark wooden tables. Pictures of diners from years past covered the walls. As Haven walked by on her way to the bar, she recognized a few royals, faeries, and djinn whom she assumed were diplomats. She took a seat with several other guests and ordered a beer and dinner, then lost herself in her book.

One stack of fries later, Haven wiped her face and placed her napkin on her empty plate.

The bartender set down the glass he was drying and cleared her dishes. "Can I get you anything else?" he asked.

Haven closed her book and stuffed it in her bag. "No thank you, just the bill."

"Your bill was paid." She opened her mouth to argue, but he pointed over her shoulder.

Larkin was sitting in a booth against the wall of the bar and tipped his beer to her. Haven approached his table as a server cleared two plates and two empty wine glasses.

"Thank you for dinner. You didn't have to do that."

"Yes, I think I did. Please, sit for a minute."

"I don't want to interrupt. It looks like you have a guest."

"She left. Please. A minute of your time." Haven sat at his table. "I owe you many dinners. And an apology."

"Really," Haven, her eyes narrowing.

"Yes. The last year at the Institute has been...humbling. I may never be a one female kind of person, but I could have been more honest with you. When I met you, I knew you weren't worldly." Haven winced at the reminder of how naïve she had been. "I took advantage of you, and I'm ashamed of that."

"Yes, you did. And it's embarrassing, still, to think I fell for you."

"I know. And I'm apologizing for that. Sincerely," he said.

"Why?" she asked, puzzled by his uncharacteristic contrition.

"Think of it as trying to rectify wrongs I've made. After a few weeks at the Institute, I really missed our pod. I took those relationships for granted. They could have been friendships if I'd shown some care. I now understand that from some painful lessons, starting with the one Ryker gave me."

"Thank you," Haven said.

"The instructors at the Academy have invited me and Avina to join you for ComSim. I'd like to, but I won't if it makes you uncomfortable."

"Are you going to try to seduce me?" she said.

"No." His amber-green eyes fixed on her. "Unless you want me to."

"Zero interest."

"Sorry, had to check," he said, grinning at her.

"You can't help yourself, can you?" Larkin chuckled. She shook her head and changed the subject. "How was your training this year? I'm assuming you finally learned how to shift to a bird?"

The outline of Larkin's body shimmered. For a moment, Haven glimpsed golden brown feathers, a sharp, curved beak, and the intense golden eyes of an eagle.

"Wow," Haven gasped.

"Like I said, I've learned a lot."

"That could be a real asset for ComSim. Check with Dax, Tristan, and Maddox. If they agree, it's okay with me." She thanked him again for dinner and left the bar. *Well, that was interesting.* Seems like they had all grown up this last year. Even Larkin. She chuckled to herself as she strolled down the street. She had to start believing in miracles now.

# CHAPTER 22

## Araine

Haven landed in front of the ministry building and found Lukas resting against a pale yellow limestone column of a portico.

"Thanks for meeting on such short notice," he said, offering her his arm.

"No problem. Glad we could make this work," Haven said. "Where are we going?"

"The Green Room, right around the corner. Sorry for making this a quick one. I have a crossing tomorrow and will leave Araine to recover."

"You aren't staying for the ball?"

"No, unfortunately. I rarely miss balls, but there's no avoiding it this time," he said. They arrived at a two-story rough cobblestone brick building. Dark wood framed the oversized windows, where diners sat at tables draped in fine white linen. They weaved their way through waiting guests to the concierge, who checked his list for Lukas's reservation.

A server escorted them to a table in the center of the restaurant, their steps silenced by the thick forest-green carpeting.

Mahogany wood paneling wrapped the room, warmed by the low lighting from two large crystal chandeliers. The muted buzz of conversation drifted around them as Haven sat in the chair Lukas pulled out for her.

"This is beautiful," Haven said. "I've never been to a place like this."

"It's a frequent hangout for the ministry crowd. My Triad is meeting at Lilith's offices after lunch to work on our crossing, so I thought this would be convenient."

They ordered lunch and Haven asked, "So what kind of crossing is this?"

"Nothing exciting, a meeting in Elsah-ra with the djinn and faeries. We have a lead on a missing Serendib. We're coordinating how to track him and who should lead the operation."

"Sounds serious," Haven said, sipping her tea as their lunch arrived.

"It's a lot of talking, really. But I expect the meeting to last most of the day, which means my recovery will be longer than usual."

They talked amicably over lunch. The dinners with Lukas over the winter had been a reprieve from her training, and a chance to forget the Academy for a few hours. But the time she spent with him had done very little to bring them together. She still felt like Lukas was a pleasant acquaintance. He was charming, personable, and polite. And maybe that was okay. But she also thought there should be more between two people who agreed to spend their lives together.

When the server took their plates away, Lukas checked his watch and asked for the bill. "I'm really sorry to cut this short, but Calaine and Xander are waiting for me."

"No problem," Haven said. "Thanks for fitting me in."

"Of course," he said, rising from his seat. Haven stood, and behind Lukas, she noticed River with an elderly female.

Haven took Lukas's offered arm and let him lead her toward the door. Before she could exit, she felt a hand grip her elbow, holding her back. She turned but held Lukas with her.

"Hello, Haven," River said. "What are you doing here?"

"Having lunch with Lukas."

"I can see that. How are you?"

"Fine. We were just leaving." Haven moved closer to Lukas.

River cocked his head, then said, "This is my grandmother, Shallah. Shallah, this is a special friend of mine, Haven." Shallah was fascinating. Haven had never seen an aged seraphim, a true rarity. The female's hair was more gray than black. Deep lines framed her mouth and fanned around her alert, green eyes, and the loose skin on her neck and the back of her clasped hands contrasted with her smooth cheeks.

Shallah said, "It's a pleasure to meet you. River has told me a lot about you."

Haven glanced at River. "Really," she said with a flat tone of disbelief.

"Yes. We saw you come in with Lukas and he's talked of nothing else." Haven was speechless.

"Haven, I really need to leave. Can I walk you out?" Lukas said.

"Oh, yes, thank you," she said. They left the restaurant and Lukas kissed her cheek, unfurled his wings, and left.

"Haven, do you have a minute?" River asked from behind her.

"Uh, sure," she said. They walked to the street as Shallah waited for them on the steps of the restaurant. "It's good to see you," River said.

"You see me at the Academy all the time," Haven said curtly, looking down the street and avoiding him.

"What's wrong? Have I offended you?" he asked.

"You mean other than assaulting me behind the dorms?" she snapped.

River took a step back. "Is that what you think happened? I'm sorry. That certainly wasn't my intention."

"I think it was."

River ran a hand through his hair. "I'm sorry. Truly. I thought you wanted me to kiss you."

"I did. But I also wanted you to stop. And you didn't."

"I'm sorry. I didn't realize...Is this why you've been avoiding me?" River reached a tentative hand to her arm and she flinched away.

"I wasn't avoiding you. But I don't trust you."

"That was not my intention. I know I keep saying this, but I am sorry." His blue eyes softened. "This is a horrible misunderstanding. I'd like to make it up to you, if you'll let me."

Haven paused, wondering if she'd misunderstood what happened between them. She had kissed him. Maybe she had led him to believe she wanted more. "Are you going to the ball?" she asked.

"No. Unfortunately, I need to leave from here to return to Damaris this afternoon. But you'll be graduating in a few months. Maybe we can talk again when you're not a cadet. I know how you feel about relationships with instructors." River exhaled sharply. "It's disappointing you think so poorly of me. If I'd known how you felt, I would have tried to change your mind a long time ago. I'm not what you think. Maybe we should try to be friends first. We can start over."

Haven wavered, then said, "Okay. But only friends."

Shallah walked down the stairs and said to River, "Your Skimmer is here."

"Thanks, Mimi," River replied. "Is yours?"

"I sent her away," Shallah said. River glared at her. "Don't give me that look. You know I hate skimming. I can walk. I'm fine."

"You're not walking by yourself. My Skimmer can take us both, then I can leave from the Garret."

"I want to walk. I'm not an invalid," she said. Haven tried to suppress a smile, watching the stubborn elder female exasperate her grandson.

"I can take her," Haven offered, then turned to Shallah. "I'm happy to walk you back. I was planning on walking myself."

"Are you sure?" River asked.

"Of course."

"Okay." He took her hand gently in his. "I am sorry about the misunderstanding. I look forward to your graduation when we can start fresh."

The Skimmer passed the concierge and took River's arm. Haven led Shallah away from the restaurant toward Falco Park, and the smile River had plastered on his face fell. His scornful eyes flicked over Haven. *Gods, she was gullible.*

Upon arrival, River walked into the small study of Lilith's townhouse and opened the bar cupboards. He poured himself a drink and sat heavily on the sofa and leaned his head back against the wall. Seeing Haven at lunch today had caught him off guard. She was stunning. Speaking with her again after all these months reminded him he hadn't convinced her to sleep with him, and in the back of his mind, that bothered him. He watched her with Lukas, wondering if he should give her another try. And Shallah was the perfect solution. If she could speak well of him, which he knew she would, then maybe Haven would overlook the disaster of their last date and give him another chance. So he blathered on about Haven all through lunch, hoping he could get Shallah and Haven to talk. And then Haven offered to walk Shallah to the Garret. River shrugged. He'd learn in a few months if his apology had sunk in. In the meantime, he had other females to keep him occupied.

Lilith and Roque entered the room and sat in the chairs across from him.

"Shocking to find your lapdog here," River said. "You asked me to come, so what do you want? And make it quick. My Skimmer is waiting outside."

Lilith crossed her legs and relaxed back in her chair, but her foot bounced with impatience. "I'll get to the point. How is your relationship with Haven?"

"Funny you should ask. Before today, I would say pretty shitty. But it might get better," River said, sipping his drink.

"That's good, because we don't have time. She is gaining control of her magic. We need you."

"Gods, Lilith, this was what you had me run over here for?" he said. He shot his drink and rose to leave. "There's no 'we' here. I want no part of your scheming. And I'm not at your beck and call. No more demands to appear, or I'll stop showing up."

Roque stepped in front of River, blocking his way. The seraphim was at least three inches taller than River, even larger than Silas.

Lilith wedged herself between the two males. "What do you want?"

"I want this idiot out of my way," he growled, unfurling his bladed wings.

Lilith touched his arm. "He means you no harm. Tell me how we can make this work for you."

"Are you begging?" River asked, his icy eyes glinting.

"Please. I don't beg any male for anything. But everyone wants something. Tell me what you want most."

"Make me a Shadowalker. I'd love to leave this entire world behind," River said.

"Something that's real," Lilith said. "And spare me the sibling envy crap. You're no Ryker."

He shook off her arm. "I used to think you were a bitch, but now I know you are. I have no interest in what you're offering."

"Think about what you want. We'll accommodate you, whatever you need."

River walked out the door and didn't look back.

"Do you mind walking with me?" Haven asked.

"Of course not," Shallah said, falling in step with Haven as they meandered through the ministry district, heading north to Falco Park. "So, I understand River was your instructor at the Academy."

"Yes, a few years ago. I'm finishing my third year."

"Oh! My congratulations, a little early. Have you decided what to do after the Academy?" Shallah asked.

"Not yet. I know it's tradition to join the Aerial training program, and I enjoyed the war game training this year."

"Oh?" Shallah said. "Did Ryker teach this year?"

"Yes, he did," Haven said. "He was my squad advisor."

"Then you know both my boys," Shallah said. "I know I'm horribly biased, but my boys are special."

"They most certainly are unique," Haven said.

"I know River enjoys the military, and Ryker enjoyed his two years in the Aerial. It can be a nice transition from the Academy to your next step in life."

Haven considered her advice for a moment. "You know, I think you're right. I'm not sure what I want to do, but continuing with the Aerial might be a way for me to figure that out."

Shallah patted her arm. "Funny when life's solutions strike you." Haven grinned at her. "So, tell me a little about yourself. Where are you from?" she asked.

"I grew up outside Ancharin."

Shallah pursed her lips. "There aren't many places outside Ancharin. Where specifically?"

Haven fell silent. "My parents had an estate outside the city."

"Why are you avoiding telling me where you grew up?"

"Sorry. It's a habit, I guess. Prince Astor is my father."

Shallah stilled for a step, then continued walking. "And you didn't grow up here in Araine? Well, of course you didn't. We would have known you."

Haven gave her a curious look. "Now that I think about it, Ryker knew. I'm not sure how, but he did."

"It's not strange at all. Shadowalkers know all the royal lines. It's part of their responsibilities, to protect royalty. I'm sure he's known of you since you were a child. How well do you know River?"

"We had a few dates a long time ago, but I wouldn't say I know him well. And before today, I hadn't seen him in almost a year."

Shallah said, "He spoke of you fondly at lunch. I'm assuming you are special to him."

"We are barely acquaintances," Haven said.

"River is often misunderstood. He's a complicated male and has had a difficult life." Haven's eyebrows rose. That certainly wasn't the impression she had of River. But then again, she knew she wasn't the best at judging character. She was working at keeping an open mind about people. Maybe she needed to rethink River, too.

They arrived at the Garret and Shallah took Haven's hand. "It was a pleasure meeting you. Would you like to visit for a little bit? I can have tea brought in."

Shallah's warm eyes and open face were irresistible. "I think I'd like that." Haven took her arm and followed her through the lobby to the main study, where Shallah summoned a sprite and ordered tea. The door cracked opened silently, and a large orange cat jumped onto the sofa next to Shallah.

"Ah, Kimo, did you miss me?" she said, stroking the cat's head.

"This cat is yours?" Haven asked. "You let a cat into your house?"

"Of course," Shallah said. "Kimo is family." He curled up next to Shallah, and Haven heard a deep, rhythmic rumbling emanating from him. Kimo looked at Shallah with half-closed green eyes. "You've never had a pet?"

"Well, no. We had cats at the estate, but they lived in our stables. I've never seen a cat like that, sitting next to someone."

Shallah stroked the cat's soft fur, and Kimo hitched over, exposing his belly. "Pets are a great comfort. With a cat in your house, you're never alone."

Tea service appeared on the low table between them, and Shallah poured a cup.

Looking around the study, Haven asked, "What exactly is the Garret?"

"This is Ryker's residence in Araine. I stay here when I come to the city. River usually stays here too. The two top floors are restricted to the Triad."

"Restricted?"

"Yes, as you know, Ryker is a Shadowalker. The Garret's wards protect the Triad." Shallah paused and listened. Haven heard it too, the faint sound of voices above them. "Excuse me." Shallah held the stairwell railing in the lobby and called out, "Ryker? Is that you up there?" Haven heard the voices quiet, then footsteps on the stairs. Ryker appeared, bounding down the stairs two at a time, and swept Shallah up in his arms, spinning her around while she giggled at his antics. When he set her down, Haven glimpsed the most dazzling, true smile on Ryker's face.

"Mimi, when did you come back?" He kissed her cheek and hugged her again.

"You're going to break me," she laughed. He pulled away and took in the sight of her. "I arrived before lunch." Shallah stroked his face. "Ah, my baby boy, how are you?"

"Better, now that you're here. And how long do I get you?"

"I'm here for a month, at least." He hugged her tight. She pulled away from him and said, "I've been waiting for you, and having a pleasant visit with my new friend, Haven." She stepped aside and Ryker's eyes went to Haven. He stiffened, and his face fell.

Haven shuffled awkwardly under his cold, penetrating gaze. She picked up her bag and moved toward the door. "I was leaving anyway."

"No, you weren't," Shallah said.

"I don't want to intrude."

"You're not." Shallah took Ryker's hand and pulled him into the study to a seat next to her on the couch. He perched on the edge, his unguarded moment gone and his face carefully neutral.

"What's wrong with you?" Shallah asked.

He stood and said, "Please, Haven. Sit. Finish your visit with Shallah. It's clear I was the one intruding." He said to Shallah, "Come upstairs later, when you're free." He brushed the hair from her brow and let his hand fall to her shoulder, then stroked her arm to her hand.

"Ryker, you're making this awkward. Why won't you stay?" Ryker was silent when Shallah tugged on his hand. He reluctantly returned to his seat next to her. "Haven was telling me of how she grew up in Ancharin."

"Actually, outside of Ancharin. I've never been to the city itself. Portos was the first city I had ever been to."

"Portos is not a city," Ryker scoffed. "More like an outpost."

"So I've been told. And now, having seen Araine and Raveno, I agree. But at the time it seemed huge."

"How is it you never visited Araine? I would think you would come to court often, even as a child," Shallah said.

"I never left my family's estate until I went to the Academy. My parents and I, we're not close. My father visited once or twice a year. I've seen my mother less than a handful of times in my life."

"Why is that?" Ryker asked.

"I really don't know. I suppose her contract with my father said she had to produce a child, and once I was born, she felt she had done her duty. Growing up, I had governesses and companions, and my cousin, Ayden, who spent summers with me."

Shallah raised an eyebrow and looked at Ryker. "Looks like you have something in common."

"I had you." Ryker took her small hand in his.

"Yes, you did."

"You're fortunate to have Shallah," Haven said.

"Yes, I am. She's a treasure," he said.

"Please," Shallah sniffed. "You didn't think highly of me when I paddled you and your brother for tormenting the kitchen staff." Ryker's silver eyes sparkled with humor, his aloof mask finally lifting and the angles of his face softening as he looked at his grandmother.

"I'm surprised we only got a paddling. We were monsters."

"Were? Who says you've changed?" She nudged his ribs.

"You hurt me, Mimi. Deeply." He covered his heart, feigning death from a mortal wound. Shallah laughed at him, and Haven couldn't help smiling at his melodrama.

Shallah said to Haven, "So I'm assuming that's why we never knew Astor had a child."

"I suppose. I've never spoken of it with either of my parents. And I certainly didn't want to talk about it to others. I felt people would assume I was a spoiled princess." She gave Ryker a hard look.

"Who would assume that?" Shallah spied the look Haven leveled at Ryker, and his slightly pained expression. "Ah. Let me guess. You acted like an ass and assumed she was an entitled royal."

"It was a reasonable assumption," Ryker said defensively.

"Right. Sounds like the jackasses who make assumptions about you because of your magic, no?" Ryker looked at her with irritation but said nothing.

Haven rose. "Well, on that note, I do need to leave. Thank you, Shallah, it was a pleasure meeting you." She said to Ryker, "It was nice seeing you too. It was...enlightening."

"Likewise," he said.

"Please come see me again," Shallah said. "You don't need the excuse of one of these boys here to visit."

"I'd like that very much," Haven said, and walked through the lobby to the street.

"Haven," she heard Ryker call to her. She turned back to him as he met her in the street. "I didn't know."

"Know what? That I was an unwanted child? That my parents kept me in a beautiful cage until they shipped me off to the Academy?"

"Yes."

"Did you even think to ask?" He said nothing. "Why would you? It was too easy to assume you knew everything." She stepped near him. "You know nothing about me. Nothing."

His cool gaze fell on her. "Wrong again. I love telling you all the things you get wrong. There's just so many." He closed the distance between them, their bodies almost touching. "You're strong and smart. And brave. But I think we all know that. What you don't realize yet is you can control your own life now."

"And I suppose you think you taught me that," she said, folding her arms.

"Yes, to some extent. You've learned how to stand up for yourself. To use your bravery to fight back."

"I've always known how to defend myself. You learn to depend on only yourself when you always end up alone," she said, and left him standing in the street.

Dax and Kit were in a beer war when Haven and Harper met them at the Outpost for dinner.

"I'm not carrying you home tonight," Haven said to Dax as he pounded his third beer. "The ball is in two days. Save some enthusiasm." She leaned away from the table so the server could put her plate in front of her.

"Plenty in reserve." He bit into his bacon cheeseburger. "They have the best burgers," he said around a mouthful. Haven couldn't disagree. "What did you two do today?"

"Shopping," Harper said, popping a fry in her mouth.

"Bummer we missed it," Kit said dryly. Harper made a face at him.

"How about you?" Haven asked.

"My cousin was in town. Stopped by my aunt's house to see him."

Silas and Trinity walked into the pub as the server cleared the table. Trinity waved at Harper and stopped at their table.

"Where's Ryker?" Harper said.

"Running late. Should be here any minute."

"Join us?"

"We don't want to intrude," Silas said.

Harper gave him a puzzled look. "Why would you be intruding?"

"Haven?" Silas said.

"Sure, please sit," Haven said. They pulled up a table and brought three more chairs. Haven sat between Dax and Silas. Ryker soon joined them, kissing Harper's cheek before sitting next to her. He nodded to Haven and Dax, then turned his attention to his sister. Haven stole glances at Ryker throughout the evening, curious to see another glimpse of the private Ryker she had seen with Shallah. He listened to a story Harper told him while he ate dinner, laughing and pausing his eating to tell her one of his own. He seemed...normal.

"Are you okay?" Dax whispered.

"I think so, yes." She watched Ryker from the corner of her eye. "You saw him with me. Sometimes it's hard to think of him as a regular person. But that is exactly who is sitting at this table, isn't it?"

"Sometimes normal people are forced to do shitty things. I know that's hard for you to see."

"That's the funny thing. It isn't hard for me to see when I open my eyes and look." Dax squeezed her shoulder.

At midnight, a band did an impromptu setup in an attached studio hall behind the Outpost. Ryker grabbed Trinity's hand and pulled her away. She resisted at first, but he cajoled her into following him. Dax ordered another round for their table.

After the server cleared the Triad's dishes, Silas said to Haven, "Want to dance? I should check on Ryker to make sure he hasn't exhausted Trinity."

"Sure. Dax?" she said. They followed Silas toward the thumping sound of the band. The music was fast and loud, and bodies packed together, writhing under the flashing lights. Silas wound his way through the crowd to Ryker and Trinity. She hung back when she saw Ryker dancing next to the stage. He had shed his jacket, and his tight black t-shirt clung to his body in the heat of the moving crowd. Sweat shone on his forehead, his body rocking as he and Trinity bumped to the music's heavy beat. He held her waist and whispered in her ear. Trinity threw her head back and roared with laughter, loud enough that Haven could hear it over the music. Ryker grinned, then laughed with her.

Dax pushed Haven from behind to get her moving again. "Normal moment?" She nodded and took his hand, losing herself in the music.

The night waned to the darkest hour, and the music's tempo slowed for the band's last song. Ryker offered Haven his hand. "Will you?" Haven hesitated. "I won't bite," he said, a smile flickering at the corner of his mouth.

She gave him an annoyed look and took his hand. He pulled her close but kept a friendly space between them. They swayed to the music and the crowd thinned, but bodies still pressed around them.

"I think I owe you an apology," Ryker said.

"Oh? For what?" Haven asked.

"For making assumptions about you because of your family. That was rude."

"Yes, it was."

He glared at her, but his eyes twinkled with mischief. "Are you going to rub it in?"

"Maybe. I think you deserve it, a little," she said.

Ryker suddenly spun her around, and she stumbled a little. He gave her a wicked smile, and she stepped on his foot on purpose. Ryker chuckled. "Fair enough." He looked at Harper and Kit dancing a few couples away from them. "You're friends with Harper. And you seem to have charmed the pants off Shallah." His eyes dropped to hers again. "I'm guessing we will see each other frequently, so we might as well try to be civil."

"I'm good with civil," Haven said. She glanced at Harper and Kit too. "And yes, I adore your sister. I've never had a friend like her before. Or like Dax."

"You've made good friends at the Academy."

"Yes, I have."

"Keep them close," he said. Her brow creased in confusion. "There are people who would drive a wedge between you and your friends to make you feel alone. To keep you isolated."

"I know what that's like. I won't give up my friends."

Ryker nodded to Dax, who was dancing with a petite brunette. "You can lean on your friends. Remember that, even when you feel like no one understands you."

"I'm guessing you know what it feels like to be isolated," Haven said.

"I do. But I have Trinity and Silas. And Harper and Shallah. Their friendship, my family, is everything to me."

Haven was silent and chewed her lip. "When you stopped training me, it bothered me that you were happy. You returned to your life, and I was stuck with the mess that is my magic," Haven said. "It made me feel alone."

His hand pressed into the small of her back. "You're not alone. Some people will define you by your magic. But your friends won't. They don't think of you that way. Don't lose sight of that," he said.

"Did you ever feel that way?"

"Yes. I escaped my training and my magic by seeing Harper. She was a child, not even a year old. But she was always happy to see me and didn't care about my magic. She only cared for me. And then I found Silas and Trinity. They helped repair my relationship with Finnian." He pulled her a little closer, his hand heavier on her waist. "Find ways to remember joy in your life. It will keep you grounded and help you through the rest of your training."

She looked down, thinking of his words, and leaned into him a little, stealing a moment of closeness with another person. He didn't seem to mind, so she moved a little closer. The heat of his body warmed her, and his hand lightly stroked her waist, offering a small comfort. The muscles of his broad shoulders coiled under her hand. A pleasant tension crept through her at the feel of him moving with her, against her. Too soon, the song ended, and she held on to him, maybe for a little longer than she needed to.

"Are you okay?" he asked.

She let him go. "Yes, but maybe it's time to call it a night. It's late."

The deserted streets of Falco Park were sparsely lit, faint pools of light diffusing from the occasional iron lamppost along the sidewalk. Sweet blooming flowers and awakening leaves from the trees lining the broad sidewalks tickled Haven's nose. And fresh ocean pine, clean and male, threaded through the scent of the chilled spring night.

"Did you have fun tonight?" Ryker asked.

She gave him an easy smile. "I did."

"Good. You should have more nights like this."

"It was also educational. I didn't know you were capable of having fun."

His silver eyes glittered. "Did you just make a joke?"

"A feeble attempt," she said.

He smirked at her. "You should work on that. I could get you a trainer."

"Gods, please tell me it's not you. You would be horrible."

"I'm mortally offended." They laughed together. She glanced up to see his smile, his hands casually hooked in his pockets, his relaxed, loping stride. And the uneasiness she felt before at seeing his happiness was gone. This time, it was infectious and warmed her heart.

Before she even realized it, they arrived at her apartment complex. Ryker said good night and walked away with Silas and Trinity. She watched as their figures started to fade into the darkness, but there was something still left unsaid between them. And it needed to be said now. Haven caught up to him and touched his arm. He stopped and turned back to her.

"Ryker, I feel I owe you an apology too," she said.

"For what?"

"I don't think I was fair to you either. I understand what you were trying to do for me. It wasn't pretty, but it was hard on us both."

"Don't apologize. It's unnecessary," Ryker interrupted. "I may have made a mistake in assuming something about you because of your family, but I'm not apologizing for what I did to train you. It had a purpose and was part of a process those of us with powerful magic have to endure. I didn't get special treatment, and neither did you."

"I understand, but still, I didn't need to make assumptions about your character either," she said.

"You have a right to feel what you did."

"I guess so," she said. "And I know you were trying to help me. You didn't owe me anything, but you still tried. So, thank you."

Ryker's eyes roved her face, lingering on her mouth before his gaze held hers. "There were days I truly hated myself. But it was worth it to know you can defend yourself. I can gain a little of my soul back knowing that."

"Do you think we can be friends?" she blurted, surprised as he was at her words. "I mean, civil is fine, if that's what you want," she trailed off. She was glad the sparse streetlights hid the heat in her cheeks.

"Do you really want that? To be friends?"

"I think so. You are friends with Finnian now, after your Bane training, right?"

"Yes, we're friends. Close friends. He trained me for ten years when I became a Shadowalker. He's like a father to me."

"Well, I don't want you as a father," she said, flashing him a pained look.

"I would make a terrible father figure for you," he said, grinning. "But I'd like to be your friend. We can give it a try."

She squeezed his hand, then let him go. "Thank you. For everything."

He flexed the hand she touched. "Good night, Haven."

# CHAPTER 23

## Spring Equinox

Ryker, Silas, and Trinity entered the ballroom and wound their way through the throng of guests waiting to greet the king and queen. They joined the receiving line and eventually passed by the royals. Trinity pulled Ryker through the crowd of people, socializing where required. After an hour, he'd had enough and escaped with Silas to a quiet corner for a break from the mindless chatter.

"Hopefully that was the worst of it," Silas said. "Trinity can cover for us for a while." They watched her move expertly through the packed room.

"I'm kind of pissed we didn't have a crossing this week," Ryker said. "I haven't recovered from the torture of the Winter Ball. Would have been nice to have a reason not to be here."

"Lukas had the only crossing scheduled, so he lucked out."

"Of all of us, Lukas should have been here tonight. He loves these things," Ryker said.

"I'll talk to Trinity about cutting it short." Silas scanned the crowd, and his face suddenly changed. "Wow." Ryker ignored him. There was always at least one female Silas chased down at these events. Silas elbowed him. Ryker followed his gaze and saw Harper and Kit near the bar.

"What, Harper? Yes, she looks lovely. But you know she's off limits. Find someone else."

"Not Harper," Silas said, glaring at Ryker and rolling his eyes. "Look there, behind her."

Ryker spotted Haven and his mouth dropped open slightly. She wore a scandalous deep red dress. The low-cut square neckline and snug bodice emphasized the swell of her breasts and slim waist, the silky fabric dripping over her curves before flaring and falling to the ground. Her chestnut hair draped down her bare back in soft, loose curls. Dramatic, dark liner set off her blue eyes, and her deep red lips made Ryker's head spin.

Silas watched Ryker and said, "Looks like another one that's off limits." Ryker stared at Silas in confusion. Silas laughed and clapped his back.

Dax handed Harper and Haven each a flute of champagne. "Harper really picked one for you this time," he said.

Harper glanced at Haven's dress. "That's not on me. Although I applaud her choice, one hundred percent."

"I chose it," Haven said. "I liked it." Haven found the dress during one of her wanderings through Araine last week. While not technically a spring color, she had fallen in love with the deep red dress. Haven looked at her gown and smiled to herself. She felt bold. And covered in flames.

"It doesn't leave much to the imagination," Kit said. "And for the record, I love it."

"I disagree completely," Ryker said from behind her. Haven turned to him and lost her thoughts in his silver eyes. "I think every male here has their imagination running wild at the moment."

Harper's face brightened at the sight of her brother, and she brushed past Haven to hug him. Ryker's gaze never left Haven as he held his sister.

"You both look lovely tonight," Silas said, kissing Haven's cheek. "Will you dance with me?"

"Of course. I'd love to," Haven said. Silas led her away to an adjoining dance hall where couples swirled in rhythm to lilting, classical music.

"No mosh pit tonight," Silas said, pouting as he swept her into the rhythm of the other dancers. "Only classical dance. The Spring Ball is my least favorite."

"It's nice to have a mix, I guess. We had the Outpost a few nights ago. I suppose we'll survive this," Haven said. She knew Silas was a skilled warrior, but she discovered he was also graceful on his feet. She had always found Silas's humor and quick wit to be infectious, even when he was challenging her in the most rigorous wing training she had received so far at the Academy. But this version of Silas was downright charming, and his sense of humor had her breathless from laughing while trying to keep up with his dancing. The music faded and Silas bowed slightly, offering his arm as he led her back to her friends. Haven and Silas arrived as Kit and Trinity left for the dance hall.

"Come on," Harper said to Ryker, taking his hand and Dax's. Haven trailed behind and watched Dax and Harper dance. Ryker stood beside her with his hands behind his back, casually elegant in black dress pants and a gray linen shirt under a traditional black stand collar jacket with dark gray embroidery on the right chest and cuff.

"I thought you liked to dance," Haven said.

"I do," Ryker said, watching the couples. "I love music."

"Then why aren't you dancing?"

"Is that an invitation?" he asked, smiling down at her. Haven glared at him, then looked at the dancing couples. Ryker stepped in front of her and offered his hand. She took it and followed him to the floor. He pulled her close and picked up the rhythm of the dance, expertly merging into the other couples.

"You look handsome tonight," Haven said.

The corners of his mouth twitched up. "Formal clothes make everyone look nice. And are friends supposed to say things like that to one another?"

"Why not? It's true. I don't think anyone here would say otherwise."

"Silas might."

Haven rolled her eyes. "He doesn't count." Ryker said nothing but continued to look at her. "Do you have something on your mind?" she asked.

"Lots of things." Ryker's eyes dropped lower.

She arched an eyebrow. "Like the view?"

"Very much." He took his time looking, then slowly raised his eyes back to hers. "You've set up a masterful display." He gave her a slow smile, sensual and contagious. Haven avoided his gaze, but her face heated. She could see him staring at her, willing her to look at him. "But I'm rather enjoying the entire scenery tonight," he said. Haven glared at him. "What? Should I not think you look lovely? I thought you said friends could say that to one another. Besides, I'm assuming that was the effect you were going for. So, well done." Haven was transfixed by his eyes, the changing colors of gray and silver. But his perfect mouth curled in a mocking smile that irritated her.

"I really don't care what you think. I dressed for me tonight, and I'm not apologizing for it," she said, not backing down from his gaze.

He pulled her closer as he turned her gracefully across the dance floor. She could feel his hips subtly pressing hers to signal his movements. She melted into him, her body responding to his by reflex. He leaned closer to her, his cheek resting near her ear. "I don't think that's the case at all." He spun her in a sweeping arc that flared her skirt and left her breathless. The music stopped, and so did Ryker. He held her to him as their halted momentum swirled the fabric of her skirt around his legs before it fell.

Haven stepped away from him, flushed and winded from more than the dance. She held his eyes and curtsied low, tipping her shoulders forward slightly and giving him an eyeful down her bodice. She rose slowly. "Thank you for the dance. And the compliment. I hope your views tonight continue to be picturesque." Ryker's smile spread, then he laughed at her sass. Haven flashed him a wicked grin as she walked away.

Ryker tried to pay attention to the minister Trinity introduced to him, but his attention strayed and found Haven wherever she went. The minister excused himself and Ryker barely noticed. Trinity started to scold him for being rude, then followed his intent look. "She's lovely, but a difficult choice for you to make."

He gave her a blank look. "What are you talking about?"

"Remember who you're talking to. I can feel you. And her," she said, nodding in Haven's direction.

Ryker stared at Haven. "You must be confused."

She huffed at him. "Right. Because that happens frequently."

"She's lovely, and yes, I find her very attractive tonight. But she's not my type."

Trinity snorted. "Gods, sometimes you're as thick as a brick wall. She's beautiful, smart, and a good person. And she doesn't take your shit. Oh, and she's not afraid of you. Like, not even a little. She's exactly your type."

He had always thought of Haven as one of Harper's friends, too young to be of any interest to him. From across the room, Ryker's gaze found his sister. Kit rested his lips on Harper's temple and she slipped her arm around his waist, pulling him close to her. Harper wasn't a child any longer. And he realized her friends weren't either. The voices around Ryker fell away as his focus centered on Haven. There was something about her tonight. He had always thought she was attractive, but tonight she was stunning. He watched her in animated conversation with her friends, touching Dax's arm, Kit handing her a drink as he moved to stand beside Harper. She smiled brilliantly at Kit before laughing at something he said. Ryker was bewitched.

Inevitably, Haven caught him watching her, but he didn't flinch, and held her gaze with his own. A slow smile played across her deep red lips, and his throat tightened while his heart stammered uncomfortably. Dax spoke to her, forcing her eyes away from Ryker, then led her to the dance floor.

Trinity remarked, "You're going to have a stroke if you keep looking at her like that." He scowled at her and took Silas's arm and headed for the bar.

Silas allowed Ryker to drag him along. "I'm rather enjoying seeing you squirm. Almost as fun as seeing you get dumped."

"Silas, if you're going to be an ass, I'm going to find Lilith and tell her you want to dance all night. And that's no empty threat." Silas snickered and clapped him on the back.

The music faded, and over the din of the crowd, Ryker heard a long tone. He watched Dax lead Haven off the dance floor to the dining room, then lost her in the crowd, seeing only glimmers of red between the pastels and black slacks and jackets of the other guests.

"Ready?" His attention fell to Trinity, who took his arm. "You can find her later."

"I don't know what you mean," he said, leading her through the crowd.

"You're a stubborn, shitty liar," she laughed.

Lilith sat stiffly in her chair, the voices at her table a low buzz that needled her nerves. The council member to her left finally gave up trying to talk to her and turned his attention elsewhere. She watched the drama unfolding at the king's table with dread and anxiety that writhed in her stomach.

She overheard the king say, "You were a no show at the last three Advisory Board meetings. Should I assume you have no further interest in that role?"

Lilith tensed, her fork slipping out of her hand and clattering on her plate.

"Oh, I'm still interested. But I've been rather busy lately." Liam looked away from the king, and his eyes devoured his date. Another young female Lilith had never seen before.

"Too busy to advise the king of Berinia?"

Liam either ignored the trap or was oblivious and stepped right into it. "I'm sure Lilith represented Valena's views adequately. From what I understand, the issues you've discussed have been rather minor, anyway."

Aric's face flushed. "Well, my apologies for assuming the *king's* issues are less important than yours."

Lilith cringed to the bottom of her soul.

Throughout dinner, she watched the king either disregard Liam or look at him with such disgust and anger that Lilith wanted to slink away herself. But Liam continued to provoke him, unaware of his increasingly precarious position. The server asked if she was finished with her dinner. She nodded, and he took away her barely touched plate. Another tone sounded and the crowd rose, dispersing to the dance hall for the king and queen's Ostara waltz.

Lilith pushed aside her anxiety over her father and walked to the neighboring table. Hopefully the Ostara would distract her for a moment. It certainly would be the highlight of a disastrous evening.

"Ready for our dance?" she said to Ryker.

He brushed her aside without looking at her. "Not tonight. I've promised this dance to someone else." Lilith gaped as he walked away without another word.

"Well done. You might want to close your mouth. You look like a dying fish," her father hissed from beside her. Lilith snapped her mouth closed. The unease that had been simmering all night erupted into anger. Liam's smile faltered, then Lilith's dread returned with a vengeance.

"I thought I made myself clear on many occasions." Liam jumped at the sound of the king behind him. "Leave the Palace, now. I'm banning you from Regency social events until you can show our traditions a minimum of respect." Liam sneered at the king, but Aric stepped close to him. "Shut your mouth. I will have a guard escort you out if you say one more word." Liam's bluster faded in the face of the king's wrath. Even Lilith could see he knew he'd crossed the line. Silently, Liam took his date's arm and led her to the Palace foyer.

The king escorted the queen to the dance hall without a glance toward Lilith. The edges of her vision rippled with fury, tunneling to her father as he strode out of the ballroom, the female next to him struggling to keep pace.

Lilith followed Liam outside the Palace and grasped his arm before the Skimmer could take them away.

"Just what the fuck do you think you're doing?" Lilith said.

"Don't speak to me like that," Liam said, jerking his arm from her grip.

"This is how I speak to petulant children who need an attitude adjustment," she said. Her cold eyes fell on the female standing beside her father. "Leave. Now."

"You don't make decisions for me," Liam said, his eyes flaring.

"I said now," Lilith said to Liam's date. The female took a step back, then hurried to the group of Skimmers. Lilith wheeled on her father. "Don't ever do that again." Liam was momentarily speechless. "I've put up with your bullshit with Aric for years. You are destroying us with your childish games. From now on, you'll do exactly as I say."

"Or what?" he asked, his face a thundering cloud. "You are forgetting yourself, Lilith."

She remained steady and confident in the face of his anger. "I know exactly who I am. I'm who you made me. I lead the Rift Council. I'm a powerful advisor to the king and a confidante to Hope." She let out a curt laugh. "The king has already lost all respect for you. It's an easy step to ask him to remove you as cesare and appoint me in your place."

Liam's eyes widened. "You can't do that."

"Watch me." Lilith said. "I love you. With all my heart. But you've become an embarrassment and a disgrace, and a liability to our family. Go home and let this evening blow over." She stepped closer to him, her eyes like daggers. "Do not come to Araine without Skye again. I don't care where you stick your dick, but keep it to yourself and learn discretion. The next time you force me to clean up after you, I will have you removed and banished to Cantos permanently." She left him standing under the Palace portico, gaping.

Lilith stormed back to the ball, determined to fix the mess her father had left in his wake. She entered the dance hall and froze as she saw Ryker dancing, his gaze intent on the female in his arms. She willed him to look at her, and his mouth curved in a beautiful, sensual smile. The smile she saw so rarely yet never failed to stir her senses.

But his smile was not for her. Lilith backed out of the dance hall, then vanished.

Ryker leaned back as the server cleared his plate. "How much longer before we can leave?"

"At least an hour after the Ostara. Are you sure you want to leave?" Silas said, nodding his head toward Haven's table. Ryker had gathered himself during dinner, relaxing with the help of Finn and Corde's company and conversation. But as he watched Haven rise, the tension in his chest returned.

He barely noticed Lilith standing next to him. "Ready for our dance?" she said.

His eyes never left Haven as he said, "Not tonight. I've promised this dance to someone else."

Silas choked back a laugh as Ryker left the table. He walked to Haven, then held out his hand. "Will you dance?"

Haven shrank away from him. "I don't know this dance. I'm afraid I'll embarrass you."

Ryker grinned. "I'll help you." He reached for her hand and pulled her forward, but she resisted.

"Seriously, Ryker, I'm awful," she said.

He folded her hand into his arm and dipped his head to whisper, "I insist. Do I have to drag you? I will, you know."

She made a face but relented and walked with him to the dance hall. "Fine, but you dance at your own peril."

Ryker stood with her next to Corde and Finn, who waited with the king and queen.

"Good gods, just the three of us?" Haven whispered to him, looking around as the crowd filed into the room to watch the traditional spring waltz. "Nothing like having a spotlight on your weakest skill."

"I told you I would help you," he said, trying to suppress a laugh. "But I need to keep you close. Are you okay with that?"

Haven blew out a heavy breath. "Lead the way. And I'm apologizing in advance to your poor toes." Ryker smiled and pulled her even tighter.

The music began, and Ryker swept her into the dance. Haven let out a small squeak at the pace he set, but he supported her first stumbling step and didn't let her fail.

"Relax your hips. Let me move you," he said, encouraging her.

"It's pretty fucking hard to relax with a thousand people staring at me," she seethed.

"You're doing fine," he said. Her iron grip on his arm relaxed just a bit, and her body followed. He could feel her moving with him, their steps becoming more fluid. More couples joined them, and their dance became more restrained in the crowd. "Less of a spotlight now. Are you okay?" She nodded and looked up at him and smiled. His own smile faltered as he lost a moment of time in the joy that lit her eyes. The tension he had felt all evening when he was around her curled inside him, writhing in his stomach and warming his body with feelings he hadn't felt in years.

The music ended and Ryker held her close, absorbing her smile, the curve of her cheek, the shine of her hair. He reached out and touched a lock, absently pulling it through his fingers.

"Thank you, princess," he said.

Ryker's lips curved into a sensual smile and Haven's breath caught. His silver eyes glittered under his black lashes, those strange eyes that seemed to see straight through her.

"I...You're welcome," she stammered. She gathered herself and stepped away from him, breaking the moment between them. "I hope I didn't embarrass you."

"Not at all."

She stood in the middle of the milling crowd, unsure whether to leave. Dax saved her and took her hand.

"My turn," he said, and pulled her away. She looked over her shoulder at Ryker, who remained where he was, watching her leave. He winked at her as he walked away. She turned her attention to Dax and caught him smirking. "I'll make it a quick one."

She frowned. "I'm always happy to dance with you."

Dax picked up the rhythm of the dance and swung Haven around. She glimpsed Ryker standing with Silas and Trinity, his gaze still on her. "I know," he said. "But it's okay if your preferences lie elsewhere."

"My what?" she stammered.

"This is going to be fun to watch." He smiled at her confusion as he spun her through the crowd.

Haven drifted from room to room for the rest of the evening, meeting ministers and diplomats and dancing with her friends and new acquaintances. But she always knew where Ryker was in the room and who he was with, his voice reaching out to her.

Haven hovered at the edge of the dance floor with Harper, watching the couples dance to one final Ostara. While the dance steps were the same, the tempo of this rendition was quicker, more upbeat. Haven and Harper clapped to the music, encouraging the dancers. Kit and Ryker stood next to them, and Kit began clapping too.

"This version is my favorite," he said as he pulled a laughing Harper onto the floor. Haven watched Kit swing Harper through the last few bars of the dance. They laughed and embraced as the music ended with a crashing crescendo. Ryker looked down at her and smiled.

"That is a fun dance. You should try it."

"Oh gods, no. Not without years of lessons." Haven's smile faded a little, and she tilted her head. "I thought we were going to be friends."

"We are. Am I not being friendly?"

"Yes, but why haven't you asked me to dance again? Not that one, though." She pointed to the exhausted red faces of the dancers as they filed around them. "I've danced with Dax four times tonight."

"I've asked you twice. You haven't asked me. As a friend, you're perfectly capable of asking me." She glared at him. "Well? Are you going to ask me or just stare?"

Haven's face flushed. "You're an arrogant shit, you know that?" she said.

"That definitely doesn't sound like an invitation," Ryker said, crossing his arms. "I'm thinking you really don't consider me a friend." His silver eyes sparked, and his mouth quirked in a barely suppressed laugh. Haven gritted her teeth and walked away. Ryker's arm slid around her waist, and he moved her gracefully to the dance floor. "Seems I found yet another thing you could use instruction on—social niceties."

"I hate you," she said.

"No, you don't." His eyes danced. "At least not right now." He pulled her close and swept her through the crowd. "See, if you want to dance with a friend, you only have to ask. And since it's a ball, it's usually best if you are polite. Do you need specific examples?" Haven scowled at him. "And probably best if you don't kill your dance partner either. Merely a suggestion." He looked past her to the other couples and clusters of people talking around the room, then said, "Although sometimes at an event like this I wouldn't blame you for wanting to kill some of these people."

Haven swallowed a laugh, but her mouth twitched. His cheek touched hers, his lips brushing her hair. "Go ahead and smile, princess. It makes you even more lovely," he whispered.

"That's very close to flirting. I didn't think friends did that."

Ryker's eyes held hers and a smile danced across his own face. "I guess I'm still trying to figure out what you want from me. As a friend," he said. The music ended and Haven tried to move away, but Ryker held her close. "Now it's my turn to ask. Will you dance with me again?"

Haven agreed, and Ryker moved her again as the music started. Haven tried her best not to feel him against her, the graceful way he moved. *Gods, he could dance.* It was impossible to resist. She leaned into him and closed her eyes, feeling the rhythm of the music and their movements together. When the music ended, Ryker's hand fell from her waist, but she didn't move away. Instead, she pressed into him, not ready to lose the closeness, the warmth of him. She opened her eyes and saw Ryker watching her. He brushed a lock of hair from her brow. "It's good to see you happy. Are you happy, princess?"

"Yes, but I hate it when you call me that," she said.

"But you are a princess. And it suits you in so many ways." The music started again, and Haven didn't move, one hand kept in his and the other resting on his chest. "What do you want, princess?"

"I...I don't know." She avoided his shimmering silver eyes.

"I think you do. You just have to ask."

Haven flashed him a look of irritation. "Why do you have to complicate everything?"

He grinned at her, then laughed. The couples moved around them. Ryker stepped away and brought her hand to his lips. Haven watched his kiss, mesmerized by the feel of him on her skin.

"Thank you for the dance. I truly enjoyed it," he said, and walked away. Haven lingered amongst the dancers, trying to remember how to breathe.

She joined Dax and Kit and watched Harper dance with a Council member she had seen with Lilith earlier in the evening.

"Are you okay?" Dax asked.

"Yes, I'm fine. I think Ryker and I are friends now. Although he's really annoying."

"Annoying in a good way or a bad way?"

"Is there a good way to be annoyed?"

"Of course," he said. "I've seen you flirt with males before. I'm surprised you can't see this. He's trying to provoke a different response this time."

Haven saw Ryker dancing with a beautiful female with flaming red hair. "What are you saying?"

"He's attracted to you."

Haven blinked, words failing her. "No, he's not."

"Why wouldn't he be?" Dax watched her watch Ryker. "I think you like him too."

"That's ridiculous. I've barely started thinking of him as a friend."

"That's a great place to start, but it isn't ridiculous at all. You both experienced something intense and traumatic together. It would make sense if you felt connected to him emotionally."

"I should hate him for what he did to me. I'm actually shocked I don't. How is that even possible?"

"Maybe because you know he was trying to help you? I don't know, but you should give yourself permission to feel whatever you feel. And that includes being attracted to him."

"I'm not," she said, a little too quickly.

"Come on, Haven."

"Okay, yes, he's attractive. I'd have to be blind not to see that. But he's not interested in me like that. He thinks of me as a student, like I'm a kid."

Dax gestured at her dress. "Something tells me he figured out tonight you're not a kid."

Haven ignored him. "Besides, remember my rule. No more males."

Dax took her hand and led her to the dance floor. "You also owe it to yourself to be honest. Not every male is a shithead like Larkin. You should try it again."

"Me? What about you?" she asked as he moved her to the music.

"What about me?"

"I've seen the way you look at Tannys." Dax flushed bright red. Haven squeezed his arm. "You're adorable when you're flustered."

"Shut up, or I'll stomp on your toes," he said, scowling at her. She laughed and hugged him tight.

Late in the evening, the music struck a resonant tone. Harper said to Kit, "Last dance?" He took her hand and kissed it and led her to the dance floor. Haven watched them walk away, and her gaze caught on Ryker talking with Trinity and several Council members.

Dax nudged her and nodded toward Ryker. "Be brave."

Haven elbowed him back but corralled the courage that was attempting to abandon her completely. She walked to Ryker and touched his arm. "Last dance tonight?"

He glanced at her. "I'd love to." He took her hand in his and moved into the flow of the other dancing couples. "Now, that wasn't hard, was it?"

"Can you not be irritating for five minutes and dance?" He laughed and pulled her tighter to him. Haven let herself enjoy the feel of him moving her around the floor. The slow, melodic rhythm of the music blended with the press of his hips. His hand stayed low on her back, the warmth of his touch radiating through the fabric of her dress, and the brush of his fingertips on her bare back sent her thoughts reeling. The music faded and Ryker stilled. Haven stayed close, losing herself in him. "Thank you," she breathed. "You're a lovely dancer."

"First you say I'm handsome, and now you compliment my dancing. If I didn't think we were friends, I might think you were flirting with me."

Haven rolled her eyes. "I'm sure you're used to having females throw themselves at you. I could see how you would misunderstand."

"I don't think I misunderstood at all." He brought her hand to his lips. "And I like it."

Trinity and Silas joined them, then Ryker said to Haven, "Thank you for a lovely evening. You made this ball a pleasant surprise." They wished Haven a good night, and Ryker left with his Triad. Dax found her and led her to the crowd of Skimmers waiting to transport the guests home.

"Well?" Dax said.

"I've never been more confused in my entire life," Haven grumbled. Dax laughed and held her hand as the Skimmer took theirs and vanished.

# CHAPTER 24

## Falco Park

Haven slouched on a sofa in the apartment's common room, reading a book. Kit sat next to her, his own book open on his lap and his head resting on the back of the sofa, having lost the battle with sleep. The volatile spring weather had succumbed to winter overnight. The sun hid behind ominous clouds, blanketing the day in a dull gray. The temperature plummeted, and a blustering wind pelted the glass panes with half-frozen raindrops. Haven was distracted by the icy chunks sliding down and puddling on the sills.

"Gods dammit, Harper," Dax barked from the table next to Haven. Kit jerked awake.

"Face it. You'll never beat me," Harper gloated after winning her fourth game of petteia.

"How the fuck do you do that?" Dax asked, studying her closing move.

"I'm not giving away my secrets," she said.

Haven closed her book and yawned. "I'm taking a nap this afternoon," she said, rising and stretching. "Any plans for this evening?"

Dax said, "I'm meeting my parents. They're in Araine for a few days."

"Kit and I are having dinner with Ryker and Shallah at the Garret," Harper said.

Haven's shoulders fell. "Have fun. I'll see you all tomorrow." She walked to the stairs.

Harper pulled her arm. "Come with us."

"I don't want to intrude on an evening with your family," she said.

"Intrude? That's ridiculous. You're always welcome. Meet us in the lobby at six." Harper shivered at the weather. "We'll find Skimmers to take us there. I'm not walking in this."

"It's only three blocks," Kit said, stretching.

"You can walk, but I'd rather not be a frozen, drowned rat," Harper said.

Later that evening, they were skimmed to the lobby of the Garret where Silas waited for them.

"This is a surprise," he said to Haven.

"I hope you don't mind," she said, glancing at Harper.

"Mind? Of course not." He asked Harper, "Ready?" Silas took her in his arms and vanished. He reappeared, then skimmed Kit. When he reappeared again, he said to Haven, "I need to stand close to get past the wards of the loft. Is that okay?"

"Uh, sure," Haven said. A heartbeat later, she was standing in Silas's arms in the middle of a large, open living area.

Silas said to Ryker, "I'm out tonight. Have Trinity tap me if you need anything." Ryker nodded to him, and Silas vanished.

Haven joined Kit at the bar across from the kitchen, admiring the expansive apartment. The open architecture, exposed metal beams, and polished dark hardwood floors were a stark contrast to the large but cozy overstuffed couch and chairs surrounding a blazing fire. Kit helped himself to a beer and poured two glasses of white wine. He handed one to Haven, then to Harper. Haven sipped her drink and looked through the glass doors to a large balcony that ran the length of the loft. Even with the bad weather and dark skies, Haven could see the views were stunning. Tiny rivers of reflected light from Lucine and Araine streaked down the wet glass.

"Where's Shallah?" Harper asked.

"She's on her way with Trinity," Ryker said from behind Haven. Haven turned to him. "Glad you could come tonight."

"I hope you don't mind. Harper invited me."

"Not at all. Friends are always welcome in my home. Can I get you anything?"

Haven raised her glass. "Kit took care of me." Shallah's orange cat wound itself through Ryker's legs, his striped tail wrapping around his calf.

"You're out of red wine," Trinity called to Ryker from across the loft.

"The queen bee calls. Excuse me." He leaned down and stroked Kimo, then left to help Trinity.

Haven followed Kimo to the sofa and sat next to Shallah. The cat jumped up between them and curled into a ball. Shallah stroked him absently, and Haven found his soft rumblings soothing.

She lost herself in conversation over the next hour. Dinner appeared in the kitchen delivered by the Garret's hobs. After dinner, Kit and Trinity collected plates, and Harper and Silas cleaned the kitchen.

Ryker sat next to Shallah. "How do you know each other?"

"We met a few days ago. I had lunch with River at The Green Room and met Haven there. Haven and River are special friends, I think."

Ryker stiffened. "You're seeing River?"

"No," Haven said quickly. "I'm not interested in him that way."

"I think he cares for you," Shallah said. "He spoke of you fondly. And at length."

Haven squirmed in her seat. "We dated a few times two years ago."

"When you were a student?" Shallah asked.

"Yes. Probably not one of the best decisions I've made."

"River should have known better," Shallah said.

"Rules have never much mattered to him," Ryker said.

"Ryker, be nice." Shallah scolded. "Regardless," she said to Haven, "if you don't think of him that way, you should tell him."

"I have, many times. I'm only interested in him as an instructor, or maybe as a friend. We're working on that."

"I doubt he'll get the message by telling him. River isn't interested in female friends," Ryker said.

Shallah clucked at him. "River lives his life differently than you do. But he's still your brother."

"Yes, and I know him well. Trust me, he has females in every city in Berinia."

"That seems extreme," Haven said.

"That's no exaggeration. And I'm sure he'd be happy to add you to his stable," Ryker said.

"Well, I'm not interested in him that way."

"What about Lukas? I understand from River you are connected?" Shallah asked.

"Lukas?" Ryker asked.

"No, not Lukas either," Haven said quickly. "I'm not seeing anyone right now."

"Sorry, I must have misunderstood? I saw the two of you at lunch together," Shallah said.

"Well, our parents agreed to an enosi contract," Haven said, her eyes dropping to her fidgeting hands. "We're trying to get to know one another to see if it's something we can live with."

"Really?" Ryker said. "And what do you think of that?"

"I don't know what to think yet." She raised her eyes to his. "It's an archaic thing, an arrangement like that between two strangers. But I've spent the last seven months getting to know Lukas and he's nice. He's a good person. And his situation, as a Shadowalker, could offer a unique safety. Or so I'm told." Haven looked around the loft. "If his living situation is like this, it wouldn't be terrible."

"It's a hard thing to live with someone you're not in love with," Ryker said. "Don't you think you deserve that?"

"Love?" Haven said. "I might grow old and die before I experience that."

"That's a little cynical," Shallah said. "You're young. I'm sure the right person will come along."

"Were you ever in love?" Haven asked Shallah.

"Of course. To Ryker's grandfather. He was much older and has since passed away, but I loved him dearly," she said, glancing warmly at Ryker.

"Well, there are worse things I can imagine than being with a friend," Haven said. "And I would say Lukas is my friend."

Harper joined them, moving Kimo to the floor and sitting next to Shallah. "Are you still planning to go to Damaris? I understand you are going to my father's house for a stay." Harper said. Kimo stretched, then jumped back on the couch and settled next to Haven.

"I'm thinking about it. But I'm not comfortable staying there by myself." Shallah asked Ryker, "Would you come with me?"

"Mimi, you know the answer to that. Have you asked River?"

"No, not yet, but I need to see your aunt. You know she's not well. They moved her to a remedial center, so I can't stay with her. I can stay at Ronan's house, but I would feel more comfortable if you or your brother were with me."

Ryker said, "I'll speak to River for you."

Harper yawned and offered Kit her hand. "It's late. We should go," she said.

Ryker walked to the kitchen and rustled through a drawer, then offered Harper a key. "The weather sucks. Stay in a suite on the second floor. It'll be hard to find a Skimmer, and Silas isn't around tonight." Harper took the key and walked toward the stairs.

"Umm...," Haven stammered, unsure of what to do. Ryker offered her another key.

"There are four suites on the second floor. You can stay too. Or I can have Trinity try to find you a Skimmer, but it may take a while."

The pelting rain was a constant staccato on the dark windows. Haven took the brass key and turned it in her hand, noting the letter 'D' engraved on the head. "Thanks, I'll stay."

"There are guest supplies in the suite. Trinity can get you a change of clothes if you need anything," Ryker said.

"That's okay," Haven said, pulling on her jacket. Ryker walked her to the stairs. "Thanks for letting me crash your party tonight. You have a lovely family."

"Thank you." Ryker lingered at the stairs. "If I can give you some unsolicited advice, I wouldn't make any rash decisions about a commitment to Lukas. You shouldn't give up on the idea of finding love and passion in your life."

Haven could feel heat rising on her neck. "I can't see how my love life would be interesting to you," she said, turning to leave.

"I think you would be surprised to know what interests me." She turned slowly back to him. A hint of a smile played over his lips.

"Really," she said dryly.

"Yes. Really," he said.

"And how do you know I don't feel passionately for Lukas?"

"I thought you said you were friends."

"Friends can feel that way about one another."

He moved closer to her. "One could hope that was true. But it only works if the feelings are mutual."

Haven's breath stuck in her throat. "I don't know what Lukas feels."

"Sorry, were we talking about Lukas?" His silver eyes paled, almost colorless, and seemed to see straight through her. Haven opened her mouth, but words failed her. "Good night, Haven. And let me know if there's anything else I can do for you."

Haven drifted down the stairs, not sure what had happened between her and Ryker. Lost in her thoughts, she ran into River on the second-floor landing.

"Oh! Sorry," she said with a start.

"What are you doing here?" he asked.

"I had dinner upstairs with Harper and Kit."

River ran his hand through his wet hair, water drops splattering on the floor. "Since you are here, can I interest you in a nightcap? I'd love to continue our conversation from lunch. I'm prepared to grovel. Extensively."

Haven avoided his eyes. "That's not necessary. It's late, so I'll pass."

"I would think you would enjoy seeing me on my knees. I'd certainly like the view." She took a step back and he chuckled. "I'm kidding. But it may be weeks until we see each other again, not until your squad walks The Loop. I understand I'm assigned as one of your advisors."

"What's The Loop?"

"A fun four-day hike in the mountains, near the Aerial. Come in, and I'll tell you all about it." River moved across the landing toward the door of his suite. Haven felt an uncomfortable pressure in her mind. A shivering tension rolled down her spine, and her stomach twisted a little. River's icy blue eyes were dazzling, his shining black hair dripping water down his carved cheeks, his soaked shirt clinging to his broad chest and arms. She took a step closer, drawn to him. Staying with him sounded very appealing.

"I thought I heard voices," Kit said from the door next to River's. Harper stood in the doorway, glaring at River. Kit took Haven's hand and pulled her toward her door. "Are you having trouble with your key?"

"N-no, I didn't try it yet." Haven lurched sideways and grabbed Kit's arm, her stomach churning and her head spinning. Kit took her key and opened her door. "Are you okay?"

Haven's vision cleared, but her stomach still felt unsettled. "I think so. Thanks Kit." Kit walked to his door, bumping River's shoulder as he passed him.

"Don't you have somewhere to be?" Kit growled. Haven heard River's bitter laugh as he slammed the door to his suite.

Haven slowly closed her own door and rubbed her stomach under her jacket. The longer she stood in the cool, dark suite, the more the feelings she just had for River faded, then felt *wrong*, like they were thoughts that belonged to someone else. Seeing River brought back memories of the poor decisions she made with him two years ago, and with Larkin. She shuddered and pushed those thoughts away too. Those decisions belonged to a version of her that no longer existed.

She flicked on the lights to the suite and walked to the bedroom. She unwrapped a clean toothbrush and brushed her teeth, then splashed water on her face. The bracing cold helped drive away the last wispy memories of River. She stripped off her jeans and bra and slid into the bed in her t-shirt and underwear. As sleep took over, Ryker handsome face loomed over hers and she felt his touch, warm and gentle on her back. His smile was dazzling, his face open. Kind and reassuring. And his playful eyes were a sparkling silver.

# Chapter 25

## The Academy

Haven returned to the Academy and immediately missed Araine. It took her a few days to leave her vacation behind and shift her mind back to the routine of lectures and physical training. Her two weeks in Araine made her acutely aware that her time at the Academy was almost over.

She also resumed training with Kaden and Shane, but without Ryker, her Phoenix form remained elusive.

"I'm surprised you haven't lost patience," Haven said to Shane.

"I'm frustrated, but what choice do I have? Ryker won't train you. And he's not entirely wrong. You should learn how to use your Phoenix form without being provoked." He sighed heavily. "It would have been easier if he had stuck it out for a few more months before turning it over to Kaden."

Haven walked in silence, lost in thought. "What was his Bane training like?"

"About like yours. And like you, he needed to learn fast. Finnian went at him hard. It was unpleasant for them both. But Finnian pushed Ryker until he could control it."

"How long did that take?"

"Close to a year."

"Yikes," Haven said under her breath.

They stopped in the plaza at the foot of the stairs to her dorm. "I can try to speak with Ryker next week when he's here. Would you be willing to train with him?"

"Yes," Haven said. "Thank you."

The next week, Ryker was with Shane when Haven and Dax entered the clearing. Haven could see by his taut expression he didn't want to be there.

"Thank you for coming," Haven said. Ryker gave her a curt nod but said nothing. She braced herself and waited, but no magic touched her. "What are you waiting for?" she asked.

"Why do you want to do this?" he said, his voice flat.

"Because Kaden's way isn't working. We're friends, remember? I trust you." Ryker turned his back to her, the tension obvious in his shoulders. She said to Dax and Shane, "Can you leave us?"

When they were alone, Haven said, "I won't hate you again."

"I don't know why I agreed to this," he muttered, and started to leave. Haven held his arm.

"You came because I need you." His arm flinched under her hand. "Please." His face was expressionless, but a muscle ticked in his jaw. Smoke trickled from his hands and wrapped around his arms. She squirmed as his magic enveloped her, tickled her. "What are you doing? Only Bane works. This feels funny."

"My magic isn't always fear." A smoky tendril caressed her face. She swiped at the smoke and it vanished in a puff, then reformed around her waist, squeezing, binding her gently.

"Quit screwing around." She squirmed at the magic tethering her feet to the ground.

"If you don't like it, fight it." She slipped a tendril of Light around his wrist and flared it. He hissed at the red mark on his wrist.

"I've learned a little since you stopped training me. I'm not a naïve cadet anymore."

"No, you're not, are you," A tendril of Bane wrapped around her wrist. Haven felt the fear envelop her, and her eyes burned.

"What do you want?" Ryker asked.

"More," she said. Ryker tightened the Bane spiraling up her arm. Haven's red feathers emerged from her back, and fangs slipped from her mouth. Flames danced along her feathers and across the apex of her wings.

"Your control is good," Ryker said. "Now use your magic."

"What kind?" Haven said, her deep voice not her own.

"Skim, if you can." Haven vanished and appeared behind him outside the bindings of his Shadowalking and Bane. He turned to face her.

"What do you want?" Her white eyes shone, but she kept a distance between them.

He swallowed hard. "I don't know."

"That's a lie. I can see your heart." Ryker flushed. "Be brave," she said.

Ryker withdrew his magic, and Haven's eyes darkened to blue and her wings disappeared. He studied her face and saw the fatigue in her flushed cheeks and drooping lids.

"How do you feel?" he asked.

"Exhausted," she said. "Are you okay? Did I hurt you?"

"No, I'm fine. Let me look at your wings, to check for burns," he said, changing the subject. Haven unfurled her membrane wings. "What do you remember?" he asked, his hand falling to her shoulder as he turned her around.

"I remember skimming. I think. But it feels like a dream?"

"You did skim. You're learning how to control and use your magic. May I touch your wings?"

"Yes." He gently lifted her wing. He touched the joint, pulling her shirt away to examine her lower back. He dropped her wing and did the same to the other. She squirmed and said, "That feels funny."

Ryker quickly dropped her wing. "Sorry, I didn't mean to make you uncomfortable."

"I wasn't uncomfortable. It tingled. It felt kind of nice."

"I could make it feel a lot nicer. But that isn't what friends do."

"What do you mean?"

"You've never had a male touch your wings during sex?" he asked.

"That really is none of your business." Haven's cheeks flushed. He grinned, which seemed to make them redder.

"You asked. I'm just a friend, trying to help," he said. "But I'm assuming from your red face the answer is no. You should try it. It can feel much better than a tingle."

"This conversation is over." She turned away to hide her flaming cheeks.

Ryker laughed loudly. "There's nothing wrong with sex, particularly when it's done well."

"Over, I said."

Ryker chuckled. "Your wings are fine, by the way. You have two minor burns low on the joints, but a healer can treat them in one sitting. I suggest you seek a female healer if a male's touch makes you uncomfortable."

She furled her wings. "I'm not a child. I know the difference between a healer and a lover's touch."

"I know you're not a child," he said, stepping closer to her. "But it seems you've had some lovers who were in a hurry. You should make better choices."

Haven's face reddened again. "Why is this any concern of yours?"

"Just looking out for you. As a friend." He did his best to suppress a laugh. From the scowl on Haven's face, he knew he wasn't entirely successful. She ignored him and gathered her things.

"There's nothing wrong with the choices I've made," she grumbled.

"Really? And Larkin was a brilliant choice."

She glared at his mocking tone. "He may have been an asshole, but the sex part was great."

"I doubt that."

Haven slung her bag over her shoulder. "Well, I guess you'll have to take my word for it. And the next time I have sex, I'll tell you all the details and you can give me pointers." Ryker's gaze held hers. "Well? Isn't that what friends are for? Gossip and advice?" Ryker watched her carefully but said nothing. "What, no smartass comments?"

"No, I think we've said enough. Can I walk you to the medical wing?"

"If you want," she said. They walked in silence across the square.

"I'm happy to see you walking around after this shift. That's progress. But don't push it. After the healer finishes, you should rest. If the dorm is too noisy, stay here."

"Thank you," Haven said.

He nodded. "You're welcome."

Haven watched him walk away. "Ryker," she called to him. He turned to look at her. "Will you see me next week?"

He paused, then walked back to her. "You want to see me?" His silver eyes sparked, and Haven's stomach tightened.

"To...to train again," she stammered.

"Sure. I'm happy to help you with whatever you need practice with." Haven watched his face, mesmerized. He leaned down and added, "Now who's speechless, princess?" He flashed her a look of smug revenge. Haven watched him walk away, a tension knotting her stomach and heat flooding her body. Probably from the acute desire to murder him. She watched his confident stride, his broad shoulders, his powerful thighs. The heat turned into achy tingles, and Haven hurried away, desperate to dismiss the other thoughts running through her mind that felt even worse.

Haven sought a healer, who relieved the blistering burns around her wing joints. Without the pain keeping her on edge, exhaustion overwhelmed her. She took Ryker's advice and found an empty bed in the medical wing and asked the healer to wake her before dinner. Haven had barely closed her eyes when an assistant healer gently shook her awake. She thanked him and hurried across the square to the dining hall and sat next to Dax.

"Where have you been?" he asked. "Did you shift?"

"Yes. I was resting."

"Are you okay?"

"Yes, I'm fine. I was just tired. Gods, I'm starving." In between bites, she said to him, "I think I'm going to take your advice."

"Oh? And which advice is that?" He reached for another roll.

"Dating. It's been two years. I think being alone is making me see things that aren't there." Dax gave her a confused look. She shrugged. "I don't have a lot of faith in my judgement where males are concerned."

"I'm sure your judgement is fine. You're not the same person who chose Larkin."

"Let's hope I've learned at least that much," she muttered.

During sparring training the next day, Haven viewed the squad with a fresh eye. Over the past two years, she had several males ask her out, but she always declined and quickly set boundaries. Knox had persisted more than any other, in a friendly, respectful way. She liked him. He was nice, attractive, and funny. She often sought his company when their squad socialized together, and had been tempted to go out with him, but she always chickened out. She hadn't been ready to see anyone in that way. Now, he seemed like a reasonable choice to try dating again.

Through the week, Haven made a point to speak with him socially when their pods sparred. He picked up on her interest quickly and asked her to dinner.

"We can skim to Portos, if you're up for that," he suggested.

"That sounds great," she said. Saturday night, they had dinner together and skimmed back to the Academy late in the evening.

They walked to their dorm, close, but not touching, and deep in conversation. They passed through the common room and stopped in front of Haven's door. She tensed as they both fell silent.

Knox took her hand. "Thanks for a great evening. I had fun, and I hope we can do this again." He let her go, and a small smile played across her mouth as he walked away. She surprised herself by realizing the evening *had* been fun. Just simple, quiet fun.

Dax put down his book when she returned to their room. "Well? Did you like it?"

"Yes, I did. And I think it was the first date I didn't have to fight someone off. He didn't even ask for a kiss."

"Knox is a gentleman. I know him well. I told you, not every male is a jerk."

Haven hopped up on her bunk and folded her legs under her. "It was kind of nice."

"Sounds like a normal first date," Dax said, and opened his book. Haven lay back on her bed. A normal date. That had to be a first.

The following Monday, Haven's squad assembled in the Yard for their war gaming session, an early April drizzle slowly drowning them. Before she realized it, Haven was soaked to the bone. She shivered in damp misery and thought fondly of her spring break in Araine. Only two weeks had passed, and already the routine of the Academy made the vacation feel like a lifetime ago.

Ryker paced in front of the squad. "This is your last session before the end of the year. This scenario is different. There are four teams in the field, and we will stay overnight. The goal is the same, to capture flags. This exercise will prepare you for ComSim, two months from now. Your packs for this exercise are in your quarters. Gear up and meet back here in an hour."

Haven and her pod retrieved their packs and returned to the Yard. A Skimmer took her hand and Tristan's, and they vanished, reappearing in a clearing at the top of a ridge. The drizzle had stopped, and the sun broke through the gray clouds. Ryker gathered the squad and described the surrounding terrain and alternatives for evading capture. She listened to the lecture, but her attention drifted. She wanted to consider offensive strategies, not defensive tactics. "I'm going to scout," she said to Maddox and Dax. "I'll be back within the hour." She unfurled her wings and launched into the air.

When Haven returned, she paced outside the squad, lost in thought. An idea came to her, and she found Dax. "Get the pod together. I have a plan and I need you all." Dax gathered the pod while Ryker watched from a distance. She nodded to him. He gave her a level look, then nodded in return. "Come with me," Haven said to her pod, and unfurled her wings.

They flew under the tree line to the top of the ridge and landed, crouching low. Her pod followed and huddled around her, kneeling in the damp grass. "Look here." She pointed to three camps arranged in a semicircle in the valley below. "The three squads are camped close but far enough away they can't see each other." From their elevated position, they could see the three squads camped in the north, east, and south of a wooded plain below them. "I'm sure the squads know the layout of this valley and where the other squads are located. If we use three teams, we can trick the northern and southern squads into thinking attacks are coming from the squad in the middle to the east. They will expect it and have defenses heaviest on those sides. We can distract them while a smaller team infiltrates from the weak side. But we need to focus on the middle squad in the east first." She said to Kit, "We need you to slip into the squad. And this has to happen tonight. Tomorrow, the squads will have planned. We need to hit them now while they are still setting up and considering strategies."

Haven and Tristan decided to lead the teams targeting the squads to the north and south, while Maddox and Dax took the flag. "You need to protect it," Haven instructed them. "You will be our smallest team. We need the rest of the squad for the north and south exercises, so we'll be most vulnerable in the next few hours. Expect the worst and be alert. We can't have a team flank us."

Dax and Maddox agreed with her plan. "Not crazy about sitting this one out," Maddox grumbled.

"Trust me. This will only work if we have a strong defense. And you and Dax are the best. The rest of us are really just a small stealth strike team and noise."

"I got it," Maddox said.

Haven and Tristan left their teams to wait on the ridge as they crept with Kit to the edge of the eastern squad's camp, where they found a guard. Kit crept up behind him, slipped a hand over his mouth, and dragged him away from his post. Tristan's Wind took his breath until the guard fell unconscious. Kit studied his face, turning it from side to side. Haven's riveted gaze took in Kit as his features slowly changed, his eyes turning a medium blue, his nose more pronounced, and his lips thin. After a moment, the guard's face stared at them.

"That never gets old," Haven said.

"I heard him talk before I captured him. How do I sound?"

"Not at all like you," Haven said. "Be safe, and good luck."

Kit flew away, and the rest of the pod waited anxiously for his return. Half an hour later Haven heard a rustling through the trees. She motioned for the team to take their positions, and Kit entered the clearing with two cadets from the eastern squad, one of whom held a flag. Haven and Tristan ambushed the party and eliminated the cadets. As Tristan bound them, Haven asked, "Any problems?"

"No," Kit said. "It worked like a charm. They thought I was the guard and were so distracted with mobilizing their team to fend off an attack I warned them about, they jumped at my suggestion to hide the flag. It was easy."

"But they sent two guards with you," Tristan said.

"I suggested it so they wouldn't be suspicious." He nodded at the silenced guards. "It wasn't an obstacle."

"Well, we won one flag," Haven said. She turned to Tristan. "We're up next. Good luck." Haven took her team and headed north. She landed south of the northern squad with Kit, Harper, and a small team. Haven whispered to Knox, who was crouched next to her. "Use your Echo and take my Light. Send a flare when you're in position."

"Will do. This will feel weird," Knox said.

Haven felt a pull at her magic, like someone was sipping at her strength, that left her nauseated and clammy. "Ugh, that does feel weird," she said.

Kit and Harper slunk away through the woods with their small team. Fifteen minutes later, a tiny flash shot from the trees into the sky, and Haven rallied her team. "Spread out and move in, but stay back fifty yards. And make as much noise as you can. Draw them into the woods and scatter them."

The team dispersed in a semicircle around the campsite and broke into a screeching uproar. The camp dissolved into chaos. Haven could see cadets rushing into the woods, chasing phantom noises from every direction, or flying overhead, looking for enemy squads from the south. Haven fought off two cadets who rushed her from the site. Whirling, she struck one in the side with a dagger and sliced the other across the throat. Both cadets writhed in pain on the ground and glowed blue from the mortal sparring wounds. A second flare of Light appeared above the campsite, and Haven shouted to her squad, "RETREAT, now!" Her squad disengaged and withdrew, then flew back to their campsite. Kit, Harper, and Knox landed beside her, Harper holding a flag in her hand. Haven paced the campsite, waiting for Tristan to return. A few minutes later, his team approached from the south with a flag in hand.

"You did it," she said, beaming.

"I lost four cadets, but we got the flag," Tristan said.

"I lost three."

Haven glanced at Ryker, and the brief, begrudging approval in his smile was almost more satisfying than the win. Once the squad reassembled, he said, "That was excellent work. I don't think I've ever seen all three flags captured on the first night of this exercise." He turned to Haven. "Well done." She glanced at Dax, who gave her a small fist pump. She ducked her head, but couldn't hide her grin, nor the elation she felt at being in her element.

Haven relaxed with her pod by the campfire that night. Their success had concluded the exercise, winning them a return to the Academy in the morning. She sat with Knox and Dax, listening to Tristan and Kit retell their experience of the exercise. Their stories grew more outlandish and then downright comical as they tried to outdo one another. Their improbable exaggerations had the squad howling. Knox slipped his hand in hers, laughing at Kit's exaggerated version of the actual flag stealing. She joined in, but her gaze was drawn across the campsite to Harper and Ryker.

"Excuse me for a minute," she said, slipping her hand out of Knox's.

"Do you want me to come with you?"

"No, I just need to check with Ryker on the schedule for tomorrow. I'll be right back." She walked around the fire and asked Ryker, "Are you staying tomorrow?"

He looked up at her. "I was expecting the exercise to last through tomorrow, so yes."

"Would you be willing to train me when we return?"

"Are you up for it?"

"Sure." Knox drew close to them and slipped his hand in hers.

"Would you be interested in a walk?" he asked. Haven nodded but glanced back at Ryker as Knox led her away. She noticed Ryker's gaze drop to their clasped hands. His eyes caught hers, and a muscle ticked in his jaw. She looked down at their twined fingers, then at Ryker, but he had turned his attention back to Harper. Haven lingered, then opened her mouth to speak with him, but Knox tugged her along. She caught Ryker's eyes flicking to hers just before she followed Knox into the forest.

They strolled the perimeter of the campsite while Knox recounted the details of how they infiltrated the northern squad and captured their flag, laughing again at the outlandish stories from the exercise. Haven watched Knox as he talked, his sandy blond hair curling at his collar and falling across his forehead and into his warm amber eyes. He slipped his arm around her waist and pulled her closer as they walked. She felt his warm body move with hers and...liked it. She slid her arm around his waist too.

"You're from Phirot, right?" she asked.

"Yes, from Raveno."

"Did you know Maddox before the Academy?"

"No, we never met. Raveno is a big city. My family lives on the north side in the shipping district."

"I've been there once. It's lovely."

Knox stopped outside the tree line and touched her cheek. "Haven, I'd like to kiss you tonight."

She hesitated, surprised that he'd asked permission, then nodded. His kiss was gentle and hesitant at first, and his lips felt soft and warm. His hand on her hip gently pressed her closer as he deepened the kiss. When their bodies touched, Haven lightened their kiss, and he let her go. His hand stroked the small of her back as he led her back to the campsite.

Haven lay in her bedroll that night, thinking of Knox. She liked him. And their kiss had been nice. She felt comfortable with him. Maybe this was how good relationships were built—slowly, not in a burst of flames like she had experienced with River and Larkin. But there was still something missing. She thought of Maddox's parents and sighed. Haven enjoyed being with Knox, but felt there should be something else.

A spark in her heart. And maybe just a little fire.

The next morning, Ryker met Silas in the Yard as the squad reassembled from the exercise. Ryker dismissed them, and they dispersed to their dorm. Silas picked up his bag and handed Ryker's to him.

"After lunch for training? Does that work for you?" Haven asked Ryker.

"Yes, that's fine."

Knox walked to Haven's side and slid his free hand into hers. "Walk you to your room?" he said.

"Sure." She followed him but glanced at Ryker as she walked away.

Silas watched Haven leave and Ryker's silver eyes tense and turn gray. A muscle feathered in his jaw.

"The good ones don't stay single for long," Silas said. Ryker scowled at him and walked toward the instructors' apartments. Silas followed him. "What's with you?"

"What do you mean?" Ryker asked.

Silas pulled his arm, halting his stride. "I've never seen you hold back like this when you're interested in someone. Is it because Haven is a student? Or because of her Phoenix training?"

"I don't know." Ryker stared past him, and Silas turned and caught a glimpse of Haven as she walked with Knox up the steps to her dorm. "Maybe. I don't know how I feel about her."

Silas smirked. "I do." Ryker glared at him. "What? If you're honest about how you feel, you'll know what to do."

"And what do you think I feel?"

Silas shrugged. "You like her. More than any female I've seen in a long time. Enough to have you acting like an ass half the time."

"She's too young. And she's a student." Ryker ran his hand through his hair.

"All valid, but also lame excuses to stand by and watch her find someone else," Silas said, folding his arms across his chest and raising an eyebrow.

"And I don't know what to make of her, whether she would be interested in someone like me."

Silas barked a laugh. "This is worse than I thought. She has you feeling insecure? Wow, that's got to be a first." Ryker shook his head and continued walking. Silas fell in step beside him. "You're used to females meeting you halfway, where you don't have to put yourself out there to make a connection. I think this is different." They paused at the door and Ryker looked at him. "She's taking you out of your comfort zone."

"Obviously," Ryker said.

"Well, you better figure out what you want before the chance slips away."

# CHAPTER 26

## The Phoenix

Ryker entered the clearing and found Haven waiting alone. "Where's Shane and Dax?" he said.

"I don't think we need help anymore, unless you think differently."

"It's up to you." He avoided her eyes and rolled his shoulders.

"Are you okay?" Haven asked.

He looked at her finally, but his face was distant and impersonal. "Yes. Are you ready?"

"Yes," she said, closing her eyes and slowing her breathing, employing Kaden's meditation techniques.

Smoke drifted from Ryker's arms, enveloping her. "Try to think of your magic and shift without Bane."

She opened her eyes and frowned at him. "I've tried and it doesn't work."

"Let's try it again today. Think of what Bane feels like." He tried to encourage her to shift for the next hour without Bane. Nothing worked. Finally, Haven threw up her hands and paced away from him.

"Why are you holding back? I thought you were here to get me to shift."

"I told you, it's better to learn to shift without fear and hate."

"Well, it isn't working. Maybe I'm not ready for it yet. Shane said it took you a year to learn to control your Bane without Finnian." Ryker turned away from her. "I won't hate you. I asked for your help. There is a difference between your magic and intent, and I know you don't mean to hurt me."

"I'm not crazy about you fearing me, either."

"Fear you? That's unlikely. I've never feared you."

"Yes, I know. That's rare. Most people who feel Bane will always have a residual fear of me. That's one reason I chose Silas and Trinity. Neither of them ever feared me, either."

"Well, I won't. Your Bane has touched me for over six months. We're good. Can we get to work now?"

Ryker wove black tendrils through the smoky wisps encircling Haven's waist. A Bane thread wrapped around her and she tensed, her face paling at the fear Bane evoked. Her eyes whitened.

"Unfurl your wings," Ryker said to her. Haven spread her red feather wings. Ryker walked around her. "Fire?" he asked. The tips of her feathers flamed, then flickered out. "That's good. Show me fire in your hand." Haven held out her empty hand.

"Harder," she said in an eerie, low voice. Ryker tightened his fist, and the Bane tendril cut into her arm. Flames danced across Haven's hand. Ryker let her go, and the flame disappeared. "Again," Haven said. Ryker clenched harder, and flames engulfed Haven's wings. Ryker stepped back and released her. The flames disappeared, but Ryker could see wisps of smoke drifting up behind her and smelled burning flesh. She stepped near him. Ryker enveloped her in smoke, holding her away. "I won't hurt you," she said.

"You may not be able to control it."

"Yes, I can. You want to help. I can feel your magic." Haven's fangs dropped, and she moved toward him. Ryker stepped back and held her tightly. "Don't fear me. This is how it should be." Ryker enveloped her throat in Shadow and Bane. Haven choked, and her hands encircled her neck as she fell to her knees. Her eyes shifted to blue, and her wings became membrane, the joints smoldering. Haven wrinkled her nose and turned her head to look at her wings.

"Did I hurt you?" she asked. Ryker shook his head.

He moved behind her, examining her wings. "Can I touch you?"

"Yes."

He lifted her wing and pulled back her shirt. "That's a nasty burn. Still trying to find the right amount of help you need, and that was a little too much." He lowered her wing, and she flinched. He raised her other wing. "This one isn't bad." She flinched again as he gently released her. He peeled her shirt from her back, revealing a red, raw patch above her wing joint. "But that's a nasty one too. Sorry."

"It's not your fault," Haven assured him.

"That should be enough for today. Do you remember anything?"

"Not really. I remember being hot."

"You could control Fire in your hand." He held her hand, palm up. "See? No burns." Haven inspected her hand, flexing her fingers.

"You should see a healer for your shoulder and wings. They aren't too bad, but the one under your wing may need two sessions."

"Will you come next week?" she asked.

"If you want, yes."

Haven watched Ryker leave the clearing, confused by his brusque demeanor. She didn't remember him smiling at her once. She jogged to catch up to him, and they walked together to the square outside the dorms. "Why are you behaving this way?"

He halted. "I don't interfere with females who are dating other males."

"Interfere? What is that supposed to mean? I thought we were friends."

"We are. But I can assure you Knox would not appreciate our friendship."

"Well, I can choose who I want as friends. And if he's not okay with that, then he's not for me."

Ryker smiled at her for the first time that day. "I already know he's not for you. That's obvious."

She frowned at him. "What's so obvious?" Ryker said nothing. "You make such a big deal that I should make my own choices. Well, this is me, choosing."

"Being able to choose isn't the same thing as making bad choices."

"How is Knox a bad choice?" she asked. "He's nice, funny, and a gentleman. Sounds like you're just another person making choices for me."

He glared at her. "And insulting me won't make it a better choice either."

"Are you judging me?"

"Judging you? Why would I do that?" Ryker said. "There's nothing wrong with dating. I've had my fair share of relationships, some good and some bad."

"What is it exactly about Knox you think is bad?"

"You tell me. How does he make you feel?"

"Safe."

Ryker rolled his eyes. "That's the first thing that comes to your mind? That sounds like code for boring."

"There's a lot to be said for going on a date and not fighting the male off at the end of the night. And Knox is a gentleman."

Ryker bristled. "A male who can't control his feelings is weak. I'm sorry you had that experience."

"Yes, River taught me to be wary of males, a lesson I'm taking to heart."

"River? Did he hurt you?" he asked, stepping toward her.

"No. But he came close to crossing a line. I think he would have if Kit and Harper hadn't shown up when they did." Haven watched

Ryker's eyes fade to a dark gray. "How...How do your eyes do that?"

"Do what?"

"Change color like that. They changed from silver to gray. I've never seen anything like it."

"It's Bane. It affects my eyes. Finnian's do the same." He turned toward the instructors' apartments. "I'm not trying to pry into your personal life. And I'm certainly not trying to choose for you. But dating someone you don't have feelings for isn't fair to the other person. I'm guessing Knox has feelings for you, and 'safe' wouldn't be the first word he would use to describe how he feels."

"Maybe this is how a good relationship starts. Slowly. As a friend first."

"It can." He took a step closer to her. "But unless there's a spark there from the start, it isn't something that comes with time. It's there or it isn't. Don't you think you want that?"

"Maybe. But every time I've had a spark, I've been burned."

"Every time?" His eyes held hers for a moment.

Haven's stomach rolled a little. "What are you saying?"

He moved closer to her and drew a lock of her hair through his fingers, then dropped it. "I'm saying sometimes what you're looking for can be right in front of you."

"I don't see anything," she said, her voice catching in her throat.

"Then you're not looking hard enough. Go see a healer for your wings. I'll see you next week, if that's what you want." He turned and walked away.

Haven lay in her bed that night, unable to sleep. Ryker's words haunted her, both about Knox and seeing what was in front of her. She was attracted to Ryker. There was no sense in denying that. But she was also sure whatever she was feeling couldn't possibly be the way he felt for her. And she'd be damned if she was going to chase after him like some moony, lovestruck adolescent. Gods, males were complicated. She was starting to think dating again was one of her worst ideas.

Haven hustled through the door of The Common with her pod, shedding her coat and shaking the rain from her hair.

"Gods, I'm sick of winter," she groused to Dax. "I wish it would make up its mind. Winter or spring. Just pick one."

Dax ran a hand through his wet hair as he led her to a table. "A few more weeks, if we're lucky. At least it's getting warmer."

Haven sipped her beer and spied Knox playing pool with some of his podmates. He motioned to her, and she joined them. She watched them play a few games, laughing at their friendly competition. When Knox slipped his arm around her and smiled, she knew Ryker was right. Knox was a great person, but when he looked at her, she felt nothing. She couldn't pretend she had feelings for him, hoping that someday she would wake up and miraculously have fallen in love. And letting this go any further would only hurt him. She had been on the other side of that feeling before and had no interest in hurting someone that way, particularly someone as decent as Knox. She excused herself and walked back to her pod.

Dax sat up as Haven sat at the bar next to him and ordered a whiskey. "Dating sucks," she grumbled. He snickered and clinked his shot glass on hers.

The next week, Ryker met Haven in the clearing. "Ready?" he asked as he dropped his bag next to hers.

Haven was already working on her breathing exercises. "Yes."

Ryker rippled Shadow toward her but didn't touch. "Shift without me."

"Not this again," she said, hands on her hips.

"Just try it. Humor me." She tried to shift for the next hour without success.

"Ryker, *come on*," she said through gritted teeth. Ryker could see her frustration turning to anger. He wrapped her legs in smoke, stilling her pacing and tethering her to the ground.

"Fight it, princess. Or should I call your boyfriend to fight your battles for you?"

"Not that it's any of your business, but Knox is not my boyfriend," she snapped.

"Oh? So you decided I was right?"

"I decided it wasn't fair to him. Because I like him, but not that way."

"So basically, yes, I was right," he said, grinning at her.

"Is this your solution? To be an ass rather than use Bane?"

"Maybe. It's also a lot more fun for me. You're cute when you're mad."

"*Cute?* I'm not a puppy, Ryker." He laughed loudly. "Use your Bane, or this is over." Threads of Bane swirled in the smoke writhing around Haven's legs. "Do it," she said.

He wrapped a tendril around her wrist and tightened. Haven's eyes turned white, and her red wings erupted from her back in flames.

Ryker swore. "Haven, can you hear me." He withdrew his Bane, but Haven burned. She snarled as her fangs punched down with a splash of blood on her cheek and chin. She hissed at Ryker and lunged for him. He fell back, holding her as she bit at his face.

"Haven!" he shouted, struggling against the strength she shouldn't have. She pushed through his grip, inching closer to him, wrenching his hand from her shoulder and snapping at his neck. Her fang grazed him, and blood trickled into his collar. Haven's nostrils flared, and she pushed him back until he slammed into a tree. His foot slipped on a root just as she lunged for him again, missing him by an inch.

"Enough!" he yelled and encircled her torso in writhing rings of Bane. Her grip loosened, then she toppled over as a cloud of Shadow enveloped her.

She gasped, and through the clouds of Shadow, her ocean eyes stared at him.

"So maybe anger wasn't the right way to get you to shift. Sorry," he said. Ryker released her, his Bane and Shadow evaporating into wisps of black and gray.

"Did I hurt you?" she asked, holding her neck.

"No, I'm fine."

She noticed the blood running into his collar. "Are you sure? You're bleeding."

Ryker rubbed his neck and looked at the blood on his hand. "It's nothing. A scratch." He offered her his hand, helped her stand, then moved behind her. "May I touch you?"

Exasperated, she snapped, "Are you going to ask me that every time?"

"Yes," he said, and blinked. "Your wings are...personal."

"A tingle is not personal," she said.

"Your wings can do a lot more than tingle." He stepped closer to her. "Do you want me to show you what I mean?" he said, his voice low. "For educational purposes, so you know."

Haven wavered, then gave a small nod. Ryker's fingertips touched the apex of her wing and slowly drifted along the edge. She tensed at the sensation. Her stomach did more than tingle— her entire body heated. Ryker's mouth quirked as his eyes roved over her face. His hand dropped, and his fingers slowly traced up the inside of her wing toward the apex. Haven closed her eyes, and a groan escaped her as the tension in her body increased and settled between her legs. Ryker dropped his hand and the tension eased, but the ache remained. She slowly opened her eyes and willed her breathing to be normal.

"Probably something friends shouldn't do." He watched her, then moved away to collect his bag. Haven tried to relax the raw desire rippling through her body, her slow breathing making her lightheaded. "Come with me. I'll take you to the healer." She followed him, still unable to speak.

Ryker left her with a healer who treated her burns. She returned to the dorms and showered, then had dinner with her pod. Dax and Tristan carried on an animated disagreement over their last lecture on defensive strategies, which Haven barely listened to as she walked between them on their way back to the dorm. They crossed the plaza, but she stopped at the foot of the stairs. The thought of sitting in her room with seven other people crowded her already full mind.

"I'm going for a walk. I need some space to think."

She wandered under the dark canopy of trees until her mind finally slowed and she could think rationally about the moment with Ryker that afternoon. She felt more than a spark between them, she had to admit. She was attracted to him, and not because of what he did to her wings. He was thrilling to be around. River had been thrilling too, but also dark and threatening. Ryker made her feel alive, even though she sometimes wanted to kill him. And she knew she was well past thinking of him as a friend. He was flirty; she knew that. But was he just being friendly? She didn't have a great track record of reading people correctly. Her face burned with embarrassment at the idea that Ryker would know her feelings while she was wrong about his.

She drifted through the Academy buildings to The Common. She considered stopping in to see if Dax, Harper, or Kit were there, but decided she was not ready to be social. As she passed by the door, Silas and Ryker came out. She kept her head down and hurried past the building, moving toward the shadows to avoid the bright lights of the square.

Ryker fell into step beside her. "What are you doing out so late?"

Haven jumped. "I went for a walk. It helps me think sometimes."

"I do that too. Walking helps me relax. Particularly when I'm overstimulated." She glared at him and caught the flash of a smirk before she dropped her gaze to the path again.

"Don't you have somewhere else to be?" she griped.

"No, not right now. I like being right where I am." Haven sighed loudly in reply. They walked through the Academy Green and past the lecture buildings toward her dorm. "You're awfully quiet tonight," he said.

"I was trying to find some peace. That doesn't seem possible right now."

"Are you feeling okay? How are your wings? Still aching?" She ignored him but picked up her pace. He kept up with her, then put a hand on her arm, stopping her.

"I'm sorry. That wasn't fair." She could see the silent laughter in his eyes. "But at least you now know why I won't stop asking for your permission to touch you." He stepped a little closer. "And maybe it has raised your standards of what to expect from males." She gave him a dirty look and pulled her arm from his grip and continued along the dark path home. He followed beside her.

"There's nothing wrong with my expectations or my experiences, thank you very much."

"Really? I'm not so sure about that. I'm thinking you need some lessons on the fundamentals. I'm wondering if you've ever been properly kissed."

Haven stopped between the dorm buildings outside the light of the square. "Why are you interested in how I'm kissed? I'm pretty sure this isn't on the list of things friends should wonder about one another."

"I disagree. Didn't you say once friends should be there to offer advice? Think of it as a little tutoring on the side." Ryker's silver eyes glittered. "You should have someone kiss you who knows what he's doing."

"Really. And you think that's you?" She crossed her arms, a look of disbelief on her face.

"Maybe." She held his eyes and waited. Ryker said nothing and didn't move.

"You certainly like to talk a lot." She marched across the square, determined to put some distance between them.

"I may talk, but your answer to everything is to walk away," he called after her.

She stopped in her tracks, then stomped back. "That's rich coming from you. And maybe I walk away because I'm sick of waiting," she said. She was only partly angry at him, but also at herself for admitting as much.

"And what exactly are you waiting for?" His lips curved in a way that made Haven's stomach tighten and tingle, which also infuriated her.

She leaned closer to him, her face inches from his. Her eyes flashed in anger. "You're so clever. You figure it out," she seethed. His smile broadened and he laughed softly. Her face flushed, and she walked away again. Ryker grabbed her arm and spun her to him, and his lips were on hers. One hand slid to her waist as his other hand laced behind her neck into her hair.

Haven pulled away from him in surprise, but he held her tight. His kiss was soft and slow, but she felt his cool restraint melting away. He deepened the kiss, his lips demanding a response from her, but lightened his grip on her waist, giving her the choice to move away. Haven felt Ryker's hard body pressed to hers, and the tension and ache she felt earlier and forced down came roaring back. Her resistance vanished, and she leaned into him. His hand on her waist slid lower to her hip, gently pulling her tighter. Her tongue teased his lips, and he groaned, their tongues touching, tasting, and exploring. Haven ran her hands up his arms, across his broad shoulders, and laced them into his hair.

In what felt like a heartbeat from the first touch of his lips, Ryker eased his body away from her and slowly lessened the intensity of his kiss. His lips stayed close, gently playing with hers, brushing hers. "That's how you should be kissed," he whispered, stepping away from her. "Just my opinion."

He left her alone in the dark shadows, her heart racing, her lips tingling. Gods, he was not wrong. Gods damn him.

Haven's stomach twisted in knots as she approached the training clearing in the woods. She had thought of Ryker's kiss all week. Her mind and heart tangled up hopelessly, and she felt she was on dangerous ground. There was no use denying she'd enjoyed his kiss. Probably too much. And she wanted more, but she was unsure of his intentions. She felt vulnerable, that the feelings she had for him were not the same as his. And if she was being completely honest, she wasn't sure what she felt for him. Until she could sort through her own feelings—which flittered stupidly between excitement, her old insecurities about reading people, and fear that this meant something different to him, when she still wasn't even sure what it meant to her—she wasn't ready to take a risk with a male again. Her relationship with Ryker needed to stay within the boundary of friendship, at least for now. She didn't regret the kiss, but she was afraid. She would admit at least that. She needed to protect her heart until she decided what to do next. What that was, she wasn't sure. *How did you know?* Maybe she should ask Harper. No, that would be weird, the whole brother and sister thing. Maybe Dax.

Haven entered the clearing scatterbrained and deep in her own thoughts and didn't notice Kaden standing with Shane until she had dropped her bag. "Where's Ryker?" she asked.

"He had a crossing yesterday and will be in recovery for a few weeks. Kaden and I will work with you until Ryker can return," Shane said.

Haven exhaled in relief while her stomach turned with disappointment. Her jumbled brain told her this break from Ryker might be exactly what she needed.

# Chapter 27

## Araine

Roque was waiting for Lilith when she entered her office in the Council chambers. She closed the door behind her and walked around to the seat behind the desk.

"Have you made any progress with River?" Roque asked. This was becoming a daily conversation.

"No. He still refuses to work with us."

"I think it's time to pressure him."

"Why?" she asked, concern rising in her voice. "Have you learned something new?"

"The Phoenix's control is growing. And she's spending more time with Ryker." He paced in front of her desk. "This is dangerous. We need them separated. They cannot, under any circumstances, create a Pair."

"Why are you against this Pairing? I understand having River control the Phoenix is ideal, but I'm thinking there's more to this." Roque stared at her but said nothing. "Not ready to tell me everything? Fine. But pressuring River the wrong way won't work. We have to make him want to work with us. I'm bringing River back from the Aerial in two weeks for a Council meeting. I have an errand in mind that would be perfect for him. It would get him used to working with us. Hopefully, one thing will lead to another. As far as Ryker goes, I sent him on a crossing to help the djinn. He's recovering at his safe house, which will remove him from the Academy for at least three weeks. I can also keep him as a priority on the crossing rotation. We can always find demons to hunt."

Roque stood. "Whatever method you use, be quick about it. We need her bound. We're on borrowed time."

River walked into the ministry building and down the hallway toward Lilith's office. His rotation for the Aerial meetings wasn't due yet, and he'd expected to be away from Araine for at least half the year. The command to return had come from the colonel, but he knew Lilith was behind it. From their last encounter in March, he knew she was getting desperate about Haven. He wasn't sure what irritated him more, Lilith's demands that he come to Araine or her reasons. But it was time to have it out with her once and for all. He opened the door to Lilith's office and closed it behind him.

"Don't you ever knock?" Lilith snapped.

"No," he said flatly. "And let me guess. You pulled me to this shithole of a city because the situation with Haven is an emergency. Again."

"Sit down and be quiet for once," Lilith said.

River flopped into a chair. "Hurry and get this over with. And let's skip to the punchline, the answer is no. But go ahead. Say what you need to say."

"Fine. Let's get to the point. I know you are an unregistered Persuasion. You know about me. But I have a feeling your secret is much more damaging."

"You want to play chicken with me? Let's go. Your threats are as empty as your soul."

Lilith sighed. "Really, River. We have a lot more in common than you care to admit. It would be easier if you could see this."

She walked around her desk and sat on the edge in front of him. River watched her cross her long legs. "Forget the Phoenix for a minute. Let's discuss your career."

"What about it?"

"There are other ways we can work together. There is a certain group within the Aerial that would benefit from your influence."

"My influence," River said.

"Yes. Alignment with Special Forces would be beneficial to me, and to the Council."

"Dekkar runs that group. I know him well. He's good, but sometimes not too bright."

"Exactly. If you could counsel him occasionally, we would be grateful."

"How grateful?" River brazenly eyed her legs. Lilith bounced a foot and slowly smirked at him.

"Not as grateful as I would be if you worked with us on the Phoenix." Lilith stepped from the desk and returned to her seat.

"I don't need that much gratitude in my life. But a little wouldn't hurt. And I like the idea of 'helping' Dekkar. He could use a little guidance. And controlling Special Forces would be interesting."

"Go to Damaris and meet with Dekkar."

"I can't just pop into Damaris and ask to meet with Dekkar," he said impatiently. "I have no reason to be there. And I'm not risking exposing my magic by attracting attention."

"Well, find a way to be in Damaris. You can at least be a little creative. Doesn't your father live there?"

"Yes, but I wouldn't voluntarily see him for any reason."

"Well, I leave the reason up to you. We have a Council meeting later this week. You have until then to come up with an excuse."

"Just like that? No more hounding me about Haven?" he asked.

"Why? Do you want to talk about her?"

"No," River said, rising. "I'll let you know what I come up with at the Council meeting."

River walked to the street, surprised at the turn of the conversation. It certainly wasn't what he'd expected. And he hadn't lied, controlling the Special Forces would be a step up from commanding a regular Aerial unit. But it couldn't be that simple with Lilith. Somehow, what she was asking him to do had to be connected to Haven. He knew Lilith wouldn't let it go easily, but he couldn't see her reasons yet, which meant he needed to be wary of her.

But Lilith was also asking him to risk exposure of his magic, which was out of the question. His close call with Haven a few weeks ago was a perfect example of the risks he shouldn't be taking. But she'd caught him off guard at the Garret, and without thinking, he had aggressively tried to Persuade her to come into his suite. He cringed at his stupidity and considered himself lucky she hadn't recognized his magic for what it was. It was annoying that she still resisted him. Not that he really cared about sleeping with her, but now it was a game, and one he was determined to win. But not with Persuasion. He knew better. The first time he'd used his magic on her, to get her to go to dinner with him at Falcon Ridge, he could feel she was not easily susceptible. He couldn't make that kind of mistake again.

Dekkar, on the other hand, would be easy. River had been kind when he said Dekkar wasn't bright. His malleable mind would turn quickly and stay readily susceptible to Persuasion, like a thread River could tug on whenever he wanted. And Lilith would owe him.

# Chapter 28

## The Serendib

Ryker and Silas landed in the square of the Temple, furled their wings, and quickly strode across the plaza toward the crossing wing. Dressed in black leather combat breeches covered in finely scaled armor and a matching vest over a tight black shirt, Ryker adjusted the daggers strapped to his thighs and secured the sword behind his back. Silas handed him a vambrace, which he strapped onto his right forearm. They met Trinity in the crossing room.

"What do you See?" Ryker asked.

"The djinn already crossed into Ahrima, but I detect no native luprecans in the area," Trinity said.

"Thank the gods for small favors," Ryker said. "They're a pain in the ass." Silas laughed and handed him a second vambrace.

"The daevas intercepted the djinn and pinned them in a grove. There are two daevas controlling a team of four shima. I can't see how right now, so this crossing will be unpredictable. If I had more time, I could figure it out."

"Why the hell didn't they wait for us?" he said, frustrated at having to clean up after the djinn. "I thought Lukas had worked out the combined logistics with them. This crossing was supposed to happen in a few weeks."

"Ask them when you bail their ass out. Again," Trinity snipped.

Ryker huffed and sat on the dais, then swung his legs up as he accepted Trinity's link.

"I've worked with this djinn team," said Silas. "They are competent in combat at best. You won't get much help."

"Great," Ryker muttered. He lay back, and gray Shadow swirled around his legs. "Anything else?"

"No, but be careful and stay alert. I hate these emergency crossings," Silas said. "I could go with you..."

"Forget it," Ryker said. "No way, in an emergency like this. Too many things that could go wrong. I'll be fine." Shadow enveloped Ryker's body, and he became transparent.

Ryker appeared in the shadows at the base of a cliff, knelt, and surveyed the scene. Forty feet away, a thick grove of trees sprouted from the barren, rocky earth around the mouth of the ravine that snaked away behind him. Four demons the size of a seraphim child prowled along the tree line, their red eyes glowing in the fading evening light.

*I don't see the daevas,* he said to Trinity across the link.

*They're right there, with the shima team.*

Ryker swore under his breath. *They aren't visible. There's a Cloak nearby.*

*I can send you a live feed map, so you can see what I see,* she offered. Ryker grumbled but reluctantly agreed. Live feed maps distorted his vision and made it difficult to react to what was real.

His peripheral vision narrowed and blurred, but he now saw three figures standing with the shima team.

*I thought you said there were two daevas,* he said.

*There are.*

*I see three.* Ryker inched forward around the cliff face, staying crouched and within the shadows. One of the shima stretched tall and sniffed the air. The demon turned its head toward Ryker and hissed, green venom dripping off its long fangs and sizzling on the ground. Ryker dropped to the ground behind a boulder. He heard the shima make a series of clicking sounds, and two shima bolted in his direction. Ryker unfurled his onyx wings and drew the sword from his back as the shima separated and approached his location from opposite sides. Ryker turned his back to the boulder, and a moment later, both shima rushed him from the left and right. He slashed his sword and flicked his wing, and two heads silently rolled to his feet.

He slid around the shadowed side of the boulder.

*I still see three,* Ryker said. From Trinity's live map, he saw two daevas in their native form—similar in build to the gaunt, hominoid shima but twice the size, and with the elongated clawed hands unique to the daeva. The third form was tall and resembled an adult fae or seraphim.

*One of those isn't a daeva.*

*I can't help you,* Trinity said. *I can't see it.*

*Why can I see it and you can't?*

*I don't know, but I'm sure it's the source of the Cloak.*

Ryker grunted in agreement. *Yes, since daevas can't Cloak. It looks fae, or seraphim. Or maybe a djinn. But it seems too tall to be a djinn.*

*It's tall, like a seraphim?*

*Yes, but it has long black hair and dark skin. And its ears are rounded, like a djinn or a human.*

*Gods, Ryker, that's a Serendib.*

*Fuck. What the hell do I do with that?*

*It's bound to one of those daevas. You need to kill them both. It's the only way to free it.*

*Well, the djinn won't like me killing daevas again.*

*Too bad. If the Serendib is bound to a daeva, the daeva can wield its magic. That's the source of the Cloak. And your safety is more important.*

Ryker watched the daevas turn their attention back to the grove where they had trapped the djinn team. Ryker took the opportunity to slither Shadow along the ground like a heavy fog. It reached the daevas, and Bane twisted within the smoke. One of the daeva screeched, and the outline of its figure flickered, nearly transparent. Ryker tightened his fist, and the daeva became solid again, the Shadow tethering it to the ground and preventing it from skimming.

Ryker moved from behind the boulder and walked toward the daevas. The two remaining shima rushed him, green venom spraying in a dense cloud. He sent a wall of Shadow and the venom sizzled, then vanished. A blade snicked from the vambrace on his wrist, and he shifted the sword to his left hand. He slashed one shima across the throat, spraying black blood across his chest and face, then shoved the sword into the other shima's chest and flung the body to the side. It hit the boulder with a wet thud and slid to the ground. The Serendib shielded the daevas with his body, but his movements were erratic and wooden. Ryker tethered the Serendib in Shadow, and he stilled. Ryker moved around him and slit the throat of one of the daevas. The Serendib fell to his hands and knees on the ground, and the Cloaking disappeared.

Ryker grasped the hair of the last daeva, baring its throat.

"Don't kill it!" the Serendib said, panting and raising his head.

The djinn team emerged from the grove and rushed to the Serendib's side.

"We need to bring the daeva back for questioning," one of the djinn said. Ryker reluctantly released the daeva and helped the Serendib to his feet.

"Are you okay?" Ryker asked.

"Yes," he said. "Thank you. That was the longest three years of my life."

Ryker turned to the daeva still tethered by his Shadow. "What do you want to do with this one?"

"They have nearly depleted my magic. I can't transport it back right now. Can you take it?"

Ryker flashed him an annoyed look. "Transporting live bodies isn't something I enjoy."

"Yes, but my colleagues can't transport anything living."

"Fuck," he spat. *Have a team meet me with restraints,* he said to Trinity.

*Got it.* A few minutes later, Trinity confirmed. *We're ready. Bring it back.*

Ryker encircled the daeva's neck with Bane and squeezed. The daeva struggled against the magic, wheezing and screeching, until its eyes rolled back in its head as it fell limply to the ground. Ryker grasped the demon to his chest, enveloping the daeva in smoke, and they vanished.

Ryker's body became solid in the crossing room, and the daeva immediately scrambled off his body. He swore as the demon's claws ripped across his chest. The armored vest deflected most of the damage, but a claw clipped his arm, cutting through his bicep to the bone. His arm fell uselessly to his side, blood splashing on the floor.

The demon unsheathed the dagger from Ryker's thigh and raised it over its head. A sword burst from the daeva's chest, spraying Ryker with black ichor. Silas yanked the sword from the daeva as thick, black blood seeped from the daeva's mouth. Its eyes rolled into its head, and it fell forward onto Ryker.

"Gross," he said as he pushed the daeva's body off him onto the floor. He fell back onto the dais, blood streaming from his arm. "Well, at least the djinn will be pissed at you and not me this time," he said to Silas. They both grinned at each other as the healer rushed to Ryker's side.

Ryker rested at the Villa Pandion for two weeks after his unscheduled crossing. He sat next to Silas in the smaller dining room of the Villa and poured himself a cup of tea. "I've arranged for Skimmers to meet us in the plaza on the Wedge in an hour," Silas said. "We have a meeting with the Council this afternoon."

"Can't you put it off for another week?" Ryker complained as he scooped eggs and toast onto his plate.

"No, not possible," Trinity said. "Lilith knows you're recovered, and they've been hounding me for a debrief. You may not be ready for another crossing, but you can meet with the Council."

Ryker silently pleaded with Silas for help. Silas shrugged. "She's right." Ryker glared at him and turned back to his breakfast.

An hour later, Trinity and Ryker arrived in the lobby of the Garret with the Skimmer. Ryker stopped at Shallah's second-floor suite to let her know they had returned to Araine.

She held him tight, then pulled back, searching his face. "How are you feeling?"

"Good. Almost normal," Ryker said. "We have a Council meeting this afternoon but should be back in time for dinner."

"I hate to bother you with this when you've just come home, but have you changed your mind about taking me to Damaris?" she asked. "I need to go. I don't think your aunt has much time left."

"Mimi, there is very little I wouldn't do for you, but you know that's an exception," he said. "I expect to see River at the Council meeting today. I'll ask him to take you." He kissed her cheek.

Ryker spent the first hour of the Council meeting bored to death and desperately trying to stay awake. Finally, he gave his account of the rescue operation and confirmed they had killed the daeva team that had bound the Serendib and returned the body to the djinn as requested, along with the now free djinni.

"There's still a handful of missing Serendib," a Council member reported. "We have leads on two, but the others remain unaccounted for." The Council member turned to Trinity. "Can you speak with the Serendib? Maybe the story of his bondage can help you See others that are hidden. He is still recovering from being crossed for so long but will be ready to return home within the month." Trinity agreed to speak with the djinni the following week.

The meeting adjourned two hours later. Ryker jumped to his feet and headed toward the door. Trinity held his arm, pulling him back. "Social hour this time."

"Shit, are you serious?" he said.

"Yes. You have to. Besides, River is here. You can ask him about Shallah."

Ryker's shoulders slumped. "Lead the way."

Trinity took Ryker and Silas into the adjoining chamber, which featured a bar and several raised cocktail tables scattered throughout. Ryker marched to the bar and ordered a double scotch and shot half of it. He coughed and wiped his chin. "I'm ready." Silas snickered at him. Ryker turned to Trinity and came face to face with Lilith. *Gods, this was going downhill fast.*

"It's good to see you. How are you feeling?"

"Not quite ready for a crossing, but I feel fine." He could see Silas's amusement and mouthed a silent obscenity at him.

"Excellent," she said. "And how long do you intend to stay in Araine?"

"Probably over the weekend. I need to resume lessons at the Academy as soon as possible."

"Why did you agree to teach at the Academy? Such a waste of your talents and time."

"It's my time to spend as I wish," he said, his tone hard. "I enjoy helping students, particularly when I can expose them to unique gifts. Lukas volunteers too. Finnian has volunteered most of his life. We agreed to trade years."

"Of course. It's very generous of you. But you could be much more than a teacher."

"I am more. I'm everything I want to be. I love my life exactly the way it is."

"There's nothing more you want?" she said.

"No. Definitely not. When are you going to stop asking?"

"Until you see reason. Come, let's not be shy. We could be special together. Think of the things we could accomplish." She moved closer to him.

"You mean what I could do for you. I've made it clear there's nothing I want from you."

"You're not seeing the entire picture. A life with me could open valuable opportunities." Lilith reached for his arm, but his cold gaze and a lone wisp of Bane made her reconsider.

"Nothing that would be of value to me. This is the end of this conversation." Ryker nodded tersely, then left to join a group of Council members. He spoke with the group for what felt like an eternity. From a cluster near him, Trinity finally signaled he could move on, and he politely excused himself. He passed by her and muttered, "I don't care how many social rules I break, I'm done. I want to see Shallah." He stormed away and tapped Silas on the arm, pulling him away from a cluster of Council members near the door.

Trinity caught up to him and held his arm. "Give me ten minutes. I'll make our excuses."

Ryker and Silas stood waiting for Trinity in the reception area outside the chambers when River walked down the hall.

"You're missing all the fun," Ryker said.

"How bad is it?" River asked.

"Horrible. If it helps, the bar is in the back."

River squared his shoulders in a sarcastic show of courage. "I'm diving in. Wish me luck."

"Before you take the plunge, Shallah needs a favor. She needs you to take her to Damaris for a few weeks. Her sister is ill. She was planning to stay at Ronan's but doesn't want to stay alone."

River blinked, and his mouth gaped. "You want me to stay in Ronan's house?"

Ryker's smile thinned. "Yes. It's a lot to ask, but Shallah needs you."

"Why don't you do it?"

"Why do you need to ask that," Ryker said.

River's lips curved into a thin smile. "Just like old times. I'm always doing your dirty work with Ronan."

Ryker stiffened. "This isn't for me. Go with Shallah. You owe her."

"You owe me. Take the last training exercise at the Academy for me in two weeks, and I'll go with Shallah."

"Fine," Ryker said. Trinity emerged from the reception hall, and they moved toward the lobby of the building.

River snickered. "They're walking Lucifer's Loop," he called out to Ryker's back. Ryker whipped his head to River, his eyes wide and his shoulders drooped.

"Fuck," he muttered. River laughed out loud.

# CHAPTER 29

## The Loop

"This will be your last exercise at the Academy," Kilian said, pacing in front of the squad assembled in the Yard. "You will start at the Aerial training facility. From there, you will have four days to complete a seventy-mile hike through Valena's mountain range, affectionately known as Lucifer's Loop." The cadets' complaints rumbled through the plaza. Kilian held up his hand, and silence fell over the sour faces. "No wings allowed—walking only. And you'll find there's a reason the Azmar river is vast. It snows in the mountains most of the year. Pack warm, and enjoy your first visit to the Aerial training facility," Kilian said.

Dax threw up his hands and looked at Haven and Maddox standing in formation next to him. "Why don't we have training exercises in southern Phirot? I could use a nice seventy-mile beach hike with a beer in my hand."

Maddox clapped him on the back. "Come on, it builds character."

"I don't need any more character," Dax groused.

Haven appeared in the middle of a square surrounded on three sides by imposing red brick structures. Appearing in pairs around her, the squad dropped their heavily laden packs and quickly re-assembled in the square. She tensed as two males approached.

"Welcome to the Aerial." The peace Haven had found during the past three weeks fled like a coward in the night at the sight of Ryker prowling toward her.

"What are you doing here?" she blurted out. "Where's River?"

"He had other commitments this week," Ryker said. "Why does it matter?"

"It doesn't," Haven stammered.

Ryker said to the squad, "Check your packs carefully tonight. No weapons allowed, except a hunting knife, which we provide for you." More grumbling sounded through the crowd. "You will spend the night here. Your quarters are in the building on the east side, with pod assignments on the doors. Muster is just before dawn, starting with a pack check. Hike starts tomorrow at dawn. Early lights out tonight. We will need to average twenty miles a day."

The squad milled around Haven and rifled through their be-longings. A stack of weapons, mostly daggers and arrows, began piling up near Silas and Ryker as cadets repacked their belongings and trickled in pairs and small groups to the dorms. Haven watched Ryker, her thoughts stubbornly lingering on the kiss they'd shared. He glanced at her and caught her staring. Haven winced as he moved near.

"Can I help you, cadet?" he asked, looking down at her.

"I...no, I'm fine." She turned to gather her bag.

"Are you sure about that?"

"Yes, of course."

"Did you miss me?" he whispered, his silver eyes shimmering.

"No," she said quickly, lacing her arms through her pack and hitching it on her back.

Ryker grinned. "That sounds like a lie. Rest up, cadet."

Haven lay in her bunk that night, knowing she needed to sleep but unable to calm her mind. Ryker got under her skin like no male she'd ever met. He always managed to make her feel unbalanced. She traced her lips, remembering their kiss, frustrated by how quickly her mind scrambled and her emotions ran wild when he was near. She was drawn to him, almost hungry to be near him, a craving she had never felt with any male, not River, nor Lukas. Not even Larkin. Thinking honestly with herself, she realized she wanted to be closer to him. Much closer. She flushed at the thought of their bodies together, his lips on hers. Then she thought of her entanglement with Lukas. And even though she had no interest in River, she knew he wanted more, which made choosing Ryker complicated. Maybe that was why she pushed Ryker away. To admit she wanted to be with him would cause a cascade of hard conversations and disappointed people. And she wasn't sure what he felt for her, if the Ryker who kissed her was real. Gods, she could drive herself crazy thinking about this. Her other relationships hadn't been easy either, each in their own way. But Ryker brought a new set of challenges she was unsure how to overcome. She sighed and turned on her side and chased sleep in frustrating circles all night.

The first day hiking through the mountains was torture. The temperature neared freezing, and a strong wind blew in their faces all day. Even with the vigorous pace Kaden and Ryker set, an hour into the hike, Haven couldn't feel her hands and toes and was chilled to her core. Their pod collapsed at the first campsite an hour before sunset.

Ryker dumped his pack in the middle of the clearing. "Don't get comfortable and don't stop moving. You'll never get up again. Pair up. We need firewood and tents. Divide up the work and get it done. I want camp set before dark."

Haven hauled Quinn to her feet, looking at the fading sun inching below the mountain. "Come on, you and I are on firewood duty." Quinn grumped and shuffled toward the forest. They returned to the campsite later and dumped two armloads of wood near the pod's tents.

"Dax, light the wood," Maddox said. Soon they had a small fire crackling in the middle of their four tents. Maddox added wood to the kindling while Tristan blocked the wind. But despite the cheery, crackling fire, the mountain was frigid.

The shivering pod huddled next to one another as Ryker inspected their setup.

"It's a good start, but you can do more," he said. Haven sent a canopy of Light over the campfire. Heat undulated from the glow, and the team visibly relaxed. "Better. And food and water? Quinn, you pulled water from the wood to dry it. Why didn't you refill the canteens?"

She gave him a blank look. "Because the water was dirty?"

"Are you telling me you can now move wood with your magic?" he asked.

"Well, no."

"Earth?"

"No."

"So what makes you think the water would be dirty? It's water. Try it."

Quinn focused on the pile of kindling stacked beside their camp. A cloud of mist billowed from the wood, pooling into a water ball. Ryker scooped a handful and drank it. He motioned for Quinn to do the same. She brought a handful to her mouth. "Tastes like water."

"Imagine that." Ryker clapped her shoulder. "Now fill your canteen." Quinn frowned quizzically, then her face lit up and she shaped the water into a cone. She held her canteen underneath, and the water funneled inside. "Good," Ryker said. "Be practical, but also remember magic can't last forever. And you have limited food. If you aren't prepared to take care of your body, use your magic sparingly. You will need to pair up and keep each other warm."

At the beginning of the hike, Haven thought the main point of the exercise was to torture the cadets and freeze them to death. Now she understood the practical applications of their magic and what the instructors were trying to teach. They carried minimal rations, but if they could find additional food, they could use more magic to keep themselves protected and comfortable. But Haven was no hunter, and it was dark. Tonight they would do without, though she was determined to increase their food supply.

She paired up with Dax and slept sound and warm.

The next day was worse. They moved out before dawn, and the path ramped higher with rougher terrain. Their pace slowed, and they didn't reach the next campsite until well after dark. Haven illuminated her pod's area to set up camp, then followed Dune and Kit to search for firewood.

Picking up a soaked branch, she asked, "Do either of you know how to hunt?"

"No," Dune admitted. "But Tristan does. His family has a cabin in the mountains, and he's hunted for sport since he was a child."

When they returned to the campsite, Haven pulled Tristan aside. "Are you up for a little late-night hunting?"

"Unlikely we will find much in the dark, but I'm game to try."

"I can light the way. Come on," she said, tugging his hand.

They returned from their venture with three hares and four ptarmigans. The birds were delicious. The hares were tough and bland, but it was food. Haven felt full for the first time in two days. She watched Ryker from the other side of the campfire. He paused and smiled at her before walking to the next pod.

Haven lay on her back in the tent she shared with Maddox, unable to sleep. Exhaustion weighed on her, but she felt on edge, like too much energy was running through her veins. She slid from under Maddox's arm and pulled on her coat, then passed by the dead campfire and wound through the deserted site, her breath billowing clouds in the frigid mountain air. As she entered the forest, the peace of the trees finally quieted her mind. She breathed deeply, the scent of pine and loamy dirt easing the edginess she'd felt all day. For the first time since she opened her eyes before dawn this morning, she didn't have to think about her pod, the hike, or ways to keep from freezing to death. She could just be Haven. She tightened her woolen hood around her head, keeping the frigid night from biting her ears, and stuffed her hands deep in the warm, lined pockets of her jacket.

"You should be asleep," a voice said from behind her. Haven squeaked in surprise and jumped back against a tree. Ryker's silver eyes flashed in the dark, the light from the last campfire illuminating parts of his face and shadowing others.

"Gods, you scared me," she whispered. "I know, but I can't sleep. I thought I'd go for a walk."

"Walking helps me sleep at night too. It's peaceful." Ryker moved closer to her. "Walk with me?"

"Sure." He led her through the trees, helping her step over a fallen log and holding back a branch. They found a worn path deeper inside the forest. Haven stubbed her toe on an unseen rock, and he held her arm to prevent a fall.

Ryker said, "So what do you think of the hike so far?"

"Joyous. Much better than spending a week at the beach." She pulled her coat tighter against her.

"I hate this hike," he said. "I hated it when I did it at the Academy and the handful of times I've done it since then. It's miserable."

"Why are you here? I thought they assigned River."

"I took his rotation so he could take Shallah to Damaris."

"That was nice of you."

"I'm not a complete asshole all the time."

She nudged him with her elbow. "You're not even an asshole half the time. But when you are, it's so spectacular it makes us forget all the times you're decent."

He choked on a laugh. "You know, you may be right."

"Gods, mark the day and time. He said I was right."

"Don't get used to it. I'll likely not make that mistake again," he said. They came to a break in the trees and entered a small clearing.

"Look," Ryker said, pointing up at the sky. Haven's gaze followed his gesture to the two moons of Praesia. The smaller one glowed a soft orange and the larger one a bright gray, their edges almost touching.

"That's called the Lover's Reunion," he said.

"It's beautiful." She looked at Ryker, at the smile that played across his lips. Subtle shadows softened his chiseled features, the moonlight enhancing his cheekbones and the two days of stubble darkening his chin and jawline. He turned that smile to her, and Haven's heart stumbled. Her eyes fell to the path where it entered the trees across the clearing.

"Are you cold?" he asked.

"Of course. I've been cold for two solid days," she grumbled. Ryker chuckled, and she glanced at him again. His hand found her waist, a brief touch to guide her back to the trees.

"Let's keep moving then," he said.

They continued walking in silence. She could feel his eyes on her, but she avoided him and kept hers on the ground. His fingers trailed on her hand, two of his lacing through hers, and she looked down at his tentative touch, then at his warm eyes. Her stomach tingled, and she laced her hand into his and squeezed. He squeezed her hand in return. They walked the perimeter of the camp in silence, circling back to her pod's tents. Haven's hand in his felt like fire, making the smallest point of contact her world. She tried to tear her mind from his skin on hers and focused on the surrounding trees, the smell of the pines, the frosty, rich fragrance of the earth under her feet. And a subtle hint of...cinnamon and cloves, with a warm undertone, like wood burning in a fire. A scent misplaced in the forest.

Ryker led her to the edge of the tree line, just behind her pod's tents. Haven lingered in the dark, not ready to leave him.

"You really should try to sleep. Tomorrow is the worst day," Ryker said, still holding her hand.

"How much worse can this get?"

"It's awful. We'll be at the highest altitude tomorrow. It is a steep twelve-mile climb. Half the times I've done this hike, it snowed."

"It's fucking *May*. We should be in shorts and t-shirts."

Ryker huffed. "Tell that to the mountain. It's always winter here. Wait until you're deep into year two of the Aerial service. You'll think you'll never be warm again."

Haven groaned. "Sounds amazing." She reluctantly lessened the grip on his hand. He tightened his fingers, then let her slide her hand out of his. He stood near her, then reached up and pulled a lock of her hair through his fingers, tucking it back into the hood of her jacket.

"You're a natural for this kind of work. You're an asset to your pod."

"I'm no camper."

"Think of it as survival training. And you certainly are good at surviving."

"That sounds suspiciously like another compliment."

"Possibly." His quiet laugh reached his silver eyes. Haven's heart tightened, and she reached for him, her fingers brushing his lips, tracing the line of his jaw, then trailing down his neck. She pulled her hand back at the look of surprise on his face.

"Sorry. I..." she stammered, retreating from him. "Good night, and thank you for walking with me." She turned to her tent, but Ryker's arms slipped around her and pulled her back. She tensed at the unexpected feel of him, then relaxed and leaned into his hard body, her head resting on his chest. He pulled her hood back and dipped his head. She felt his lips travel slowly up her neck, below her ear. Her body tightened low in her stomach. He turned her slowly in his arms, his head staying low in her collar.

"I want to kiss you," he whispered, his breath a warm caress on her skin. "I shouldn't, but I want to." A small whimper escaped her as his lips grazed hers. "Badly."

"Yes. Badly." His mouth found hers, and she stepped into him. He wrapped his arms around her, one hand low on her hip and the other hand twining through her hair. His lips moved softly on hers, exploring. Haven slipped her hands inside his jacket, feeling the warmth of him, his muscled back flexing under her touch. Ryker deepened the kiss, his tongue tracing her lips. She opened to him, and his tongue flicked inside her mouth, teasing her tongue, tasting her, hinting at what he could do with that tongue. Haven moaned and laced her hand through his hair. His kiss hardened, more insistent. Haven responded with the same intensity, her hips pressing into him. He pulled her to him, and Haven felt a rumbling growl vibrate his body.

He eased the tension of their kiss, pulling at her bottom lip with his. His forehead rested against hers, his chest touching her with every uneven breath.

"I don't understand this," she rasped. "What does this mean?"

"There's no simple answer to that." Frustration touched his voice. "What if I told you I wanted more?"

"More? How much more?"

He slowly backed away from her. "I want it all. Everything."

"Everything?" she whispered, the word catching in her throat.

She saw the tension in his eyes, half hidden by the shadows of the trees, and the tight smile on his face. "Good night, and get some sleep." He turned and walked away. Haven stared at the empty forest where he'd been only a moment before, touching her tingling lips, real evidence to her numb mind that he'd kissed her and she hadn't imagined it.

She picked her way through the campsite back to her tent and shed her jacket, warming the tent with a soft glow of Light as the tip of her nose defrosted. She slipped under the blankets and lay next to Maddox, her mind stubbornly clinging to Ryker's words. Everything. *Everything?* That was a big word, and a very messy one. But she couldn't deny how that one word made her heart race and ache for something she wanted too. What seemed improbable only an hour ago now had a glimmer of possibility.

She felt farther from sleep than she had before the walk.

Ryker was right, the next day was hell. The path through the summit narrowed and grew treacherous, almost vanishing completely. The temperature plummeted, and snowflakes carried by the gusting wind pricked their faces. Despite the physical activity of the hike and her layers of clothing and heavy parka, Haven shivered all morning.

"Don't get comfortable," Ryker warned when they stopped briefly at midday for a quick meal of hardtack and water. "We need to keep moving and pass the summit in the next hour." He looked doubtfully at the sky. "The weather is getting worse. We may need to find real shelter for the night."

"I remember a series of caves on the other side of the summit," Silas said. "It's off the path, but they are extensive and will hold everyone."

"Let's make the call in an hour," Kaden said. "I know those caves. But if we stop there, the hike the next day will be grueling. Twenty-five miles at least."

"Twenty-five miles?" Haven blurted, glancing at Dax in alarm.

Ryker nodded. "Brutal, but doable." He scanned the ominous black clouds gathering in the sky. "The weather may hold," he said with no genuine conviction. "Let's get moving."

Dax pulled Haven to her feet, and the squad rallied and pushed over the summit during the next hour. Haven lingered at the top, momentarily captivated by the stark, eerie scenery. The lifeless terrain was still except for a few pelting snowflakes, completely devoid of even the scrubbiest trees, with boulders and rocks the only markers along their barren path. It was beautiful, in an inhospitable and frigid way. For a moment, she let herself enjoy the thrill of making it to the peak. Ryker walked by her and said in a clipped voice, "No sightseeing. Keep moving, cadet." She trudged a little faster in the blistering wind to catch up with her pod.

A mile past the summit, the sky fell on them. The weather changed in minutes, blanketing the squad in a dark cloud. Snow whipped around them, and the treacherous path vanished under Haven's feet. Visibility shrank to the body trudging in front of her, and she could hear Shane and Silas urging them on from in front and behind.

"Hold my hand," she said ahead to Dax and to Dune behind her. Linked together, they fought their way through the rocky terrain in the bitter, blinding cold until a wall of stone suddenly appeared. Shane and Ryker guided the squad through a narrow opening and into an expansive cavern, the squad's shuffling and soft voices echoing around her. Shaking hard enough to rattle her bones, Haven illuminated the space over her pod with a gentle heat that warmed them.

"Don't do that for long," Ryker said, passing behind her. "Conserve your energy." Haven nodded, but kept her Light over her team, a brief blanket of reprieve from the elements. She raked her hands through the Light, the warmth bringing a painful tingle to her frozen fingers.

"Where's Harper?" Dax asked, looking around the cave.

"She was just behind me," Kit said anxiously. He hurried to the entrance, searching the faces in the crowd as the last of the squad filed in.

Haven found Ryker and said, "Harper is missing."

"Stay here." Ryker walked into the blizzard and returned a few minutes later. "She's not out there."

"How do you know?" Kit said, his voice strained.

Dark gray smoke trickled from Ryker's hands. "I can't feel her." He said to Silas, "I'm going back out."

"I'll come with you." Silas pulled on his wet jacket.

"No, stay here and help the squad. I'll take Haven and Dax."

"Fine, but be careful," Silas said.

Kit stepped forward. "I'm coming too."

"No, you're not. Haven can light the way and Dax can help heat us if we need it. I can't look after you too," Ryker said. Kit opened his mouth to protest but Ryker shut him down with a look. "It's not up for debate. You're staying." He held Kit's shoulder. "I'll find her." Kit swallowed, then reluctantly agreed. "Grab your packs," Ryker said to Haven and Dax, and they left the protection of the cave and headed into the howling blizzard.

They combed the area the best they could in the blinding snow, Ryker's magic snaking away from him, probing for anything alive. After backtracking along the path for half a mile, Ryker stopped. "I can feel something. Haven, light the area there." He pointed to a small drop off the path. Haven emitted a wave of Light, the heat melting the swirling snow. They found Harper lying on her stomach between two towering boulders. Ryker knelt next to her and rolled her over.

"She's cold but breathing." He smoothed her black hair from her face. "Nice bump on the head."

Dax picked her up. "I have her. Lead the way."

Ryker turned to the path, but it had vanished in the swirling snow. He swore in frustration. "We need to get her out of this weather. Now." Ryker held Haven's hand, and she held Dax's jacket. They trudged through the snow to the wall of stone, and Haven lit the wall as Ryker dragged his hand along the rock face, searching with both sight and touch for any gap. He halted abruptly. "In here." He led them through a small opening. Dax turned sideways to pass Harper through and followed the ball of Light Haven projected in front of them.

Ryker shook the snow off his soaked black hair. "Put her here." He cleared small rocks from a flat, sheltered alcove away from the mouth of the cave. Haven lifted the Light above their heads to the center, illuminating the entire space. It wasn't a large cave, thirty feet long by twenty feet wide, and barely high enough for Ryker and Dax to stand up.

Kneeling beside Harper, Ryker felt her pulse and forehead. "She feels okay. Maybe a little cold." He sat back on his heels. "I think she's okay," he said, breathing a sigh of relief.

"She'll be fine," Haven said. Ryker nodded, then removed Harper's pack and pulled out her blanket. He gently placed the pack under her head and covered her, then rose and walked to the mouth of the cave. "Change your wet clothes. I'll see if I can find anything we can burn. Haven, see if you can warm her up a little and bring her around."

Haven and Dax unslung their bags. She dug through her pack for clothes, changed, and draped her soaked shirt over her pack to dry. Haven took her blanket from her bedroll and slung it around her shoulders. She huddled next to Harper and saw her shivering under her blanket. She projected a haze of Light over them that emitted a comforting warmth.

"More heat." Dax trailed his frozen fingers through the glowing Light. Haven slowly raised the temperature. Her brow furrowed in concentration, careful not to turn the cave into an oven. "That feels fantastic."

Haven could feel an ache radiating from her spine through her back, and the beginning of a headache. The conditions of the hike and her Light usage over the past two days were finally catching up to her as she felt the bottom of her magic reserves.

"I don't know how much longer I can do this," she said.

"Just focus on Harper, then."

Haven's Light contracted, and a small canopy covered Harper. The color on her face looked pinker, her lips less blue.

"Harper," Haven said, stroking her black hair away from her face. She said her name again and gently shook her. Harper moaned, her hand rubbing her head. "Can you hear me?"

"Yes," Harper said. "Where are we?"

"We're in a cave. We lost you in the blizzard. Can you tell me what happened?"

"I tripped and hit my head. I think. That's the last thing I remember." Harper sat up slowly, rubbing the large bump on her forehead. "Ouch."

"You should see it," Dax said. "Big. And purple."

"Great," Harper said.

Ryker returned with an armload of wood. He dropped it and knelt beside Harper. "How do you feel?" he said, his fingers tracing the purple bump on her head.

"I'm okay. It hurts and my head is throbbing, but I'm fine."

"Good. Because I have a job for you." He pointed at the woodpile. "It's wet. If you dry it out, we can have a fire. And dinner." He held up three rabbits.

Dax's eyes lit up. "Excellent. I'll take care of them." He took the rabbits from Ryker, unsheathed his knife, and walked outside the cave.

Haven and Ryker cleared a space at the front of the cave for the fire. Harper focused on the pile of wood Ryker had dropped, pulling the water from the logs and small branches. She straightened and took a step back, panting.

"Do you have the energy to dry me out?" Ryker asked, pulling his soaked shirt away from his body. "I can change if you're out."

"I'm okay," Harper said.

"Thanks," he said. "Food will help all of us. Hang in there."

A small ball of water hovered in front of him, growing larger as his clothes dried. Dax returned, and an hour later they sat in front of a cheery, warm fire, eating a hot meal of roasted rabbit. Haven wiped her hands and face with her still-damp shirt drying on her pack next to her.

She asked Harper, "How do you feel?"

"Much better." She'd regained her normal coloring, except for the large, purpling bump on her forehead.

"Good. In that case, can you get water from outside and bring it in here?" Harper focused, and a cloud of fog drifted to hover near Haven. It swirled together and became a slowly growing pool of water. When the ball of water was a foot in diameter, Haven said, "That's good. Hold it there." Light glowed within the water, and steam wafted from the ball. Haven stripped off her shirt and splashed the heated water on her face, hair, and upper body.

"My turn next," Harper said. A stream of mist from the front of the cave joined the ball. Haven used her shirt to dry herself off, then pulled it over her head.

"Harper, could you take the water from my hair and bra?" Harper concentrated, and a soft mist enveloped Haven, then gathered in a small ball of water in the air, leaving her hair and clothes dry and clean.

"Hey, a little heat would be nice." Harper pointed at the large ball of water hovering between them. The meal, as meager as it was, eased the strain on Haven's magic, but as she illuminated the ball of water, she still felt an ache in her temples. Harper and Dax both stripped and washed. Ryker joined them, removing his shirt and splashing the hot water on his torso.

Haven released the Light from the water and rubbed her head.

"Are you okay?" Ryker asked.

She nodded. "A headache."

"Then that's enough from you," he said. He cupped his hand and flicked water in Harper's face. She flinched away from the splash and glared at him. The ball of water flew to Ryker's head and dropped. Haven and Dax laughed as Ryker spluttered and wiped his face. He shot a gray mist of magic and pinned Harper to the ground and wrung his shirt over her head. She squealed, collected the water, and shot it back at him. He shielded the spray with a flat gray cloud, bouncing it back to her. Haven and Dax egged Harper on, roaring at the sibling squabble.

Ryker pecked Harper's cheek. "Okay, enough for tonight. Save your energy and magic." He unpacked his bedroll and laid it on the ground against the wall. "We don't have enough wood to keep the fire going all night. Pair up, it will get cold." Water trickled down Ryker's back from his wet hair and beaded on his bare chest. Haven got hung up on his defined, muscular arms as he dug through his pack for a dry shirt. When Harper set her bedroll next to Dax, Haven realized that meant she was paired with Ryker. She bit her lip, desperate for another option. Being that close to him was...disturbing.

"Wait, I can share with Dax," she offered. "You share with Ryker. He's your brother."

Harper shook her head. "Forget it. I've had enough of him for one day. I get Dax." Dax and Harper unpacked their bedrolls and arranged them together on the opposite side of the dying fire.

"I save your ass and all I get is sass," Ryker said. Harper gave him a dirty look and stuck out her tongue. Ryker laughed as Harper flopped on her bedroll and flung her blanket over her.

Haven forgot herself, distracted by the coiling muscles in Ryker's back and taut stomach as he pulled on his shirt. He ran a hand through his damp hair and caught her watching him. She flushed and looked away, fighting the ridiculous urge to feel those muscles moving under her fingers. She folded her arms tightly across her body, trapping her traitorous hands that had unruly thoughts of their own.

Dax watched Haven squirm, then patted the ground next to him. "Looks like it's you and me," he said to Harper. Haven gave him a pleading look, and Dax winked back.

She could already feel the chill coming in from the mouth of the cave. "Can't you get more firewood?"

"No, unless we tend to it, a fire won't last," Ryker said. "And you can't heat the cave all night."

Haven gave up and arranged her bedroll several feet away from him.

Ryker frowned. "What are you doing? You need to be close to share body heat." He reached for her bedroll and pulled it close to his.

"I'm not sleeping with you."

He grinned at her. "Now wouldn't that be fun. But unfortunately, we would have an audience tonight."

"That's not what I meant. You know what I meant," she said, flustered.

"Don't worry, you're safe with me." His eyes glittered as he patted the ground. She sighed and lay on the bedroll, her back to him. He leaned close to her and whispered, "Unless you don't want to be." She threw an elbow into his side. He grunted, then rested his head on his pack. "You have no sense of humor," he said.

"I didn't hear anything funny."

"Humorless and cruel," he teased.

"Gods, just be quiet," Haven grumbled. She could hear Ryker's quiet laughter behind her.

The flames of the fire dwindled to barely glowing embers. Dax and Harper's whispers quieted, then their breathing evened out to soft, rhythmic snoring. She could barely see the outline of their bodies, a shapeless mound of blankets in the darkness. Her thin blanket did little against the blustering wind slipping into the cave. She shook as the last flames of the fire flickered out.

"You're shivering," Ryker whispered.

"I'm okay." Haven tensed as she felt Ryker move closer to her. "What are you doing?"

"I'm cold. And if you don't keep me warm, I'm moving next to Harper and Dax and you'll freeze by morning." Ryker doubled their blankets over them both, his front cradling her back. He draped his arm across her waist and rested his chin on her head. "No joking. I said you were safe with me. I mean that."

Haven had to admit she was warmer. She relaxed and moved back into his body. He slid a leg between hers, pulling her closer to him, and she felt his chest touch her shoulders with each breath he took. A soft rustle sounded, and Ryker's raven wing draped over her. She closed her eyes, but sleep drifted farther from her at the feel of him behind her and the warmth radiating from him, his broad chest, his hips against her backside, his hard thigh between hers. Her pulse throbbed, and her heart skipped painfully. What she feared, what she knew she would feel when he was this close to her, burned her cheeks. She fought the blooming ache inside her, the need to touch him, knowing a single touch was a danger to her heart.

And then her better judgement fled like a coward in the night. Her fingers trailed down his arm, sneaking a tiny feel of his bare skin. He lowered his head, resting his lips against her hair and caught her fingers as she pulled them away. He tucked her hand in his, possessively holding a small piece of her. Her stupid heart leapt in her chest and neared the edge of an abyss that was him. She wiggled away, desperate for space to gather herself, to escape the fall that terrified her.

Ryker's hand flattened against her stomach. "I'd stop moving like that if I were you." She froze, and he gently pressed her into him. She felt him hard and thick against her backside. Haven knew from the countless times she had slept next to her male podmates over the last three years that biology affected them all at some point. She had learned to ignore it, but this reaction from Ryker was different. The surrounding air grew heavier and hard to breathe as his hand pulled her harder into him, and the same misplaced hint of warm cinnamon and rich cloves from their walk in the forest seduced her senses. Ryker's lips grazed her neck below her ear.

"Or you could keep moving. I like it, obviously. And I think you do too," he whispered. Haven fixated on his hand covering hers. The kiss they shared last month and again last night played through her mind. The phantom memory tingled across her lips, his kiss hungry, but with a gentleness that had surprised her. His words last night tumbled through her mind. *I want it all. Everything.* The tautness grew stronger, an aching heat pooling between her thighs. Haven knew it would be safer to push him away, to do what was expected, what everyone else wanted from her. But that wasn't what she wanted.

"Haven," Ryker whispered. At that moment, the only thing that mattered was what she felt for Ryker. And she wanted him. She wanted everything from him. She wouldn't deny any longer what her heart told her to reach for and take for herself. With the sound of her name still on his lips, Haven stared into the abyss and jumped.

She rolled her hips into him. Ryker's hand on her stomach clenched, and she moved her hips harder, grinding into him. Ryker gasped into her hair. His hand slowly stroked up her stomach, his thumb tracing the heavy curve of her breast. Her hand found his and he froze, then pulled away. She turned her head to him and raised his hand to cup her breast. He studied her face as his thumb grazed her nipple through her thin t-shirt. Haven closed her eyes and arched into his touch, focusing on the aching, tingling sensation skittering around her stomach, and the pressure building between her thighs. Ryker's lips touched hers lightly, softly.

"Kiss me the way you did before," she said. He lowered his head and did as she asked. There was nothing tentative about this kiss. Ryker took what he wanted from her mouth, his thumb brushing her nipple again. His hand stroked down her stomach and found the gap in her shirt and pants, his fingertips sliding just below the waistband of her breeches, stroking her bare skin, the softest, smallest of touches. Haven shuddered at the feel of his skin on hers.

"I want to touch you," he said, his voice tight. "But I won't unless you want this too. So, tell me what you want from me."

"I want this." Her hand covered his and moved it lower between her legs. "What's happening between us, I want it to be real."

His fingers pressed into her center through her breeches. Haven closed her eyes, her body aching for his touch. "What's about to happen between us right now won't be nearly enough for me. But it's all I can give you with an audience," Ryker said. "And it's real. It's always been real. But if I touch you, I want you to be sure."

"I'm sure," she said, slipping her hand between them, feeling the hard outline of him through his breeches. Dim moonlight from the mouth of the cave threw dark shadows over his face. She could see his jaw feather at the pressure of her fingers on him. His mouth crushed hers, and her body felt electric, the friction against his thigh wedged between her legs making her ache for more. She slid her fingers beneath the waistband of his breeches, feeling the blazing heat of his soft skin. He pinned her hand between them with the weight of his body, and his lips traveled over her neck, pulling at her pounding pulse as his tongue traced the groove of her neck to her shoulder. He cupped her through her breeches, his fingers sliding along the seams, down the middle of her. She felt his body rumble with a low growl as she writhed in his hand.

"Let me touch you," she said into his lips, trying to free her hand.

"Not tonight. The first time you touch me, I want it to be just you and me." He kissed her forehead, her cheek, and found her lips again. "Just relax." Ryker slowly unbuttoned her breeches, pulled the cloth down, and slid his hand lower. Cupping her, he dragged his finger through the middle of her, from her drenched center up to her bundle of nerves, and lingered there, circling and stroking her. Haven's head fell back, and a quiet moan escaped.

"You like that?" Ryker whispered into her hair. His finger stroked her entrance, the tip of his finger pressing into her. Haven held his arm, pulling at him, the world around her fading to nothing but his touch.

"Gods, yes. More," she whimpered, her knees falling apart, her hips arching into his hand. He kissed her and sunk deep into her, swearing softly.

"You are beautiful, Haven. You're perfect," he said into her kiss. His finger moved inside her in rhythm with her writhing hips while his thumb rolled over her ridge, pressing into her as deep waves of pleasure rippled through her body. Haven's breath quickened and grew shallow, the tension in her body building with every stroke. She buried her head in his shoulder, her hand grasping his hip. "Look at me," he whispered. Her gaze held his silver eyes. "I want to watch you when I make you come."

Haven flushed, her hips rocking on his hand. Her head fell back, and she gripped his shirt. Ryker slipped a second finger inside her, and she tightened around him.

"Ryker," she said, her voice tensing with her body. He covered her mouth in a kiss, swallowing the gasp as her climax broke. She shuddered, and Ryker slowly stroked her through the pulsing waves. When she finally relaxed, he drew her limp body into him, resting his head on hers and pulling her leg to his hip. His racing heart thundered on her cheek pressed to his chest. She ran her hands up his back, then trailed her fingers along the underside of his wing that was still draped over them. Ryker jerked and pinned her with his hips, his hardness pressing into her softest part. He muffled a groan into her shoulder and retracted his wings.

"Fuck, Haven," he said, his voice quavering.

"I remember your lessons well." She kissed his neck slowly. "That's for not letting me touch you."

"You almost didn't need to," he said.

"You're right, it's not enough for me either," she said, squirming under his grip, trying to move against him. "I want to feel you."

He pulled his hips back, trying to catch his breath. "Trust me, I want more too." They held each other tight, feeling the unfamiliar thrill of their bodies tangled together. Haven touched his cheek, her fingers tracing his lips.

"Ryker, what is this to you?" He tipped her chin up and looked into her eyes.

"What do you want?" he asked.

"I want..." Her voice trailed off. He waited for her to find the words she needed to say. "You said you wanted it all. That you wanted everything. What does that mean?"

He kissed her forehead, his lips brushing her skin. "It means I want this. I want to keep you for myself. I don't want to hide how I feel about you. I want to be your friend and your lover. And everything in between." She pressed her face into his chest, drinking in the hint of heavy winter spices. There was a warmth to it, like embers from a fire. *His* scent. Rich, lush, and heady. He tucked her head under his chin and pulled the blanket over her. "I know that's a lot to ask, to choose me. If you're not ready to think of me that way, I understand."

"I already think of you way too much." He smiled broadly and kissed her lips. "I made a choice a while ago," she said. "I think I'm only realizing it now. Saying it out loud, though. My life is...messy." She wrapped her arms tightly around him.

"Nothing worth having is ever easy. But for now, sleep. We still have work to do tomorrow."

"Just please tell me I'll wake up and this will be real. That we won't go backwards. I don't want to hide or pretend I don't have feelings for you."

"I don't either. I told you it was real, and I meant that. But I'm also your instructor, at least through the end of the week. I will need to be that person too. We'll figure this out." He stroked her back until they both slept.

Haven woke the next morning wrapped in Ryker's arms. She never wanted to leave this moment. She slowly kissed his neck, sinking into the warmth of his body, drinking in his fresh ocean and pine scent. She opened her eyes and found Ryker looking at her.

"Hi there. Ready to return to instructor and student?" Haven gave him a nervous nod. "And yes, it's still real." He rested his lips on her forehead. She could hear Harper and Dax waking and untangling themselves. Ryker pulled her tight to him, brushed her lips with his, then let her go.

Dax yawned, his breath fogging in front of him. "Looks like the blizzard is over. I can't wait to slog through the snow." He eyed the high snowdrifts spilling into the cave and partially blocking the entrance. "Brrr..."

Haven focused, and the roof of the cave illuminated, a soft heat rolling down to them. "Ahhh," Harper said. "That's nice."

"Pack your things. We need to catch up," Ryker said. They hurried through a meager breakfast and left the cave. The crisp, crystal-clear sky almost hurt her eyes.

They slogged through the drifting snow and caught up as the squad was moving out of the larger cave only a quarter mile from where they'd spent the night. Kit hung back and swept Harper into his arms. "Thank the gods, I was worried sick."

"I told you I'd find her," Ryker said. "Did you doubt me?"

"No, not really," Kit said, keeping Harper pressed to his side. "But my mind went to a dark place."

Harper rubbed the knot on her forehead. "I'm fine. Bump on my head still throbs, but I'm good."

"Fall in. We have a long hike today and some distance to make up," Ryker said.

They caught up to their pod, and Ryker found Silas.

"You're good?" Silas said.

"Yes, I'm fine," Ryker said, watching Haven out of the corner of his eye.

"I think you had an interesting night," Silas said. Ryker avoided him and slung his pack over his shoulder. "This will get complicated. I don't want you telling River without me there, you hear me?"

"River? There isn't anything between them."

"That's what she says. I'm not sure he feels the same way. I've seen him around her."

Ryker sighed. "He won't do anything. He can try, but I can handle him. I always have."

"You're not listening," Silas's voice was quiet so only he could hear. "This isn't a negotiation. You don't talk to him without me there. You know River's temper, particularly if he feels something is being taken from him."

"Fine, if you insist," he said dryly.

Light in the Shadows

"I do." Silas gripped his arm. "I'm happy for you."

Ryker's gaze followed Haven as she walked ahead with her pod. "We aren't there yet. You're right, this is complicated. But it's worth it."

"Should be really fun telling Lukas. And his parents. And her parents. Oh, and let's not forget the king," Silas said, grinning.

"Very funny," he said, and gave him a dirty look.

Silas clapped him on the back. "You're making my job interesting, at least."

The hike down the mountain was long, cold, wet, and exhausting. The squad arrived at the Aerial a few hours after dark. They formed up in the square, half of them barely standing.

"Congratulations on completing the Loop," Kilian said. "Dinner is available at the dining common for the next two hours. Tomorrow morning, we will return to the Academy. Dismissed."

Ryker found Harper and took her arm. "Come with me. You need to see a healer."

"Before a shower? And dinner? I'm fine," she complained, but let him drag her along.

"Healer first. Now."

# Chapter 30

## Cantos

Ryker walked Harper back to the barracks, the bump on her head mended. "I'm sure your pod is dying to eat. Walk you to the dining common?"

"I'd give anything for a shower first, but yes. No need to keep everyone waiting," she said. They crossed the square and entered the hall. Harper sat with her pod, and plates of roasted chicken, rare grilled lamb, and steaming potatoes and vegetables appeared on the table. "Okay, maybe eating first wasn't such a bad idea." She reached for the warm bread. "I'm starving."

Ryker kissed her head. "Enjoy yourself."

She held his hand that rested on her shoulder. "Do you want to join us?"

"Thanks, but I need to speak with Silas. I'll check in with you later tonight." He ruffled her hair, and she swatted his hand away.

Ryker watched Haven, and she glanced at him, then dropped her eyes to her plate. She looked at him again from under her dark lashes, and his heart leapt as thoughts of what they shared last night flashed through his mind. Her kiss, the feel of her soft skin, the sounds she made when he touched her. He gave her a slow smile. Haven bit her lip, but he saw her mouth twitch up at the corner as she piled food on her plate.

Ryker sat next to Silas at the instructors' table with Kaden and Shane. "Have you heard from Trinity?" He reached for a plate and helped himself to the hot food in the center of the table.

Silas said, "Yes. We need to leave early tomorrow morning. We have a crossing in two days. She's already done the legwork, but we need to catch up."

Ryker groaned. "We had one a month ago. And does the Council know we hiked the Loop? Can't Lukas or Finnian do it?"

"I doubt they care what we are doing in our free time," Silas said sarcastically. "Finnian can't, and it's a hunt, so Lukas is out. The future of the world rests on your shoulders."

"Smartass." He took the bread Silas handed him. "You up for skimming us?"

"Yes, after this dinner and a good night's sleep, I'll be fine." He glanced at Haven across the room. "Have you talked to her since last night?"

Ryker focused on the roasted lamb on his plate. "No, not really. There's a lot to work through. I don't even know what she really wants."

"Don't be dense. Or stupid. If you piss this away, I'm going to have to kick your ass," he said in between bites.

Ryker laughed. "I'll let you know if I need a good ass kicking."

"Oh, I'll let you know well before you know." Silas nudged him. "Don't be a dick. Go talk with her."

"I will. I needed to take care of Harper. And eat. Gods, I'm starving."

"Don't come up with more excuses."

"I got it, mother." They finished dinner and Ryker returned to his apartment to take a long, hot shower and change his clothes. He threw on a jacket and crossed the courtyard to the cadet barracks, making the rounds with each pod to ensure they were settled and recovering from the hike. Most of the cadets were already snoring in their bunks. Ryker fought his own fatigue as he visited Haven's pod last. He spoke with Harper and checked on her head one last time. The healer's work was superb. Nothing remained but a faint greenish tint on her forehead.

As he readied to leave, he said to Haven, "Cadet, Shane asked to see you."

"Can't it wait? What did I do?" Haven complained.

"How the hell would I know?" He said good night to the pod as Haven sulked, threw back the blankets, and reached for her breeches.

Ryker waited deep in the shadows of an alcove until she crossed the square toward him. She passed by, and he pulled her from behind into the pitch black of a recessed doorway.

She immediately struggled against him. "Shhh...It's me," he said, turning her around.

"You bastard, you scared the shit out of me," she said, swatting his arm.

"Sorry. I've wanted to see you all day." Ryker wrapped his arms around her and buried his face in her neck, losing himself in her fresh jasmine scent. She lifted his head and kissed him hard, pushing him deeper into the darkness, against the wall. He lifted her up and pulled her legs to his waist, then turned around and pinned her to the wall, grinding his hips into her.

"You can't stay long," Ryker said, breaking their kiss.

"I thought you said we weren't hiding."

"Not here. Not while you're still a student." He kissed her slower this time, playing over her soft lips, tasting her, sweet and warm.

"I'm starting to think I'll never have a relationship out in the open," she grumbled. She kissed him again, running her hands through his hair.

"I don't like it either, but you won't be a cadet for long. A few more weeks. Sorry, my rules." He cupped the curve of her backside, and she tightened her legs around him. Ryker reeled from the pressure, his imagination racing to what was separated by only the thin cloth of their breeches. They both groaned together.

"I hate your rules," she said, pressing into him. He swore and pushed her harder against the wall. "But I don't want our first time together to be against a wall in the freezing cold."

"I hate your rules," he said. She giggled, and he rested his forehead against hers. "I'm leaving first thing in the morning."

Haven's face fell. "Where are you going?"

"Araine. I have a crossing in a few days and will need to recover for a week or two after that. I didn't want you to think I was slipping away and vanishing on you."

"When will I see you again?"

"You want to see me?" He ran his fingers through her hair, his lips brushing hers.

"What do you think?"

"I don't want to assume. What happened in the cave was, well, a unique situation. It doesn't have to happen again, if that's not what you want."

She touched his face, tracing the curve of his lips. "What happened there was my choice, and I want more." Her kiss was soft, her tongue tracing his lips. She slid her hand down and cupped him through his breeches, slowly stroking him, her thumb pressing into his tip. His kiss deepened, the hunger for her slipping free, and his heart raced at the thought that she wanted him as much as he needed her, needed every moment together, every new touch and smile. Her kiss. The taste of her skin, the sound of her laugh. With each new detail, he felt her hold his heart a little tighter. He slid his hand under her jacket, his fingertips finding a gap in the layers of clothing to the warmth of her bare skin. She flinched away from his touch and smiled into his lips.

"Your hand is freezing," she said. He wormed his hand farther inside her clothing.

"You're warm," he whispered, his kisses trailing down her jaw to her neck. His fingers slid inside the waistband of her breeches.

She gripped him through his jeans, her thumb stroking him. "I want to feel you," she breathed.

His hand dropped from her waist to hold her wrist. For one last moment, he thought of the intimacy he craved. Not just the physical, but those parts of her heart he imagined and hoped she would share with him. But tonight was impossible.

He pressed into her touch, then removed her hand. "No more," he said, his voice desperate. "Or our first time will be right now. I don't give a shit how cold it is." She laughed, then kissed him slowly until both of their bodies relaxed.

"For real, when do I get to see you again?"

"After your graduation. Will you come to Araine?"

"Yes, for the Graduation Festival, before ComSim. But that's two weeks away," she said.

"I'm glad you can count, cadet."

"Smartass." He laughed softly and found her lips, his tongue tasting her, sending his thoughts spinning into inappropriate places again. "Gods, that seems like years from now," she mumbled into his kiss.

"I know. Let me know when you arrive in Araine." He kissed her again, then slowly dropped her legs to the ground. "You should go back to your pod." She stepped away, and his fingers tightened on her hand, holding on to her a few seconds longer. "Don't forget this is real."

"Don't forget me."

He pulled her in and kissed her one last time. "Not a chance," he whispered, resting his forehead on hers and stroking her lower lip with his thumb. She backed away once more, and his fingertips reluctantly let her go. He waited in the shadows, listening to the sound of her footsteps fade away, and already felt a space in his heart where she should be. Where she fit perfectly. If she wanted it.

The next two weeks were a blur of lessons, exams, and wrapping up three years of living at the Academy. On her last day, Haven's squad gathered in formation in the Yard. She found comfort in the familiar faces around her, the routine of the assembly and the Academy that had been her home. It felt like yesterday that she'd arrived in Portos, almost vomiting from the warding.

"Last day," she said to Kit and Harper. Kit did a small fist pump. Although their time together at the Academy was ending, most of their pod was joining the Aerial for the two-year rotation. Haven was even looking forward to seeing Larkin and Avina later in the month for ComSim.

Kilian paced in front of the unit. "You started here three years ago, when there were close to a thousand of you. There are less than seven hundred of you assembled today. You should be proud of this accomplishment. For those of you joining the Aerial in the fall, you will build on what you learned here at the Academy. Enjoy your summer off. We always welcome our graduates back to the Academy. We will contact you throughout your lives to ask you to give back to new students. Each seraphim is unique, and your gifts and experiences are vital to the next class coming through. Don't forget us here. It was an honor to have you. You are dismissed."

The unit exploded in a collective whoop and fell into chaos. Haven hugged the forty cadets left in her squad. They planned to skim to Araine that night for a celebration with her fellow graduates, who were all being housed in the Academy apartments in Falco Park for the summer.

Haven's pod returned to their quarters, where she packed her belongings. She brushed her hand across her now empty bunk. Memories of her years at the Academy flooded her thoughts, and she could barely recognize the scared, inexperienced, closed-off version of herself who had first slept in this bunk. She knew she still had a lot to work on, but at least now she could recognize those elements of herself as flaws, leftovers from an unusual and maybe even cruel upbringing that she desperately wanted to put behind her. But she had also discovered her strengths, not just mastering the difficult gift of wings, but also learning the skills she needed to be an effective, contributing member of Berinia. And her magic. Haven sighed. She still needed training next year when she went into the Aerial. Kaden had already connected her with another fae trainer who would visit once a week for a lesson. But she knew she could master that as well, because the most important thing she had uncovered was her mind. Her logical thinking was her greatest strength and had shone during the war gaming this year. She had also honed her will, her ability to discover her own path and choose it, a gift she knew she could take with her from the Academy, hold close, and depend on for the rest of her life.

She felt more focused, more sure of herself and what she wanted. She certainly didn't have all the answers right now. But she trusted that she could find a solution to any problem life threw at her. A little melancholy seeped into her heart, and a smile crossed her face at the thought of her pod, of their silly adventures, the laughter and struggles they shared, knowing she had friends she could rely on when she needed them, but also to give herself to. She cherished those relationships, the people who had helped her uncover her true self, not just to them, but also to herself in preparation for the next phase of her life and, maybe, for a relationship that could mean everything. Ryker. She knew the person she was when she came to the Academy could never have contributed to a loving relationship. This version? It was possible.

"Ready?" Harper said, reaching for Haven's hand.

"Yes. Let's go," she said.


They appeared with a Skimmer in the expansive lobby of an apartment building. Against one wall was a table with two advisors, dressed in the Academy's red uniform shirt, ready to check in the arriving cadets to their assigned apartments.

An advisor said to Haven, "The apartment will be yours until you report to the Aerial in October. You can leave your belongings here when you return to the Academy for ComSim." They lugged their gear up three flights of stairs to the fourth floor and found their assigned rooms.

The apartment was small, but clean and modern. Haven walked down a short hallway to the compact kitchen to her left, separated from a living area by a small dining table. She moved to her right and opened the door to a bright, airy bedroom with an attached bath. After unpacking, she returned to the living room and took in the best part of the apartment—the large balcony. She slid back the glass door, the early summer sun warming her face. The apartment complex was one of eight similar buildings that enclosed a sizeable park in the center. Large trees shaded the lawn areas where she could see several groups of seraphim lounging on blankets, enjoying the weather.

Haven summoned a windsprite and sent a message to Ryker.

*Just wanted to let you know I'm in Araine.*

Ten minutes later, the sprite returned. From the tiny glowing faerie, she heard Ryker's voice in her mind. *Welcome, and congrats on your graduation. Working today. Stop by the Garret tomorrow for lunch?*

She sent back a response. *Would love to.*

Haven heard a knock on her door. She opened it, and Kit said to her, "Are you up for dinner out tonight?"

"Sounds great."

"Meet downstairs at seven? Looks like the squad is invading the Outpost."

Later that evening as she changed for dinner, another windsprite appeared.

Lukas's voice said, I heard you were back in Araine. Would you like to have dinner tomorrow night?

Haven steeled herself. The first step in choosing her own path started with him. She knew this arrangement wasn't part of the life she envisioned. She sent the sprite back. *I'd love to. I look forward to seeing you.*

# CHAPTER 31

## Falco Park

River waited in the office of Lilith's Falco Park townhouse. For once, he was happy to be back in Araine. His visit to Damaris had been productive, but he was glad for a brief reprieve from his father's estate. Memories were hard to escape there. He had settled Shallah in their former residence in the north wing of Ronan's estate, but he also knew he couldn't leave her alone for long. His presence added a layer of friction around her that kept his father's sharp tongue at bay.

Other than his required weekly check-in at the Aerial, he had been stuck in Damaris for two weeks and expected to be there at least another month. On the bright side, this brief trip to Araine would also give him the opportunity to see the female he had met recently. Tonight could be an interesting new adventure and welcome release of tension.

Lilith entered the office and sat in a chair across from him. She poured herself a cup of tea from the tray on the table between them. "How did it go with Dekkar?"

"About as I expected. He will be easy to control. What do you want from him?" River said.

"This afternoon he will be in Araine to meet Roque. I'd like you there to ensure the meeting goes smoothly."

"Easy enough. I ended up seeing Dekkar a few times when I was in Damaris, so now it looks like we're friends. In the future, setting up a meeting with him will seem normal."

"Excellent." Lilith's eyes roved over River. "You look well."

The corners of his mouth slowly turned up. "I am. Glad to be out of Damaris, for once."

"Would you be interested in having dinner with me tonight?" she asked, crossing her long legs.

River watched her skirt ride up her thighs and raised his brows. "Are you asking me out?"

"Sure, why not? I know we don't always see eye to eye. Maybe a private conversation would help us understand one another a little better."

River appraised Lilith with a fresh eye. "I'm busy tonight."

"That's a shame," she said, standing. "I'm planning on having drinks with a colleague at The Green Room later this evening. Please stop by if you find yourself available."

River rose. "I doubt it, but you never know."

River pulled the blankets back and eased out of bed. The dozing female rustled and rolled over to the spot where he had lain sleepless in the dark. He searched for his clothes in the faint predawn light trickling through the window and dressed quickly, closing the bedroom door soundlessly behind him and leaving the brownstone in Falco Park.

His meeting with Dekkar and Roque yesterday had gone well. With his subtle influence, Dekkar had agreed to work with Roque. If Roque met resistance from Dekkar in the future, River would only need to tug on the thread of his magic in Dekkar's mind. But for simple things, Dekkar would be pliable and willing.

He found this new working relationship with Roque and Lilith to be productive, and mutually beneficial. But he would need to return to Araine more frequently. His footsteps tapped a faint echo in the empty streets of Falco Park. He really needed to find a different living situation. His extracurricular activities would not sit well with Ryker or Shallah. Not that he cared much about Ryker, but Shallah's opinion mattered and he didn't want to disappoint her. This new lover changed everything as he didn't see the relationship ending anytime soon. Females rarely surprised him, but this one was an exception. She matched him in bed, as did her aggression, enthusiasm, and indifference, which was liberating. And made him want to come back for more. This relationship, as well as his others, needed to stay private, and that was unlikely to happen while staying at Ryker's house.

He entered the lobby of the Garret and started up the stairs. Ryker was staring down at him. "Slithering in at this hour? I wonder if the poor female even knows you've left."

River barely acknowledged him as he walked by. "Why are you awake," he said flatly.

"Some of us work for a living."

River gave him a nasty look. "Yes, the Prince of Shadowwalkers slaving away." He opened the door to his suite. "You used to enjoy yourself more. You got boring."

"I'd rather be boring than a gutter rat." Ryker walked up the stairs to the loft.

River peeled his eyes open. The blazing sun told him the hour was late. He glanced at the clock and jumped out of bed. He had scheduled a lunch appointment with a general of the Aerial at the Palace to help conceal his meetings with Roque and Lilith and the increased frequency of his trips to Araine. Now he was going to be late. He dressed quickly, splashed water on his face, and ran a wet hand through his hair. He bounced down the stairs to the lobby but halted when he spied Haven sitting on the couch through the open door to the study. Shit, he really couldn't believe his bad luck. First Ryker, now Haven. He cocked his head, wondering why she wanted to see him. He entered the study, and Haven leapt to her feet and took a step back from him.

"Well, this is unexpected. You should have told me you were coming by. Is something wrong?" he asked.

"No," she fumbled. "Actually, I didn't know you were in Araine. I thought you were in Damaris with Shallah."

"I was, but I needed to be in Araine for a few days." River narrowed his eyes. "So why are you here at the Garret?"

"I..." Her voice trailed off.

"I asked her to come," Ryker said. River wheeled around to face his brother. Silas loomed behind him, his gray wings unfurled, but tucked tight.

"Oh? And why is that?" River asked.

"Because I wanted to see her."

"Really. You wanted to see her." River turned to Haven. "And did you want to see him?"

"I did, yes," she said.

River looked from Haven to Ryker, whose gaze never moved from hers as his mouth curved in a slow smile.

"Interesting," River said, turning back to Haven. "I'm surprised. I can honestly say I didn't expect you to fuck my brother."

"It's not like that," Haven said.

"Don't answer him," Ryker interrupted. River felt Silas's imposing presence looming behind him. "And were you going to explain to Haven why you came home at dawn? Who were you with last night? Or do you even know her name?" Ryker asked, his voice heavy with contempt.

River stiffened. "I don't appreciate the accusations."

"Not accusations. I'm positive they are facts," Ryker said, moving closer. "Because I can smell the sex on you. You should have showered." River glanced at Haven as her eyes widened and her mouth fell open before she snapped it closed. The anger flashing in her eyes irritated him.

"This is none of your business," River seethed at his brother.

"The hell it isn't. Did you think I would keep your dirty little secrets? That I would cover for you while you seduced Haven but kept your string of females on the side?"

"Is that true? How many females are you involved with?" she asked.

"Did you actually think I'd wait for you? Besides, now that you are spreading your legs for my brother, why do you care who I'm with?"

"Easy," Silas said.

"Piss off, dog. Ryker, put a leash on him," River spat.

"If you call Silas a dog again, we are going to have a big problem," Ryker said, his voice dangerously low.

"I don't care who you're with," Haven interrupted. "I've told you for a year I wanted to be friends, and now I know that decision was the right one. I think you know I'm not interested in being one of a string of anyone's lovers."

"Really. What a little hypocrite," River sneered. "Does Lukas know you're sleeping with someone else? I'm sure that prim prick would care too."

She glared at him. "Not that it's any of your business, but I haven't slept with any of you."

"Gods, you females are ridiculous. It's just sex. Maybe a little screwing would make you less uptight and insufferable to be around." She winced as he moved closer to her. Ryker bristled, angling his body between them. "It would have been fun to fuck a princess, at least the first few times. But I need more than a simpering female in love to keep my interest," River scoffed as his gaze raked over her.

"Then you should be relieved because I was never in love with you," Haven fumed.

From behind him, River heard the snick of metal, and saw the tips of Silas's steel blades.

"Keep your distance," Silas said. "You've worn out your welcome. I think it's time you leave." River took a step back from Silas but said nothing.

Ryker reached behind him and found Haven's hand and walked to the door of the study, keeping his body between River and Haven.

He paused and said, "I think it would be best if you found another place to stay when you come to Araine."

Ryker left the Garret with Haven, while Silas stayed behind, blocking his access to the front door. River stormed to his suite and slammed the door. Gods damn his brother to hell. He called a windsprite to tell the general he would be late to their meeting, and went to the bath to shower.

River squirmed in his seat the entire meeting with the general. He couldn't wait to leave Araine. He had enough of this city to last a lifetime. His recent interactions with Lilith made him see new ways to use his skills in the Aerial, but the political responsibilities that came with it were killing him. And he needed some space away from Ryker. His brother's involvement with Haven shouldn't bother him as much as it did. But it stung. And that made him furious.

The meeting finally ended, and River excused himself and made for the door as quickly as he could. He marched to the garden and unfurled his wings, impatient to return to Damaris.

"River, a minute of your time," he heard a familiar voice call to him. His shoulders sagged in frustration, and he turned to see Roque with Lilith. *Gods, how much worse could this day get?* He folded his wings and waited for them to catch up.

"What do you want," he said.

"Let me be blunt. The situation with the Phoenix is critical, and we need your help," Roque said.

"I've heard all this before. It's always a critical situation with Haven. There's nothing in this scenario that would benefit me."

"Her situation changed because now she is connected to Ryker," Roque said, eyeing him closely. River kept his face neutral. "She cannot, under any circumstances, Pair with a Shadowalker."

"You didn't have your panties in a twist about her being involved with Lukas."

"Lukas has limited magic. Without Bane, he is unlikely to provoke her to create a Pairing," Lilith said. "You say there is nothing in this for you. Tell us what you want. We can make it happen."

"I want my brother dead," River said.

"Don't be petty," Lilith said. "Something you really want."

"I want out of the politics of this city."

"That's easy. Consider it done. I'll speak to your colonel tomorrow and tell him your skills are wasted in Araine."

"Just like that?"

"Yes. I have significant influence over the diplomatic staff here in Araine. I can keep you with your unit, where you belong anyway."

River looked at her with suspicion. "What exactly do you want from me?"

"Pair with the Phoenix. Then we can control her," Roque said.

"What else do I have to do to Haven?"

Lilith said, "Do to her? Whatever you want. I don't care about anything other than her magic."

River snickered to himself. Maybe this wasn't the worst thing he had ever heard of. He could kill three birds with this stone. Rid himself of politics, finally bed Haven, and take what his brother thought he had.

"Fine. Tell me what I need to do."

"Not here," Roque said. "We can meet tomorrow night. Lilith will contact you and tell you where."

# Chapter 32

## Araine

Haven's throat felt tight, and her face burned. She focused on the patterns of cobblestones as she walked with Ryker through the streets of Falco Park. He had been right about River, and she felt foolish. She knew she didn't feel anything for River, but she should have put the pieces together and seen him for who he really was. The clues were there, but she had been almost willfully blind where he was concerned. And why? For the attention? That made her feel almost stupid.

Ryker glanced at her and reached for her hand, his fingers lacing through hers.

"I'm sorry," he said. "I know that wasn't pleasant. I didn't mean for you to have that conversation before you were ready."

"It's okay. It needed to happen. I'm more embarrassed than anything else. I should have believed you." She sighed. "I know there are more conversations to come, but hopefully they won't all be like that one. I have a hard time imagining Lukas calling me a slut."

Ryker scowled. "River is an ass. Please don't take what he said personally." He stopped walking, turning to face her. "I know this is difficult. It doesn't help I'm River's brother. I understand if you need time alone."

Haven took a deep breath. "I'm okay. It's a shock, though."

Ryker brushed her hair from her face and twisted a lock through his fingers. "Tell me what you need."

"I don't know what I need right now."

He tipped her chin up, forcing her eyes to his. "I know when I feel like crap, a nice greasy burger and a beer helps."

She huffed a small laugh. "As long as it has double cheese. And fries."

"I can make that happen."

She played with a wrinkle in his shirt. "Thank you. For being here."

He pulled her close, and she slipped her arms around his waist. "Any time."

Haven had finished her fries and moved on to stealing Ryker's when he asked, "So what are your plans tonight?"

"Lukas invited me to dinner. I hope you're okay with that."

"Why wouldn't I be? You're free to see who you want."

She gave him a hard look. "I'm not sure how to take that."

"Why?"

"Because I'm not the kind of person to see more than one person. Are you?"

"No, I'm not. I didn't realize your dinner with Lukas was a date. I assumed it wasn't."

"It isn't. This is a strange conversation." She threw him an arched look and ate another of his fries.

"I'm going to break your fingers the next time you steal my fries," he snarled at her. She looked at him from under her lashes and stole another fry.

"You can try, but you have to come get me first."

"That is a challenge you shouldn't be making," he said, his eyes shimmering.

"Why? It could be fun tangling with you...over a fry," she said and reached for his plate. His hand snagged hers.

He leaned forward and whispered, "You didn't want our first time to be against a wall in the cold. How do you feel about bent over a table in a bar?"

"Hmmm...tempting. But I think I'll pass," she said.

"To clarify our conversation about Lukas before I started thinking of you naked, I don't care who you see and why. You can have friends without me saying you can. I'm also not that kind of person. I trust you, is what I was trying to say." He took her fingers in his hand. "You said 'seeing more than one person'. Is that how you think of me? Of us?"

"Yes." She gave him a steady look that she hoped hid the anxiety running rampant through her. "I'm hoping you see it the same way."

"Yes, I do." He pulled her hand to his soft lips. "You're not alone. Remember, we'll figure this out together." Her fear faded a little and her breath came a little easier. "Will you tell Lukas tonight? Do you want me to come with you?"

"Yes, I'll tell him, but I think I should do it alone. Lukas is a gentleman and a friend. I suppose if I hadn't found you, I could have been happy with him. He's nice. Good-looking. Funny. Gorgeous smile." Haven grinned at Ryker.

"Please, go on," he said, glaring at her. "I love hearing all the things you love about Lukas."

"Jealous?" she asked.

He laughed. "No. Annoyed? Yes."

"Anyway, I'm sure Lukas will be fine." She faltered. "His parents? I'm not looking forward to that conversation. Not with my parents, either. But it needs to be done. Aside from us, the arrangement with Lukas isn't for me."

"I'll do whatever you need me to do," Ryker said, squeezing her hand.

His touch sparked a ripple of mischief inside her. "Really? Whatever I need?" she breathed.

"Anything. Any time. Particularly if it involves you being naked."

"I've been naked a few times in this conversation."

"You haven't. Not once. And that's a tragedy." He rose and took her hand. "As much as I would love to continue the conversation of all the ways I'm thinking of you naked, which, by the way, are numerous, I need to get back to work. Walk with me back to the Garret?"

They strolled through Falco Park, enjoying the breezy, warm summer day. Ryker led her through the lobby of the Garret to the study, where he closed the door behind him and locked it.

"I thought you had to work," Haven said.

"I do. But I can steal a few minutes." He pulled her close and kissed her. She ran her hands across his shoulders and down his arms and under his shirt, stroking his ribs and up his back. Feeling his skin on hers for the first time was better than she had imagined. Warm. Soft and hard at the same time. His muscles flexed under her touch. And so *alive*. His hand drifted from her waist to her hip, then lower, cupping the curve of her backside and pulling her tight to him. "I missed you," he said into her lips. His kiss became more insistent. His touch burned, not just her body, but every little nerve. She was almost painfully aware of her surroundings, of her connection to him and what he was offering her. Haven's hand drifted lower and slid between them, feeling the hard strain in his jeans.

"I missed you too," she said, stroking him. His breath caught, and he picked her up and in two strides had her on the desk. He pressed his hips between her legs, one hand bracing his body and one lacing behind her head. Haven stroked him harder.

"You need to stop that," he said, pushing into her hand.

"I don't want to," she purred, watching him close his eyes slowly, his lips parted and his breath uneven. She could see his pulse throbbing in his neck. His jaw tensed, and his eyes shone with a glassy heat, his gaze never leaving hers. His reaction to her touch was intoxicating. She wanted more. She wanted all of him.

He gently removed her hand. "You're killing me."

She kissed him, biting his lower lip. He groaned, his kiss desperate before backing away. "I'm all for a quickie in the afternoon, but not now. Not like this. I'm not rushing this."

"Okay. But I could still make you feel good. I owe you."

Ryker's eyes flashed. "Are you keeping score?"

"Maybe," she said. "Maybe I want to see your face when I make you come." Ryker's smile faded and he swallowed hard. She pulled him back to her and unbuttoned his jeans. His hand stayed on her wrist but didn't stop her. She slid her hand lower, stroking him, then freed his thick, hard length. Her eyes widened at the size of him filling her hand.

"Haven," he growled. "You don't have to do this."

"Did you not hear me? I want to. Let me touch you." She ran her hand up him, her thumb circling the sensitive tip, then stroked down. He swore and closed his eyes, pushing into her touch. She stroked him again, harder, her own pulse pounding at the feel of him. "What I really want is to have my lips on you," she whispered in his ear. "I want to taste you here." She thrilled a little at the desperate look that crossed his face. Her fingers traced the grooves of his tip, and his breathing shallowed as he watched her hand move on him. She could see the tension in his body building with every stroke. His movements, his pleasure at her touch, heated her center, her own ache for him almost painful. She held his eyes with hers as his body rocked, thrusting into her hand. His eyes glazed and his chest heaved as his hand on her hip gripped her tightly.

"*Haven*," he gasped as his climax broke, his body shuddering as he pulsed into her hand. Haven's heart thundered as his release crested, then ebbed. She kissed him, her lips and tongue playing with his.

"You are beautiful," she said. He rested his forehead on hers as he relaxed into her, holding her close.

"I don't want to leave you."

She kissed his lips, his cheek, his jaw. "I'm thinking a no-show at work would cause a scandal."

He kissed her nose, his hands roaming her hips and backside. He slipped his hand between her legs, his fingers pressing into her through her jeans. She arched into his touch, her need for him suddenly acute. "A no-show might be better. All I can think of is you anyway." He dipped his head and kissed her breast through her shirt. Haven's thoughts narrowed to the feel of his lips on her, imagining what his kiss would feel like on her bare skin.

"And I'll be thinking of this," she said, stroking him again, "when I'm having dinner with Lukas tonight." She could feel him thicken in her hand, despite the release she'd wrung from him.

"Naughty," Ryker said, reluctantly pulling away from her. He pointed across the study. "There's a washroom through that door." She hopped off the desk, kissed him, and washed up.

Ryker had managed to piece himself together by the time she returned. He drew her into his arms, his kisses trailing along her neck, then finding her lips again. He kissed her deeply and held her tight to him.

She pulled away, her fingers tracing his jaw and the curve of his lips. "You're making me regret agreeing to see Lukas tonight," she said, pulling his mouth to hers again.

"I hate it." He deepened the kiss. "I need more than this. I want to feel all of you."

"I'm leaving. Now. Or I'm taking you upstairs."

"I could be convinced to skip work."

She pressed into his hardness. "I can tell." Ryker grinned and kissed her nose.

Haven took his hand and led him to the lobby. She stood on her toes and brushed his lips in a quick goodbye, then stepped into the street. Before she rounded the corner, she looked back at him, lounging in the doorway of the Garret, his hands casually in his pockets. Just before she lost sight of him, she saw him smile.

Haven met Lukas at a restaurant in Araine, a few blocks from the border of Falco Park. They sat at the table and started the evening with cocktails.

"Before we order dinner," Haven said, "I feel I need to be honest with you."

Lukas said, "This sounds serious."

"It is. I've started seeing someone recently. And I think it's serious."

Lukas sat back in his chair. "I guess that isn't surprising. But please tell me this isn't River."

She quickly shook her head. "No, definitely not." She hesitated, then said, "It's Ryker."

Lukas blinked. "Well, I didn't see that coming."

"I will always appreciate what you've offered me, but I've decided we shouldn't go through with the enosi contract. You are a wonderful person, and you deserve to be with someone who loves you. It's just not me."

"Thank you for that. And I appreciate your honesty. And while I think we could have developed an affection for one another, the reasons I offered you our own deal are less important now. Ryker can offer you the same protection I could."

"Honestly, I hadn't thought of it that way. My feelings for Ryker are beside the point. I refuse to live in a cage again, even if it's filled with delightful people."

"I appreciate your decision, but protection is still something you will need. Why do you think Shadowalkers have such secure residences? All of us with powerful magic need a place to feel safe," Lukas said.

"I agree, but there's a difference between safety and confinement." She sighed. "I will always be grateful for your willingness to help me. It came when I really needed a friend, and you were there to make what was an unpleasant situation tolerable. But I think we both deserve more."

"And you are my friend. Security and safety aside, you chose well. Ryker is a good person. I hold him in high regard."

"I can understand if you'd rather spend the evening doing something else. I wanted to tell you before we ordered, in case you preferred to cancel our evening."

"Absolutely not. I enjoy your company and would love to have dinner with you. As a friend."

"I will always be that. Your friend."

Lukas walked Haven back to her apartment after dinner. "I'll tell my parents about our choice. There may be some resistance, but I will do my best to clean it up from my side."

"I'll do the same. My father will support me, but my mother..." she trailed off.

"Let me know if I can help." They arrived at her apartment building, and Lukas kissed her cheek. "Good luck." Haven silently wished all the conversations to come—her parents, Lukas's parents, the king—would go this well.

Haven returned to her apartment and sent a windsprite to Ryker. *I'm back from dinner with Lukas. All is good.* She changed into a t-shirt and slipped into bed, exhausted from the evening.

A windsprite circled her head, glowing softly in the dark. *Thanks for letting me know. Are you okay?*

She sent the sprite back. Yes, just tired. I miss you.

A few minutes later, Haven heard rustling on her balcony and the door sliding open. She got out of bed and found Ryker standing in the open doorway, leaning on the frame, his wings tucked tightly behind him.

"I miss you too," Ryker said. "I needed to see you, to be sure you're okay."

"I'm fine. Lukas was exactly as I expected. A gentleman, and supportive." She frowned. "Are you going to stand outside the entire night?"

"I don't want to bother you. I know you're tired."

"I may be tired, but I'm not dead."

His gaze lingered on her bare legs. "You look sexy."

"I'm in a t-shirt. That's not very sexy."

"Yes, it is. You're almost naked," he said, his silver eyes sparking.

"Almost? I have a feeling I could be fully clothed in a parka and you would still say I'm almost naked."

Ryker laughed. "I have a very good imagination."

"You have a dirty mind." She folded her arms across her chest. "Would you like to see me naked? For real?"

"What do you think," he said. Haven held his intense, hungry gaze and stepped out of her underwear, her t-shirt covering her to the top of her thighs. Ryker didn't move, but swallowed hard, his eyes glittering.

"More?"

"Yes," he said. Haven removed her shirt and stood naked before him, the shadows hinting at her feminine swells and curves. Ryker's eyes moved over her, and she let him look.

"You're more beautiful than I even imagined," he said, his voice low and thick.

"Why are you still standing outside?" She idly stroked her stomach.

His gaze followed her hand, hypnotized. "You haven't invited me in."

"Please, come in." Ryker furled his wings and stepped through the doorway. Haven walked past him and closed the door. "Do you want to touch me?"

He let out a heavy breath. "Yes."

"Then why aren't you?" She moved closer.

"Do you want me to? And before you answer that, if I touch you, I won't want to stop with my hands this time. I want all of you." He brushed the hair from her face, his fingers trailing along her lips. "So think about what you want before you give permission."

"Permission?"

"Yes. Always."

She stepped close enough her bare body touched his. His hand fell to her shoulder, and he stroked her arm. "Touch me, Ryker. I want everything from you."

Ryker pulled her close, his hand cupping her cheek. His fingers slid behind her neck and twined through her hair as he kissed her, his lips exploring the feel of her. Haven's hands rested on his hips and pulled his body to hers. His hand circled her waist, drifting down to her backside. He kissed her jaw, then ran the tip of his tongue along her collarbone, and she shivered at the sensation, the intimacy of him tasting her, exploring her. He bent his head and slid his tongue across her nipple, pulling at the sensitive skin with his mouth. She arched into him and shuddered as a tingling pleasure skittered through her body. "Gods," she moaned, tugging at the back of his shirt as he pulled it over his head.

"I've wanted to do this since I saw you in that red dress." His tongue circled her nipple again, his hand cupping her other breast, his thumb brushing her nipple.

"Oh? You liked that?"

"I told you then I did." He pulled her nipple into his mouth again, nipping at her. Haven groaned and unbuttoned his jeans.

"I thought friends don't have those kinds of thoughts."

He toed off his shoes and stepped out of his pants, tossing them aside. "I had many thoughts that night. None of them were as a friend," he said, kissing her lips again. She ran her fingers down his chest, over the corded muscles of his stomach, moving lower, feeling him thick and hard in her hand. She gently stroked him from the base to the sensitive tip.

"What else did you want to do?" His silver eyes glazed as she stroked him again.

Ryker squeezed her hip, a small muscle in his jaw ticking. "Lots of things. I'm about to show you a few." He picked her up, and she wrapped her legs around his hips, burying her face in his neck, losing herself in his warm, rich scent. He took her to her bedroom and laid her on the bed, covering her body with his. His thigh slid between hers, and he pulled her leg to his waist, their bodies tangling together.

He looked down at her. "Last chance, friend, to keep this clean."

She pressed into him, feeling him twitch against her stomach. "I think we're well beyond that, don't you?"

"Yes, thank the gods," he said into her kiss, then rolled her under him, kissing her slowly, his comforting weight resting on her. He settled between her thighs, and she lifted her legs higher, wrapping them around his hips. She stroked his powerful arms, her touch trailing across his broad shoulders, his muscles cording and flexing under his smooth skin.

She bit at his lip, the tip of her tongue grazing his, and felt him jump against her and deepen the kiss in response. Ryker's hands twined in her hair, his thumbs stroking her cheekbones. He broke the kiss and touched her forehead with his. His hips rocked up and back, and she felt him drop and press into her center. She shook with need, ready to feel him for real and not just what her mind imagined. She kissed his neck and stroked his back, down his trim waist to the swell of his backside. She pulled him to her, his tip entering her. Ryker hissed and pulled his hips back.

"Not yet," he whispered.

"Yes. Now." Haven gripped him again.

"I'm not in a hurry," he said, kissing her. "Seems I need to teach you yet another thing. Patience."

She raked her nails along his ribs. He swore and flinched away, and laughed into her lips.

"Brat," she snarled, but let him go.

"Maybe. But relax. Let me enjoy you," he whispered. Her heart leapt, and she lost herself in the taste and feel of his skin, his kiss, his lips so warm and soft and gentle. He found that spot on her neck that tickled like hell, and she pulled away, goosebumps rolling down her ribs. "Ah, I like that spot," he said, his tongue flicking over her neck, making her squeal as he growled with pleasure.

He rolled to her side, and his fingers traced the swell of her breast, his thumb skimming her nipple. Haven arched into his touch, gripping his arm, almost desperate to feel more of him. He stroked the warm skin of her ribs to the curve of her hip, and lower still, down the lean muscles of her thigh. His touch brushed like feathers up the inside of her leg, slowly moving higher as his lips played with hers. Haven's hips reached for him, her hand pulling at his arm, needing him to touch her where she ached for him. Her knees fell apart, her body begging for more, and his finger slid through her drenched center, stroking her hard ridge. Haven shuddered and rolled her hips against his hand. She felt Ryker's body rumble as he slid a finger inside her.

"Tell me what you like." His lips moved slowly along her neck to the top of her breast. "Is it this?" he said, as he slipped another finger deep inside her, pressing against her sensitive walls. Haven jerked her hips and gasped. "Or this?" he said, taking her nipple into his mouth, his teeth nipping at her, his tongue swirling over her sensitive skin. She clung to him, her breathing shallow as his fingers slid inside her again.

"All of you. Everything," she whispered, slipping her hand between them and stroking him, her fingertips brushing the grooves of his tip. "And this."

He groaned as her grip tightened on him and stroked down. "I'm looking forward to that, very much," he said, as his thumb found that sensitive bundle of nerves between her legs.

"Gods, Ryker," she whispered into his neck.

He pulled away from her grip. "But right now, I have other things on my mind," he said, as he kissed her neck, then her breast, his tongue finding her nipple before roving down her stomach. He withdrew his hand from between her legs and she whimpered, rolling her hips at the loss of his touch. His hand pressed her inner thigh, moving her leg and baring her fully to him. He nipped at the inside of her thigh, his teeth and lips brushing her skin as he settled between her legs. Haven quivered in anticipation. "Like this," he said, dipping his head, his tongue sliding over the ridge of sensitive nerves. Haven gasped and clenched the sheets. "I've definitely been thinking of this." His tongue caressed her again and dipped lower to her center. Her hips moved against his teasing tongue.

"Such dirty thoughts," she said, gripping his shoulder.

"Mmmmhmmm...less talking," he said. She laughed, then moaned, her hips writhing against his mouth as he increased the pressure on her with his tongue, taking her into his mouth, sliding his tongue inside her. His finger joined his tongue as he tasted and teased her, and she ran her hands through his hair, her body coiling, her release building along her spine.

"Ryker," she said, her voice low and urgent, the tension in her center unbearable. His hand pressed her hips, pinning her, his mouth and tongue devouring her. Her hips ground against him, and she cried out as her climax shattered her body. She felt his rumbling growl on her as his lips held her still and his tongue slowly caressed her. The pulses of her release intensified before finally ebbing. Haven lay panting and blinked, stunned by what he had coaxed from her body. She shuddered, her body luxuriously liquid to her bones. He kissed his way up, lingering at her breast, then found her lips.

He settled between her thighs, and she wrapped her legs around his waist. She felt him nudge her, slipping just inside. "Tell me you want this. I want to hear you say you want me," he said, his voice rough.

"Gods, yes. I want you," she urged, her nails digging into his lower back as she rolled her hips, pushing him in a little further. Ryker's silver eyes watched hers as he slid slowly inside her. She groaned at the thickness of him as he stretched her, filled her. He waited for her to adjust, then withdrew a little and pushed in farther. Haven's head dropped back, and Ryker kissed her throat, finding that place where her pulse hammered. He pushed again until he was seated deep inside her. He swore as his body trembled.

"Gods, Haven you feel...I may burst into flames."

Haven grinned. "That's my trick."

He laughed softly onto her lips. "Are you good?" he asked.

She nodded and canted her hips, wrapping her legs around his back. "More," she said into his kiss, her hands stroking his arms. He drew back and moved slowly inside her.

"Like that?" he said.

"Yes," she breathed. "More of that. A lot more." He stroked into her slowly, and she clung to him, moving her hips in rhythm, trying to increase his pace. He kissed her deeply and did as her body asked. Haven's world became him, his rough hands on her smooth skin, his hard angles against her curves, the warm pressure of his body coming together with hers, his soft lips, his teasing tongue. Haven held on to their connection, greedy for an intimacy that was more than physical. And that threatened to tear her heart wide open.

Ryker lifted his shoulders off her, bracing his weight on his hands as he rocked his hips into her. She matched his rhythm, meeting his strokes, pulling him deeper. Ryker's pace increased, and she gripped his back, her release coiling as she tightened around him.

Ryker's control crumbled. Haven brought her knees higher, holding on to him as his strokes deepened, his pace unhinged. She clung to him, feeling the straining, corded muscles of his arms and back, his breath warm against her cheek. Ryker groaned, their bodies moving together, taking what they needed from each other, the need perfectly the same. Haven's body became taut, almost painfully, then her release ripped through her, waves of pleasure coursing along her back and thighs. Ryker kissed her eyes, her cheek, her neck as he stroked her through her climax, a heated, tingling sensation heightening each wave. Then he tensed and thrust deep inside her as his body shuddered. She held him tight, stroking him as he gasped, his back arching and straining as she felt his pulsing release deep inside her. He collapsed onto his elbows, resting his head on the pillow next to her.

"Holy shit," he said, his body quivering.

"Tell me you felt that," Haven breathed.

"Like tingling electricity?" he said into her neck.

"Yes, but in a good way." He raised his head and held her eyes. "In a very good way." His lips were gentle and soft, his tongue caressing hers. She ran her hands through his hair and gripped his waist with her legs, not ready to let the moment go. He eased out of her and rolled to the side, keeping her close, idly stroking her back, feeling the curves of her hips and backside.

She kissed his chest, enjoying the quiet feel of his arms around her, their bodies twined together.

Haven was afraid to move, afraid she would break this feeling between them. She had never been with someone who made sex intimate, who had demanded this kind of response from her body, who cared about her experience the way Ryker had tonight. His fingers trailed down her spine, caressed softly to her hip, then flattened on her backside before tracing back up her spine, exploring the shapes of her body with lazy, slow touches, feeling what his body instinctually needed to feel. She kissed his neck, her lips feeling his still-racing pulse. She could lose herself, her soul, in a moment like this. Her heart ached, and she pulled him to her. His arms tightened around her, and he kissed her head, her forehead, her cheek, then her lips as she tipped her head to him.

"Have you ever been in love?" she asked.

Ryker's hand stilled on her back. "Are you asking me—" he started.

"Don't. Don't say anything about us right now," Haven interrupted him, anxiety blazing in her heart. "After what we just did, it would be too easy to say things you don't really mean. And I've been lied to before."

Ryker pulled back and stroked her lips with his thumb. "I would never lie to you about how I feel."

"You may not intentionally. But people say things in bed they later regret." She curled her head against his chest, and the steady thrum of his heart soothed her own painful beats. "So, have you? Have you ever been in love?"

"Yes, a long time ago, a few years after I left the Aerial."

"So why aren't you with her?"

"Because the feelings weren't mutual."

She raised her head and stroked his face. "I can't see how that's possible," she said, kissing him.

"Some people are fine with affection and sex if it also brings power. She wanted the lifestyle I could offer as a Shadowalker. How I felt was of little importance."

"That's an awful reason to be with someone."

"I agree," Ryker said. "I was inexperienced and naïve. And unfortunately for me, I didn't understand the difference at first. It was a painful lesson, and not a good time in my life."

"What happened?"

"Let's say I lived enough like River to know casual sex isn't for me." Haven relaxed against his chest. "What about you?" he asked.

"No. At first I thought I might have been with Larkin, but it was more infatuation with a pretty face."

"Ah, yes, those pretty fae faces." Ryker squeezed her to him. "Don't forget their perfect bodies."

Ryker buried his face in her hair, his lips finding that ticklish place behind her ear. "Perfect? That's a lot to live up to."

Haven giggled and hid her neck from his kisses. She ran her hand down his broad back to his trim waist, feeling the curve of his backside to his powerful thigh resting between her legs. "You're good. Better than good." She kissed his chest, her tongue rolling over his nipple. Ryker hissed, and she felt him thicken against her stomach. Her hand slipped between them, her fingers tracing him. "You're perfect," she whispered. She gently rolled him onto his back and straddled him. He gripped her hips as she leaned down and kissed him, her hair falling around them. He laced his fingers through the silky waves, pulling them behind her head. "You're not the only one who had thoughts friends shouldn't have. Would you like me to show you what I was thinking?"

Ryker's eyes closed as she slid down him. "Yes," he growled. Her lips found his again. She kissed his neck, her fingers tracing the intricate, swirling tattoo on his left side that covered his ribs and curled under his chest. She nipped at him, her teeth grazing his ribs, and her tongue traced the design of the tattoo. Ryker hissed, his fingers tightening in her thick hair. Her kisses moved over his hips, following the muscles that led lower. Her tongue caressed his sensitive tip, and she felt Ryker's hand in her hair clench. She explored his grooves before taking him into her mouth. Ryker groaned, and she pulled at his tip with her lips and tongue. She wrapped her hand around the base of him, stroking him as she took him deeper. Ryker's head kicked back, his hips rolling in a shallow rhythm to her mouth and hand. His breathing grew quick and heavy, his body tightening with every stroke.

"You need to stop," he said, his voice taut. She took him deeper. "Fuck," he rasped. "Haven, I'm not kidding." His voice was nearly desperate. She stroked up him, her lips and teeth pulling at his tip. "*Haven*," he cried out as his release broke. She kissed his stomach and held him in her hand through the pulsing waves of his climax.

Ryker shuddered, then his body finally relaxed. He pulled her to him, rolling her under him and holding her tight.

"Gods, Haven," he growled into her hair.

"I love what I can do to your body," she said, kissing his neck. "Feeling you respond to my touch, seeing you undone like that, gets me wound up tight." She kissed him, tasting their sex on his lips. "Besides," she whispered into his mouth, "now we're even again."

"You're welcome to keep score any time you like," he murmured as he nipped her ear.

"Any time?" she asked.

"Definitely."

"That could be interesting. And quite embarrassing."

"Don't care."

"You're shameless."

"I am," he said. She smiled into his chest, and he pulled her tight again. She melted into him, willing the moment to last forever.

# CHAPTER 33

## Graduation Festival

Ryker sat on a chair and pulled on his socks and shook his head, flinging water from his hair. He ran a hand through the strands and reached for his shoes. Haven was asleep on her stomach, the blankets around her waist, her chestnut hair a tumble over her face and shoulders. Ryker's heart pulled toward her, and his body heated at the sight of her bare skin. She had been such a surprise. He had to admit he thought of her as young and inexperienced. But she had come alive last night in a way that had rocked him. He knew she was fearless, aggressive in combat training, and a leader. She was not afraid of anything or anyone, and certainly not afraid of him. That fearlessness had drawn him to her. And he was surprised and delighted to find that carried over to sex. She welcomed his aggression, challenged him, and doubled down with her own. She was also soft and vulnerable, and gentle and careful with his own unguarded emotions.

He stifled a deep yawn. They had talked late into the night, sharing their stories and their bodies. They spent hours discovering small things about each other. She loved chocolate and had never tried coffee. She wasn't bad at horseback riding and was an excellent swimmer, and deathly afraid of spiders. Ryker smiled at the memory of her admission. He had laughed at the idea of her terrified of an insect. She could stare down any seraphim warrior but would flee from a tiny bug. His playful kidding had led to a wrestling match, and he had ended up inside her again. He knew she was ticklish on her neck behind her ear. And that biting her hips drove her mad. Last night was the beginning of a deeper intimacy he had craved for decades. Maybe his entire life.

Ryker moved to sit next to her, the bed dipping under his weight. He pushed her hair back from her face as her eyes fluttered open.

"Good morning, beautiful," he said. She purred at his touch, then frowned.

"You're dressed. Where are you going?"

"I need to meet with Trinity and Silas and the Council this morning. It's early, I didn't want to wake you, but I also wanted to say goodbye," he said, kissing her forehead.

"Work," she grumbled, sliding her hand up the inside of his thigh. "I want you all to myself."

"You have me. But you'll have to share a little." His lips moved up her neck, then found her mouth. "I'm free after lunch all day. We can go to the Graduation Festival if you want."

"Go? You mean go together? No hiding?"

"No hiding. You're officially graduated and no longer a student." He looped a lock of her hair through his fingers, feeling the softness. "Although I will follow your lead on that."

"Really? Because I was planning on climbing to the rooftop buck naked and telling the world."

Ryker burst out laughing. "Wow, what a visual."

She laughed with him. "No hiding. The only one that matters to me is you."

"I'll stop by here around noon and pick you up. Go back to sleep."

He rose to leave, but Haven held his hand. "I can't convince you to stay a little longer?" She kissed his hand and pulled him back, rising to her knees in front of him.

"You're naked." Ryker traced the curves of her breasts.

"Yes, glad you noticed." She pulled up his shirt and stroked his taut stomach.

"You know how much I like it when you're naked." He bent down and took her nipple in his mouth and bit her, just the right side of pain. She gasped, her hand drifting to the stretched front of his pants.

"You're going to make me late," he growled.

"That's not my problem." She guided his hand between her thighs. "But you're free to leave if you want." He stroked her slick center and slipped in a finger.

"Gods, Haven," he whispered. She unbuttoned his pants and pulled him to the bed, rolling him onto his back and straddling him.

"Shhh...," she said, her lips finding his. "Less talking."

Ryker was late to his meeting. Trinity tapped him as he was dressing.

*Ryker, where the hell are you?* she said after he accepted the link.

*Something came up. I'm on my way. I'll meet you there.*

*You better hurry. You know we can't start without you.*

*I'll be there in ten minutes.*

He kissed Haven. "I'll be back after lunch." She burrowed into the covers and smiled at him.

Ryker walked to the balcony, unfurled his wings, and flew to the ministry district, south of the Temple. He walked into the Council chambers ten minutes after speaking with Trinity and took a seat next to her.

Trinity's nostrils flared. "Something came up? I bet it did," she said, glaring at him.

"What do you want me to say?" His grin widened to a toothy smile, and Silas nudged him with his elbow.

"Gods, you two are children," she said, shaking her head. Ryker laughed and kissed her cheek. She swore at him and pushed him away.

Finnian gave his report, and a council member asked Ryker for a review of his upcoming crossings.

"I don't see anything for the next few weeks," Trinity said.

"And we should discuss ComSim. They will need advisors and referees on site," Ryker said. "Silas and I volunteered as advisors. Trinity, Lukas, and Xander are acting as referees. That ties us up for the next four weeks at least. But they need people."

"Very well," Lilith said. "Finnian can stay in Araine to cover any emergency."

The meeting droned on for another three hours. At last, Lilith convened the session. "The Graduation Festival is today. Council members who are not previously engaged should be there. We also expect the Triads to attend. The royals will be there, so should we."

Trinity eyed Ryker and said, "I'd suggest you shower and freshen up before meeting her parents."

He smirked at her. "Yes, mother. I'll meet you both there."

Ryker landed on Haven's balcony an hour later.

"Ready?" she asked, stepping out of the apartment to meet him.

"Yes," he said, kissing her. "I heard today in my meeting that the royals will be at the Festival, including your father and mother. I thought you should know."

She pressed her forehead to his chest. "I'm ready, as long as you're there."

"I'm not going anywhere."

Haven looped a hand through his arm. "Come on, let's go have some fun."

They flew to the Palace grounds and landed in the gardens off the main ballroom. The Graduation Festival was massive. All seven hundred graduating cadets were in attendance, along with extended families. Haven surveyed the mob that sprawled through the gardens and spilled onto the distant green lawns. The royals were assembled on the ballroom patio to welcome the cadets and their families. Ryker gripped Haven's hand to keep from losing her in the crowd's crush.

"What do you want to do first? Fun, or parents?" he asked.

"Parents. Let's get this over with." Ryker kissed her head and led her to the patio.

Trinity tapped him, and he accepted. *Where are you?*

*Going to the royals to say hello. Wish me luck. You and Silas?*

*Same. Will meet you there.*

Ryker and Haven approached the king and queen, bowing low. "Ryker, Haven, it is good to see you both. Congratulations on your graduation," the king said.

"Thank you, sir," Haven said.

The queen raised an eyebrow at Haven's hand in Ryker's. "I thought you were committed to Lukas. Do you have something to tell us?"

"Yes," Haven said, glancing at Ryker. "Lukas and I will ask to have the enosi contract voided. He's a dear friend, but Ryker has my heart." Hope's brown eyes snapped to Haven, then narrowed. Haven squeezed Ryker's hand at the sight of her mother's anger.

"I see," the king replied. "Submit a petition and I'll consider it. Again, congratulations on your graduation. Very well deserved."

"Thank you," Haven said. Her mother's piercing eyes never left hers. Haven remained still, unflinching from her mother's gaze. "Mother, Father, it is nice to see you both."

"Congratulations. We're proud of you," Astor said warmly. "It is an accomplishment to graduate from the Academy, particularly with the gifts you've discovered."

"It seems you have discovered something else as well," Hope sneered.

"Easy," Astor said curtly. Haven felt Ryker stiffen beside her. He stepped closer to her, and she felt his hip brush hers.

"Yes, I plan to ask the king to release me from the enosi contract with Lukas. My heart lies elsewhere." Ryker slid his arm around her waist. She leaned into him, strengthened by his warmth and presence.

"Your heart? That is of little importance," Hope said icily. "We made a commitment to Lukas's family. You need to honor that commitment."

"I'm sorry you feel that way, but this is my choice. You can't force me," Haven said.

"No, I can't. But the king can," Hope said.

"If Haven doesn't want the match, we won't stand in her way," her father said. "We arranged the commitment for her safety. I'm sure Ryker could offer the same."

Ryker said, "Her safety is of primary importance to me, along with her happiness."

Hope turned away from them.

"Enjoy the day, and don't worry," Astor reassured her. "Your mother and I will discuss our differing views."

"Thank you," Haven said. She and Ryker bowed low again. Hope said nothing as they walked away.

Ryker pulled her close. "We're okay."

"What if my mother persuades the king to force me into this contract?"

"We'll deal with that if it becomes a problem. Let's not worry about it now. Your father supports us, and he's a prince. Don't underestimate the value of his opinion to the king and queen."

Trinity and Silas joined them, and they walked back to the gardens where Haven finally relaxed. "Well, I guess that could have been worse. Thank you for being here."

"Of course," Ryker quickly replied. "Where else would I be?"

"Well, this thing with Lukas is my problem. I warned you, my life is messy."

"And I'm the reason you have a problem. I will always be there to help you."

Haven stared at him. "Sometimes I wonder if you're for real."

"I am," he said, and kissed her. "Come on, let's get a beer."

"Oh, thank gods," Silas said. Ryker scowled at him. "What? Things got way too serious. This is a party. Let's go find one."

"I'm with you, Silas. Lead the way," Haven said, looping her arm through his. They walked through the gardens to the Green where palace servers bustled among tents that offered a wide variety of food and drinks. An open area near the tents featured live music and dancing. In the far distance, she could see organized sporting events across three fields, with crowds surrounding each, cheering on teams. She also spied a sparring ladder tournament, with warriors and cadets alike testing their skills in a progressive elimination competition. They passed through a break in the food tents to a row of tables offering drinks of every kind.

Ryker said to Silas, "Welcome home." Haven laughed, and Silas flipped him off.

"Want something? Beer or wine?" Silas asked her.

"Whiskey."

"Gods, I'm in love." He passed Trinity a cup of milky white liquid and Ryker a beer.

Haven pointed to Trinity's drink. "What is that?"

"Raki. It's a human specialty," Trinity said. "Here, try it."

Haven sipped the cool liquid and coughed at the biting taste of anise. "Gods, that's awful."

"It's an acquired taste," Trinity said.

"I don't know." Silas smacked his lips. "I kinda like it."

Ryker said, "You like anything with alcohol. It tastes like horse piss."

"And you drink horse piss frequently?" Trinity asked.

"No, but I sip that shit often enough to be reminded not to."

Haven tensed as Harper, Kit, Dax, and Dune approached them through the crowd.

"Go talk to Harper," she said, nudging Ryker.

Dax stood beside her after Ryker left. "Is there something I should know?"

"Ryker and I are seeing each other," she said to Dax, while watching Harper intently.

"About fucking time," he said under his breath. She flicked a glare at him, and he elbowed her in the ribs. Harper's eyes widened, then focused on Haven. Haven flushed but didn't flinch.

Harper walked to Haven and hugged her. "You're okay with this?" she said into Harper's ear.

"Yes. He's happy," she said, and pulled back to look at Haven. "And you are, too. I can see it all over both of you." She glanced over her shoulder at Ryker. "I haven't seen him speak like that about someone in decades. Maybe ever." She turned back to Haven. "And you, you're positively glowing."

"I am happy," she said, her eye catching Ryker's. "He's an amazing person. But I don't want this to be weird for you."

"It isn't. I was a little surprised, but to be honest? I'm actually excited. I don't know about you, but I've been dreading the end of the Academy a little. I'm not going into the Aerial like you, so I'm already missing our pod."

"I feel that too."

"Now, I'll have an excuse to see you more." Harper squeezed her hand. "And maybe even more of a reason to call you family."

Haven stared at the ground, feeling her cheeks heat a little. "One step at a time," she said. "It's really new between us. But I'm hoping this one is real."

"I'll keep my fingers crossed for you both." She tugged on Haven's hand. "Come on. Let's get a drink. I need to catch up."

Dune fell into step on the other side of Harper. "Well, one more exercise together before we scatter," Haven said. "We'll have to make ComSim a farewell party too."

"You'll have to tell me all about it," Dune said.

Haven blinked. "What do you mean?"

"I'm not going."

"Why?" Harper said.

"Come on," Dune said, tilting her head and smiling at them. "I'm not the greatest strategist. I barely got through the third year."

"I thought you did well," Haven said.

"Well, the instructors thought differently. I barely passed."

"Ryker failed you?"

"No, his marks were fine, oddly enough. It was Shane." Haven and Harper glanced at each other and shared a confused look. "It doesn't matter. I've been accepted into the healer training program in Raveno. It's where I belong."

Haven took her hand. "That's not for another two months. One more exercise together."

Harper nodded and took her other hand. "Please reconsider. It won't be the same without you."

"Maybe," Dune said and grinned at them both.

Dax took a beer from Silas and joined the group as they strolled through the tents. "I thought you were done with pretty boys," Dax said to Haven under his breath.

She grinned at him. "I'm a hopeless sucker."

"This one is different. I'm happy for you." He wrapped his arm around her, and she laced her arm around his waist as walked together through the crowds to the open area around the band.

The group danced through a set of upbeat music, then continued exploring the Festival tents with Ryker's fingers laced through hers. It was a strange feeling, to be with him in the open, their relationship visible for everyone to see. She watched him casually speak to Silas, naturally comfortable being by her side in the crowd. She took his cue and relaxed, and enjoyed a public event with someone she cared for deeply—the first step in building a shared life together.

Ryker sat with Haven on a blanket under the trees on the Green, the sun setting in a riot of pinks, oranges, and deep violets. He handed her the last bite of his pom tart, a gooey cinnamon fruit confection common to Elsah-ra that was one of his favorites. And by the way she'd wolfed hers down, one of her new favorites too. She took the bite, and he took her empty plate from her lap and tossed it in a nearby trash can, brushing his hands off on his jeans. Trinity stared into the distance, her face somber. He sat next to Haven and touched Trinity's arm as he tapped his head.

*What's wrong?*

*Look there, in the woods.*

Ryker saw River, his gaze focused on Haven. Ryker's face hardened.

*I feel something not right,* Trinity said.

*About me?*

*No, and that's the weird part. It's Haven. Seeing River gave me a blurry image, but one that makes me anxious.*

*Got it. I'll let Silas know.* Ryker's stomach tightened. Despite the sorry state of their relationship, he didn't want to hurt his brother. He knew River was a terrible match for Haven and doubted he had any genuine feelings for her. But he also didn't like to see his brother in pain, particularly if he was causing it. He stood and Silas started to follow, but Trinity held his arm and shook her head.

"Let him go. It's okay," she said.

"I'm good," Ryker said to him, and strode into the woods.

River watched Ryker approach but didn't acknowledge him.

"I'm sorry," Ryker said. "I know this isn't easy, and I didn't intend to fall for Haven."

"Why are you here?" he asked, his voice low.

"I wanted to say I was sorry for hurting you."

"Does that mean you're giving her up?"

"No, I can't do that."

"Then take your insincere apologies and kindly fuck off."

Ryker sighed. "River, please. There's no reason for this to escalate."

"I'm sure you see it that way since you won. Again," River said.

"Gods, not everything is a competition. And Haven is not a prize, like a toy at a carnival. Did you ever listen to what she wanted?"

"Why do you always take what I have?" River said, ignoring Ryker's question.

"What exactly have I ever taken from you?" Anger shrouded his face, but River said nothing. "What's really bothering you is I woke up one day and decided I was done whoring around with you. I had a bad time in my life, but I got through it. I tried to convince you to think better of yourself, and now you hate me for not being like you."

"That's your opinion, which I don't give a shit about. After all the things I've done for you..." he said under his breath.

"Like what? What have you done that's so worthy of giving up on a person I've grown to care for? Just so you can toy with her, then throw her away like you do with every female."

"You know nothing about me," River seethed. "I'm not kidding. Stay the hell away from me."

"Don't do this. You're my brother."

River gave a rough laugh. "We haven't been family for years." He unsheathed a dagger and kept it by his leg.

"Fine. But I'm warning you, don't go near Haven. Trinity can feel your intentions toward her. I will not let you harm her." Ryker walked away from River and sat between Silas and Haven, who reached for his hand and moved closer. He glanced back at the woods, but River was gone.

The sun had long vanished when Dax and Dune said their goodbyes.

"I'm already missing our pod," Harper said as she watched them walk away.

"Our pod is the closest I've had to a family," Haven said wistfully. "I feel I'm losing them."

Harper held her hand. "You have us."

"I don't think you understand how lucky you are."

"I do," Ryker said. "I never knew my mother, and my father barely tolerated us." Haven stroked his hand. "I know what it's like to have a disinterested family. My father allowed Shallah to stay with us, and for that, I'm grateful. Without her, River and I would've had no one."

"That's not true. You had me," Harper said.

"True, but not when we were kids. You didn't come along until the Academy. But I still like having a bratty little sister." Ryker tugged on a lock of Harper's hair. She swatted his hand away and he laughed.

"You're obnoxious," she said.

"You love me that way."

They walked back to the Palace together. Lamps spaced every twenty feet threw puddles of soft light onto the paths that wound through the gardens.

Haven walked next to Silas and asked, "Where is your family?"

"Right here," he said, looking at Ryker and Trinity, his arm draped over her shoulders.

"Your parents?"

"Dead. No siblings."

"Not that I wish my parents were dead, but honestly, sometimes I think it would be easier."

"I get it. But you should realize you have a choice. You don't have to claim your family because of blood. You can claim a family of your own, one that you love."

"That's beautiful. You're a real softie, Silas."

"Only to pretty females."

"And a shameless flirt."

"Guilty," he said. She elbowed him, and he squeezed the arm she had looped through his. They walked through the Palace gardens to the patio off the main ballroom.

Silas said, "What are your plans for the evening?"

"Your call," Ryker said to Haven.

"My place again?" she said.

"Not a good idea," Silas said. "One night is fine, but without wardings, too much of a risk. I can skim you to the loft."

"Do you mind?" Ryker asked. "Silas has rules even I have to follow."

Haven shrugged. "Sure."

Silas stepped close to her, his arms circling her waist. "Ready?" They vanished and appeared in the Garret's loft.

A few minutes later, Ryker landed on the loft's balcony with Trinity. He released her, and she said good night to both as she walked down the stairs to her suite.

"I saw you speaking with River," Haven said to Ryker when he sat next to her on the sofa.

"Yes. I know I hurt him, but I don't think I can fix what's broken between us."

"I feel like I'm standing between you."

Ryker tipped her head up. "You aren't. River and I have had our differences for longer than I can remember. We may be twins, but we aren't alike."

"I used to think you were identical. Now I can't see how I ever thought that."

"I don't want to think about River. I've reached out to him countless times, and he never reaches back. He is who he is, and he makes his own choices."

"What happens to us?" Haven asked, playing with the buttons on his shirt. "I have to go to ComSim. I committed to the Aerial. How do we work?"

"Look at me." Haven stared back into his intent silver eyes. "You need to know I don't casually sleep with females. I'm not like River."

"I know. But I don't know what I should expect from you, from us, together." She sighed heavily. "I'm not that person who makes demands from the start. And whatever you want is fine. But it's better to know now to avoid disappointment."

"I told you I wanted everything. I didn't say that to sleep with you, then run away. I meant it."

"Gods, 'everything' is such a big word."

"Do you really think I would put you through breaking your contract to Lukas, taking you from my brother, and the wrath of your parents and the damn king if I wasn't serious?"

"First, you didn't take me from your brother," she interrupted him.

"I'm not done," he said, silencing her. She pinched his ribs. He flinched and squeezed her knee. "If all I wanted was sex, there are easier ways to get it. I had other options." She scowled at him. "Just being honest," he teased, kissing her gently.

"I don't even know how to think about that. Right now, I just want to punch you."

Ryker's eyes glittered. "A little hand-to-hand combat training? That could be fun. Particularly if you're naked."

"You're sick."

He scooped her up into his lap and wrapped her legs around him. His hands cupped her backside and pulled her to him. "You like me like that." Being close to him, feeling his hands on her, was quickly becoming her new favorite thing.

She kissed him and said, "I guess that means there's something really wrong with me." His breath hitched as his gaze dropped and watched her hips slide up him.

"We'll make it work. The Academy. The Aerial. My job. All of it. I want to be with you. All the rest sounds like noise."

"And if I'm gone for months at the Aerial?"

"I'll miss you horribly. And I may become too familiar with my hand." Haven raised her brow and laughed in surprise. "What? I thought you wanted honesty."

"Maybe not that much honesty," she said.

"Well, if it's any consolation, you do a better job." His grin reached his shimmering silver eyes.

"Gods, you're awful," she said, relaxing a little as his humor took the edge off her anxiety. He stroked her back, his fingers lacing through her hair.

"I guess what I'm trying to say is I'm not going anywhere. I want to be with you. Being away from you doesn't change that."

"Okay," she said, running her hands over his chest.

"So, in the meantime, do I get to see you naked?" he said. Haven smiled and rested her forehead against his. "I know this is new, and you really don't know me. But I enjoy your company, your mind. And your body. I wasn't looking for this either. I know it's unsettling. But exciting too. And it's what I want."

"We'll figure this out together?"

"Yes." She felt Ryker's hands on her, circling her hips and cupping her backside, drawing her closer, harder, to him. She needed to be even closer. To feel his touch, his skin on hers. "Just like this. Tell me what's on your mind. I'm here to listen."

"Are you listening now?" she said, grinding into him. Ryker blinked slowly.

"Definitely," he said.

# CHAPTER 34

## Araine

River prowled the murky streets of southern Araine, running from the anger roiling through his mind and clouding his vision. His meeting wasn't for another hour, but if he relaxed, the feeling would creep out of the darkness where he had pushed it down for years. Ryker. He had protected him for decades, shielding him from the realities of life with their father. That was his role, what his father had groomed him for his entire life. And having Ryker by his side made that role bearable. Then Ryker left him. For fifteen years, he had buried that loss, cloaking it in anger. And now that anger surged, growing ugly and vicious as he struggled to contain his past.

He'd moved from the Garret to a small Aerial apartment in Araine. Not as convenient or comfortable as the Garret, but he was already enjoying the freedom the anonymity of the new quarters offered. And right now, River wanted to remain unseen. It was when he felt most like himself. When he could simply *be*, away from everyone's judgement and disapproval.

River ceased his roaming half a block from where his meeting would be, the darkness concealing him and allowing him to survey the surrounding area. He didn't trust Lilith, and Roque even less, but he really needed to leave Araine as soon as possible. The deal he struck with Lilith would finally get him away from Araine, but Ryker had blindsided him and now stood squarely in the way. If it had been any other person, he would have eliminated the obstacle. But as much as he hated Ryker right now, he knew he didn't really want him dead, though he certainly wasn't above inflicting some pain. He hoped this meeting with Roque would help him find a solution.

Roque walked down the street toward him, and from the shadows, River could see he was alone. River checked his daggers and emerged from the darkness. "Thank you for meeting me," Roque said.

River leaned against the building. "What's your grand plan for Haven?"

"To get right to the point, in order to capture the Phoenix, you must Pair with her."

"I know that," River said with an exaggerated sigh. "I didn't need to meet you in the middle of the night in a dark alley to hear that. But my relationship with Haven has chilled, and Ryker now stands between us."

"Yes, that's why I'm here, away from Lilith. I think you misunderstood me. I would gladly eliminate Ryker, particularly if it means keeping him from Pairing with the Phoenix. Lilith forbids it. She has a fondness for Ryker. She always has, and it's a weakness."

River's eyes narrowed. "What are you saying? Lilith is in love with Ryker?"

"Really, do you think Lilith can love anyone?"

He snorted. "Probably not."

"She covets him. She wants him, to control and use his power. She also is attracted to him and wouldn't mind sleeping with him."

"Ryker has no interest in her. I may not know my brother well anymore, but I know that. He'll never get anywhere near Lilith."

"I agree with you, which is why I said her obsession with him is a weakness. She is blind to him, unfortunately." Roque paced the street. "Forget Lilith for a minute. Let's discuss the Phoenix and what I can offer you. What Lilith didn't tell you, because she doesn't know, is that to Pair with the Phoenix you need a blood bond. Specifically, the Phoenix must share your blood."

"See, this is exactly the type of nonsense that isn't helpful," he said, annoyed. "Your talk of dark magic is mysticism."

"I know more about the Phoenix bloodline than you ever will. Trust me. If Haven shares your blood, she will be bound to you for life. She can't harm you, and you can direct her power. And her magic will enhance your own. And since your magic is Persuasion, your influence over her will almost be control."

"She isn't susceptible to Persuasion," River said.

"That will change through a Pairing." Roque's voice faded a little, softened, but became more urgent. "And I know how to get another magic. One of immense power. I'm guessing this would interest you."

"Change my magic?" River challenged. "Now we are really entering the realm of ridiculous."

"Not at all. And the person who can help you is right in front of you. Adrien. It isn't without risks, but from what I can see, you're a risk taker. Would you like being a world walker?" River blinked, curiosity slowly replacing his disbelief. "I know how much you envy your brother's power. I'm offering you a way to have the same gift. If you then bind the Phoenix, you will become as powerful as Gabriel."

River swallowed, his mind reeling with the chance to be different. A better version of who he was. "So how do I do this?"

"Get the Phoenix to share your blood. She needs to be in her Phoenix form when she bites you."

"Are you kidding me? Have you seen the Phoenix? It's like a wild animal."

"You're resourceful. And an officer in the Aerial. I trust your combat skills are excellent."

"Yes, in warfare, against soldiers. I'm not a wild animal tamer," River said.

"Well, you better become one."

"And how do I get her to shift into the Phoenix? She's only done it a few times."

"Provoke her. The Phoenix will respond to threats or danger."

River's face darkened. This sounded like more fun all the time. "Those happen to be my strengths."

"Why do you think Lilith and I approached you? We know what you're capable of. I can give you a rune that will limit her Light magic. Unfortunately, it won't work on the Phoenix's magic, so make sure you contain her before you get her to shift."

"How the hell will you limit her magic?" he asked.

"The rune is a transfer of Canceller magic."

"Seraphim don't have Canceller magic, and neither do fae or faeries," he said, taking half a step away. "What are you?"

"That's none of your concern. Take the rune. You'll need it."

River balked. A plan formed in his mind. He would need this magic to pull it off, but he would be stepping into the realm of darkness, further than he'd ever gone before. At some point, there may be no return. But he could think about that later.

He lifted his shirt. Roque's hands glowed, and River winced as Roque forced the magic into his skin. "This will only last a day or two. We will give you an opportunity tomorrow to get Haven alone."

"And a new magic?"

"Talk to Adrien. But focus on the Phoenix for now. The situation with her is urgent." Roque drifted away into the darkness of the night.

# CHAPTER 35

## Falco Park

Haven rested in Ryker's arms, feeling his chest move with hers in that steady, deep rhythm of sleep. The echoes of what they shared last night lingered on her body, in her full, bruised lips from his kisses and the pleasant ache between her thighs. In these moments, where she was awake and Ryker was asleep, she consumed the feel of him, his relaxed body heavy and solid against hers. Careful not to wake him, she stroked his powerful leg between hers, felt his arms around her, took in the smell of him. Crisp pine, and a freshness, like being near the ocean. Different from his lush, warm scent when he was ready for sex.

Her heart ached in a way that was thrilling but also made her anxious. Her emotions seemed to tangle up in a knot when she was with him. And then there was what they shared in his bed, the physical responses he provoked from her body, sensations she never knew she could feel. Even the small things sent her emotions reeling, like when he held her hand or pulled her into his arms, simply to touch her, to feel her. The way he supported her and stood beside her, not in front or behind, but willing to do either if she needed him. Her heart was starting to need him, and that was unnerving. She ached at the thought of him being gone. Or worse, if he didn't feel this too.

She sighed to herself and pushed away her fears, drowning her uncertainties in the feel of him. She couldn't help herself, and kissed his neck, slowly, to his chin. He stirred, then lowered his head and kissed her deeply, his full lips soft on hers, his tongue teasing.

"When you hold me like this, I believe we can have anything," she said.

He held her tight, and his scent shifted, deepened, became richer. "We can," he whispered. He rolled her under him, settling between her legs. She tipped her hips, and with a single stroke, he slid inside her. He kissed her, and Haven forgot the rest of the world.

Haven sat at the kitchen table and popped the last of her blueberry muffin into her mouth.

"Finished?" Ryker asked. She nodded and drained the last sip of tea. He took their dishes to the kitchen, rinsed them, and stacked them in the sink.

"Trinity just told me we're meeting with your parents this morning," he said, coming back to her. "They want us there within the hour."

"Why would my parents want to talk with your Triad?"

"Well, it's unusual but not completely unheard of. Occasionally, the royals take an interest in crossing politics. Sometimes they ask our opinions." He shrugged. "I'm not sure when I'll be back. You can stay, but you can't leave the loft. Once you walk downstairs, the wards will seal this floor."

"I'm trying to wrap my brain around the crazy security you have," Haven said.

"I know, it's a lot to take in. The wardings, Silas..."

"It means you're special." She wrapped her arms around his waist, and he huffed.

"I know it can be overbearing, but there isn't anything I can do to change it."

"I'm not asking you to change. Honestly, your security and protocols don't matter to me. If you had to pick a gatekeeper, Silas is the best. But what do you mean there's nothing you can do about it?"

"Silas and I are bound to one another. He can compel me to obey him."

"Really? Wow."

"That's why it's important to have a strong relationship between a Shadowalker and a Warrior. There needs to be respect and trust. And there certainly is between Silas and me."

"Has Silas ever compelled you to do something?"

"Never. Not even close. He doesn't ask unless he feels strongly. If he asks, I do it. Although, I swear he has compelled me to have one too many drinks. Which he denies. But I think he's a liar," Ryker said.

Haven giggled. "I can't imagine Silas asking you to do anything you wouldn't normally agree to, so I'm going with Silas on this one."

Ryker grinned. "You clearly haven't spent enough time with Silas at a bar." Haven laughed with him as he brushed her hair back, lacing a lock through his fingers and feeling the softness. "You are beautiful when you smile. And when you laugh, my heart stops."

"You need to stop talking or take me back to bed."

"Don't tempt me." He ran his thumb over her soft, full lips, and she shuddered against him.

"Ready to go?" Trinity's voice floated up from the stairwell.

"Yes, ready." Ryker asked Haven, "Are you staying?"

"No, I'll go back to my apartment to clean up and see Harper. I should catch up with my pod. There's only three days before ComSim, and we've scattered this week."

Ryker walked her to the lobby where Silas was waiting. "I'll let you know when the meeting is over."

Haven waved and walked the short distance to her apartment complex. The lobby was bustling with cadets coming and going and lounging together in the building's first floor common area.

She hung out in the lobby for an hour, visiting with a few of her squad she hadn't seen since arriving in Araine.

Eventually, she excused herself and walked up the stairs to the fourth floor where she entered her apartment and plopped on the couch. She hadn't really been alone since arriving in Araine and was grateful for the silence. The way her life had changed since she first walked through the door of this apartment was bewildering. She could hardly believe it was only three days ago. But she wouldn't change a thing. Her thoughts ran through the memories of the last time she was in this apartment, of what happened in her bedroom with Ryker only a few short days ago. She traced her lips, almost feeling him, tasting him. She took a deep breath, shaking off the ache that thoughts of Ryker always seemed to cause, and returned to the present. A nice, hot shower sounded divine. Or maybe a cold one. Her lips twitched in a smile just for herself as she took off her shirt and walked toward the bath.

She paused as a subtle breeze caressed her face. The door to the balcony was closed. So was the window. But the breeze grew stronger, lifting the hair off her shoulders. The air around her felt thick and hard to breathe. In a single movement, she spun and unfurled her silver wings, slashing behind her.

River jumped back, but not fast enough. Her wing sliced him across the chest. Not a deep wound, but he bled through his armored vest. He hissed, "You bitch—" Before he could get the next word out, Haven's fist connected with his jaw. She swung her leg, catching him in the ankle and tripping him in the same movement. River went down hard. She pulsed a wave of Light, and ripples of heat surged toward him. The magic moved around River, and he jumped to his feet and slammed his fist into her temple. Haven spun and landed on her side, her vision narrowing as she shook her head to keep from losing consciousness. Her head jerked back as River fisted her hair and pulled her to her feet. She slammed her elbow into his ribs. He grunted, but yanked her closer.

"Keep fighting me, I like it." Her initial surprise and fear shifted to disgust and anger. Haven curved her silver blades toward him again, connecting with his. Her throat constricted, and she gasped. "Put your wings away, or I swear I'll suffocate you," he snarled. Haven choked as River's magic removed the last bit of air from her lungs.

"Go to hell," she rasped, and dropped to her knees as her world went black.

Ryker cocked his head at Hope. "You asked us to come here to discuss rifts between Praesia and Hura? Why are you concerned with this?"

Ryker and Trinity sat on a sofa across from Astor and Hope. Silas leaned against the wall, his gaze occasionally catching Ryker's but mostly locked on Hope's guardian, who hovered behind her. He kept his gray feathered wings unfurled and on display but tucked tightly.

Astor said, "We were told the hurak incursions have increased. It's concerning. Since the daeva invasions have ceased, we are wondering if the huraks are taking their place, if they have formed a new rift. So we were curious how rifts are formed."

"Why are you asking me? Shouldn't you be asking a guardian? Besides, to the best of my knowledge, huraks can't form rifts. And even if they could, they aren't dangerous."

"Yes, but we don't allow them to enter Praesia. You've seen many rifts, though, correct?" Hope asked.

"Yes," Ryker drawled.

"Can you describe them? What do they look like? Are there differences in rifts between worlds?" Astor asked.

Ryker answered their questions the best he could for the next hour. Finally, he said, "A guardian like Adrien will know more. You should ask him." He rose to leave. Even Silas was frustrated by this entire pointless conversation.

"Ryker, could we have a moment alone?" Astor requested. Silas stepped closer to Ryker, his eyes hard. "We would like to discuss your relationship with Haven. If you have a few minutes."

"Is that what all this questioning was about?" Ryker asked.

Astor shifted uncomfortably in his seat. "Yes and no. Hope and I were trying to get a sense of you. The rifts into Berinia do concern us, so it seemed like something we could talk about."

Ryker raised an eyebrow. "If you wanted to talk with me, you could have asked. I'm happy to speak with you about anything, including my relationship with Haven."

Hope said, "You're right, we should have been more direct. Our apologies for that."

Astor said to Silas, "We will only be a minute. We can keep the door open."

"Fine," Silas relented, moving closer to the door to keep Ryker in his eyesight as Astor and Hope followed Ryker into a private study. Hope's guardian lurked just inside the open door, his face expressionless but blocking Silas's view.

Silas moved toward the guardian to move him out of his line of sight when Trinity sat straight and whipped her gaze to him. "You need to leave. Something is wrong with Haven. Go now. I think she's in her apartment." Silas drew a knife from the sheath on his thigh and vanished.

Haven's eyes flew open as someone slapped her face.

"Wake up," River snapped. She immediately struggled and reached for her magic but felt nothing. Her arms and legs were bound to a chair. An iron band locked around her ribs contained her wings and muffled her magic.

"I knew you were a bastard, but really? This is extreme. What the hell do you want?"

"Well, I used to want you, but not now that my brother has polluted you." He dipped his head to her hair and scented her. She jerked away from him. "I can smell him on you. Must have been quite a night."

"It was fantastic. Do you want to hear the details? How many times we made love? And how? Where his mouth was on me? Where mine was on him?"

"Not really." His eyes were cold as he grabbed her hair and drew a dagger. He sliced her cheek to the bone, from nose to ear. She grunted as blood ran down her face, the pain dulling her surprise, then fueling her anger. "Keep talking like that and I'll start carving up pieces."

"The first time we made love, he was on top of me. The next time I—" Haven screamed as River stabbed her shoulder, twisting the handle and pushing the dagger to the hilt, the tip emerging from her back.

"Keep it up. I love watching you bleed."

She ground her teeth and steadied her breathing, controlling the pain as he withdrew the knife. She refused to give him what he wanted, though the panic welling inside her threatened to break through the thin bravery she clung to. Blood splashed into her lap, but she gritted her teeth and continued, "But I forgot to mention, before he was inside me, his tongue was on my—" River's fist slammed into her face again, splitting the cut on her cheek further. Her head exploded in pain, and the world faded.

"Bitch, you need to shut your mouth. Right now."

"Fuck off," she growled, shaking her head to cling to consciousness. She felt tiny drops of blood splatter on her chest.

"Seriously, I will cut you into little pieces if you don't shut up. Starting with your tongue," he said.

"You want to fight? Unbind me, you coward," she spat. The room blinked into darkness. Haven shook her head again, and River's wary face came back into focus. Drawing blood from each shoulder and between her breasts, he sliced her bra, exposing her chest.

"You do have great tits." He leered at her full breasts. "You're a little too big for me. Too tall. Too hippy. I like my females petite, slender. But I'd still enjoy myself, I think." He dragged the tip of his dagger across her chest under her collarbone, drawing a line of blood that ran down her ribs.

"You should see what your brother does to these tits," she taunted. He grabbed her by the throat.

"I'm going to enjoy having you as my slave," he said, his cold eyes holding hers as his hand circled her neck. He dropped the knife and brought his other hand up to grip her throat, his thumbs pressing in and closing off her windpipe. Haven struggled against her bindings, against his grip, and her world flashed in a burst of red flames.

Fangs slid from Haven's upper jaw, and a thin stream of blood ran from her mouth over her lips. The Phoenix hissed at River, growling low in her throat.

"That's it. Now bite me."

His fist slammed into her cheek again. Her head snapped back, and she roared and lunged for him.

But he wasn't there. A huge blond male slammed him to the ground and stabbed him in the chest with his dagger. He screamed.

"That was an inch from your heart." The blond's voice was low and even. Confident and commanding. He straddled River's chest, his knees pinning his arms to the ground. "The only reason this knife isn't deep in your heart is I'm saving you for Ryker to kill. Get your ass out of Araine within the hour. And if I see you near Haven again, the next time I won't miss. Understood?" He withdrew the knife and sliced River's cheek. The Phoenix felt the burn of her own similar wound. The male released River, who scrambled to his feet, holding his chest and wiping the blood from his face. He stumbled to the balcony and flew away.

The Phoenix scanned the warrior's unfamiliar face, his large frame, the bloody knife in his hand, then hissed at him, baring her fangs. "You're hurt. Let me help you," he said, his voice low and soothing. He took off his shirt and approached her. "I need to remove the iron banding."

She growled at him, and the deep rumbling halted his advance. She could feel his wariness rolling from him. "Ssshhh, it's okay. I'm here to help you." She hesitated, then reassessed him, the tone of his voice, his willingness to keep his distance until she allowed him near.

"Who are you," she snarled.

The blond man took a small step forward. "I'm Silas. You know me."

"I've never seen you before."

"Haven knows me. Who are you?"

"I'm her heart. Her courage." The Phoenix raised her head and looked at him with disdain. "And *I'll* protect her."

"I know you will. But so will I. She's important to me. And to Ryker." Silas held out his arm. "Feel this, my bond with Ryker." She gripped one of the swirling tattoos. Silas winced as flames seared his arm. But she felt the link.

"You're a friend."

"Yes, always," he gasped. "Let me help you." The Phoenix released him and nodded. He untied her arms and legs and reached behind her, unclasping the iron from her chest. He slid his shirt over her head and helped her to her feet.

"It's okay now. I'm going to take you to a healer." Holding her tight, they vanished.

# CHAPTER 36

## The Garret

Ryker never had time to speak with Astor and Hope. As soon as Silas vanished, Trinity barged into the conference room and pulled Ryker aside. A few words from her and Ryker unfurled his raven wings, scooped her into his arms, and flew through the Palace, over the gardens and toward the Temple. They landed in front of the medical wing and rushed inside and found Silas and Haven in a treatment room with a healer.

Haven was a mess. Silas's shirt was covered in the blood that dripped from her face and welled from her shoulder. Her face was swollen and purple, and a ring of bruises around her throat was turning black.

"It's not that bad," she said.

Ryker could barely contain his rage at her bravery. He touched the cheek that wasn't cut and brushed the hair from her face. "It's pretty bad. You should see yourself. You look awful."

"I got in a few good hits. He bled."

His voice grew dangerously calm. "I will kill him. He'll do more than bleed."

"Save some for me. I want to cut off a few pieces first."

Farna walked in and waved at the crowd, shooing them. "Everyone out. I'll let you know when she can have visitors." Ryker didn't move. "Ryker, that means you, too." He bristled. *Not a chance.* Farna held his arm. "I know what you're thinking. I need to talk with her to make sure she's okay," he said gently. "I don't need long, but give us some privacy."

Ryker clenched his jaw, then nodded and reluctantly moved toward the door. He looked to Haven, "I'll be right outside. Call me if you need me."

He let Silas pull him away, then wheeled on him as soon as they were outside. "Tell me what happened. What did you see? Why is she wearing your shirt?"

"He didn't...he hurt her. He made her bleed. But he didn't rape her if that's what you're thinking," Silas said. Trinity sat heavily on a bench, and Ryker paced in the hallway. "He bound her in iron and stabbed her in the shoulder and cut her chest and face. She...she was naked from the waist up, though. That's why I gave her my shirt."

Ryker halted. His face contorted, and his hands trembled as a thread of Bane slithered up his arm. "While I was sitting at the Palace, babbling on about rifts to Hura. Gods," he said with disgust.

Silas continued, "She got him too, you should know. He had a good slice across the chest and a bruise on his jaw. I think she also tried to use her magic. I could see scorch marks on the wall. She put up a good fight before he got her bound."

"What the fuck? Why did he do this?" Ryker said.

"I don't know. But when I got there, she was in her Phoenix form." Ryker's head whipped to Trinity, and he saw the same gaping look on her face. "He was, I don't know, egging her on. Provoking her. He told her to bite him."

"River is sick," Ryker said. "Perverted. Pain is erotic to him."

Silas blanched. "Gods, I didn't realize it was that bad."

Ryker felt Trinity's touch on his arm. "I'm sorry I didn't see this earlier," she said, her voice tight. "I could have prevented this."

Ryker stopped pacing. "You cannot seriously be blaming yourself. She's probably alive right now because of your vision. How did you See her anyway?"

She shrugged. "Maybe because you're connected to her? I really don't know. It came to me fast and clear."

"I didn't kill him, but I came close." Silas told him what he did and what he said to River. "If you want to hunt him, let me know. I'm ready any time you are. But it's your call whether he lives. I got close enough to his heart he won't be coming after her any time soon. I'm thinking the only way to be sure is to put him down. But it's your call."

He gripped Silas's arm. "Thank you."

Ryker sat with Trinity and Silas while Farna worked with Haven. An hour later, Farna emerged into the hallway. "She's fine. I've healed the cuts on her chest and her bruises, mostly. The cut on her face and the stab wound will need another session to fully heal them and remove the scars, but she should be fine. She will be sore for the next day or two, though. Emotionally, she's a little rattled, but she's pretty tough. She's okay. Go gentle for a while, but she's more pissed than upset."

Ryker exhaled loudly and ran his hand through his hair. "Can I see her now?"

"Yes, of course," Farna said, opening the door for him.

The bruises on Haven's face were healed, but the green-tinged marks on her throat were still visible. The cut on her cheek was a red line, but healed. Ryker walked to her and took her in his arms. She felt solid and warm. And alive. He felt her strength as she pushed her way into the aching spot in his heart she had claimed for her own. She returned his embrace, sliding her arms around his waist.

"I'm okay," she said.

"Tell me what you need," he said, desperate to be useful again.

"Can we go back to the loft?"

"Of course." He stroked her cheek. "I want you to stay there until you leave for ComSim. I need to keep my eyes on you."

"I'm okay. You don't have to do that. I don't want to get in the way."

Ryker gently kissed her forehead. "I'd like to say you don't have a choice, but you do. I want you there. Not because I want to cage you, but because I want you with me." Haven rested her head on his chest again. "Before we leave, I want Silas to give you an access rune to the Garret. You can come and go as you please. It will only last a week or so, but at least you won't be a prisoner or have to rely on Silas. Are you okay with that?"

"Yes," she whispered. Ryker left to get Silas and find a guardian who could apply the rune. He returned a few minutes later, and Silas and Trinity followed them into her room. Haven said to Silas, "Thank you."

"Any time. Although I'm not sure you really needed me. I think you were about to rip out his throat."

"I wish I had."

"So do I," Trinity said. They shared a fierce look.

"Usually, I apply runes like this to your ribs. Is that okay?" the guardian asked. Haven agreed and lifted her gown. The guardian placed his hand on her ribs above her hip and touched one of the swirling tattoos on Silas's arm. A minute later, he removed his hand.

Farna said, "You can leave whenever you're ready. Rest for the next few days. No flying, and avoid magic if you can. Give yourself time to heal. And come see me again before you leave and I'll clean up the scars."

"Thank you, Farna," Haven said.

"Are you ready?" Ryker asked. Haven nodded and reached for Silas, but Ryker took her hand. "You don't need a skim. I'll take you." Ryker walked her to the courtyard. He unfurled his raven wings and held her close, and with one downstroke, launched into the air. A few minutes later, they landed on his balcony. He gently set her down and held her hand as he led her inside. "Farna said you should rest. What do you want?"

"Actually, resting sounds great. I'm...just tired." He led her into his bedroom and pulled back the blankets, and Haven crawled into his bed. He covered her and lay next to her, holding her tight until he felt her breathing deepen. He drew in her warm jasmine scent and swore to himself nothing, no one, would hurt her again.

Haven woke in the dark, briefly disoriented. She buried her face in her pillow, and a hint of fresh pine and ocean calmed her, reminding her she was in Ryker's bed in the loft. She rose and walked to the living area and found him sitting on the balcony, a drink in his hand.

"How are you feeling?" he asked.

"Okay. My neck and shoulder are sore, but I'm fine."

"Hungry?"

"Yes, a little," she said.

Ryker called a windsprite and ordered her dinner. "Trinity went to your apartment and brought some of your things here. I hope you don't mind."

"Thanks. I'd love a shower."

He walked to her, took her hand, and led her to the second bedroom where she found a bag sitting on the bed. "You can use the bath here, or mine. By the time you're done, dinner will be here. Take your time." He left her and closed the door behind him.

Haven showered, her soapy hand lingering on the puckered scar on her shoulder. Pain and fear lurked in the edges of her thoughts, waiting for any weakness to rend her emotions. But she gathered herself and shoved it down, embracing her anger to give her strength. Fucking River. She'd kill him if she ever saw him again. She froze, surprised by her own venom. *He's Ryker's brother.* She rinsed her body and turned off the water and pressed the soft towel to her face.

The situation couldn't be more complicated.

She dressed in a shirt and leggings, then joined Ryker on the balcony. Her hands glowed as she ran her fingers through her hair.

"Better?" he asked.

"Yes. Would be better with one of those." She pointed at his drink. He walked to the bar, and by the time he returned, her hair was dry.

"That's a neat trick."

"One benefit of having heat as part of my magic." She sipped the cocktail he handed her.

"I'm so sorry, Haven," Ryker said.

"It's not your fault. I don't want you thinking it was. There is something really wrong with River, and that's not on you."

"Do you need to talk? If you're not comfortable talking to me, I can get Harper. Or Corde. You haven't met him, but he's a Sympath. Very good at what he does. Or anyone else you want."

"I'm fine. Really. I want to *kill* River, but I'm okay. And honestly? I don't want to talk about it. Maybe someday, but dwelling on it will give River power over me. And that will not happen." Ryker watched her carefully. "What?" she said.

"You are one of the strongest people I've ever met. I'm a little awestruck right now." Haven stared at her empty drink, hoping he couldn't see the heat in her cheeks in the dark.

Ryker rose. "Your dinner is here."

She looked up and saw a covered plate on the counter that hadn't been there moments before. "Thank gods, I'm starving," Haven said. Ryker brought the food to the table and sat next to her, keeping her company while she ate. "Did you eat already?"

"Yes, hours ago. It's close to midnight."

"Oh! I didn't realize I'd slept that long." They talked about small things through dinner and into the dim hours of the morning.

Eventually, Ryker stifled a yawn. "Unfortunately, I didn't get a six-hour nap this afternoon. I'm beat."

"Sorry, I didn't mean to keep you up," Haven said, rising with him. She led him to his bedroom, and he remained in the doorway as she slid under the covers. She patted the bed next to her.

Ryker stripped, and as he pulled on loose cotton pants, she caught a shadowy glimpse of muscles and skin, of powerful, toned arms and broad chest. Strength that she needed to feel, to lean on. He slid under the covers, and she wiggled in close, surrendering to the warmth and comfort of his embrace.

The sun dragged Haven to the surface of a sleepy fog the next morning. She rubbed her eyes, blinded by the rays streaming through the floor-to-ceiling window. She rose, rifled through Ryker's closet, and slipped into a thick robe, then padded silently into the loft. Ryker looked up from his desk in the corner on the far side of the stairs and set down his pen.

"How do you feel?" he asked.

"Pretty good. Starving."

"I'm not surprised. It's after noon."

Full daylight streamed through the doors, heat radiating from the glass and warming the floor under her feet. "Why didn't you wake me?"

"You needed the sleep. Do you feel up for going out?"

"Sure. What do you have in mind?"

"Nothing fancy. Get dressed, and I'll show you."

She emerged from the bedroom. "Too casual?" she said, looking at her jeans and t-shirt.

"No, that's perfect." He slung a large bag over his shoulder, took her hand, and led her through the streets of Falco Park to an open, grassy park. As he unpacked and spread a blanket, she toed off her flats and wiggled her toes in the soft grass. She sat down, tilted her face to the sky, and closed her eyes. The late spring sun bathed her in warmth, chasing away the ugly events of yesterday and promising fresh starts.

She felt Ryker's fingers trace the red scar on her face and opened her eyes. He smiled at her, then kissed the mark softly, then her lips.

"Are we going to eat?" she whispered, distracted by the heat in his silvery eyes.

His eyes dropped to her breasts. "Yes. I'm starving."

She grinned at him. "We're in public."

"What? I am hungry." He clucked at her. "You have a dirty mind."

She rolled her eyes. He pecked her cheek, unpacked a small platter, and arranged fruit, cheeses, and bread, as well as cured and roasted meats. "I didn't know what you liked, so I had the hobs pack a little of everything." He removed the lid from a container of olives and stuck a small knife into a block of creamy goat cheese.

"This is perfect," she said, popping a grape into her mouth.

"Except fries. I know how much you like those."

"I like them best when I'm stealing yours," she said, looking at him through her lashes.

"Oh? Thievery deserves a harsh punishment. Especially something valuable, like fries."

Haven crawled to him on her hands and knees, inches from his lips. "You're full of empty promises." A slow smile spread across his face, and his lips brushed hers. She leaned toward him, but he pulled away. "Tease," she said.

"A gift," he said, and handed her a book. Haven sat back and took it from him. Her eyes lit up when she saw the cover, and she beamed.

"This was on your nightstand at your apartment. Trinity brought it along with your clothes. I have some work to do but thought the fresh air and sunshine would be better than being cooped up inside." Haven rifled through the pages before setting the book aside and taking the piece of bread he handed her.

She spread cheese and piled shaved roast beef on top. "Two more days before ComSim. Then the Aerial. Did you like it?"

"It was okay. I liked the strategy and war gaming, but I'm not much for the military."

"Do you like being a Shadowalker?" she asked. "With your magic, I'm assuming you knew what you would do with your life even before the Academy."

"I knew world walking was an option, yes. And I do like it. But when I went to the Academy, I didn't know if I had Bane. And world walking without Bane is a limited field. I knew I wasn't in-terested in politics the way Lukas is. So yes, there was some uncertainty at first."

"I wish I knew what my options were. At least to narrow the possibilities."

"You will. There's no rush. Enjoy your time in the Aerial. You'll figure it out."

"Did you say 'enjoy the Aerial'? I think you mean 'endure it,'" she corrected.

Ryker laughed. "Yes, you're right. But it's a challenge I think you'll also enjoy. The training is much like the lessons and war gaming of last year. From what I saw, I'm sure you'll excel. Although beach clothes are out of the question," he said, giving her a knowing look.

"I hate being cold," Haven grumbled.

Ryker's silver eyes glinted in the sun. "I know." She scowled at him. He chuckled and kissed her, then offered her a slice of apple.

The sun dipped below the trees, casting the first shadow of the afternoon. Ryker glanced up from his papers at the setting sun. Haven's head rested on his lap, her book fallen closed an hour ago when she'd drifted to sleep. Her breathing was regular and deep, her face serene and relaxed. He brushed the hair from her forehead, and she startled awake.

"I fell asleep," she said, stretching like a cat.

"You did. You were snoring."

"I don't snore." She poked him in the ribs.

He flinched away and grabbed her hand. "Ow, wench."

"That didn't hurt, you big baby." He laughed, then kissed her fingers.

"It's getting late. Trinity tapped me and suggested going to the Outpost for dinner. I told her probably not but wondered if it sounds good to you."

"Actually, it does. I think I'd like that," she said.

Ryker brushed off his jeans and packed the remnants of their lunch in the bag. "I'll let her know."

After a quick dinner, Haven and Ryker said good night to Silas and Trinity on the third-floor landing. In the loft, Ryker watched Haven stretch and walk toward the bedroom.

"I need a shower. Rushing around today, I didn't have time to clean up." Ryker followed her into the bath and leaned in the doorway.

"Are you joining me?" she asked, shedding her clothes.

"No, just enjoying the view," he said. "Do you like baths?"

"Yes, sometimes." She turned on the shower, but he shut it off, then led her to the copper tub.

"Hot?" he asked.

"Scorching." He gingerly tested the temperature, then added an oil to the steaming water. The fresh, soothing smell of lavender with a tangy hint of eucalyptus permeated the room. When the tub filled, she eased herself in, and he pulled a stool next to her.

"Are you sure you're not joining me? There's plenty of room," she said, swishing the water around her.

He shook his head. "Wet your hair." Haven closed her eyes and slipped beneath the water, then resurfaced, wiping the water from her face. Ryker slipped his hands through her hair and slowly massaged shampoo into her scalp, then gently kneaded her head and neck. She purred in delight, and he was smugly gratified by the small bumps that appeared on her arms from his touch. He eased her back under the water and worked the suds from her hair. Once she sat up, he tipped her chin and poured fresh hot water over her hair from a pitcher to finish the rinse, then lowered her against the tub and tucked a small towel under her head and neck. "Rest. I'll be back in a few minutes."

He left her to soak, but after thirty minutes and no sound from the bath, he stepped silently through the door and noticed Haven had slipped farther into the water, her chin resting on her chest, fast asleep. He touched her arm through the tepid, almost cold water, and she cracked her eyes and sat up, rubbing her wet hands over her eyes.

"I'm cold," she said.

Ryker held a towel open for her. "Let's get you dry. That will help." She stepped onto the mat, and he folded the towel around her. He led her to his bed and pulled the covers back. Haven sat on the edge of the bed, her hands glowing as she dried her hair. Ryker took his shirt off, then his jeans, and pulled on a pair of cotton pants.

"No," Haven said.

"No? No what?"

"No clothes. I want to feel you on my skin."

Ryker hesitated. "That might not be a good idea."

Haven slid under the blankets and reached for him. "It's a great idea. The best I've had all day."

Haven woke early the morning she was due to report for ComSim. She eased herself from the bed, careful not to wake Ryker, and showered. She slipped into the second bedroom and dressed and sent a windsprite for breakfast. Ten minutes later, a blueberry muffin, fruit, and tea service appeared on the counter in the kitchen. She took her muffin and tea to the balcony, the sun's first awakening rays glittering across the rooftops of Araine.

Her throat tightened a little at the thought of leaving the city. She felt a different peace, one she had never felt before. She was happy here and loved everything about being with Ryker. His Triad, Harper and Kit, the way Ryker lived his life, the way he cared for her. And honestly, the way she was falling in love with him. This new feeling was both thrilling and terrifying. She had never felt her heart bound to anyone before. Not her parents, her family, or a friend. Certainly not a male. And Ryker had stolen her heart. She sighed, but the ache in her chest was relentless. Before she could stop, a tear slid down her face. She brushed it away in surprise.

"Why are you crying?" Ryker said. She turned to him. He was leaning in the doorway, loose, cotton pants slung low on his hips, his chest bare and his hair sticking up in every direction, a cup of steaming tea in his hand. She smiled at his rumpled look, at how he could make even that look sexy.

"I was thinking of leaving Araine, and it made me sad. I'm happy here. Probably more than I should be." She swirled the last bit of tea in her mug as Ryker sat beside her.

"There isn't such a thing as too happy."

Haven sighed, relishing the warmth of the morning sun, the view of Araine in the distance, and the peace of the loft. "You have a lovely life. I'm envious of it, to be honest."

"You can have as much of it, of me, as you want."

"I think I want too much. You once said you want everything. I do too. But I'm afraid my 'everything' isn't the same as yours."

His fingers traced hers, stroking her hand. "I doubt it."

She shuddered, then abruptly rose. "I should go to the Temple. I need to see Farna before I leave."

Ryker stood with her. "Say it, Haven." She stared at his silver eyes, then looked away. He set his mug down and put a hand low on her hip. "Say it," he said softly.

"I don't think I can." She gripped his waist, avoiding his gaze.

"Do you want me to say it first?" His hand slid behind her neck, his fingers twining in her hair. He tipped her chin up so she had to look at him.

"Yes. Because I'm a coward."

He grinned, then kissed her nose. "You are the least cowardly person I've ever met." His lips brushed hers. "I love you."

She pulled his head down and kissed him. His lips trailed over her jaw, her eyes, then nestled in her neck as he pulled her tight. "I love you," she whispered.

"See? That wasn't so hard, was it?"

She pressed her lips to his chest. "Yes. And terrifying."

He rested his forehead on hers, and she stroked his face, her fingertips playing with the rough stubble on his cheek.

"You're letting this grow," she said.

"You don't like it?"

"It's different. I like it both ways." Ryker's eyes lost focus and the stubble disappeared. He scratched his smooth cheek.

"Itchy. It's better if I do that right after a shower."

"You didn't have to."

He shrugged. "I was being lazy." He scratched at his chin. "Go see Farna. I'll get cleaned up and help pack your things. Big day today." Haven stepped away from him, her fingertips grasping his, reluctant to leave him even for a moment.

"Go. I'll be here when you're done."

She unfurled her wings and flew to the Temple, where Farna was waiting for her. She hopped up on an exam table, and he turned her cheek.

"It looks good. How do you feel?" he asked.

"Good."

"This might be a little tingly." His glowing hand touched the scar, and a faint electric pulse ran down the nerves in her neck to her arm. He handed her a mirror, and she saw nothing but smooth skin.

"You're a master," Haven said.

"Scars are easy," he said. "Now your shoulder. It would be easier if you removed your shirt." She peeled her t-shirt off, and he pulled the strap of her bra down. She felt the same tingly burning sensation and looked down to see the puckered scar had vanished.

After thanking Farna, she flew back to the Garret and landed softly on the balcony. Ryker was packing his bag when she walked into the bedroom. She showed him her cheek.

"All pretty again," she said.

"Please. A scar doesn't make you less pretty," he said, zipping the bag. He studied her face, then frowned. "I don't know. You may have looked better with it. More dangerous. Like a pirate." He grinned at her.

"I didn't realize pirates were a thing for you," she said, crossing her arms.

"You're a thing for me." He pulled her to him and kissed her neck, his hands roaming to her backside. He squeezed her to him.

"This is a thing for me."

"What, a big butt?"

"Curvy. Round and sexy." He stroked her backside, his hand slipping low between her legs.

"Ryker," she whispered, squirming away from him. "We need to leave." He lifted her leg to his waist and felt her through her pants.

"We do." He kissed her lips, his tongue caressing hers. "But all that talk of dangerous pirates and firm asses distracted me."

She laughed. "That's quite a combination to get hot and bothered about."

"Okay, so maybe it was more the firm ass that did it." He unbuttoned her pants and slid his hand inside.

"Gods, how am I going to make it through a month of ComSim?" she mumbled, kissing him and rocking her hips to his hand.

"I have no idea," he said, sliding her pants down. He knelt in front of her and lifted her leg to rest on his shoulder. He tasted her, his tongue sliding over her. She dropped her head back and laced her hands through his hair, her legs weak. "Let me have you," he whispered.

"Yes, now," she said, rocking her hips against his mouth. He stood and kissed her lips, walking her backwards until her knees touched the bed. He turned her around on her stomach and stroked her backside, nipping at her. Kissing the curve of her hips, his lips traveled up her spine, his hands sliding under her to cup her breasts. His knees gently spread her as he lifted her hips to him. She felt him slide inside her, slowly stretching her. Gods, the feel of him. He stroked into her, his fingers circling her bundle of nerves.

"Hard, Ryker. I want to feel you days from now."

"*Fuck*," he growled, kissing her neck.

"Exactly. Do that," she said breathlessly.

# PART 3 :

# WAR GAMES

# CHAPTER 37

## Araine

River landed in a dark street between two empty warehouses in southern Araine. He rested against a building to catch his breath and clutched his chest. Blood seeped between his fingers, and he shook his head to clear his fading vision. On weak legs, he lurched down the street into a narrow alley and pounded on the door of a small townhouse. He pushed his way inside when Adrien opened the door, then fell to his knees as the blood loss finally caught up with him.

"Adrien, heal me," he gasped. Adrien eased him flat to the floor and opened River's shirt. He swore under his breath. River's eyes cracked open and caught the glowing blue of his hand as Adrien treated the hole in his chest. He gritted his teeth, then relaxed as Adrien touched his temple and eased his pain.

"What have you done this time," Adrien scolded as he mended the cut on his face.

"None of your business. Just patch me up. I'm going back to Damaris."

River could barely keep his eyes open as Adrien worked on the chest wound. Adrien was quiet, but his blanched face told River the wound was serious. River's eyes sagged, and he heard Adrien tsking to himself about how close the wound was to his heart.

"That seal should be good. At least the bleeding has stopped," Adrien said. "Although you'll need another treatment tomorrow to further clean up the injury inside your chest." River felt the pressure of a skim, and Adrien eased him onto a bed, where he finally slipped into a dreamless sleep.

River woke the next morning aching and weak. He tried to stand, but Adrien pushed him down. "You need to rest for a few days. Your blood loss was profound. I regenerated some of it, but my Light reserves are low. I can replenish it today and treat you again tonight to repair the worst of it." River sighed and realized he was in no condition to travel. "You'll also need another session in a few days to completely heal the stab wound and remove the scar from your face." He sat in a chair next to River's bed. "Do you want to tell me what happened?"

"Not really." In the light of a new morning, his urge to flee had tempered. Now that he was rested and could think clearly, he realized if he wanted another chance at Haven, he was staring at the one person who could help him. He recalled Roque's suggestion to seek Adrien. "What do you know of the Phoenix? You're an expert. Have you ever seen that kind of magic?"

"No. It's even less common than Shadowalking and Bane."

"What makes the Phoenix special? It's just magic, right?"

"No, it's completely unique," Adrien said. "Why do you ask? Why are you interested in Haven?"

River closed his eyes. He would never get close to Haven again, not by any regular means. He was lucky he had gotten as far as he had. Now that Trinity knew of River's interest in Haven, she would See anything he had planned. He cursed under his breath. There had to be another way to bind her.

"Do you know of a way to transfer magic permanently from one seraphim to another?"

Adrien watched River warily. "Why would you ask me that?"

"Oh, come on. I know you're the keeper of a lot of dirty little secrets. Like you help unregistered seraphim avoid detection. It's a specialty of yours, isn't it? Since you are unregistered yourself." Adrien turned slowly to River. "You may have registered your Amplify magic, which gives you a cushy job as a guardian. But the Council doesn't know you're also a Cloak, do they?"

"Yes, I know a lot of secrets. Did you get stabbed because you finally tried to Persuade someone who wasn't susceptible?" Adrien said, a bitter tone in his voice River had never heard before.

"No need to be hostile. We're on the same side."

"I doubt that. You're never on anyone's side but your own. What do you really want?"

River sat up slowly, easing back to the pillows. "I want to know how to...collect someone's magic. Permanently."

"That sounds like a fantasy," Adrien scoffed.

"That's not what I heard. I was told you know how to do this."

Adrien's eyes narrowed. "By whom?"

"Roque. I'm assuming you know him. You're both historians, so you travel in the same circles."

Confusion clouded Adrien's face. "Roque? I've never heard of him."

"Tall, broad as a house. Dark hair, short beard and brown eyes. He's hard to miss."

"No, I don't know him. How do you know him?" Adrien asked.

"We have a mutual friend."

"Who?"

River cocked his head. "I'd rather not say. But are you telling me he's wrong? You don't know how to transfer magic?"

Adrien gave him a hard look. "You mean you want to steal someone's magic."

"Such ugly words. Let's not say steal. How about 'share'..."

"I won't help you harm a seraphim."

"I don't want to harm anyone. What's wrong with borrowing someone's magic? Echoes do it all the time."

"For registered Echoes, seraphim donate it willingly. And it isn't permanent. You know this. As soon as the store of magic is depleted, it can't be used again until it's replenished."

"Can you transfer Echo magic to me through a rune?"

"That's not how Echo works. But there are other life forms that have magic like an Echo. Tell me specifically what you are looking for. And why."

"Why?" River rubbed his eyes. "Because I'm tired of being common."

Adrien's face softened. "You're not common. Quite the opposite. What makes you common is your anger toward everyone."

"Spare me. I don't need a Sympath. Are you going to help me or not?" River said, his voice cold.

"Why should I help you gain magic so you can harm others? That seems like the worst idea you've ever had in a long list of terrible ideas." Adrien paced, refusing to look at him.

"Please," River said, his voice quavering.

Adrien halted and his eyes brightened. "Ah, I see where you're going with this. If you use Echo to collect another magic and are bound to the Phoenix, her magic will enhance yours. Thus, a borrowed magic becomes permanent. Is this what you hope to accomplish?"

"Yes. I've been in love with Haven since I first met her, before I even knew she was a Phoenix," River lied. "I feel like we're meant to be together. And I could protect her. Why shouldn't she be bonded to me?"

Adrien wavered. River patiently watched the guilt Adrien carried inside him worm its way through his reticence, eroding his common sense as it always did where he and his brother were concerned.

"You truly care for her?" Adrien asked.

"Yes, I do."

"What you're asking for is dark magic. If not used properly, you could find yourself in a living hell. Much worse than living with unfounded feelings of inadequacy." River shot him a daggered glare. "Oh, I know why you feel common," Adrien said. "It's hard having a twin like Ryker. But you've forgotten he loves you for who you are."

"Well, he doesn't anymore. I'm sure he will put the next hole in my chest. And he won't miss my heart on purpose."

Adrien gave him a pained look. "Why do you provoke him? You used to be so close. What you're doing to Ryker, and the sorry state of your relationship, would have devastated your mother."

River's eyes turned cold. "Then I guess you're glad she's dead so she doesn't have to see it."

"Sometimes that mouth of yours goes too far," Adrien said, and abruptly left the room.

# CHAPTER 38

## The Valley

Ryker and Haven walked the few short blocks to her apartment complex and arrived in the park as Kilian was announcing advisor assignments. He glowered at Haven as she quickly fell in line with her pod. Ryker walked to the front of the unit and took his position beside Silas and Trinity with the other advisors and referees.

Haven silently greeted Larkin and Avina, who stood behind Tristan. Dune was the only one from their original pod who was absent. Somewhere in the back of her mind, Haven thought she might have a change of heart, and was disappointed they wouldn't finish this final exercise together.

"Officially, you have graduated and are no longer cadets. My congratulations to you all," Kilian said. "For those joining the Aerial in the fall for the post-graduate training program, you are now considered rangers. If you complete the two-year program and enlist in the Aerial, you will earn the rank of warrior. For everyone joining the Aerial in the fall, ComSim is mandatory. For the rest of you, this is the last chance to change your mind. Once we assign you, we count any departures against the squad." None of the rangers moved. "There are approximately six hundred of you here today. We will divide you into squads, so twelve groups, each with an advisor. The referees mediate conflicts." Kilian gestured to Lukas and Xander. "Lukas is the lead referee and will have final say over any dispute."

Kilian distributed the pods to their advisors, their normal calm broken by the momentary disarray of moving into new groupings.

Their squad for ComSim was the same squad that had shared their floor for the last three years. Two new pods joined them to round out their numbers.

Kilian barked, "Settle down, people! We will assign your squad to a site for the first week. Each squad will receive a flag and a token. You must protect both. If your flag is captured, we will penalize you. If you capture a flag, we will reward you. Each squad's token is different, and it can be anything. If your token is captured, we will dismiss your squad from ComSim.

"After the first week, you are free to seek another site. If your flag is captured after the first week, we will disburse your squad to other squads. Your squad's size will grow as you capture flags. Learn to integrate new members. This will happen in the field when teams rotate in and out. When the number of squads is reduced to four, we will redistribute them down to pods, and the exercise will start again until only one pod remains.

"Your advisor will help you interpret the rules. Don't ask for advice on strategy. You will use sparring weapons, which you should all be familiar with. Each ranger is allowed two deaths on the field. On the third death, we will dismiss you from ComSim. Advisors and referees will record kills.

"Any further questions, ask your advisor. ComSim starts at dawn tomorrow. Good luck."

Haven's pod assembled in front of a tall, broad-shouldered female Haven had never met. She bellowed at Haven's squad, "My name is Fallon. I've been a captain in the Aerial for thirty years. This is my tenth ComSim. Questions before we get started?" The squad remained silent. "Your ComSim packs are in your apartments. Skimmers will be here shortly. Hustle, people!"

The squad scurried toward the apartment building. Haven had not returned to her room since the attack but found it cleaned and neat, with no evidence of the violence she had experienced. In the bedroom, she found her ComSim pack and a set of fatigues and boots on her bed. She quickly changed her clothes and inventoried the contents of the pack, adding warmer clothes, a heavier blanket, and extra food before slinging the pack on her back. She rushed back to the park and fell in line as the Skimmers arrived. Ryker and Silas lined up with their squad across the park. Ryker's gaze found hers, and he touched his heart. She touched her lips. A Skimmer held her hand, and she and Quinn vanished.

Haven appeared with Quinn on the edge of a forest. The dense pine trees faded to oaks scattered around an open, shallow valley half a mile wide. A swift river ran through the center and broadened to a small lake five hundred yards from the flat plain where Haven and her squad gathered. The light breeze skittered across the lake's surface and rippled through the lush green grass that reached Haven's knees.

"We're screwed," Dax said.

"Totally," Tristan said. "How the hell are we supposed to defend all this?" He waved his hand at the vast, open space around them.

Haven said, "Let's make the best of it. We need a good watch and an escape plan."

"With almost fifty people? Did I mention how screwed we are?" Dax said.

Tristan said, "She's right, it's the best we can do. We're stuck here for a week."

Haven and Tristan scouted in one direction, while Dax and Maddox took the opposite direction. Both groups circled the perimeter and met where they started.

"I see two possibilities for camps," Haven said. She pointed to a clearing on the side of the valley halfway up a ridge. "That area is slightly elevated, and the cliff slopes up high on the back side, which will protect us from an attack from the top. Downside is the area is small, and we'll be clustered pretty tight. Also, the escape route is down, which isn't ideal." Dax and Tristan agreed. "The second is on the valley floor. Obviously bad because everything is elevated from there, but there are two natural escape routes and a third concealed from the tree line." She pointed to the side of the clearing to her right. "Just beyond the trees, there's another clearing that is too small for a camp, but it's elevated and feeds into the ridgeline. We can use it as a launching point for an escape."

Dax said, "What makes that a good escape route is also a way in."

"Gods, there are ways in everywhere," Maddox said.

"Agreed," Haven said. "We'll need to expand the guard assignments. This isn't a two guard, two shift type of setup."

They chose the valley floor for the first night and assigned eight guard locations in pairs, one for stationary guarding and one to rove between stations. They divided the squad into thirds, with each guard pair assigned to three-hour shifts. Haven sent Maddox, Avina, and three other rangers to hunt for food. On the far side of the lake, they discovered a wild fruit orchard and other edible vegetation in abundance. The stream of fresh water pooled beyond the clearing and teemed with fish, thankfully helping them eat well that night.

Sitting at the evening campfire, Fallon gathered the squad. "Your token is this." She held a silver cube the size of her fist. "The rule for protecting your token is a person must carry it." Dax stepped forward and took it from her.

Haven asked, "What of other groups' tokens? Do they have the same rules?"

"Good question. No, they don't. Every group's token is different," Fallon said.

"How different?" Maddox asked. "What was your squad's token when you last advised ComSim?"

"It was a ranger," Fallon said. Dax examined the silver cube, turning it in his hand. "You decide how you want to protect it."

"We need to rotate it," Dax decided. "I'll take it tonight." He put the token in his pack, and they settled for the night.

Haven slid into her bedroll next to Tristan. "I have a bad feeling about this."

"I agree, but get some sleep. The first guard shift will wake at four. That should be plenty of time to scout for early intruders." Tristan was snoring softly minutes later.

Haven lay next to him, her mind too busy to sleep. She could still feel the dull ache from her morning with Ryker. She held onto that feeling, missing his company, the sound of his voice and the feel of him lying with her in his bed.

She was uncertain when she finally fell asleep, but woke in the morning to a searing pain in her chest and her body covered in a blue glow.

A ranger's face appeared over her and said, "You're dead."

She wasn't the only one. Ten minutes into ComSim, the invading squad killed her entire squad and captured their flag. The attacking squad jeered as everyone lined up and Fallon recorded the kills with a referee. Haven sulked during the inspection, glowing blue and feeling furious. The penalty for losing their flag was iron banding for the day, eliminating magic and flight.

Fallon warned, "If you lose your flag again, the penalties become more severe."

Haven grumbled to Dax, "What the hell happened to the guards? Find out who was on duty and where our lines failed."

Dax discovered Larkin and his partner had scouted at the start of their guard shift but fallen asleep. They also found a gap in the tree line they'd missed in their initial scouting. Haven spied Larkin dumping a pile of firewood, and his partner cleaning a string of fish.

"They will be busy all day," Dax said. "I have a list of chores a mile long."

Haven was still fuming over the early kill. "How the hell did they know our site at dawn on the first day?" she muttered.

At dusk, a referee removed their bands. Haven unfurled her wings and said to Dax, "I'm scouting. I'll be back in an hour." She launched into the air.

Haven marched straight to Dax upon her return. "I need you, Tristan, Larkin, and Kit. I have an idea." When Dax gathered their pod, Haven laid out her plan. "We need to do this tonight. They won't be expecting us to recover and retaliate now. Quinn and Harper, you need to stay and organize the rest of the squad. Set guards and monitor them. We can't let anyone in again." Harper and Quinn and the rest of their pod faded into the woods to return to the camp.

Haven led the small team on foot for two miles to the edge of a clearing on the back side of the ridgeline. They dropped to their stomachs, and Haven explained. "I saw them from the air. They're posting single guards." She pointed to a guard sitting on a rock a hundred yards from them. "That's the same guard that was there earlier, so a shift change should happen soon. Larkin, you're up."

Larkin sprouted feathers over his entire body, then shifted to an owl. He hooted and flew away. Haven caught a glimpse of his magic the night she ran into him in Araine but had never seen him fully shift before. He may have been limited to birds, but for what she had in mind, that was perfect.

An hour later, an owl landed beside them, and Larkin shifted back.

"Their token is a dagger. They aren't even trying to conceal it." He shook his head. "By the way, their advisor is an Aerial soldier named Dekkar. He's also leading them."

"What the hell?" Haven spat.

"That's how they knew where to attack us. I listened to Dekkar describe this area and their maneuver this morning. He had the squad set to ambush us at sunrise. Not saying what I did was okay," he said, glancing at Dax and Haven. "But we never had a chance."

"Well, revenge is the best medicine. Dax, come with me," Haven said. Silently, they approached the guard who was sitting on a boulder watching the camp. Dax grabbed him from behind, his hand muffling the cry. "Don't kill him," Haven whispered. "The camp will see the blue light." Tristan took his breath away until the guard fell unconscious, then dragged him deeper into the shadows of the trees. Haven illuminated his face. "Kit, your turn."

Kit viewed the guard's face from every angle. His own face shifted, and the guard peered back at them. "I'm a little taller, but I don't think anyone will notice. I didn't hear his voice, so I'll try to say as little as possible."

Haven nodded. "Hurry, the shift change could happen any time." Kit jogged through the trees and sat on the boulder. Moments later, another guard relieved Kit, and he walked into the camp. Haven said to Larkin, "Your turn again." Larkin shifted into a massive black eagle, almost invisible in the dark. He spread his wings and flew into the air. In the tense silence that seemed to stretch forever, Haven heard an eagle scream, two short bursts. They retreated and flew back to their camp.

When they arrived, their squad was in an uproar. In the middle of the clearing, Larkin held the dagger high in triumph. Fallon and Lukas confirmed Dekkar's squad had lost their token and was thus eliminated from ComSim. A few minutes later, Kit landed and furled his wings, his entire body glowing blue. He had sacrificed one of his kill lives, but their squad had gained an enormous advantage.

Lukas asked, "Any request for your reward?"

Haven thought of Ryker's loft and blurted, "I want the valley warded for the week. No one comes in but us." The pod stared at her.

"That's an excellent idea," Dax agreed.

"I can't do it for the entire week. Three days, max," Lukas said.

"Four," Haven countered. "Come on, Lukas. We eliminated a squad in the first twenty-four hours of ComSim."

He folded his arms. "You also got your entire squad killed on the first day." Haven flushed. "Three days. Or I'll pick the reward."

She scowled at him. "Fine. Three days." Haven and her pod worked with Lukas and Xander to define the area, making sure it included the orchard and the small lake.

They relaxed a little for the next two days. The squad kept busy storing food and scouting for better sites once the embargo was lifted and they could leave the valley. Search teams regularly tracked which squads were still in play. Two days after guardians cast the wards, Maddox and a scouting team intercepted another squad attempting to invade the valley. They watched from the trees as the team charged, hit the wards, and fell back stunned, then swarmed in for the easy kill.

While Maddox and Tristan monitored security and intelligence on the other squads, Dax and Haven worked on a plan to win another token. Haven and Larkin searched the area and found five squads within six miles of them.

"We know the leaders of two of the squads. They are smart and effective. They won't be as careless," Haven noted. Larkin searched the other three camps in his owl form. They quickly eliminated one site as impossible to access.

"They have an ideal location," Larkin said. "It would be great to eliminate them, then move into their spot."

"We can't afford a risk like that right now. We need a sure way to get another token," Maddox countered.

"The other two are good candidates," Larkin finally agreed. "I'll try to discover their tokens tonight."

In the fading light of the setting sun, Larkin and Haven flew together to investigate a site. Larkin left Haven to scout from above while he shifted to a small, dark gray screech owl and silently landed on a high branch just outside the encampment. Using the owl's exceptional hearing, he caught two rangers discussing their token.

"I hate having this thing near me," one ranger complained.

"We all have to take a turn. I had it yesterday," the other ranger said.

"But I have no magic with it. I feel naked."

Larkin silently flapped into the air and found Haven circling high above. He led her to a secluded, heavily wooded area and shifted back to fae. "This group's token is iron. That will be impossible to take by stealth. The token will force me to shift back to fae, and Kit will lose his Glamour."

Haven swore. "Let's try the next one." Larkin shifted once again into the small gray owl, and they both flew to the next campsite. Larkin watched from the trees until the squad bedded down for the night and was quiet for the rest of the evening. At midnight, Larkin began to despair that they would ever discover the squad's token.

They were running out of time. The wardings around their own campsite would expire at midnight, leaving them exposed. They *needed* a token.

Larkin shuffled from foot to foot and ruffled his feathers, trying to stay alert. He spread his wings, about to give up for the night when he noticed four rangers gather in the center of the campsite.

"My turn is over. Here, take it." A ranger reached over his shoulder and pulled an arrow from his quiver. Larkin blinked. The arrow was unremarkable, except for a gold tip. He had to risk the theft now, before it was indistinguishable among the other arrows. The ranger handed it to another, who swung it behind his head. Larkin dove from the branch, and before the ranger released the arrow into the quiver, Larkin snatched it from his hand. He swooped up, screeched, and banked to the right as an arrow skimmed his breast. Larkin screeched again and flew low through the trees, as if chased by Abaddon's own demons.

Haven heard the first screech and unfurled her wings. The tense sound of the second screech had her flaring her wings in anticipation. She heard Larkin screech a third time, much closer. Then, through the trees, he came barreling toward her, an arrow in his claw and three rangers close behind. Haven pulsed a wave of

Light at Larkin and the rangers. Larkin dipped low to the ground, and the wave passed over him, the wall of scorching heat hitting the rangers. One ranger screamed and tumbled to the ground, her wings smoldering. In mid-flight, a ranger drew his bow and shot an arrow. Larkin screeched and erupted in blue light, an arrow protruding from his chest before it disintegrated. He shifted to fae and fell to the ground thirty feet from Haven, kicking up a flurry of leaves and dirt. As he fell, he tossed the arrow at her. She swept her wings down and lurched forward, catching the arrow before it fell into the forest's underbrush.

Haven shot into the air, through the canopy of trees. It had been ages since she had needed to fly with speed, and she thrilled at the power she unleashed. With three strokes of her wings, she was beyond the rangers' arrow range. Larkin had sacrificed another life, but the squad was now protected until they could leave the valley.

After their wards were renewed, Haven's squad spent the next three days storing food and preparing to move, scouting the area for a better, more defensible site. Their last night in the valley, the pod assembled around the campfire.

"Our first option is the site now vacant from the arrow token squad," Dax said. "It's elevated, fairly protected, and has a source of water close by. The downside is a scarcity of food. We could choose a better defensive location, but it isn't bad, and it's much better than this valley.

"Second choice is a site on the back side of this ridge. It's a small clearing that will be very difficult to attack. We will be clustered together, which isn't ideal, but safer than here. Unfortunately, no water nearby and limited food.

"Third location has an abundance of food, but no water. It is also elevated, but a little exposed. Very close by. We could easily fly there, which will limit our exposure when traveling."

"I think the best option is the first," Haven said. "We've stored plenty of food, and we can hunt and scavenge in other sites. But protection and water are vital." Dax agreed with her, but Tristan and Maddox pushed for the third site. They debated the benefits and risks further, but eventually Haven and Dax persuaded them. The squad prepared to leave at first light.

Dawn's colors splashed across the sky, announcing the sun's imminent arrival. Harper, Kit, and Quinn rallied the squad. As dawn broke, the squad flew into the sky as one, with Haven and Tristan leading, and Dax and Maddox following behind.

The squad arrived at the campsite as another squad appeared on the ridge. They had prepared for this possibility, and Dax and Maddox led a trailing team that attacked the invading squad from the air, firing a volley of arrows and taking down the leading edge. Haven heard Maddox's signal, and she and Tristan led the charge from the ground. Kit, Harper, and Quinn also took their cue from Maddox and split from the ground attack, flanking the squad in a surprise move that allowed them to capture the squad's flag before they fled down the mountain. Haven's squad lost six members, including Kit, who received his third kill.

"Gods, damn it Kit, why did you do that," Haven said.

"It was the only way Harper could slip into the squad unharmed. It's what was best for us."

"But now we lose you, and that's not good for our squad!" she argued.

"Maybe." He shrugged. "But it was my call and it's done. You can use Knox once. I gave him my Glamour. You'll be fine." They said their goodbyes, and Kit was skimmed to Portos.

Haven stewed on the loss of Kit all day. She now needed to find another way to steal tokens.

# CHAPTER 39

## Araine

Roque entered Lilith's office at the Council chambers and closed the door behind him.

"What are you doing here?" Lilith asked. "A little risky, don't you think?"

Roque said, "We have a problem. They dismissed Dekkar from ComSim."

Lilith swore. "Gods, he's an idiot."

"This would be easier if River was working with us."

"I think we're close. The bright side of Ryker being closer to the Phoenix is River's petulant jealousy."

Roque paced in front of her desk. "Well, that won't help us right now."

"It may. I can get River to the ComSim site."

"That would help, but it won't replace Dekkar. We need an Echo. You need to be there."

"Why me? Why don't you go?"

"I can't be near there. You know I can't be near the Phoenix."

"You keep saying that, but you never say why."

"She cancels my magic," Roque said. "I'm weakened around her."

"I gathered that much. But how?" Lilith asked.

"I have a connection to the Phoenix that is part of me. And I can't get around it."

"Is it connected to your ability to control demons?" Roque remained silent, and Lilith sighed. "Well, I can't do this without cover. My relationship with the daevas will make me an obvious suspect."

"I can help with that." Roque's face narrowed, and his jaw softened as his skin smoothed, and his hair lengthened to a black sheet that ended at his waist. His body became more compact, lithe and feminine. Forest green eyes stared back at Lilith like a mirror. She abruptly stood and took a step back.

"Have you done this before? Impersonated me?"

Roque gave her a slow smile. "Of course not."

Lilith eyed him with suspicion. "I think you're lying. And if you do this without my permission, not only will our partnership be over, it will also be the last thing you ever do."

Roque chuckled. "We're on the same side. Where do you want to be seen?"

Lilith hesitated. "There's a reception in Torella in a week. Very large social gathering, lots of people to mingle with and be seen. And conversation should be superficial."

Roque shifted back to himself. "It sounds ideal. I don't have to be there long. An hour at most."

"Fine. Getting to the site should be easy," Lilith said, rubbing the rune on her ribs Roque gave her weeks ago. "I know a certain daeva that owes me. And the shima queen is primed. How large a swarm do you want here?"

"Large enough to lay waste to the Phoenix and everyone around her," Roque said.

River spent the next week with Adrien, resting and healing. Adrien's words about Ryker had hurt worse than the knife wound to his chest. He desperately missed his brother. After their graduation from the Academy, they had been close. Then Ryker changed. He moved to Araine and accepted his role as a Shadowalker, away from Damaris, away from how he and River had lived together. He knew Adrien was right, but every time he got around Ryker, he felt *angry*, and did everything he could to provoke him and get under his skin. River didn't care for Haven. He would be fine to never think of her again. But it didn't change the fact that Ryker had stolen her right out from under him, and he'd never seen it coming.

At the end of his week, he knew he couldn't stay at Adrien's any longer. He sent a windsprite to Lilith. *I'm sure you know the plan failed. Trinity can See Haven now. We need another way. Working on it now.*

He received a return message from her. *I have a plan of my own. I need you in the ComSim arena in three days. Can you be there? I will give you an opening.*

He sent a sprite back. *Yes. And I'll have help this time.*

He received a reply. *I have help of my own. Either bind her, or she will be dead.*

Shit. He hadn't expected that. If he couldn't bind her with Adrien's magic, he never would. And then, what did he care if she was dead?

The answer was, he didn't.

The sun had set long ago when Adrien returned from his shift at the Temple. He set a bag on the counter, and River could smell the savory scent of pork and mushrooms, with a sweet undertone. Adrien took two plates from the cupboard and set them on the table.

"Dim sum for dinner. Your favorite," Adrien said, unpacking several containers from the bag.

"From The Gray Pearl?"

"Of course," Adrien said. "I came by at lunch, but you weren't here."

River reached for a carton of dumplings. "I had an errand to run." He bit into a fluffy white steamed sticky bun and watched Adrien eat. "I need to leave tomorrow. I need the magic you promised."

"I didn't promise."

"If you won't help me, I'll find someone who will. And I'll wager that person will be less skilled. I'm doing this, but the outcome would be safer with your help." River lowered his voice and honed the edge, ready to cut deep. "Are you abandoning me too, when I'm asking for your help?"

"That's low. And not even subtle." Adrien swallowed hard and looked away. "I can't do this. It's too dangerous. I'm sorry."

River stared intently at him. "I'm sorry too." He reached out to Adrien with his magic. Adrien stiffened.

"You'd force me?"

"I don't want to, but yes, I will. And you know I can."

"You're being impulsive. You would risk your future and your life?"

"That's a little melodramatic, don't you think?"

"No, I don't. You're ignoring the risks." Adrien gasped, perspiration beading on his brow.

"I really don't care. This will hurt more the longer you resist." River pushed harder, his Persuasion writhing around Adrien, then felt his magic slip inside.

Adrien relaxed, and a vacant look dulled his eyes. He retreated to his bedroom, leaving River to clear the table and wash the dishes. As River put away the last plate and closed the cupboard, Adrien returned with a wooden box the size of a book. He opened the lid and removed a glass cylinder with a long, thin metal nose and a vial of black fluid flecked with silver streaks.

"This is a needle. I will need to insert this sharp end into your vein and inject this into your body."

River's eyes widened. "Where the hell did you find that?"

"Non-magical species, like humans, use it all the time. It's quite common."

"It sounds barbaric."

"It kind of is."

"What exactly are you putting into my body?"

"Demon blood." River leaned away from Adrien. "You asked for something unique. You didn't expect there to be a cost?"

Adrien inserted the sharp end of the cylinder into the top of the bottle of black blood and drew the plunger. The fluid filled the cylinder of the needle. "Here are the rules. I need to apply a rune to your skin that will neutralize this in three days. You will have the power of this demon, which is like an Echo. Two things you can't do. First, don't get near any demon. They will sense you and think you are like them." River had never seen a demon in his life, so that seemed safe enough. "Second, this is blood magic. If you have contact with another type of demon blood, you will be trapped between magics and bound to this blood, become like it, and that will survive the rune's Cancelling magic. Very little in this world, or any world, will undo it." Adrien stalled. "River," he pleaded. "You are special, just the way you are. Please reconsider."

River hardened his eyes and pushed his magic around Adrien. "Let's get this over with."

Adrien rolled up his sleeve and held his forearm. River flinched as a blistering heat burned his skin. Adrien removed his hand, and a black, swirling rune appeared. He slid the needle into River's arm in the middle of the rune and pushed the plunger. The rune glimmered black and silver, and River's world changed forever.

His eyes burned, and so did his heart. His world became simple. And clear. That dull ache in his heart that had always been there, because of Ryker, the neglect and exploitation from his father, every slight, either real or imagined, eased when the demon blood surged through his veins. The pain subsided completely, and then there was only him.

He rolled his neck and shoulders, then leveled his eyes at Adrien. "This is the best I've felt in two decades. Thank you."

"The rune countdown starts now. Be careful," Adrien said.

River returned to his room and sent a windsprite to Lilith. *Where is she?*

Moments later, the sprite reappeared. Site Nine, above the valley. She moved there today. I will send you a surprise tonight, two hours after nightfall.

River watched the swirling magic of the rune shimmer under his skin. He felt a new sensation within him, a power he had never felt when using Wind or Persuasion. He silently opened the door to his bedroom and saw Adrien in the living room, reading a book. He reached toward him with his new magic. River could sense the Cloak, and pulled at that feeling.

Adrien's eyes flew open, and he glanced at River. "What the hell are you doing?"

"Testing this new toy you gave me. I need to Cloak myself. I can't have a Seer detect me." He could feel the Cloaking magic writhing inside him, a fourth source next to his Wind and Persuasion and the new demon magic.

"Why do you need to be concealed? The only Seers in Araine are bound to Shadowalkers."

"Exactly. And how could I take Ryker's magic if Trinity can See me?" River said.

"This isn't the answer. I know you, River. You will regret harming your brother."

River's face contorted in a sneer as he laughed bitterly. "That's tomorrow's problem. I told you I was tired of being common. After tonight, I won't be any longer. Particularly when I bind that bitch girlfriend of Ryker's to me. Thanks for everything, Adrien."

Adrien's face burned as he heard River slam the door behind him. He had underestimated River's desperation, and knew River was becoming more like his father every day.

Adrien flew to the Temple and paced his office until he saw Katalin walk down the hall.

"We need to talk." Adrien pulled her into his office. "I need you to contact Calaine and have her link with Trinity. Ryker and Silas need to find Haven today."

"Why me? Why can't you tell her?"

"Because you can say it was your reader abilities that gave you a vision. If I did it, they would know..." Adrien faltered.

Katalin's face blanched. "What have you done?"

"Don't ask. Do this for me. We don't have a lot of time."

"I don't like this." Adrien tensed, holding his breath while Katalin considered his request. She exhaled sharply. "Fine."

"Now. It's important."

# CHAPTER 40

## Site Nine

Ryker felt a tapping in his mind and flashed a concerned look at Silas. Trinity would never link to him during ComSim unless it was an emergency. He accepted her request.

*Ryker, it's Calaine. I received a message from a reader. Haven needs you and Silas. Go to her now.*

*Got it, thank you. Please contact Trinity and tell her my squad needs an alternate advisor. Also, let me know which site Haven is at now.*

*Yes, will do.*

He jogged to Silas, who sat with several cadets around the campfire, listening to their strategy session.

"Gear up. We're leaving," he said. Silas leapt to his feet and hurried to his pack. Ryker strapped his daggers to his thighs and his sword to his back and slung his pack. Silas returned, adjusting the weapons he'd hastily thrown on, and Ryker filled him in as he received the message from Calaine with Haven's location.

"Site Nine. Do you know where that is?" Ryker asked him. Silas nodded, held Ryker's arm, and they vanished, appearing in a clearing on a mountain ridge.

Ryker searched for Haven in the squad clustered around a campfire. They quickly strode across the clearing, and Ryker pulled her aside.

"Is everything okay?" he asked.

"Yes," Haven said. Dax joined them as Haven nervously scanned the site. "Why are you here? Is something wrong?"

Fallon marched across the clearing. "Ryker, you're not supposed to be here. It violates the rules."

"We received a warning from a Temple reader," Ryker said to Haven. "Specifically, that you were in trouble."

Haven's jaw set, her chin rising in defiance. "River?"

"I'm not taking any chances," Ryker said. "Silas and I are staying until we know the danger has passed." He turned to Fallon, "We aren't here as advisors. Think of us as guards. We'll try not to interfere, but we aren't leaving." Fallon nodded, then left them to rejoin the squad. Ryker looked at Haven. "I need you to stay within the campsite, away from the tree line."

"That won't work. I need to scout. We have an excursion planned for this evening."

"You're not going."

"The hell I'm not," she snapped. Ryker glared at her. "That's not for you to decide," she said, her hands on her hips, prepared to dig in.

His eyebrows rose. "You're choosing to be stubborn right now? Over this? You're no use to your pod dead."

Haven rolled her eyes. "That's a little overdramatic, don't you think?"

"No, I don't. Do you remember what happened to you a week ago? Because I sure as shit do." She threw up her hands and walked a few paces away from him.

"What happened?" Dax asked. Ryker gave him the short version. "Gods, Haven," he murmured.

Silas said to Haven, "If River is targeting you, we can always take you out of the equation by skimming you to Araine."

"You too, Silas? I swear, you're like two grannies. I'm not leaving. I'll be fine."

Dax said, "I'm with them. You realize River is an elite soldier in the Aerial. And he is clever and fights dirty. Don't let your pride get the best of you."

Haven gave Dax a dirty look. "I hate you all." Ryker moved to follow her as she walked away, fuming, but Dax held him back. He shot a killing look at Dax's hand on his arm. Dax didn't budge.

"She gave in and is pissed. Let her stew. She'll do the right thing."

Haven paced the campsite for an hour like a caged animal, ignoring Ryker, Silas, and Dax. She finally stopped, then marched to Dax. "Fine. I'll stay here, but I am not quitting ComSim. We can revise the plan for tonight. Come with me. You and Quinn are leading."

"We need to bring in others from the squad if you want the excursion to happen now. I think the pod should stay near you," Dax said.

"You're joking."

"No. I'm not leaving you. I know for a fact they won't want to leave you either. We protect our own." Haven stared at him, her throat thickening.

"Dax..." she said. He walked to her and hugged her.

"I'm not leaving you. You can't force me. If you want me to lead the excursion, delay it. Our plan will still work tomorrow night. Even a week from now. It's not worth the risk."

"I still think you worry too much," she grumbled, but held him tight.

"It's one night," he said. "There are still plenty of chances for you to outwit the gaping jaws of death tomorrow." Haven chuckled into his chest.

An hour before sunset, a ranger approached Haven and told her nine of their guards were missing. "It was my team's turn to guard, but all five posts were empty. The guards that we were supposed to relieve were already gone, and no one has seen them. When I made my rounds to my team's posts, I found only one of my own team remained. The rest are gone."

"Take two of your best fliers and search the area. Scout from the air," Haven said. The ranger returned to the site to assemble a team. Ryker and Silas stood a few feet from her. She had not spoken to Ryker since they'd argued, when he and Silas arrived at the site. She broke the silence and said, "I'm assuming you heard that."

Ryker nodded. "Let's see what the aerial scouts find."

Haven sighed. "I'm still mad at you. But I know you're only trying to help."

His lips curved in a half smile, and he moved closer to her. "I like it when you're mad. Maybe a little hand-to-hand sparring later?"

She huffed and crossed her arms. "You're an ass."

He grinned. "You're beautiful."

"That will get you nowhere," she said.

"Yes, it will." Haven called him a filthy name as she walked away to check on the evening meal preparation. She could hear him laughing softly behind her.

When they gathered at the campfire for dinner, eight more of her squad were missing, and the three rangers that left for aerial surveillance had not returned. Dax kept the pod near Haven and rotated other squad members to guard duty while they sent another scouting party to search for the missing rangers. After an hour of searching on the ground and the sky, the guards were nowhere to be found.

Ryker prowled the perimeter of the clearing, his magic slithering around him and into the woods, trying to sense what was lurking beyond the trees. Haven's heart skipped a beat as she watched him patrol the campsite. She knew Ryker was a skilled soldier, and was intimately familiar with the power of his magic and training to know he was deadly. There was nothing soft or tender about the male striding around the clearing, fully armed, his onyx blades unfurled, flared and curving around his arms, his magic swirling around him in a gray cloud. He was a hunter, a demon killer, dangerous and slightly terrifying.

Ryker returned to Haven after two turns of the perimeter. "I can't sense anything other than animals. But this isn't right."

"I agree. Something feels wrong," Haven said.

"Now that it's dark, we should stay within the clearing. Bring the guard posts in tighter and keep them where we can see them."

"Outside my pod, we are now down to less than twenty rangers." Besides Kit, they had lost four more to kills in skirmishes with other teams since arriving at the ridge.

Ryker said to Dax, "Set up guards at six points around the perimeter. Keep inside the tree line." Dax left to organize the night guard.

"It will be fine," Ryker said. Haven saw the wisps of Bane circling his arms and the tension in his body and the fire in his eyes.

"I know," she said.

They both knew it was a lie.

River found a Skimmer who took him to Portos, then flew to the forest outside Site Nine. Through the trees, he spied Ryker and Silas speaking with Haven and Dax. They were both fully armed with bladed wings unfurled and ready. River swore under his breath. Stealth would be impossible without a little help from Lilith. In the meantime, he could try to even the odds.

He disabled half the squad by picking off rangers throughout the evening. His magic felt boundless with the demon blood running through his veins. He had Persuaded the guards around the campsite to leave their posts, walk three miles, and fall asleep for twelve hours. Some didn't respond to his suggestions, but most had, including the three aerial scouts. Now that the guard posts had consolidated inside the clearing, it was unlikely he could get any other rangers to walk away without being noticed. He had less than an hour to wait at this point but felt he had significantly improved his situation. He now needed to depend on Lilith's plan. It had better be a good one.

After they finished the evening meal and set the first guard rotation, Haven sat next to Ryker. He moved over to share his bedroll, and she slipped an arm around his waist. The night's darkness blanketed the site, consuming the dying embers of the campfire.

"I missed you," she said.

"I thought you hated me." His eyes sparkled silver in the last flickering flames from the campfire.

"I do."

Ryker laughed softly and pressed her tight to him. "I missed you, too." She looked up at him, and he dipped his head and kissed her thoroughly.

"You're breaking all your rules tonight, aren't you?" she asked, breathless.

"I don't care." He kissed her again, softer this time, his fingertips grazing her cheek.

"Good, because I don't either." She looked up. "It's going to be a frosty night, I think."

The crystal-clear summer sky was a canopy of glittering stars. "Looks like it might snow."

"I'll get my blankets. We can share body heat to keep from freezing." Haven moved her bedroll to his and covered them with their blankets. She snuggled into his side, her head resting on his chest, the steady beat of his heart soothing her taut nerves. She stroked his arm, his ribs, and up his stomach.

"I really missed you," she whispered. His hand that had been stroking her back in slow, lazy circles, dropped to her hip and pulled her closer. The subtle scent around him shifted from crisp, fresh pine to rich winter spices and fire.

"Don't start something you can't finish," he said into her hair.

"I have no idea what you're talking about." Her hand drifted up the inside of his thigh wedged between her legs.

"Yes, you do. I can tell, you know. You smell sweet and tangy, like warm honey and blackberries, when you want me." Her face heated. "I could always tell when you lied," he said, grinning. Her face burned, thinking of all the conversations they had that were a little flirty, the times they had danced, argued, and even fought, while she had been aroused. And he had known.

"I really want to punch you right now," she said. He laughed and kissed her hair.

Haven felt the surrounding air change, as if she were suddenly under water. Ryker scrambled to his feet and looked at Silas.

"What is that?" Silas said, rising quickly, his steel blades unfurled. The pressure intensified, then released, popping their ears.

Ryker's onyx wings flared. He reached under his pack and drew his sword. "That was a new rift."

Lilith slipped between the trees and stopped at the edge of the campsite. Her Glamour shifted, the square jaw and stubble fading to feminine curves and smooth skin. Even using her Amplify, the Glamour magic she'd stolen off a seraphim was fading. She knelt in a shadowed cluster of trees, cursing Dekkar for the hundredth time. Dekkar's Echo magic made him the perfect pawn. She had ensured they selected him as an advisor for ComSim to position him to create a new rift, and had transferred the rift magic she had bartered from Vannin to him. But because he was an idiot and had to show off, he was now dismissed from the games. She had met with Dekkar that morning and reclaimed the magic, and now rubbed at the rune on her side, still tingling from the transfer.

Lilith watched the squad settle for the evening and waited until the fire died and the dark enveloped the site. She could feel River near her, despite being Cloaked. She frowned. He felt different. Darker and more dangerous. She stretched her Echo magic to him and jumped to her feet. *What had he done to himself?* Lilith could feel the demon magic coursing through his veins. Now she understood how he had Cloaked himself. He stole the magic. Her eyes narrowed. There was only one person she knew who could have given River the demon magic. And he was also an un-registered Cloak. Adrien. She also knew the demon magic writhing inside River was dangerous and unstable. *Hopefully, he won't do anything truly stupid.*

Lilith Amplified the rift rune on her ribs, and the surrounding air thickened, pressing on her ears until they popped in sudden relief. Ten feet from her, a pair of red eyes glowed within the trees.

Then all hell broke loose.

Ryker glimpsed the red glowing eyes just as the first shima bolted from the forest and took down a guarding ranger. His magic streamed from him, enveloping the shima as four more demons leapt from the cover of the trees. Silas and Dax rushed to help the guards as shima came from both sides of the clearing, charging the unsuspecting rangers. Ryker clenched his fist, and his magic crushed the demon, stifling the scream as the demon crumbled to ash.

He moved to help the ranger as another demon leapt at him from the trees. He flicked his wing and the demon's head rolled to the ground next to him. He grabbed the ranger by the collar and dragged him to Haven as two more demons broke from the tree line toward them. A wall of smoke appeared before him, and the demons bounced off the shield, falling on each other. The wall of smoke crested over the demons, enveloping them in a crashing wave as they screeched, then turned to ash.

Ryker knelt beside the ranger and knew he would be dead shortly. Blood pumped from a deep wound in his neck, the bright red mixing with a green froth. A spiderweb of glowing green covered his neck and face as the poison crept under his skin and through his veins. Haven came to his side and covered her nose and mouth. Ryker too wrinkled his nose at the soured milk smell of the poison leaching from the skin in a noxious vapor.

Silas appeared with the body of another ranger and laid it next to Haven. "This one won't make it either. The demons are shima. Unless we have a healer treat them within minutes, they'll die from the poison." Ryker checked on Haven, who blanched at the grisly sight as the ranger with the neck wound took his last breath.

"Are you okay?" he asked her. Her stunned eyes fell on him. "Haven, are you okay?"

"Yes," she said, as her shock eased. Dax brought over two more rangers, also bitten and poisoned.

Ryker said, "Haven, Dax, warn your team. Help them."

Haven unfurled her silver bladed wings and followed Dax to the rangers fighting off the demons. "These demons are poisonous! Don't let them touch you!" Ryker heard her shout repeatedly through the teams of fighting rangers. He leapt to his feet as two shima burst through the tree line toward them, but he watched Haven and Dax quickly fall into one of their practiced defensive stances and fight efficiently as a team. She stabbed a demon in the chest, and Dax swung his wing and sliced it in half. Together, they drove the remaining demons back into the forest. The demons prowled the perimeter, their red eyes glowing in the dark between the trees.

Haven helped Dax and Tristan move the wounded cadets to the center of the clearing, careful to avoid their poisonous wounds. She gently closed the eyes of a dead cadet, then stood to see who she could help next and looked into the dead eyes of Quinn and

Larkin. Haven stumbled back into Ryker. He caught her, his powerful arms steadying.

"Oh my gods," she whispered.

"I know," Dax said.

She turned into Ryker, and he held her tight, then reluctantly released her and wiped at her face.

"Keep gathering the wounded," he said gently. "Your pod needs you right now."

"I'm okay," she hiccuped, and gathered herself. He squeezed her hand and gave her a wan smile before helping a struggling ranger who was dragging two bodies to the center of the clearing.

At the perimeter of the woods twenty yards from him, Silas fought off two demons. He stabbed one through the chest, and when the second flanked him, he vanished and appeared behind the demon, cutting off its head.

The site calmed. Ryker's heart dropped at the bodies lying everywhere. Fallon's empty eyes stared at him, her throat bloody and covered in green froth.

He began to feel a strange pull at his stomach as he took in the scene. Silas rushed to him and held his arm. "What's wrong with you?"

"I don't know," he said, feeling his magic slipping away from him. He saw River emerge from the perimeter of the trees, Bane threads swirling around his arms.

"No wonder you feel powerful," River said, his mouth curving in a humorless grin. "This is fantastic."

"What the hell have you done?" Ryker said, his voice cold and furious.

"What I've always wanted. I've taken what *you* have, for once. And now I'm going to take that bitch girlfriend of yours."

"Over my dead body," Ryker growled.

"Not my first choice, but happy to make that happen," River taunted.

"I think you'll find that a lot harder than you imagine." Ryker splayed his wings, black blood dripping from the blades. He drew the dagger from the sheath on his thigh.

River lowered his chin, his lips pressed to a hard line, and struck the Bane at Ryker.

Lilith watched as River emerged from the trees. She jumped to her feet as she saw the Bane swirling around his arms. *Oh shit. He's in deep trouble and doesn't even know it.* She tried to activate the rune on her side that Roque had given her, to control the threat she had brought from a place she didn't even know. Roque had assured her this demon would follow the commands he had taught her to implant in its mind. And when she used the rune, she could feel those orders locking in the animal's mind, an unbendable, undeniable force. But now the rune had burned out, and her magic was nearly depleted. She was helpless to undo what she had done, to redirect the golden-eyed demon that crept behind River, programmed and compelled to kill a Shadowalker.

Bane tendrils streaked from River toward Ryker. Ryker twisted away from the writhing magic and rolled to the ground, flaring his black blades as a shield in front of him. The magic swirled around Ryker's splayed wings, seeping into the metal. River's eyes widened, and he stopped in his tracks. Ryker rolled to his feet and prowled toward him.

"Did you really think you could use my magic against me?" Ryker laughed.

River stalked him, Bane writhing around his arms. "Actually, I did. But that's a neat trick. I'll have to remember that one for later," he sneered.

"Ryker!" Dax yelled. From the corner of his eye, Ryker glimpsed a shima leaping at him. He slashed it with his wings, slicing it across the face. Green venom flew from the demon, spraying Dax's face, bare arms, and chest.

"Silas, help him," Ryker barked. Silas ran to Dax and skimmed him to the center of the site. Ryker turned back to River, crouching and fanning his wings in front of him.

He stumbled back as a black form sprang from the shadows, attacking River from behind and pulling him screaming to the ground. Ryker raced toward him, the last of his Bane snaking toward the demon. The magic touched the demon, and it screamed. Ryker skidded to a stop and thrust his sword, but it leapt back and prowled around him. He tried to get a better look at the demon, but it was a shadow in the dark. He'd never seen one like this before. It was larger than a shima, thicker across the shoulders, with narrow, wraithlike hind legs. The demon stood up and sniffed the air, almost as tall as Ryker. He felt a pressure in his mind, not unlike a Sympath's magic. He refused the magic, not letting it in, and the demon fell to its hands and knees and turned back to River. Ryker slashed at the demon again, and it hissed, then roared an earsplitting cry that vibrated his bones. Then the demon fled into the forest.

Ryker thought to pursue it, but knelt by River, never taking his eyes off the forest. He could see the demon's shadow flitting between the trees. Another screech split the night, then its yellow eyes vanished.

He blinked slowly, dreading what he would see on the ground next to him. He finally looked down at River, and his dread turned into an anguish he knew would never leave him. Blood pumped from a hole in River's throat, his spine visible in the depths of the gash. His eyes pleaded with Ryker, but the only sound he could make was a bubbling hiss. Blood dribbled from his mouth as he reached for Ryker's hand and held him for a brief second.

"River, hold on," Ryker begged, unsure how to help him and cursing his impatience with Farna's basic first aid lectures. But in his heart, he also knew this was beyond anyone's skill. River's back arched, thrashing against the pain. And his pale blue eyes dulled and became vacant.

"River?" Ryker said, shaking his brother's arm. River's head lolled unnaturally to the side, exposing the gash. Blood pumping from the wound slowed to a trickle. Ryker could barely breathe. He stroked River's cheek, then gently closed his unseeing eyes.

Ryker stared numbly at his reflection, desperate to understand a world that didn't include River. He thought they would have more time to find one another again. For River to grow out of his self-destructive phase. He tested Ryker's patience, but they were both still so young. Death? It never crossed Ryker's mind that their time together would end this soon.

A deep rumbling close to the edge of the forest abruptly brought Ryker back to the present, reminding him they weren't out of danger yet. The flitting shadow he glimpsed moments ago stilled, and yellow eyes held his with deadly intent. Ryker backed away, then ran to Silas in the center of the site.

"How is he?" Ryker said, kneeling next to Dax.

"Dying," Silas said. "Poisoning on the skin isn't as fast, but he has maybe twenty minutes. He will die if we don't get him to a healer now."

"Skim him, Silas," Ryker said. Haven fell to her knees beside them.

"Oh gods," she said, her voice quavering. She reached for Dax, and Ryker grabbed her hand.

"Don't touch him. The poison will kill you even through the skin," he said. "Where's Harper?"

"She's okay," Haven said.

Ryker said to Silas, "Take her and Dax to Portos. Get him safe."

"I can't. I can't skim them both and come back. I'm almost empty."

"It's okay," Ryker said. "River is dead. I can handle the demons. Get Dax to a healer and save Harper. Do this for me."

Silas nodded.

"Go, get Harper," he asked Haven. She jumped to her feet, returning a moment later, dragging Harper behind her. "Go with Silas. Make sure Dax lives." Harper hugged her brother quickly and took Silas's hand. Silas wrapped his arm around Dax's shoulder.

"I'm going to be really pissed at you if you die," he said. Ryker gripped his arm and kissed Harper's cheek. Silas vanished, taking Dax and Harper with him.

Lilith watched in horror as the demon attacked River from behind. She had programmed the demon to kill a Shadowalker as a distraction, knowing Ryker's skill and experience with demons. She never expected River to be the target. She saw Ryker drive the demon back to the trees, then kneel beside his brother. His head dipped, and Lilith knew the worst had happened. When Ryker turned back to help the fallen rangers, the demon reemerged from the woods and dragged River's body away.

She frowned. Why would the demon do that?

Her primary objective had failed. Roque had been explicit about the fallback when she had suggested this plan—Haven could not leave this ridge alive. Lilith hesitated as an idea formed in her mind. Maybe this night wasn't the disaster she thought it was. But she had to act quickly. She held back the last reserves of her Amplify magic and used a rune on her back to send an instruction to the red-eyed demons. The hissing and rustling grew as dozens of red eyes glowed around her. Lilith retreated to avoid being caught in the Dampening the shima would cast over the site and followed the yellow-eyed demon's trail into the forest.

Haven's breath caught in her tightening throat at the surrounding devastation. Tristan lay next to Larkin. Dead. Ryker laid Avina's body next to Tristan. "Where's Maddox?" she whispered to no one. "Where's Maddox?" she said again, her voice hitching. Ryker rose, and she caught his gaze. "*Where's Maddox?*" she yelled at him. Ryker strode to her and held her tight. She struggled, trying to shove him away, pounding his chest when he refused to release her.

"Haven," he said softly, but with an urgency in his voice, trying to reach through her panic.

"Where is he?" she said, slumping into his chest, her tears dampening his shirt.

"I don't know. We'll find him."

Ryker's voice suddenly sounded muffled. She felt him stiffen as a weight settled over them. Her eyes widened. "My magic is gone."

Ryker swore and spun Haven to his back. "That's Dampening. Shima have that magic. And there must be a lot of them to Dampen an area this big. Wings out."

"I can't," she said, struggling to unfurl her blades.

"*Shit*. Like, *a lot* of them. Here, take this." Ryker handed her a dagger. Haven saw red eyes glowing around the perimeter.

"Gods, they're everywhere."

"Keep your back to me. I won't let any come at you from behind."

She spied another dagger on the ground and lunged for it. As she gripped the handle, the eyes surged forward together. Haven and Ryker faced a wall of demons, their teeth covered in frothing, green venom.

"Focus. One at a time. They aren't hard to kill. But keep the venom off you," he said, his voice clipped and tense.

She could feel Ryker behind her, his wings whistling in the air as he moved through the wall of demons like a scythe. Haven rolled her shoulders and settled her weight into her knees. *Your best skill is speed. Use it.* She'd heard that a thousand times.

She opened her eyes and moved.

Haven slashed and spun away, avoiding the spray of venom directed at her. She was a whirlwind. All she thought of was cutting and moving, spinning and avoiding, while covering Ryker's back. But they were losing. The wall of demons pressed in, crowding them. A demon clawed her arm, and she cried out. No venom, but the cut was deep, and her arm fell useless to her side.

Another got close before she slashed its throat, its talons opening her ribs to the bone. Overwhelmed, she screamed, and felt her body burst into flame.

Ryker felt a sudden surge of heat behind him. He looked to see Haven's body engulfed in flames. The demons balked, then prowled around them, lunging but staying beyond her reach. Haven hissed, and a demon charged her. She caught the demon by the throat, and it crumbled to ash in her hand. Haven roared, and chills ran up his spine. She turned to him, and fangs dropped from her mouth over her lower lip. Ryker stood his ground, despite having no magic to restrain her. Her white glowing eyes stayed riveted on him.

"Haven," he said, his voice soothing but firm, "control your magic." She charged with unnatural speed. Ryker couldn't follow her movement until she buried her fangs into his shoulder. He swore and tried to hold her off. *Gods, she's strong.* He ripped her away, shouting in agony as her sharp fangs tore through the deep muscle. She lunged through his hands and bit his neck.

And Ryker fell into the sun.

Haven's fangs sank deep, and fire ran through his veins. He gripped her arms and pulled her away, but she didn't budge. He stumbled back and shouted her name, but then noticed the ring of demons were moving *back*, away from them. Haven sealed her lips around the bite and pulled. His blood and his body became an inferno as she drank from his neck. He cried out and struggled against her, pulling desperately at his depleted magic. And, inexplicably, his magic responded. What had been spent only moments before began to grow. Ryker felt Haven's magic flow within him, reviving his Shadowalking, his Bane growing strong. He held her shoulders, his restored magic swirling around his arms and moving up to wrap around her neck. He squeezed gently and pulled her away from him. She broke her grip on his neck, and her mouth found his. Her fangs scraped his lips, filling their mouths with the coppery taste of his own blood.

He opened his eyes to see the demons had vanished, retreating into the tree line. His magic continued to swirl around Haven, and her wings sprang from her back, making him groan with a rush of heat and arousal. He was instantly hard and kissed her fiercely. Bane laced around her red burning wings, and Haven reared back and roared. Ryker held her tight, and she exploded in a pulse of Light that turned the night into day.

Ryker's mind reeled as he ached for her, stronger than anything he had ever felt. He crushed her hips to his, panting and desperate to find any kind of control over his body.

"Ryker," she whispered. Her ocean blue eyes blazed back at him. Her fangs had disappeared, her lips stained red with his blood. She kissed him with the same ferocious need he felt. He picked her up and carried her into the dark of the woods, pressing her against a tree. Her hand slipped between them, fumbling and tugging at the buttons of his breeches.

"Ryker, I'm on fire," she hissed. He kissed her neck, devouring her mouth and grinding into her, his need overtaking any rational thought.

"I need you," he rasped. "I don't think I can stop."

"Don't. Please," she said, unbuttoning her pants. He let her legs drop and stripped her bare. He immediately picked her back up and buried himself in her. They both groaned, and Ryker lost himself. Haven's legs gripped him as he slammed into her. He could feel her tighten against him with every greedy roll of his hips. Haven threw her head back and shouted his name as she found her release. Ryker thrust deep into her and lost his soul. As his own climax rolled through him, he felt Haven in every part of his body, in every facet of his being. They held each other, both gasping for air.

"Your wings are blue," Haven whispered. "And glowing."

Ryker looked to the side and saw a blue light dancing along his onyx blades. Haven's red wings had shifted to silver and were visible behind her. White, peaked flames flickered across the apex. He bent his onyx wings to hers and slid the metal down her silver blade. Haven cried out, and he felt her core pulse around him. His eyes widened as he moaned, nearing climax as well.

Ryker could feel Haven's beating heart, her blood flowing through her veins. He could feel every part of her. Her heart opened to him, and he felt the love that had been growing for him set deep within her. It was real and unbreakable. Ryker's own heart almost broke at the feelings she sent to him. He didn't have to ask her how she felt. He *knew*. Ryker opened his heart to her because he did love her, with everything he was. His onyx wings pulsed and slid down her silver blades again.

"I love you," she said. "So much."

"I can feel you," he said. "I know. Can you feel me?"

"Yes," she said, tears spilling down her face. "I can feel your heart beating. And you love me. Like nothing I've ever felt before."

"It's real, Haven. I think my heart may burst." She laughed a little, then looked down at them. He was still hard and buried inside her.

"This is so inappropriate," she said, grinning at him.

"Totally." He rested his forehead on hers. "I'm sorry. I'm not even sure what happened."

"Don't be sorry," she said. He withdrew and eased her legs to the ground. They found her pants and dressed quickly. Ryker walked a few yards into the woods and knelt, dragging his hand across the ground.

"Ashes. Everywhere," he said, rising and dusting his hands on his breeches. "I think your pulse of Light ashed all the demons."

"Pulse of Light?" she said. "From me?"

"Yes. It was...incredible. We can talk about it later." Ryker walked to her, held her face in his hands, and kissed her lips, lingering a little. He sighed and took her hand. "We need to go back to the site. I don't think there are any survivors. Are you going to be okay?"

She took an unsteady breath. "I don't know. I think so."

They found Knox's body at the edge of the clearing, his ribs bloody and covered in green poison. Haven knelt by him and closed his eyes, her throat constricting and her eyes welling with tears. They returned to the center of the site, to the bodies of her pod. Haven knelt next to Tristan, the bloody gash on his leg edged in venom. She touched his cooling face and curled over his body, her grief pouring from her in a heaving sob. She cried for her friends who stayed to help her, to protect her, who gave their lives so she could live. Ryker knelt beside her, his hand on her back until her tears eased. He gently pulled her off Tristan and held her tight.

"I'm so tired," she said into his chest.

"I know. Stay with me a little longer. The Dampening is gone. Trinity will contact me soon. We'll get a Skimmer and I can take you someplace safe." Within minutes, a squad from the Aerial landed in the clearing, securing the area. Three of the rangers were unconscious but alive. Healers rushed to the survivors, and Skimmers arrived to move them to Portos as another took Haven and Ryker to the Temple in Lucine.

Farna met them and healed the cuts on Haven's arm and ribs.

"Honestly, she did most of the healing herself. I removed the scars. If you had been here an hour later, those would have been healed, too," Farna said.

"How is that possible?" Ryker asked.

"I think it is part of your Phoenix form," he said to Haven.

"I've never healed myself before."

"You're learning to control it and how to use it." Farna noticed a faint mark on her ribs. "Is that your access rune to the Garret?" Haven nodded. "It's depleted. I can Amplify it, but it won't last long. Maybe a day." His fingers traced the rune on Haven's ribs, and the rune darkened.

Farna turned to Ryker. "Now let me see those bites." Ryker removed his jacket and shirt. Haven gasped. The skin and muscle on his shoulder were shredded and purple, and a slow trickle of blood ran down his bare chest and back. His neck was also turning black and weeping blood, with deep puncture wounds in the center of the bruising.

"Good gods, what happened to you?" Haven said.

Ryker raised his eyebrows. "You bit me. Twice."

"I did that?" she said, her hand covering her mouth. He nodded as Farna's glowing hands pressed against his shoulder. "Oh my gods, I'm sorry."

"It was worth it," he said, a sly smile reaching his silver eyes. Haven's face heated, and she laced her fingers through his.

Farna shook his hands, then applied them again and grunted. Ryker winced at the healer's touch.

"Gods, Farna, what are you doing?" Ryker said through gritted teeth.

"The wounds don't want to heal. I'm going to seal them tonight. You need to see me a few times next week." Ryker gripped the edge of the table as Farna worked on him. Farna sealed the torn muscle and skin enough to stop the bleeding, but the marks were angry and red, the bruising profound.

"You're a mess," Haven said as he pulled on his shirt.

"I've had worse."

"I'm thinking poorly of your job right now if you get wounds worse than that."

"I want you to rest tonight, but come again in the morning." Farna eyed Ryker sternly. "Don't make me chase you."

"I got it. Thank you for seeing us this late." Ryker slid off the table and took Haven's hand. "Let's go home."

# CHAPTER 41

## Lucine

Ryker held Haven as warm water coursed over their bodies. She could stand there forever. He eventually released her, dipped his head under the water, then left her to stand under the spray. The pounding water loosened her muscles and eased the tension in her body, chasing away the tidal wave of exhaustion that threatened to overwhelm her. Her mind had difficulty comprehending the scope of what happened earlier that evening, only a few short hours ago. Instead, she shut down, emotionally exhausted and physically drained from the battle and her shift into the Phoenix. She focused on the smallest drops of water that ran down her arms and legs. The steam that billowed around her. The sound of the water sprinkling on the tiles under her feet. Letting the small things keep her thoughts away from the disaster of ComSim.

Ryker handed her a towel when she shut off the water. Passing him as he dressed, she walked to the second bedroom and rummaged through her belongings Trinity had brought last week. It seemed like a lifetime ago.

Haven joined Ryker in the living area, dressed in a t-shirt and leggings. "I need a drink."

He handed her a whiskey. "Already there."

They moved to the balcony and sat on the couch. She curled against him, folding her legs under her. They sipped their drinks in silence.

"Eventually we need to talk about what happened tonight," Ryker started.

Haven held up her hand, stopping him. "But not tonight. I feel if I go down that road right now, I'll start crying and won't stop for days."

Ryker draped his arm across her shoulders and pulled her tight, resting his lips on her forehead. "Trinity tapped me earlier. Dax is going to be okay. The healer was a good one and they got to him in time. And they found Maddox." Haven tensed. "He's in critical condition, but with a healer. We'll know more in the morning." She pulled his arm around her waist and sank into him.

"I guess I'll take my teaspoon of good news and be grateful for it."

"I'm sorry I don't have more. But it's a start." He took her empty glass and set it on the table. "Come on. You need rest."

She followed him, dragging her feet and falling into the blankets. She barely remembered his arms folding around her and holding her tight before sleep consumed her.

Haven woke to an empty bed the next morning. She pulled back the blankets and rose, rummaging through his dresser. The t-shirt she pulled over her head smelled of him, a fresh ocean breeze with a hint of pine. She shuffled into the living area, yawning and stretching, rubbing her sleepy eyes. Ryker was leaning on the rail of the balcony, his head bowed. She slipped her arm around his waist, their hips touching.

"Hey," she said softly. "You okay?" Ryker was quiet, his gaze fixed on the city of Araine. "Ryker?" she asked.

"River and I were inseparable as children," he said, looking down at her. His eyes were bloodshot, with dark smudges in the corners. There was a weariness around him she knew was from more than a sleepless night. "He was the bold one, the one that always got us in trouble. Even with my magic, he was never afraid. Not of me, not of anything. He was brave and clever. To him, my magic didn't make me different. It was a part of me. It was who I was. And believe it or not, he loved me. He always had my back, particularly with our older brother Rafael, who was a bully. And he always defended me and Shallah against our father." The pain of loss shimmered in Ryker's eyes. "He wasn't always the person you knew."

"I'm sorry," she whispered. He wrapped his arm around her shoulders, and she could feel the tension in his body against hers.

"I have been mourning the loss of my brother for fifteen years," Ryker said, his voice thick with emotion. "A small part of me hoped the brother I knew was still in there somewhere. That I could find him again. Even when I knew in my mind it wasn't possible." Haven held him, her heart breaking. "He was part of me. And now..." He faltered, his words thick and rough. "I feel I failed him."

"I don't have any siblings, let alone a twin. I can't imagine the loss you feel. But River was an adult and responsible for the choices he made. Yes, he loved you, but he was also jealous, and he let that consume him. That's not your fault." His glistening eyes roved her face as she brushed his hair back from his eyes. "Don't apologize for who you are, or for your gifts."

After breakfast, Ryker felt Trinity tap him. *Yes, Trinity?*

*How are you? How is Haven?*

*Recovering. How is Maddox?*

*Still serious, but stable for now. He has a long way to go. The healer said they should transfer him to the Temple in a day or two. Dax is okay, but also will need time to recover. At least a few weeks, according to the healer. He knows about the pod's deaths and is asking for Haven.*

*We can skim there later this afternoon. Will you stay through ComSim?*

*Yes, if that's okay with you. I feel I need to stay here. The remaining squads are understandably nervous.*

*Yes, that's fine. I'll meet up with Silas. Have the guardians and Lukas mapped the new rift?*

*That's the strange thing. It's gone.*

*What do you mean, gone?*

*Lukas said it doesn't exist. It's sealed, like it wasn't even there.*

*How can that be? Rifts don't repair themselves.*

*I don't know. You can speak to the guardians once you get here. Also, the investigations team wants to speak with you and Haven when you're ready.*

*We're okay. Tell them we can talk this afternoon. Thanks, Trinity.*

*Take care of each other,* she said.

Haven emerged from the bedroom, dressed for the day and pulling her hair into a high pony. He updated her on Maddox and Dax and was relieved to see her relax a little.

"Farna wants to see me this morning, and then, if you're up for it, we should go to Portos. It would be good for you and Dax to see each other. And I need to reconnect with Silas and see Harper."

Haven walked with him to the balcony as he unfurled his raven wings. She lingered, holding on to his hand. He waited until she was ready to let him go. "Send me a sprite when you're done with Farna and I'll meet you," she said.

A quick smile flicked across his lips. "I won't be long. Promise."

Ryker flew to the Temple and found Farna waiting for him in a treatment room. He removed his shirt, and Farna frowned.

"The bite on your shoulder may have gotten worse overnight." Farna inspected the torn, weeping flesh. "That shouldn't happen." Farna worked on Ryker's wounds for an hour, still dissatisfied with the result. "If you have the time, I'd like to have Adrien consult on this." Ryker reluctantly agreed, and moments later, Farna returned with Adrien. Ryker hadn't seen Adrien in years, by choice.

"It's good to see you. You look more like your mother every day," Adrien said.

"I wouldn't know," Ryker said coldly. Disappointment clouded Adrien's eyes before he looked away.

Farna attempted to diffuse the tension between the two males. "Ryker's wounds are not responding to healing magic. Can you take a look?"

Ryker turned away from him and heard Adrien sigh. He flinched as Adrien examined his shoulder and neck, gently probing the tender wounds.

"How did you get this bite? What bit you?"

"Haven did, in her Phoenix form," Ryker said.

Adrien's eyes widened. "And what happened when she bit you? Be very specific."

"It happened fast. She bit my shoulder and I pulled her off me. I think that's why the bite is torn."

"You pulled her off you?"

"Yes, but barely. She was strong. When I pulled her off me, she lunged for my neck and bit me again. I couldn't pull her off my neck."

"I'm surprised you could have pulled her off you the first time."

"She drank my blood," Ryker said, reaching up to touch the black, bruised puncture marks on his neck.

"Be very specific about what happened next," Adrien said.

"I'm assuming you know what happened at the site that day."

"Generally, yes. But not the details."

"River was there. He stole my magic." Ryker's eyes narrowed at Adrien's carefully guarded face. "My magic was almost empty. But when Haven first pulled at my neck, when she drank my blood, I could feel my magic grow stronger. It hurt, like my blood was on fire. Haven also said later she felt like she was on fire. And actually, she was. I used my magic to pull her off me, and she exploded in Light. The wave was intense. When she was on my neck and on fire, the demons ran away from us. Later, I found ash everywhere. I think the Light wave ashed every demon around us."

"It did," Adrien said. "Demons can sense Light, and for most demon species, it's deadly."

"Before she bit me, she was in her Phoenix form and held a shima by the neck and turned it to ash. And when the Phoenix first emerged, the demons stopped pressing their attack on us."

"Our history is vague on the Phoenix form, but mystics and the legends describing the origin of the Phoenix say its purpose was to keep the demons at bay, to restrict them to their worlds. I would assume they could feel the Light within her and feared her. It would be instinctual, if indeed the legends are true."

"Well, they certainly ran from her," Ryker said.

"I need to ask you some personal questions. Ones that may make you uncomfortable. But they are important," Adrien said.

Farna said, "I can leave if you want."

"No, it's okay. I have nothing to hide."

"What is the nature of your relationship with Haven?" Adrien asked.

"We are seeing each other. It is fairly new, about a month."

"Do you love her?"

"Yes, I do. And I know she loves me."

Adrien clasped his hands in his lap. "You say that with such certainty. How do you know?"

"Because I felt her. Our wings touched and they glowed. And I could *feel* her. What it was like to be her. I could feel her emotions." Ryker sighed. "It's hard to explain. But I'm sure of this. And I know she felt the same from me."

"I don't doubt what you felt. What you experienced was a mating bond. You and Haven are bonded."

"You mean like a fae mating bond?"

"Yes, somewhat," Adrien said. "As you know, seraphim can choose to accept a mating. Fae cannot. A fae mating bond is permanent."

"What do you mean, accept it? We just say 'yes' and it's permanent?"

Adrien chuckled. "No, nothing is that easy. Like any relationship, a bond takes nurturing before it settles. You'll have to work at it, get to know one another and see a Sympath for counseling. Setting a bond usually takes a year, and it can be turbulent. Bonds evoke powerful emotions. I know you know Corde. I would recommend him for counseling. Not only is he an experienced Sympath, but also has a mating bond with Finnian, so he knows firsthand the difficulty of coping with a settling bond.

"While the bond is setting, if you find you aren't compatible, you can still reject it. However, the blood exchange in Haven's Phoenix form bound your magic for life. You are stronger together. That's why she could restore your magic."

Ryker ran his hand through his hair. "That's a lot to take in."

"You still have a choice. If you choose not to be with Haven, you will...care for her, but not be compelled. Does that make sense?"

"Yes, I think so," Ryker said.

"However, your magic will always be connected. And Ryker, there is not a more powerful combination of magic. Shadowwalker and the Phoenix form, this combination was the original Mated Pair, between Gabriel and Fenix." Adrien smiled warmly. "For a historian, I feel privileged to see this Pairing come to life."

Farna said, "All of this is fascinating, but why can't I heal his wound?"

"It's Haven's Phoenix magic. It's stronger than any healing magic we have. She could heal it if she were in her Phoenix form, but absent that, it will have to heal on its own," Adrien said. "Keep treating it, but unfortunately it will be a slow process."

"Thank you." Ryker pulled on his shirt.

"It's my pleasure. And may I offer my congratulations on your mating. It's a rare gift and should be treasured. You're lucky." Ryker thanked Farna and flew back to the loft, his mind reeling from Adrien's words.

Haven was resting on the sofa when Ryker returned. "You didn't have to come back here. I thought you were going to send me a sprite when you finished with Farna." She sat up when she noticed his somber look. Ryker took her hand and sat next to her. "What's wrong? Are you okay?" she asked warily, reaching for his collar to look at the wound on his shoulder.

He told her what Adrien said. Haven stood and paced the room, her arms crossed and shoulders tense. Ryker watched her carefully.

"You don't have to accept our bond. I know our relationship is new, and maybe you aren't ready for that kind of commitment. We can still love each other without being bonded." He followed her and slowly turned her around. "This is your life. Your choice. I will respect your decision."

"What about you?" She swallowed hard. "I bit you and bonded you to me, against your will. You aren't trapped with me. You can choose, too."

Ryker tipped her chin. Haven's eyes glistened, and a tear slid down her face as she avoided his eyes. "I can think of worse traps to fall into," he teased.

"It's not funny, Ryker," she said, glaring at him. "I feel like I stole you." She broke away from him and walked to the balcony. He caught her by the waist and pulled her to him, kissing her hard.

"You are mine," he said into her lips.

"You want this?" she said, breathless.

"Yes. More than anything." He held her tightly to him. This time, his kiss was light, gentle. "But it's your choice too. If you don't want to commit to me, I'll do my best to give you space. But I may haunt you for the rest of your life," he said. His smile faded as he tried to put a brave front to her indecision. "Tell me what you want, if you're ready. I understand if you need time."

"I told you I loved you, and I meant that. I've never had anyone in my life that loved me." She touched his face, his lips. "I choose you. You belong to me."

Ryker pulled off his shirt and unbuttoned his pants. "I'm taking what's mine. Right now," he said, his voice low and rough. Her fingers brushed his face as he stripped off her jeans. He pulled her leg to his hip and slipped his hand between her thighs. Ryker carried her to his bed and laid her down, his eyes devouring her naked body as he tossed his jeans on the floor. He leaned over her, hesitating, waiting for a change of heart. But he saw nothing but heated longing.

"I choose you," she whispered, touching his lips. His mouth crushed hers, his need for her consuming him in a rush of lust and passion. And love. Haven writhed under him as his fingers found her center, drenched and ready for him.

"Put me inside you," he whispered. Haven reached between them and stroked him from base to tip. His eyes closed, the sensation of her touch driving him to the agonizing edge. "Now, Haven. I need you," he growled. She guided him to her, and he slowly entered her until he was seated deep inside. "You are mine. I love you, and always will."

# CHAPTER 42

## Portos

"Ready to go?" Ryker kissed the back of Haven's neck as she twisted her hair into a long braid.

"Almost," she said, turning to him. "I want to file a petition to annul the contract with Lukas this morning. I want this over as soon as possible."

They flew to the ministry building south of the Temple where Haven filed her petition, then returned to the Temple and found a Skimmer who took them to Portos.

Their first stop was the morgue, where Haven said goodbye to Tristan, Quinn, Avina, and Larkin for the last time. She held Tristan's cold, lifeless hand, his face blurring through her tears.

Ryker took her hand. "Dax is waiting. And the living need you more."

"I just can't believe this," she breathed.

"I know." He pulled her tight. "But remember him as he was. Alive, your podmate and friend. Not like this." She sniffled and nodded, and he gently led her from the room.

They walked through the Administration building to the medical wing and found a healer who directed them to Dax's room. Haven knocked on the door.

"Enter," a small voice said. She opened the door and stopped short at the sight of Dax. He was lying on his back, his face pale and drawn, dark circles around his closed eyes.

"Hi." She sat on the bed next to him and held his icy hand. He slowly opened his eyes.

"Hey," he said, smiling thinly at her. "You look good. That's a relief."

"I'm fine. How do you feel?"

"Pretty shitty." He closed his eyes again. "But I hear I'll live."

Haven sat with Dax for the next hour. She spoke to him when he could listen and kept him company when he slept. Ryker left to find his healer. When he returned, he waited until Dax faded again and told her what he knew.

"Dax will be fine, but the healers say he'll be sick like this for the next month. Shima poisoning is serious. The healers will transfer Maddox to the Temple tomorrow. Farna is familiar with injuries like this and best equipped to treat him."

Haven asked, "Why only Farna?"

"Because Farna works exclusively with Shadowalkers. And since we hunt demons, he knows how to treat rare injuries."

Haven tensed. "And how serious is Maddox?"

"Not good. They aren't sure if he'll live." He pulled his chair close to her. "He was severely poisoned. Not like Dax, which was through the skin. He was bitten on the leg. Quinn forced him to skim immediately to Portos. That's what saved his life. If he hadn't skimmed when he did, he would be dead."

"Gods, Ryker. What the hell happened on the ridge?" She wiped angrily at her tears and stroked Dax's icy hand.

"I don't know. I know River had something to do with it, but he wasn't working alone. He can't form a rift. I'm not sure who could, but someone let in a team of shima with the sole purpose of targeting your squad. I can only imagine it was to capture or kill you."

"I find that hard to believe," she said, shaking her head.

"Why? Remember what I told you that night in the woods around Portos? There are people who would seek to control your power, to bind you to them. Or eliminate you altogether if you can't be bound. I think River was trying to bind you. When he attacked you in your apartment, Silas heard him tell you to bite him." Haven's eyes widened. "And at the site yesterday, he said he was coming after you. The largest wave of shima came *after* he died. I think once he couldn't bind you, whoever he was working with tried to kill you." Haven shuddered and set her mouth in a thin line.

"I once told Dax I feel cursed. Sometimes I still feel that way," she said, stroking Dax's hand.

"You have me. I can offer you protection and safety through the Garret's wardings. But honestly, that's not enough. I know it's too soon to talk, but you need to continue training your Phoenix form. You've made a good start, but you need to develop the magic to wield it effectively and protect yourself. And I think you've run out of time. It needs to happen now, particularly if you intend to go through with your commitment to the Aerial."

"Will you help me?"

"Yes, if that's what you want. I can help you gain control, but eventually you will need to work with an expert fae trainer, like Kaden, who can train you properly."

Haven reached for his hand. "Will you stay with me through training?"

He kissed her hand in his. "Always."

They stayed with Dax for another hour, then left to see Maddox. Haven trembled as she held his ice-cold hand, unnerved by his sunken cheeks and pale, bloodless skin. They talked to his healer, who also wanted to transfer Dax to the Temple to be under Farna's care. They would move both Dax and Maddox the following day.

Silas joined them in the medical wing after they visited Maddox. A guardian renewed Haven's access ward to the Garret, then Silas took them to the investigations unit that had set up temporarily in the Admin building. They spent the rest of the afternoon speaking with the team assigned to the incident. Ryker told him of his suspicions, of River and Haven and his attack on her.

"There had to be someone helping him. Who opened that rift?"

"We can't find any evidence of the rift," a detective said.

"Well, how else did shima get into Praesia? Come on, none of what you're saying makes sense," Ryker said, his frustration creeping through his composure. "As far as I know, djinn can form rifts, but we know they would never work with shima. And while rare, some daevas can."

"There are no daevas in Praesia," an inspector said.

Ryker rolled his eyes. "A daeva doesn't need to be here to form a rift. But someone needed to be here at the site to place it. Have you asked Lilith? She has contacts with the daevas. She could have helped them."

"Ryker," Haven whispered. "Why would Lilith do that?"

"I wouldn't put anything past her."

"It wasn't Lilith," an inspector said. "We had similar thoughts and checked. Lilith was in Torella yesterday evening at a political function. She was seen by more than three hundred people."

"Well, gods damn it, someone did this!" Ryker snapped.

"We know," the inspector said. "Lilith is making inquiries with the daevas. We'll let you know if we learn anything."

Ryker abruptly stood and stormed out of the Admin building. Haven chased him into the plaza. "This is ridiculous," Ryker growled. "Is anyone taking this seriously?"

Haven held his arm. "They are trying. We need to be patient." She laced a hand into his. "Come on. Harper is joining us for dinner at the inn. Let's go check in." Ryker didn't budge, but instead glared at the door to the building.

"Something feels wrong here. More than twenty people are dead. You'd think they would have...I don't know...more outrage over this."

Haven tugged at his hand. "I have enough rage for all of us. I had to say goodbye to Tristan and Quinn this afternoon before they shipped their bodies home. I want someone to pay for that with their life. But I also know we need to go through the process. Aren't you always the one preaching patience? There's nothing we can do right now. But we can keep pressing for answers. I can speak to my father, and the king if we need to pressure the search. But right now, let them do their job and collect information."

He shook his head and reluctantly followed her into town.

Lilith sat outside the senate chamber, waiting to be called in to give her testimony. Her foot bounced, and she glanced at her watch again. Finally, she felt a tapping in her mind. She accepted the link and heard Dekkar's voice.

Ryker and Haven just left. They were the last to be questioned.

*Did he ask about me?* Lilith asked, tensing.

*Yes, but the investigators confirmed your alibi. It's airtight.* Lilith slumped in relief. *The team concluded their inquiry. Have you cleared it with the king?*

*I'm sitting outside the senate chamber now. But I won't have much to add because I wasn't there.*

*You should know Ryker pressed on the rift. He wanted to know who made it and blamed the daevas.*

*That's on the Daeva Council, which I'm conveniently not a part of.*

*But it's well known you have contacts in Elsah-ra. I'd be careful on that topic.*

*I got it,* Lilith said, annoyed at getting advice from Dekkar. She severed the Link when the senate chamber doors opened. Finnian and his Triad exited behind the escort, who came to retrieve Lilith.

Finnian walked by her without a word. "A real tragedy, this attack. Seems you have a traitor on your Daeva Council," she said to his back. He paused and looked at her.

"There's no traitor on the Council." Finnian walked to Lilith and looked down at her. "But I know who is responsible."

"Oh? Who? I want to be sure we bring them to justice."

"Play all the games you want, but this is on you."

"Me? I was nowhere near the Academy yesterday. You know that." Lilith's voice grew hard. "And I won't tolerate any accusations from *you*."

"This reeks of you, from top to bottom." He bumped her so she was forced to take a step back. She gritted her teeth in fury. "Twenty people dead. *Kids*. I will expose you, if it's the last thing I do."

Lilith held his gaze. "You pursue this, and it *will* be the last thing you do."

Finnian laughed and left her standing in the hall.

Ryker, Haven, and Silas met Harper for dinner that night at a local pub in Portos. She left after dinner to join Kit in Damaris. During dinner, Haven received a link confirming her petition hearing, which would be in two days.

She lay in bed that night at the inn in Portos, restless and unable to sleep, her mind racing through the events of the day and the upcoming hearing with the king and queen. She finally rose to give Ryker a moment's peace and wandered to the sitting area of their small chamber. Silas sat on the balcony, sipping a drink.

"Hey, kiddo," he said. She trailed her hand across his arm and sat in the chair beside him. "Can't sleep?"

"Way too much happened this week. I can't turn off my brain." They sat in silence for a while, and Haven relaxed.

"Ryker told me about your bond." She turned to him. "I've never seen him this happy in the twenty years I've known him. You have to believe he loves you."

"I know he does. I felt him, his love for me." She took in the forest surrounding Portos. "I remember the day I arrived here, on the way to the Academy. I knew I was lonely then, but I had no idea how *alone* I was. I've never had someone love me before Ryker. It's something I treasure above anything and everything. And I love him, who he is, his heart and mind. I hope you know that."

Silas said, "I know you do. He's lucky to have found you."

"We're lucky to have found each other."

Two days later, Haven, Ryker, and his Triad waited outside a meeting room to present her petition. Lukas walked down the hall toward her, his face grim.

"Can I speak with you?" Haven followed him to a small reception area. "My parents will oppose your petition. I've tried everything I can to convince them we don't want this, but they dismiss me, saying we don't have sufficient cause to break the contract."

"I'll try to reason with the king, and my father will support us. Unfortunately, my mother won't. But you should know Ryker and I discovered we have a mating bond. I won't give him up. Not for anything."

Lukas's eyes brightened. "That is great news."

"How is that good news?" Haven asked.

"Because the king will never force a mated pair into a contract with someone else. He will probably have you prove your bond through a trial, but that's simple enough to do."

"What's a trial?" Haven asked.

"It varies for each couple, but usually involves some kind of separation to test whether the mating bond is real. The time can vary from a few weeks to a few months. The longest one I've ever heard of was a year."

"A year? Gods, that's a little extreme."

"Most are usually a few months. I'm sure it will be an inconvenience, but it will be easiest for you because you won't remember Berinia or being a seraphim. A guardian will bridge you through the Pale to live in another world, with no memory of this one."

"Wait, why me?"

"Because the Council will never allow a Shadowalker to leave Praesia for any length of time. So, unfortunately, it will have to be you." He touched her arm. "My congratulations on your bond. I'm happy for you both. It's truly a gift." He laced her hand through his arm. "But we can give it a try. Let's see if we can make them see reason."

They returned to the Triad and were shortly escorted into the meeting room. Liam and Skye sat at the table with Astor and Hope. Lukas and Haven sat across from them, with the king and queen at the end of the table. Ryker and his Triad stood behind Haven, and Hope's guardian loomed behind Astor and Hope.

A ministry representative read Haven's petition to the group. Haven then described her mating bond with Ryker and the Phoenix Pairing. The king thanked Haven and said, "Lukas, your thoughts on this?"

"I support Haven's decision. I don't want the contract enforced."

The king said to Astor and Hope, "And your thoughts?" As expected, Astor supported Haven, while her mother was vehemently against canceling the contract, as were Liam and Skye.

"We all know the contract is a formality. Haven is free to love whoever she wants. I don't see how this changes anything," Hope argued. Haven looked at her mother for the first time and saw her for who she was and not who she could have been, who she should have been to Haven. She was a cold, bitter female incapable of loving anyone. Haven pitied her and despised her at the same time.

The king said, "I'm inclined to respect the wishes of both Lukas and Haven if indeed she is mated to Ryker. I will require a trial, and if the mating bond is confirmed, I will annul the contract. If it isn't, I will side with Hope, Liam, and Skye, and the contract will be enforced. It seems like a fair middle ground." He addressed Haven and Ryker, "You should both consider this carefully, but you have until Summer Solstice to decide. And if you choose the trial, you must enter it by the Solstice. From what I understand, the Solstices and the Equinoxes are the only time the guardians can start a trial, and I don't want this lingering until the Autumn

Equinox." The king stood with the queen. "Haven and Ryker, I hope your bond is confirmed. It's a rare gift."

They rose as the king left with the queen. Hope remained at the table, her hands clasped tightly in front of her as Astor, Liam, and Skye followed the king and queen. Haven stared at her mother and felt...nothing. The female was a stranger to her.

Ryker gently pulled at her arm. She slipped an arm around him and made sure her mother saw it. "Goodbye, *Mother*," she said with all the disdain she felt in her heart.

Haven sat on a bench with Silas and Trinity in the Palace gardens, watching Ryker prowl in circles, his eyes a storming gray. Haven could see wisps of Shadow rolling off his arms.

"You have to be the worst poker player on the planet," she said, laughing.

He scowled at her. "This is ridiculous. A trial? That's as archaic as you can get. I can't remember the last time a couple had to go through a trial."

Silas said, "Well, not everyone is a Shadowalker, a Phoenix, and a princess that is bound in an enosi contract." Haven giggled at the furious look Ryker gave Silas. "What? Am I wrong?"

"No, you're right." Haven said to Ryker, "I'm fine doing this. It's worth it to have this entire mess cleaned up."

"You'll be away for months," Ryker said.

"Maybe. From what I understand, it's up to the guardian and reader assigned to us. It might only be a few weeks. How is this any different from me being in the Aerial for months?"

"Because you won't remember us. At least I could visit you in the Aerial," Ryker grumbled. Haven slipped her arms around him.

"Of all the crappy things that have happened recently, this is a small thing. Seriously, I'm fine with this." Ryker sighed, kissed her forehead, and hugged her.

Trinity said to Ryker, "There is little risk to this. I can feel the bond between you both. You'll pass with flying colors. We can have a long vacation, and Haven will be back before you know it."

Ryker sighed. "Apparently I'm outnumbered. Fine. But for the record, I hate it."

Haven and Ryker filed for a trial that afternoon. They were notified their trial was confirmed and would start in a week, on Summer Solstice.

# CHAPTER 43

## Araine

Lilith paced in the shadows of the trees along the edge of the lake, beyond the Palace gardens. Roque appeared, his face somber.

"This is a complete disaster," Lilith said.

"I agree," Roque said.

"What the hell do we do now? The Phoenix is Paired to Ryker, and that can't be undone. Gods damned River. What the hell was he thinking?" She halted her pacing. "Did you know he had Adrien infuse him with demon blood? I knew he was jealous of Ryker, but I never thought he would go to such extreme lengths to steal his magic." Lilith studied Roque's veiled expression.

"It doesn't matter at this point what River did. He's gone." It was Lilith's turn to keep her face blank. She knew Roque wasn't being honest. It seemed they both had their own secrets to keep. "What matters now is how we keep them apart. They *must* be apart, Lilith." Roque paced restlessly. "Ryker and Haven believe they have a mating bond."

Lilith snorted. "I'm sure they are confusing that with the Phoenix Pairing."

"Why would you doubt that?" he asked. "From what I've heard, they have been falling in love for some time."

"How do you know?" Lilith asked.

"From their friends and family. It's common knowledge."

Lilith waved a hand, dismissing him. "Unlikely."

"Why? Just because you pine after Ryker doesn't negate the feelings he has for Haven. I think you are being purposefully blind about this." Lilith glared at him but remained silent. "If you can't be objective, you are of no use to me."

"What do you suggest we do?"

"Ryker and Haven have requested a trial to break the mating contract with Lukas," Roque said. "This may be a blessing in disguise. Find a way to influence the trial. We may not break the bond between Haven and Ryker, but we can send Haven away indefinitely. Then the bond would not be confirmed. And having her off this planet may help me. Either that, or she needs to die."

"We won't be able to get anywhere near them. Not with the security around them and Trinity connected to them both." Lilith eyed him intently. "I know where your mind is going. And you can't kill Ryker. I don't care how strong your Cloaking magic is, Trinity will See it. And Berinia needs Ryker as a Shadowalker. Killing Ryker is not the answer."

"Gods damn it, there has to be a solution here!" Roque shouted. Lilith jumped in surprise as his normally unflappable composure crumbled.

Lilith thought of Roque's earlier suggestion. "There may be a way to separate them permanently and keep Ryker in Berinia." She drummed her fingers on her thigh, trying to solidify the idea that was slowly coming together in her mind. "Their trial will need a guardian and a reader. I know of both who are in trouble right now, and they don't even know it."

Adrien walked into his office to find Lilith sitting in front of his desk, waiting for him. "Adrien, you naughty boy. You've been up to no good lately, haven't you?"

"Get out. I have nothing to say to you." He sat behind his desk and ignored her.

"I think you will have a lot to say after I'm done." Lilith rested her arms on his desk. "You infused River with demon blood." Adrien's eyes jerked to hers. "And now a commander in the Aerial is dead because of you. I'm thinking the Enforcement bureau will not like that at all." Her mouth curled in a wintry smile.

"Do your worst. Report me, I don't care." He returned to the papers on his desk.

"You know the penalty for an unregistered Cloak using black blood craft on an Aerial commander, which resulted in his death, will be your own death?"

Adrien sighed. "I don't know how many times I need to say this. I don't care what they do to me."

"You may not care for yourself, but what about Katalin?"

Adrien stiffened. "Katalin? What of her?"

"She helped you."

"She had nothing to do with this."

"That's not how it will look to the Enforcement team. And I'll make sure they know she helped you all along."

"That's a lie. Katalin warned Ryker and Haven of River's threat to her. That's it."

"Well, that's not what I'm going to tell them. And who do you think they'll believe? Me? Or you? A known liar with a well-documented history of black magic and illegal activities? They will banish Katalin from Berinia. At worst, she'll end up with you in a grave."

Hatred flickered across his face. "What do you want?"

"Get Katalin in here and I'll tell you." Adrien brought Katalin into his office and sat her next to Lilith.

Katalin balked at Lilith's presence. "What are you doing here?"

"I'd like to discuss Haven and Ryker's trial," Lilith said.

"What does that have to do with me?" Katalin asked.

"We will assign you as the reader for their trial, and Adrien will be the guardian." Lilith's hard eyes raked over them both. "And you will set a trial with an indefinite time. I want you to send Haven away forever."

Katalin's mouth dropped slightly. "I would never do that to them." She stalked to the door to leave. Adrien shook off his stunned silence.

"Why are you asking for this? You know their mating bond will be broken if they refuse or fail the trial, but the Phoenix Pairing will always connect them. And besides, that's not the way the trial magic works. There has to be an end to it," he said.

"Even the most novice readers can feel the bond between them," Katalin said. "You could send Haven away for a lifetime and their mating bond would be the same."

Lilith paced, then said, "Then do that. Send her away for a lifetime."

"Why would I do that? Because you want it? It's cruel and unnecessary. I won't do it."

"Yes, you will, or they will charge you with using demon blood craft on River, a commander in the Aerial, which caused his death. One that several people witnessed, including Ryker himself. I think you know what the outcome of a conviction would be."

Katalin's face blanched. "I didn't do any of that!" She looked at Adrien in a panic. "What have you done?" she said, quietly. "What did you drag me into?"

Adrien looked down at his hands. "I'm sorry. I didn't mean for you to be involved in this." He looked at Lilith, repulsed. "And I never thought someone so vile would blackmail you."

Lilith laughed at him. "Look who's throwing stones. What you did to River was evil."

"He begged me for it, and...influenced me. I'll regret my weakness for the rest of my life."

"I really don't care. What's done is done. Both of you need to decide if you want to work with me or face the fury of the Enforcement bureau and the king," Lilith said, walking to the door. "Their trial starts in a few days. I will have my report ready to submit to the authorities if you decide to ignore my request."

# CHAPTER 44

## The Trial

"Well, I guess this is one way to avoid the Summer Solstice Ball," Silas said to Ryker. Ryker glared at him as they waited with Haven and Trinity outside the trial wing.

"I love the balls. The Autumn Ball is where we first met," Haven said, remembering the evening three years ago. "Although you were a total jackass that night."

Ryker huffed. "You were a sassy princess."

"Oh? And was I supposed to let you be a jerk to me?" she said, crossing her arms.

He pulled her toward him, fighting her resistance. "You're sexy when you're grouchy."

"I seriously don't know how you put up with him," Trinity said to Haven. Haven pushed Ryker away from her halfheartedly. She heard the door open, and Ryker's face fell, his eyes clouding to a dark gray. She looked back over her shoulder as Adrien approached them.

"Hello, Adrien," Haven said.

Ryker said in a clipped voice, "What are you doing here?"

"I've been assigned as the guardian for your trial." A seraphim female with brown hair and rich, amber eyes hovered stiffly behind Adrien. "This is Katalin, your reader." Katalin nodded curtly and avoided their gaze. "You understand how the trial works? I will ask for your commitment to the trial as I apply the rune. Once I apply the rune, it can't be reversed. Katalin will then determine what your trial should be. After you know the terms of the trial, you will have one hour before Haven must go into stasis. You can still back out at that time. However, if you do, the rune will break your mating bond."

He asked Haven, "Do you have questions?" Haven shook her head. Ryker's icy glare fell on Adrien.

"Ryker? Do you have questions?" Ryker said nothing.

An assistant healer led Haven to a small treatment room to bathe and dress her and apply a rune to her back to ease her into hibernation and protect her body for the duration of her trial. She was sitting on an exam table, waiting for a guardian to begin the process, when she heard a knock.

Hope opened the door. "May I have a word?"

Haven started, then said coldly, "If you insist."

"I do," she said, closing the door behind her. "We aren't close, and I take the blame for that. I'm sure I wasn't the mother you wanted."

"You are not my mother. Mothers care for their children. You don't care for me at all. And why should you? I'm a total stranger to you."

"Yes, you are. I know nothing about you. And yes, that's my doing. I don't have a right to ask, but I will anyway. I don't think you should go through with the trial. It is unnecessary."

"You will release me from this contract?"

Hope blinked. "No. I think you should accept the commitment to Lukas. You can still have Ryker. But this is a desirable match for both families. It's a small thing to give to me and your father."

"You mean to you. My father doesn't think this is necessary. And I don't owe you anything," Haven said, her fury barely contained. "And what of the requirement to have a child with

Lukas? You expect me to carry a male's child when I'm in love with another?"

Hope waved a hand at Haven. "If Ryker truly loves you, he won't hold it against you. It's a small thing. One year of your life carrying a child. Then you're done."

Haven gaped at her. "Is that what you thought of me? As a year gone from your life?" She looked away, refusing to let her mother hurt her like this. Hope brushed the hair from Haven's eyes.

"Yes. Don't be a selfish child."

Haven jerked from her touch. "Get out. And don't come near me again."

An hour later, Haven walked to the trial room. Ryker pulled her close, pressing her head to his chest. Haven soaked up the feel of him, his fresh scent, his warmth. She kissed him, then stepped away.

"Ready?" she asked.

He swallowed hard. "Yes."

Adrien turned Haven's arm over, palm up. He placed his hand on her forearm below her elbow and asked her a series of questions detailing the rules of the trial and her agreement to abide by the terms set by the reader and accept the consequences of failing or refusing the trial. She tried to respond while cringing at the burning pain. Adrien eventually removed his hand, and a small, dark rune edged in raw, red skin was imprinted on her arm. He repeated the process with Ryker.

When he finished, Katalin placed one hand on Ryker's trial rune and one on Haven's. She closed her eyes, and again Haven felt the rune burning her arm. Ryker reached for her and held her other hand. Katalin eventually opened her eyes, now black, and said, "You have an unusually strong bond which will need an equally strong test. Your trial will be in Terra. Haven, we require you to live a human life, a maximum of eighty years. You will be born, live a life, and die as a human. When your human body dies, you will awake again here in Berinia, and your trial will be complete."

Katalin's eyes lightened to her normal golden amber. She avoided Haven and Ryker's shocked faces. "I'm sorry," she said.

"Wait, what just happened?" Ryker said. "Did you say *eighty years?*"

"Yes," Katalin whispered.

"No way," Ryker said. He hissed and reached for the trial rune on his arm.

"Do you refuse the trial?" Adrien said.

Haven stepped forward. "No, he doesn't. Give us a minute."

Adrien said, "You have an hour to decide. Stasis must begin immediately, or the rune will judge the delay as a break in the contract." He said to Ryker, "I'm sorry."

"Get the fuck out of here," he said to Adrien, his rage barely contained. Adrien took Katalin's arm and quickly left.

Ryker wheeled to Haven. "We are not doing this," he said flatly.

"Oh, yes we are," Haven said.

"Are you crazy? Eighty years? I'm not giving you up for a year, let alone eighty!" he raged.

"This isn't only your decision to make. It's mine too. And I want this. I'm not giving us up. Not for anything."

Ryker was stunned. "Are you seriously going to do this? You're going to leave me for eighty years?" His voice was thick and quavering.

"Yes. I've never had anything like this, the love we have together. Not from my parents or my friends. I've never had a family, and I choose you, for my friend and my lover. And my family. And I won't give it up." Haven knew the shock and pain in his eyes matched the pain she felt in her own heart, and wavered. But she thought of their bond, the sensation when their wings connected and she could see into Ryker's heart and *feel* him, the strength of his feelings, of his love for her. And that unique feeling, of knowing there was a single person alive in this world who loved her for who she was with a passion and clarity that was beyond doubt, chased away any reservations she had. "I know this isn't what you want, and eighty years is a long time to wait for me. I understand if that is too much to ask. But I'll do this for us because it's what I want. Any price is worth it."

"Please don't do this. I will always love you. I don't need a bond to love you. It's not worth it!" he begged. The devastation in his eyes was almost more than she could bear. His trembling lips and his pain hurt her beyond comprehension, but her resolve was immoveable.

"It is worth it. You're worth it. And I deserve to have you as we are meant to be, not some shadow of love because I didn't have the strength to pay the price for something special. Do this for me. For us." A tear spilled down her cheek. "Please, Ryker..."

He pulled her to him and hugged her until she felt she would break. "Gods, how will we live through this?"

"It will be easy for me. I won't remember. But it will be hard on you. And I need some promises."

"What promises?" he asked warily.

"I won't remember you for a whole life. I know I will have lovers. You know this, too." He bristled, his eyes fading to a dark gray. She tried to imagine an entire life without seeing those eyes, a clear window to a soul she desperately needed to call her own forever. She swallowed her own grief and stroked his face. And gave him the only gift she could. The gift of freedom to survive. "Please promise me you won't deny yourself the same affection and company. I can live with the end, that I've tried as hard as I can to have you. I'm telling you now, when the trial is over and if you're not there, it will be worth it to have tried. I love you, and I always will. Please, please believe that."

"I can't do this," he said, and broke in her arms. Haven held him until he could piece himself together.

She wiped the tears from her face, then from his. "You have to. Be strong, Ryker. Be strong for us both."

Haven made her way to the room that would be her prison for the next eighty years and lay on the dais, arranging her gown around her legs. Farna helped position her and placed his hand on her arm. A guardian stood next to Farna, Ryker's own Shadowalking magic from his Echo rune swirling around his arms.

"I'm sorry," Farna said to them both. "Are you ready?"

Haven said, "Yes."

Ryker refused to acknowledge Farna, holding her hand tight, his fingers laced through hers.

"Ryker, you need to let go," Farna urged. "She can't bridge while you touch her."

"I can't," he rasped, and gripped her hand tighter.

She kissed his hand. "Let me go. I'll be right back," she promised, and kissed his lips. "You won't even know I'm gone."

"I love you," he said, and let her go. Shadow crept over her body, making her flesh transparent behind the swirling magic. Haven smiled at Ryker, and touched her lips with a ghostly hand, closed her eyes, and was gone.

# CHAPTER 45

## Epilogue

From the shadow of the Temple building, Roque watched Ryker's Triad walk from the trial wing across the square. It was done. The Phoenix was no longer in Berinia. He vanished and appeared in his apartment in southern Araine and hurried to his bedroom and lay on his bed, trembling. Home. He was going home.

He closed his eyes and gripped the metal band around his upper arm, then touched his magic. His pulse raced as the edges of his body distorted. But he didn't pass through the rift in the Pale. He delved deeper, his magic swirling through him, warping the surrounding air. Sweat beaded on his brow, and his stomach soured. *It couldn't be true.* He clenched the blankets, his body bucking and convulsing as he pushed harder against the membrane surrounding Praesia. His body faded, and his heart slammed in his chest and stuttered erratically. He exhaled sharply as his body lurched back to Praesia and became solid.

Roaring in frustration, Roque turned his head to the side as blood ran from his nose, his magic draining away.

He shuffled to the bath and splashed warm water on his face. Leaning over the sink, he stared at the pink drops dripping onto the white basin. The Phoenix body still trapped him in Praesia, as she had for the last twenty years. And now she was untouchable behind the trial wing wards for eighty years. Roque ran a wet hand behind his neck, shoving his disappointment away to clear his thoughts and consider his options. His legs wobbled, and he angrily wiped at the blood still trickling from his nose. Swearing in frustration, he vanished and appeared in the Temple courtyard. He shifted into a female seraphim dressed as a healer and made his way through the courtyard to the trial wing. Through the windows, he watched the healers move inside.

His eyes narrowed as Farna and Adrien entered a stasis room. He moved closer and saw Haven's transparent body through the window. A petite fae dressed as a healer entered the room and handed a chart to Farna. Roque's features shifted to match hers. He felt the handle of the knife strapped to his leg under the healer robes and turned to enter the trial wing.

Silas appeared in the doorway, his fierce green eyes piercing. He flared his steel wings and spun a sword in his hand. "Not a chance," he growled.

Fuck. *Fuck.* Roque vanished.

Ryker stared at the wall of the loft, his mind empty. He felt nothing, other than a roaring pain in his heart that had been his ever-present tormentor for the month since Haven left. He had waited his whole life for someone like her. Someone who loved him for who he was. And she left him.

Silas and Corde appeared in the loft's living room. Ryker frowned and rose, walking silently to his bedroom. Silas held his arm.

"Oh no, you don't. You will see Corde. We made a deal."

"I don't need help," Ryker spat.

"You most certainly do," Silas said, pulling Ryker to the couch and shoving him down.

Corde sat beside him. "Ryker, your mating bond is new. I know how this feels. The first year or two is intense."

"How the hell do you know how this feels?"

"Don't be an ass," Silas barked.

Ryker held his head in his hands. "Sorry," he grumbled.

Corde touched his arm. "You're right, I don't know everything you're feeling. But I do know some. My bond with Finnian was wild at first. But we were together. We worked it out together. To discover a bond so recently, and then have your mate be absent, I can't imagine that. But you do need help. The next year will be unbearable without a Sympath." Corde looked at Silas. "And we won't risk losing you. If you're more comfortable working with someone else, I can find you another to talk to."

"I don't want anyone else," Ryker whispered.

"Then let me help you," Corde said gently. Ryker heaved a breath, then nodded. Corde's magic slipped inside his mind, winding its way through the blazing pain, the emptiness, and the unbearable loneliness. Corde's magic traveled through his thoughts, leaving a soft, dulled trail behind. Ryker envisioned Haven's face, her smile, heard her laugh. He felt her touch his bare chest, her lips soft on his. Corde's magic eased around his memories, leaving them intact. Ryker glanced at him, and he smiled and squeezed Ryker's hand. A tear slid down Corde's cheek.

"She's lovely, Ryker," he whispered. "And she will come home."

EIGHTEEN YEARS LATER

Niko walked down the hall of the crossing wing and knocked on Adrien's door.

"Ready?" he asked, poking his head inside. Adrien rose and shuffled some papers, slipping them inside a drawer.

"Yes, ready."

"Big day today. Sending my baby into the world."

Adrien smiled at him. "Thank you for your help over the last eighteen years. I know this was an unusual assignment."

"It's been fun. She's a good kid."

"I've never had to create a simulation as long as this. But I've set up Haven's acceptance to college and will drop you into that memory. You can take it from there. I'd recommend building the memory from her acceptance to dropping her off at university. I've also created your exit. You'll be moving back east to be with your aging parents. From here, we will only need you once or twice a year instead of each week."

"How have the memories held up?" Niko asked.

"Well, so far," Adrien said, holding open the door to Haven's room. "They are like usual memories. Some aspects are distinct, but not detailed. She has enough childhood memories to now be dropped into the live simulation."

"I've never been a father. This was fun."

Adrien laughed. "Well, you're not much older than Haven, so I see the irony in this. But we appreciate your help and your creativity. When we were stuck with an eighty-year trial, we weren't sure how to bridge childhood to being an adult. Your idea of weekly simulations was an excellent solution. And quite a commitment." Niko shrugged. "Now that we don't need you here every week, what are your plans?"

"I'm returning to the fae Legion to join their Special Forces squad. They need a Seer in their ranks."

"Excellent choice. Will you be able to return? We will only need you for the next five or six years. We've agreed that Haven's 'father' will die when she is twenty-five."

"Yes, they understand my ongoing commitment to this project." Niko lay on a dais next to Haven. "Linking with her now."

Niko walked across the living room of the small suburban house in Napa, California. He handed a large envelope to his daughter, who sat on the sofa playing a video game with a friend.

"I think you just got some great news." Haven looked at him with large, ocean blue eyes and took the envelope. She opened it and pulled out the letter, then squealed and jumped into his arms. He held her tight and said, "Congratulations, UCLA freshman. You're going to be fine."

# ——Acknowledgments——

My mother passed away in July 2020 from uterine cancer. From diagnosis to her death was six weeks. It was right in the middle of COVID, when hospitals were locked down so I saw her once in that time period. We weren't close, but I loved her and I knew, without a doubt, that she loved me.

The next six months were a strange time in my life. I questioned everything around me. The choices I made, how I lived my life, the friendships I had. And in the middle of all this, Ryker visited me fully fleshed out and demanded I tell a story. Then he dragged Haven into it. So I wrote a story, which was actually Light Lost. Then Haven demanded I tell her story, too, so I wrote this book, Light in the Shadows.

And, reader, these books were just awful.

I gave Light in the Shadows to my best friend, Joy Parker, and she was the pivot for me to make my stories readable. She didn't laugh at the horrible, unstructured, amateur first draft. And she told me she stayed up until 2am to finish the book, and hated me for the ending. I realized my words evoked emotions, and that, despite being an amateur attempt, I had managed to trap her in the story and make her care about my characters. I think this is the goal of any writer. So, the dedication for this book goes to Joy. Without her, these books would have stayed a first draft and be stuffed in a drawer somewhere forever.

I edited Light in the Shadows over the next year with the amazing advice of four beta readers. Two were instrumental in the evolution of this story. Jessica Ritchey taught me so much about the writing craft, and it was her advice that unleashed Lilith from the shadow of a character she was in that early draft. James A. Price helped me hone the story further, fleshing out characters, pacing and plot threads that were indistinct. And they both put up with incessant questions from me!

In February 2022, I knew my manuscript needed more, but I had done everything I could with it on my own. I was absurdly lucky to find my editor, Jaime Dill. I will give her full credit for helping me pull Haven's emotional and personal growth to the forefront, and to add the emotion to this story that I felt but struggled to convey. Structurally, she turned this book into a professional piece of writing. And I thank her for her patience, wisdom and support. But most of all, I thank her for believing in my little story and respecting the vision I had.

I also want to thank the amazing writing community on Twitter. I've asked some of the dumbest questions, and someone there always bails me out. @Dario_Ciriello, I'm looking at you. I'm so happy we found a way to work together.

And last but not least, I thank my family, and my husband. I vanished for a year, emotionally, and they all waited patiently for me to come back to them. I can't say I'm completely healed, but at least it didn't take eighty years.

## ——About——

**GEORGIA C. LEIGH** grew up in California and resides in the San Francisco Bay Area with her husband, two grown sons, a cat, two horses and the occasional gecko when the youngest comes home from college. When not working and writing, Georgia is a competitive equestrian. Light in the Shadows is Georgia's debut novel, the first book in the Shadows and Light series.

Book Two, Light Lost, is expected to be released June 2023.

For more information, please visit www.georgiacleigh.com

Made in the USA
Las Vegas, NV
17 November 2023

81029398R00285